The
Resurrection
of the
Father

by

Rob G. Lerner

The Resurrection of the Father

by

Rob G. Lerner

Pomanjer Publishing Co., LLC
2022

ISBN-13: 978-0-9992511-6-4 (Pomanjer Publishing Co., LLC)

Published 2022
Pomanjer Publishing Co., LLC

Pomanjer Publishing Co., LLC, publishes fiction and non-fiction that speaks to our hearts and catches the idiosyncratic attention of the Pomanjers.

Pomanjer Publishing Co., LLC
P.O. Box 986
Vienna VA 22183 USA

The Resurrection of the Father
By Rob G. Lerner

Lerner's latest novel, *The Resurrection of the Father*, delves into the relationship between two brothers whose father disappeared when they were children. Their stable, supportive relationship as adults is upended when a man claiming to be their father shows up and wants to start a father-son relationship with the men. At the turbulent center of the story are questions of truth, loyalty, love, and forgiveness. Lerner's answers to these questions are at once uplifting and unsettling.

About the author:

Rob G. Lerner is a California native who now lives in Virginia with his family and beloved dog. He is passionate about art (Titian), music (Jascha Heifetz and Charlie Parker), and Formula One (Ferrari, of course). Lerner has been making up stories and writing fiction for most of his life, and you can follow his literary progress on the Amazon author page at
https://www.amazon.com/author/robglerner.

Previously by Rob G. Lerner

Marta (2022)
As a young man, the narrator falls in love with and marries the beautiful, elusive Marta, who in his eyes is the embodiment of perfection. A few years after Marta's death, he marries another woman who seems to be every bit as beautiful and perfect as Marta once was. One day, in the midst of a commonplace chore, he uncovers something that threatens to upend not only his memories of Marta but also his love for his current wife. *Marta* is both a love story in the grand tradition and a warning about the dangers of commercial data collection.

Snapshot (2018)
Snapshot is a departure from Lerner's previous works and announces his intention to delve deeper into the human psyche. The unnamed narrator of the story is living in the San Francisco Bay area when he meets and falls in love with the strange and passionless Luce. Certain that he cannot live without her, the narrator orchestrates a series of tests to find out if she is capable of loving him. San Francisco, Carmel, and even Lake Tahoe crop up in this bizarre tale, and it only when everything seems lost that he finds the very thing he has been seeking. Love and insanity are two sides of the same coin in this constantly swirling tale of emotional relationships.

The Nesbit Bunch (2018)
The Nesbit Bunch pulls together all three Nesbit novels: *Chasing Shadows, The Gray Ladies,* and *Endpoint?*. Each novel is complete and unabridged, and together they detail the saga of the American Interpol Agent Nesbit, his companion, the Scotland Yard Constable Tom Thwait, and the Scotland Yard Inspector Grace Sedgwick.

Find these books and more at Lerner's Amazon author page:
https://www.amazon.com/author/robglerner

Please leave a review of Lerner's book at the Amazon page.

To PJH

THE RESURRECTION OF THE FATHER

1

I remember shivering slightly as I stepped out into the cool, early morning air. I didn't mind the temperature so much. I was happy to be outside, and I was fascinated by the tiny puddles of water that had formed overnight on the dirt driveway next to our house. Since I was up before Tom, who would sleep throughout the entire weekend if allowed to do so, I used this special time to inscribe with my fingers delicate rivulets in the mud connecting one puddle to another. I don't know how long I had been squatting down at my work, but by the time that Tom appeared and stomped into one of the larger puddles, I had created an intricate topography that connected over a dozen lakes and seas of various sizes and shapes. I jumped up and, when I noticed the mud spots on my clean clothes and then Tom's toothy grin, I charged toward him only to be pushed onto the seat of my pants before I could enact retribution.

"Off your ass, scrub," he said as he helped me to my feet.

I couldn't be too upset with him. He was my older brother, and I depended on him to keep life from crumbling around us.

"How come you're up now?" I asked as he brushed the mud off my clothes and face.

"I heard mom crying. She told me to go outside and play when I asked her what was the matter."

"Why was she crying?"

"How the hell should I know? She's always crying."

Using the toe of my right shoe, I erased most of the rivers connecting the puddles. For some reason, I didn't want to explain what I was doing. I didn't want to hear Tom tell me that I was being childish. "It was because of Daddy, wasn't it? Where is Daddy? Do you know when he's coming back?"

"No."

"Why did he go? Did I do something wrong again?"

"You ask too many questions."

"I just want to know. I don't want him to be mad at me."

"Will you shut up for a change?"

Tom was walking away when I asked him where he was going.

"I don't know."

"Can I come?"

He stopped and looked back at me over his shoulder before jerking his head in confirmation. Apart from eagerly following him around the neighborhood like a lost puppy, I don't remember much else about that particular day.

Fifteen years later, I graduated from college and returned to our hometown to visit my brother. As agreed, I went to his place of work. His secretary met me when I entered the building, and she walked me to the frosted glass door of his office and led me inside. Tom was standing with his arms folded across his chest and looking at something outside his window when the young woman announced my presence. He turned, rushed over, and gave me a bear hug. I felt out of place when he stepped back and quickly sized me up. I was somewhat unkempt, in jeans, tee-shirt, and long hair, while he was cleanshaven and dressed immaculately in a white shirt, gray slacks, a red-striped tie, and matching suspenders.

"It's about time, Goofball," he said and motioned for me to take a seat opposite him on the other side of his glass-topped desk. "You've finally graduated. You're some kind of artist now, right? You look like one."

"I'm a graphics artist, or at least I hope to get a job as one."

"Can you make any money at it?"

"I don't know. It's something I enjoy. Are you happy with your job?"

"What's not to be happy with? I'm making big bucks, I have my own office, and the company pays for my car. Aren't you interested in getting rich?"

"I think we've had this conversation before. I want to do something meaningful with my life. You know I couldn't have done anything without you, and I promise I'll pay you back for everything. After Dad left, if it weren't for you…"

"Those were tough times for all of us. Do you have any leads?"

"Not yet. Tommy, when he disappeared and Mom broke down and all the rest that happened…"

"You're sounding like a broken record, Goofball. Forget the past. I have a friend of a friend at a local firm that might be able to use someone like you. You got talent, right? Okay, contact him…" He scribbled a name and phone number on a post-it and handed it to me. "He's expecting to hear from you."

"Tommy, I don't know how to thank…"

"Don't sweat it. Do you need some money?"

"Well, I haven't…"

He held up his hand for me to pause and reached inside his desk. Pulling out a binder of blank checks, he inscribed an obscenely large amount on a check and handed it to me.

"I'll never be able to pay…"

"I don't expect you to. But if you want to pay some of it back now, why don't you stop by for dinner Friday night. Belinda keeps nagging me about you. I've been telling her that you're still wrapped up in this college business, but now I don't have any more excuses."

"I'd love to. It's been a long time."

Tom got up and walked around the desk. Gently touching my arm, he encouraged me up and then walked me to the door. "In the meantime, if you don't mind, I'm a little pressed for time today." He stopped and looked at me. "Are you still seeing that chick, what's her name?"

"No, that was over a long time ago. I'm not seeing anyone these days."

"Good. I want you to meet someone before you go." He opened the frosted door and said to the secretary, "Tara, I'd like you to meet my brother. Jim, this is Tara. I think you two have a lot in common." He winked at one of us and went back into his office, letting the glass door slowly close behind him.

I felt slightly uncomfortable. I hadn't said anything to her when she brought me to my brother's office, and now face-to-face I felt compelled to say something other than to acknowledge her presence, and I was not good at small talk. Luckily, this woman, who suddenly appeared strikingly beautiful–she had long, flowing auburn hair and large, green eyes that practically sparkled when you looked at her–luckily, this young woman was a wonderful and charming conversationalist. She spoke first, but after a few seconds we were engaged in an animated discussion that lasted until Tom reappeared and asked her to come into his office on a business matter. By that time, I had her number and promised to call.

This was, in many ways, the beginning of the best period of my life. I got the job, found an apartment close to Tom's place, and within the year married the woman of my dreams. Tara, that is.

Some twenty years later, a single phone call upended everything.

2

"Hey, Goofball," Tom said as soon as I picked up. "You'll never believe it."

Tom often called me Goofball. He coined the nickname when we were kids, and he used it back then to taunt me and to make me feel inferior. As adults, the nickname became a term of endearment in his eyes, and he often used it when he was kidding around or when he was trying to con me into something that didn't appeal to me. His business, for example. Tom had been a successful businessman nearly all his life, and he often wanted to share his largesse by getting me into something with "lots of upside potential." I've been generally wary whenever Goofball was followed by dollars and cents.

"Don't call me Goofball. I'm sure I won't believe it. Now, if you're talking about money…"

"This isn't about money," he insisted, speaking as though he didn't want to sidetracked by what at this time was probably an irrelevant subject. "Listen, I'll bet you'll never guess who I spoke to today. You'll never guess."

"Okay, I'll never guess."

"Come on, Goofball, give it a try."

Tom and I were well into our forties, and he still retained an almost boyish enthusiasm for jokes and games. Normally, I was up for his humor, but not this evening. I had just come home from a long day at work, and the only things that I could whip up any enthusiasm for were my wife, dinner, and a baseball game on TV.

"I'm not going to give it a try. Just tell me who you saw and why you're so excited."

"Goofball, you're no fun sometimes."

"I'm not, so let's cut to the chase."

"Fine, but this isn't about anyone I saw. I just got the most amazing phone call I've probably ever had. Sure you don't want to guess who was on the other end?"

"The police? You're being arrested for insider trading?"

"Don't be an idiot. Okay, I'll tell you, but I want you to sit down first. Are you sitting?"

"Sure."

"Dad called. Goofball, you still there?"

"I'm still here."

"Dad called. Can you believe? Right out of the blue. I pick up the phone and he says, 'Tommy, this is Dad.' My God, I couldn't believe it. After all these years, and there he is, speaking as if I had spoken to him only yesterday. Can you believe it, Jimmy? It's the most amazing thing I've ever heard. Dad, after all these years."

It was amazing, all right. Our father walked out of our lives thirty-five years ago, and out of the blue he calls Tom and starts chatting like it was only yesterday. I wasn't sure that I could believe it. More to the point, I didn't care. We were only children when our father left us, and not once since then did he bother to say 'hello' much less explain why he left. I'm not certain our mother knew why he left, but if she did, she carried the secret to her grave.

"So what do you say? It's absolutely amazing, don't you think?"

"I suppose."

"Come on, Jimmy, you have to agree it's something. I mean, I don't think I ever expected him to call us, did you?"

"No, I sure didn't. But he called you, not me."

"He called both of us. He didn't have your number, so he reached out to me. Do you know what else he said?"

"I don't care what he said."

"What are you talking about? It's Dad, and he wanted to speak to you and me."

I was becoming impatient with all this guessing and amazement. Dad or not, I didn't give a damn what this person said, and I wasn't being hardhearted. After decades of silence, after the destruction of our lives and family, why would I care what he had to say? Why would anyone care unless it presented an opportunity of telling him to fuck off?"

"Tommy, it's been decades. Mom's dead. Why does it matter what he wants to say?"

"Goofball, you're impossible sometimes. Listen, he called and said that he wanted to speak to us one more time to apologize and make amends. Isn't that wonderful?"

"Isn't what wonderful? That after all this time he finally wants to say he's sorry? I can't imagine what he could possibly say to make up for deserting us. You remember everything as well as I do. Who cares if he wants to apologize?"

"I don't think you understand…"

"I understand just as well as you. I understand how he left without a word, I understand how we grew up without a father, and I understand how mom was destroyed because of his behavior. Have you forgotten how she fell apart after he left? I think I understand everything."

There was a slight pause, and for a moment I thought that he had hung up. "No, I don't think you do," he said without his previous enthusiasm. "We spoke for a few minutes, and he couldn't stop saying how sorry he was over everything. He said it was all his fault and didn't expect forgiveness. He wasn't asking for forgiveness. When I wanted to know why he was calling now of all times, he told me he was dying and wanted to speak to us before it was too late. Our Dad is dying, Goofball, and he wants to speak to us. We're the only family he has."

I couldn't believe that Tom of all people was concerned about some dying old man who wanted to feel good before the end. My brother was a tough, pragmatic businessman, and this odd sensitivity for someone he didn't know seemed completely out of character. I've always been more emotional than my brother–I'm an artist, after all–but it was too much even for me. Our father should have spoken to us when he was healthy and in the prime of his life–when Tom and I were still boys.

"Tommy, I don't give a damn about him. He'll have to deal with his regrets on his own. I'm not wasting my time to help him feel good before he kicks the bucket. Let me finish. I also don't understand how can you be so positive that some guy calling out of the blue–some guy you can't even see–used to be our father. Did it occur to you that this might be a phone scam designed to rip off your money? You're a rich man, buddy boy, and more than a few people would like to get their fingers in your pocket for your change."

"You're not serious, are you? Listen, we should hear what he has to say. We owe him that much…"

"We don't owe him shit…"

"He's our father, and I'm willing to give him a few minutes to talk. And, by the way, I don't believe it's a phone scam. God, I don't know where you come up with these things."

"I didn't come up with anything. It happens all the time. How can you be so sure it's not a scam?"

"I'm sure, that's all. I'm sure."

"But how can you be sure? We haven't heard from him in how many years? People change a lot over long periods of time–you and I have changed a lot since he left–and so how do you know this guy is who he claims to be?"

"I know. Can we…"

"How do you know?"

"Okay, Goofball, he said some things that only I could have known. No one else, and that's how I know. Satisfied?"

I could sense Tom's anger rising. He didn't like people pushing back, not even me.

"No, I'm not satisfied. What are these secret things that you two shared? Tell me, so I can be satisfied, too."

"God, Jim, do you have to act like this? He said some stuff…he referred to a time when he and I walked around the neighborhood. I was seven years old. That should be good enough. Look, I don't have the slightest doubt it was him…"

"It's not enough for me."

"I don't care. He also said something else. He said he wanted us to come see him at the hospital so that he can speak to us in person. If you want proof one way or another, that's where you'll find it."

The other shoe dropped. Some old man wanted to speak to us for a reason that wasn't exactly clear to me, and we would have to go to a hospital to have that conversation, presumably sitting next to his death bed. I could practically see him holding one gnarled hand out for someone to take it. Well, I wasn't going to speak to him on the phone, and I certainly wasn't going to sit by his bedside much less touch that offensive hand, and I didn't care whose feelings I hurt. "That's great, Tom," I said. "You can go see this stranger and chat with him until the cows come home, or until he expires. I'm staying here."

"Christ…that's no way to talk. If you don't believe he's the real McCoy, this is your chance to see for yourself. And if you're still sore over his absence, this is also your opportunity to tell him so, face to face. You won't get another opportunity like this one. He's dying, Jimmy."

"Okay, I'll assume for your sake that he's the real McCoy. But I'm still not going to waste my time speaking to him. I don't care how sorry he is. I don't care what he has to say. He made his bed and now he can die on it, for all I care."

There was a short pause, and I knew that Tom was doing his best to quell his rising frustration. My brother was a little tense at times.

"You have a right to be upset, Goofball. I am, too. But I want to hear what he has to say. I want to understand why he left and what he was doing all those years. I may not forgive him, but I at least want the opportunity to decide, based on the facts. Do you see what I'm getting at, brother?"

"I sure do, brother, and I wish you a good time. I'm not going with you."

"Damn you, Goofball, you're a real pain in the ass sometimes. Listen to me. I don't care what you feel about the man. I don't even know what I feel about him, either. But I need to see him. I need to hear firsthand. If there's forgiveness in there, fine. If not, fine, too. I have to go."

"Have at it."

I could practically hear my brother swallow, and his voice assumed a serious, businesslike tonality. "I have to do it, Jim, and I can't do it without you."

"What are you talking about? Since when have you ever needed me to do anything?"

"Since now. I've never asked you for anything, Jim, and I've given you plenty. I only want you to do this one thing for me."

Tom was right. He was only four years older than me, and yet he practically assumed the role of father when our father deserted us. Later, when he was on his own, he paid for my college and helped me out with money and advice. I would always be grateful for everything that Tom's done for me, but I hated the idea that he was using my debt to him to push me into something that I wouldn't have done in a million years. "Tom, I owe you my life, but this is something…this is something that makes my skin crawl."

"Please, Jim. This is important to me."

I was in a bind. I couldn't let him down. But then it occurred to me that if I could put it off for a while, the old man might croak and render all this pointless. "Okay, brother," I responded with a magnanimous tone. "I'll do it for you. I don't want anything out of it."

"That's fine with me. But I think…"

"Don't push it. Let me check my calendar, and I'll get back to you in a few days."

"Jimmy, we don't have that much time. He's dying…"

"Okay, I get it. I'll find a date and talk to you tomorrow or the day after."

"No, Jimmy, now. He's not going to last that long."

"All right, all right, let me grab my tablet…"

"I'm not asking for that, either. I'm asking for you to come with me right now. We don't have time. We may not have another hour. It has to be now."

Another shoe? I felt as if I had been kicked in the stomach. "What? Come on, I just got home, there's going to be a game, and I haven't spoken to Tara."

"You can watch a game anytime, and your wife will understand why you're out of the house. I want you to leave now and pick me up. I'll be waiting outside."

"Jesus Christ, Tom…"

"Right now." He hung up. Tom knew that I wouldn't let him down. Since he had asked me to meet him at his house, I also knew it meant that we were going in one of his flashy, expensive cars. If there was a bright side to any of this, I suppose it was this.

3

Did I mention that my brother was successful? Upon graduating college, he landed an important position at a major brokerage firm and quickly moved up the corporate ladder. A few years later, he branched out on his own and began acquiring small firms that he built up and sold at an enormous profit. As a result, Tom had money to burn, as well as a big house and several "getaways," numerous cars, and art–he was always on the lookout for some find or unique piece that he could turn over for a substantial profit. Shortly after college, he married Belinda and they had a wonderful daughter, Chelsea, who was a young teenager (I've never been able to remember her exact age).

As I noted earlier, Tom had always been more than a brother to me. In the absence of our father, I looked to him for guidance on virtually everything that normal people seek from their fathers, and there were many times in our younger years when I sought, and received, his protection from bullies and others who wanted to harm or abuse me. Shortly after high school, I went through some tough times and, if it hadn't been for my brother, who helped me both mentally and financially, I don't really know how I would have coped with life. Because of his support, I became a successful graphics artist for a small, privately-owned advertising firm. It was also through him, as I noted earlier, that I met the lovely lady who would become my wife. I suppose I should add that Tara started out as an accounts-payable clerk at Tom's firm, and through her energy and diligence she rose to become his personal secretary. Shortly before marrying me, she finished a degree in psychology at night school and has since been counseling patients, as well as advising companies like my brother's, on a wide range of mental-health issues. It was fortunate that Tara was not only close to my brother but also developed a similarly close relationship with Tom's wife, Belinda.

Well, it was for my dear brother that I reluctantly left my cozy home, my loving wife (she hadn't yet come home from work), and the baseball game to help him through something that I knew would be a complete and foolish waste of time. It took me about thirty minutes to reach his house. As I inched up his driveway, I was a little surprised that the place was dark except for the outdoor flood lights illuminating the base of the building. Instead of a beautiful, secure home, the lights made the rest of the structure look like a menacing shadow hovering over Tom's property. Like I always did, I angled the car away from the building to park in my usual spot, and just before I stopped the headlights briefly illuminated the slacks and sports shirt on a man's body. The slacks and sport shirt immediately fled from the lights, and an instant later they got into the passenger side of my car.

"Let's get going," Tom commanded.

"I thought you were going to drive."

"No time." His eyes seemed glued on something in front of us. Some distant shadow?

"All right," I grudgingly agreed. "Where to?"

"Hang a right on First...."

"Just give me the name and address."

Tom hesitated as if it were a secret. When I asked again, this time not disguising my irritation, he said Saint Mercy.

"Are you kidding me?" I stopped and put the car into park. "What the hell is he doing at Mercy?"

"Why does it matter? Let's get going before it's too late."

"I'm not going anywhere until I know." I didn't want to be a pill, but the hospital was halfway between our respective houses, and I had been there with Tom more times than I could count. Tom thought of himself as an amateur athlete, and I had taken him to Mercy numerous times over the years for everything from concussions to broken bones. I never understood why he would subject himself to such punishment, especially since many of his competitors were much younger than him. But what bothered me most was that the man claiming to be our father was dying in a facility intimately familiar to Tom and me and so close that we could have walked past it on any given day. "It doesn't make sense," I insisted. "Of all the places in the world, why the hell is he there?"

"Dying, Goofball. Now, let's get moving."

"Wait a minute. Don't you find it odd that a man we haven't seen in a lifetime is dying practically in our backyard?"

Tom turned and, in the dim lights inside the car, I could sense his questioning stare. "Here or someplace else, it doesn't matter. Dying is dying. If you're really concerned about it, you can ask him when you see him."

I didn't know what to say, and so I put the car in gear and started driving. I couldn't understand why it apparently didn't bother Tom that this man was at Mercy and not some place a thousand miles away. Wouldn't any reasonable person want to know the answer, especially since Tom and I hadn't grown up in the area?

When we reached the hospital parking lot, I pulled inside and started looking for a space toward the back of the lot. I had a new car (new for me, that is), and I wanted to find a space where someone wouldn't bang their doors into mine.

"What are you doing?" Tom demanded when saw that I wasn't going to park close to the building.

"I'm protecting my car. Unlike you, I can't afford to replace it when it gets a scratch."

"We don't have a lot of time to spare. I'll pay for the damage."

"It's not going to take that long."

"Why can't you take my recommendation? We're going to be late. I told him we'd be here on the hour."

"You told him we'd be here on the hour? You didn't tell me that."

"Sorry, there wasn't time. Let's get closer before he gets…don't worry, I'm paying."

Once again, I stopped the car, this time in the center of one of the throughways. Was there something else that he had neglected to tell me? "What do you mean, 'before he gets'?

"Nothing, nothing, just a slip of the tongue. Let's park a little closer and get in there."

Tom once told me that I can be obstinate at times. He was right. I can be obstinate when I suspect that someone is pulling something over on me. This was one of those times. "You tell me what you meant, and I'll get a little closer."

"It was nothing. I meant before he gets…gets to the end of his life. I didn't want you to think that I was pushing you. It was, as I said, a slip of the tongue."

It almost made sense, and so I reluctantly dropped it. Nevertheless, I didn't park as close to the building as Tom wanted. I wasn't pleased to be here, I wasn't interested in seeing some old patient, and I wanted to express my displeasure to Tom, albeit in a mild way.

Tom was silent as we approached the brightly-lit, glass hospital doors. Once inside, we proceeded directly to the information desk near the back of the reception area. No one was at the desk, and so Tom leaned against it and started drumming his fingers rhythmically on the top of its empty surface. While he was impatiently occupied, I stood next to him and looked around. If the overhead lights hadn't been on, I would have assumed that the hospital was closed. No one was there, not a single person either waiting for treatment or expecting to see someone. What was even more curious was that the place looked filthy. It looked more like an old bus station than a clean, modern hospital waiting room. There was a newspaper and other debris on one of the chairs, and on the table with a coffee machine were used cups, empty bags of sweetener, stir sticks, and other trash that people (and it had to have been more than one person) left rather than tossing them into trashcan next to the table. What was even worse was the couch across from the coffee machine. It was covered at least a foot high with newspapers and what looked like old rags.

Shaking my head over the change in this place (even though it had been some time since I had been here, I couldn't recall a time when it ever looked like this), I turned back to Tom. He now seemed as strange as the waiting room. He was no longer tapping but feverishly filliping the thumb and middle finger of his right hand. His feet were moving, too. I could see the tops of his toes tighten and release through the soft Italian leather of his shoes. It was as if he was ready to leave any second. I, too, was ready to leave, but I wasn't anywhere near as antsy as my brother. Without warning, he reached across the desk for the service bell and slammed it down on the desk in front of him. When the bell gave off a faint, pathetic tingle, he pounded it several times with the side of his fist.

"Jesus, what's the matter, Tom?" I pulled the bell away from him. "You're supposed to be quiet in a hospital. People are trying to relax and heal." Frankly, I really didn't know why one had to be quiet in a hospital, but I hoped that my words would silence my brother and maybe temper his increasing anxiety.

"Where is everyone?" he said loudly as he scanned the empty area behind the desk.

"I don't know, Tom." I put a brotherly hand on his muscular shoulder. "There's no reason to be upset. Someone will come soon enough."

Tom faced me. "He's dying, and not a single person is around to help us see him before the end."

"I'm sure someone will be here in a minute," I was explaining but stopped when Tom started hollering at the back of the room.

"People need help here," he shouted. "Does anyone work in this goddamned place?"

"Chill out, brother," I said and again touched him lightly on the top of his forearm. "You're only waking people. Shouting isn't going to make anyone come any quicker."

He yanked his arm away from me and again insisted, "Is anyone here?"

"They heard you the first time," I had just said when an old woman appeared seemingly from nowhere and silently sat down on the other side of the desk.

The woman could have been in her late eighties. She had a stern, unsmiling face that was covered with a complex network of lines and furrows, and her yellowish hair was bound tightly behind her head in a small bun. She was also wearing a tight-fitting, pink-and-white striped dress that seemed more suitable for a sixteen-year-old. Without a word, she scooted her chair to the side and facing a large computer monitor, flipped a switch beneath it, and typed in her password. Once the computer was up and running, she turned to me and, her dentures slightly protruding, demanded to know what I wanted. Tom elbowed me aside before I could answer.

"Can you hear me? Fine." He squinted at the small name tag over her left breast. "Grace, we're here to see our father. He's very ill and quite possibly dying. Can you or somebody else take us to him?"

The old woman wasn't in the least bit intimidated by my brother, whose tall, muscular form practically hovered over her. "Visiting hours ended three minutes ago," she responded in a voice that was unexpectedly strong and unwavering.

I moved in between them to prevent an international incident. "You don't understand. This may be the last time we get to see him, and so only a few minutes would be extremely useful." I smiled foolishly to apologize for this exception to the rules.

The woman didn't immediately respond. She narrowed her eyes at me for a few moments before looking over my shoulder at Tom. "Name," she demanded and started typing something into the monitor, the back of which faced us.

"Thomas Reid…"

"No," I interrupted and again positioned myself in front of my brother. "You want to know the patient's name. The first name is probably Bill, and the last name is…"

"The last name is Reid," Tom announced over my shoulder, "just like mine."

"I'm not deaf, Mister…what's your last name?"

"Reid," I interjected. "He's Tom Reid, and he wants to see a Bill Reid. The man claims to be his father."

Tom shot a furious glance at me and turned back to the woman, who appeared to looking for his name in the computer files. He started to say something but it was her turn to interject.

"You say he's here for what?" The woman looked back and forth at Tom and me.

Tom, hardly a person to suffer anyone lightly, was practically shaking.

"He's extremely ill," I said before Tom could respond. "I'm talking about the patient, that is, and that's the reason we're here. If it weren't the case…okay, his name is Bill Reid. Can you find him?"

"Bill Reid? Just like the name of the other gentleman." She indicated Tom with a short nod.

"Not quite, but Bill Reid will do."

"Just a minute, please." She began typing something else into the computer. Several minutes later she shook her head. "I thought so," she said quietly to herself. Turning to us, she said, "What did you say the last name was?"

I repeated it and spelled it out.

"No one here by the name of Bill."

"Bill Reid," Tom interjected.

"No Bill Reid," the woman reiterated just as strongly, looking straight at Tom. I could see a slight movement of her dentures inside of her lips.

"Are you sure?"

"Of course, I'm sure. Everything's alphabetized, and in this hospital there's no Bill what's-his-name."

"Bill Reid," Tom practically shouted. "Bill Reid, Bill Reid, Bill Reid. Is there a Bill Reid in your goddamned system? The last name is spelled R-e-i-d. The first name is Bill or William. Do you need to have me spell these, too?"

She raised one wrinkled white eyebrow and went back to the computer, shaking her head and mumbling something. A few moments later, she looked back at us and reiterated that there was no Bill Reid at the hospital.

"Did you spell the name correctly?" My brother demanded.

"I certainly do know how to spell, Mister whatever your name is."

"Maybe he's listed under William. William Reid," I interjected.

She went back to the monitor, her dentures now visibly sliding around in her mouth, and a minute later announced, "Yes, I have a Reid, William J. Is that the one you're looking for?"

"Yes, that's the one. How is he doing? When can I see him?"

"Hold your horses," the woman said to Tom. One of her eyebrows was slightly higher than the other. "In the first place, I can't tell you how he's doing. That information can only be disclosed to relatives…"

"I'm his son."

"…disclosed to relatives with the patient's permission."

Tom took a step forward. "I don't understand. I'm his son, and I should be able to at least know how he's doing."

"What's your name?"

15

"Reid, Thomas Reid."

"You don't have to shout. I can hear you very well. The regulation is very clear on this. Unless Mr....one moment, please. Yes, unless Mr. Reid, William J. has signed a waiver permitting you to have access to his records, there's nothing I can do."

"I don't want his records. I just want to know how he's doing. And I need to see him right away."

"There's nothing I can do unless Mr. Reid, William J. gives you written..."

"Permission. I got it. Can you at least tell me if he's still alive?"

"Yes, as long as you have the appropriate permission. Now, if there's nothing else I can do for you..."

"Wait a minute," Tom said as he practically shoved me out of the way. "I need to see Reid, William J. He called me to come and get...I mean to see him, and here I am. I'm his son, Reid, Thomas."

I was now standing to the side, and the old woman looked at me and asked who I was and what I wanted.

"Nothing," I said. "I'm just a bystander."

Tom frowned in an ugly, lowering way. "Please, just take me to my father, Reid, William J."

"I'm afraid I can't."

"What?"

"In the first place, visiting hours are over. And, in the second..."

"What the hell is this? He's dying, for God's sake. Why can't I see him? Can't you make an exception in a case like this?"

The woman had a perplexed look on her face. "Who's dying?"

"Reid, William J."

She glanced at the monitor and then looked at Tom. "To my knowledge, he's not dying."

"What are you talking about? I'd like to see him."

"As I said...please, let me finish. In the first lace, visiting hours are over. In the second place, he's been discharged."

"Oh, for God's sake, you couldn't tell me this earlier? Okay, when did this happen and where is he now?"

Again, she looked at the computer screen. "Two hours ago. He checked himself out. Highly irregular. We are not responsible if the patient refuses to follow hospital guidelines..."

"Oh, for...do you know where he was going?"

"Absolutely not. Even if I did..."

Tom turned his back to her and looked at me with an expression of deep concern. I couldn't tell if it was real or not, and so I smiled blandly and raised my shoulders to let him know, if it was necessary, that I, too, was perplexed by this strange turn of events.

"What the hell happens now?" Tom asked as much to himself as to me.

"Are you looking for….Mr. Reid, William J.?"

Tom faced the old woman again. He glowered at her for a few seconds, the muscles throbbing in his jaw. "Yes, I want to know where to find him."

"He's over there. If he's not going to follow hospital regulations, it would be most appreciated if you would help him exit the facility." She directed us with a couple of flapping movements of her right hand to the couch on the other side of the room, where all the newspapers and rags were piled. "It would also be nice if he cleaned up his mess."

Tom and I turned in the direction she indicated. An instant later, Tom sprinted to the mound while I remained at the desk with the old woman, who observed him as if she had never seen anything like him in the hospital. Maybe she hadn't.

I, too, was amazed. Tom stood next to the mound of rags for a few moments and then kneeled next to one end and appeared to be speaking to it. Seconds later, he looked up and, with a big sweep of his left arm, asked me to come over. Before I could determine what to do, he called out, "Jimmy, come here, quick."

4

I strolled over to where Tom was kneeling and stood to one side. Tom looked up, and I noticed big tears in his eyes.

"Here," he practically howled as he leaned back so that I could see something.

I glanced downward but I couldn't see anything but papers and what appeared to be a dirty bathrobe. I was about to go sit down in one of the chairs on the other side of the coffee table when I heard a strange gurgling and then a loud, drunken snort. Both came from the rag pile.

I again bent slightly over and looked carefully at the place from which the snort emanated. There was another snort and the rags suddenly came alive. The man or whatever it was, sat up and, like a scene out of a bad movie, the papers fell to the floor and the bathrobe slipped to what I assumed was the waist. The reveal wasn't uplifting. There was a heavyset, unshaven man with a bald head wearing a dirty tee-shirt. He slowly opened his bloodshot eyes and looked blindly around. Tom, as if on cue, hollered, "Jimmy, it's Dad. Do you see? It's Dad."

I looked, and the old man blinked blindly at something in the distance.

Tom didn't wait for response and reached solicitously toward the old man, as if the poor soul was about to roll helplessly off the couch. "Dad, be careful. How are you doing? It's me, Tom, your son."

The old man made chewing movements with his mouth and looked up at Tom, probably trying to identify the source of these moving sentiments. "Tommy, is that you, boy?" the man asked, his voice momentarily unsteady as if he had just risen from the dead.

"Yes, Dad, it's me, Tommy. God, it's good to see you. Please be careful. Don't move too much. Are you in a lot of pain?"

"Tommy, is that really you?" The man lifted one fat, dirty arm and histrionically reached for Tom's shoulder.

"Yes, Dad, it's really me. And Jimmy, your other son, is here, too."

Tom kept his eyes fixed on the old man. I couldn't tell if he was mesmerized by this unexpected resurrection or if he was afraid that if he looked away, the man might prove to be a figment of his imagination. Or, maybe…

"Tommy, is that really you?"

"Yes, and Jimmy's with me."

The old man smiled in a creepy, snarling sort of way. "It's good to see you, Tommy. I'm glad you came, son."

"Jimmy and I came as quickly as we could. You know how traffic is sometimes."

The old man stirred, moving his fat shoulders back and forth, and then dropped his bare feet to the floor. His feet made heavy, muffled thuds as they landed on the tops of a pair of dirty half-slippers and eased inside.

"Jesus, Dad, please be careful. It must be awfully painful. Where does it hurt?"

The old man struggled up and off the couch. Once he was erect and solidly on his flat, ugly feet, he glanced around and motioned for Tom to hand him his bathrobe, which was now dangling around his ankles. I was thankful that he didn't try to retrieve the bathrobe himself, for he had nothing else on below the waist except his dirty underwear.

Unexpectedly feeling as if we were being watched, I looked over at the woman behind the counter. She immediately turned away and started typing something into the computer. I looked back at the scene in front of me just as Tommy had just finished cinching the bathrobe belt around the old man's fat waist. The robe was once probably white, but it was now yellowish with brown spots on one edge. Stretching his round, mountainous shoulders, the old man started looking for something on the floor.

"What is it, Dad? Let me help."

"My glasses. They're in my bag. I'll bet one of those SOBs stole my bag. Couldn't trust them as far as I could throw them."

Tom reached down and pulled a brownish, beat-up canvas bag out from under the couch. "Is this what you're looking for?"

The old man squinted at it and grabbed it. "Thanks, son. I can't tell how much I endured here from these idiots." He zipped open the top of the back, shot a stump-like arm into it, and seconds later pulled out a pair of heavy, black-rimmed glasses. Putting his glasses on with one hand, he shoved the bag to me with the other. I held onto it instinctively. It wasn't very heavy.

"Okay," he said to Tom. "Let's get the hell out of here. Did you bring the car?"

I stopped for a moment before following them out of the hospital. Did he actually say, 'Did you bring the car'? It was a strange thing to say, given that Tom insisted that the initial conversation on the phone was short and that we were only going to see the old man, not take him some place. What was equally odd was Tom's response.

19

"Of course, Dad."

I don't know what I expected to see, but it wasn't this. The old man didn't resemble anyone I knew. He didn't resemble anyone that I knew in our extended family, either. Omitting his grubby appearance (a bath and clean clothes would fix that), there was nothing about him–neither his physical mannerisms nor the sound of his voice–that bore the slightest resemblance to either Tom or me, or to what I remembered of our mother and her brother. The old man was crude (he resembled a child's drawing of an old man) and uncouth, and he stomped out of the hospital like a thug on the prowl. When we were a few yards into the parking lot, I had to do something to stop whatever was going on.

"Tom," I called out, "shouldn't we call a cab for this…gentleman?"

The old man kept stomping while Tom hesitated and looked back at me. "No, it's okay, Jimmy."

"What do you mean it's okay? Where's he going? Are we supposed to drive him there? I thought he was dying?"

The old man, perhaps sensing that he was getting too far ahead, stopped and scanned the parking lot in front of him. "Where's your car, Tommy?"

"Don't move, Dad. I'll be right there." Tom trotted over to me and whispered, "Don't worry. I'm sorry we have to take your car right now, but there's no choice. I'll make it up to you." Without waiting for a response, he ran to the old man, calling out as he moved, "To your left, Dad. I'll take you there."

Now, I wasn't trying to make this event or whatever one called it more painful than it already was, but I wasn't interested in using my car as a taxi for anyone except my brother. I didn't want this dirty, foul-smelling old man soiling the seats and the rest of the interior, and I especially didn't want him dying in the car if there was the slightest chance of that. I was going to say something to Tom about this, but he reached the car before I had an opportunity and positioned himself next to the driver's door, telling the old man, who had not yet reached the car, to get in on the passenger's side.

"What gives?" I asked Tom as I walked up to him.

Tom told me in a hushed tone not to worry. "Everything will be okay," he assured me. He also said that he wanted to drive so that he could help the old man, if needed. He was in a lot of pain, Tom explained, and it would therefore be easier for him to get into the front seat. But, my brother offered with a firm pat on my shoulder, it was my car and, if I wanted to drive and sit next to the old man, it was fine with him. Like a lamb, I handed over my keys.

As I waited for Tom to open the doors, the old man finally lumbered over to the car but stopped a couple feet away. Putting his fists on the sides of his extensive hips, he stared at the vehicle as if he couldn't quite believe what he was seeing.

"Tommy, my boy, what kind of godawful color is this? Lipstick red? Jesus Christ. Is this piece of crap yours?" he asked with a disdainful look on his flaccid face. "I thought you were doing much better than this."

"No, Dad, you don't understand..."

"This kind of car is for losers and pimps." He raised one swollen hand for Tom to be quiet while he scratched behind his bathrobe. "Listen, son," he said to Tom with a warm smile when he was ready, "Get yourself something better. You can afford it. You shouldn't be driving a car that makes you look low class, like you don't have a real job. Hell, the color alone is enough to make you look like a little prick."

I wasn't going to let this slide, but Tom silenced me by flashing his right palm. "That's good advice, Dad. But this car isn't so bad. It's solid and reliable, and it will get you anywhere you want to go."

"Don't snow me, son. You got money, a fine house, and a lovely family. It isn't about reliability. It's about presenting yourself to the world as the winner you are. The clothes you're wearing are worth more than this..."

I was proud of that car, and I couldn't keep from highlighting the old man's ignorance of fine automobiles. Speaking across the top of the car, I informed him that it would beat anything he had. I guess it wasn't the smartest statement I ever made, and, judging from the expression on Tom's face, it didn't impress him, either.

The old man squinted at me for a moment and then turned to Tom.

"Who the hell's he, and what's he doing here?" he asked, as if I weren't in fact there.

"It's Jimmy, you other son, Dad," Tom replied like a hopeful puppy. "We're both here to see you."

"You are, are you?" the old man said to me and sniffed the air. Shrugging his shoulders, he walked over to the passenger door and waited for Tom to open the door. I got in behind the driver's seat and watched as Tom ran around to the other side of the car and carefully helped the old man into the front seat, sacrificing his clean hand to keep the old man's slick, tender head from banging the car's solid, unyielding metal frame. Once the old man was settled in (and not without several histrionic groans and numerous complaints about his rapidly declining health), Tom ran back around to the driver's side and got in.

I thought the issue of the car was more or less over at that point, but as Tom struggled to get the driver's seat into position, the old man took Tom's repeated efforts to move the seat back as another opportunity to express his disdain for everything associated with the car, including the seat, the seatbelt, the dash, the door, the window, the interior room, and so on. "Pure crap," he mumbled and shook his head.

Determined for Tom's sake not to argue, I asked the old man in a loud voice what his immediate plans were. "Where can we drop you? Someplace close, I hope, because you shouldn't spend your precious time in this horrible car."

He acted as if Tom, not me, was the one who asked the question.

"I don't know, Tommy. You can drop me off at the nearest motel, I suppose. I'm glad you came, but I don't want to burden you."

"God no, Dad," Tom responded eagerly. "We can take you anywhere you want." He started the car and sped out of the parking lot, heading back in the direction from which he and I came. "Have you had anything to eat lately?"

"Not much, son," he replied, the subject of a motel now ostensibly over. "It's impossible to eat the slop at these places. But don't bother about me. The fact that I'm sitting next to you is enough to fill my belly."

It was almost more than I could take. There was the phone call, the hospital stuff, and the car business, and now there was the easy familiarity between two people who supposedly hadn't seen each other or heard from one another in decades. And if these weren't enough to raise red flags, the old man, as run down and as ugly as he appeared, seemed to be in good health. Of course, I didn't know at the time what a dying person was supposed to look like, but I was reasonably confident that such a person wasn't as hale and hearty as the old man. I kept my mouth shut, though. There was no sense in creating more problems at this point. I was, however, determined to have it out with my brother as soon as we jettisoned the sneaky-looking lump of flesh whose rancid smell was permeating the interior.

"You know," I said, doing my best to sound pleasant, "There's a motel right around the corner. We could drop you there. How about that?"

The old man angled his head back at me and then looked at Tom. "Wherever works for you, Tommy. I don't need nothing special."

I was about to ask my brother what he had in mind when he went around the opposite corner and headed up a familiar street.

"No way, Dad," Tom said firmly, "I'm not going to drop you off at some fleabag motel. You're coming with me."

I didn't like the direction that the conversation was taking, and I almost shuddered when Tom pulled into his driveway and drove into the little turnabout in front of his main doors, which were now illuminated by several pale, overhead lights. Tom was the most streetwise individual that I had ever known, and yet he was doing something that was not only stupid but possibly dangerous. Father or not, the old man was a complete stranger. We had no way of knowing at this juncture if he was on the up-and-up or if he was plotting something sinister that my brother had just bought into. No, the old man couldn't have taken Tom one on one, but old men can be every bit as dangerous as young men in the right circumstances.

5

I jumped out at the same time that Tom was exiting the car. While the old man fumbled with something (he clearly wasn't getting out without help), I went up to Tom and whispered, "What the hell are you doing? Why are you bringing him here? You should have dropped him off at a motel."

Tom straightened his shoulders. "What are you talking about? Goofball, this is our chance to talk to him. Let's not waste it."

"We could have talked to him at the hospital or at a motel."

"No, this is the best place. He'll be more comfortable here, and we can ask him anything we want. Aren't you interested in hearing what he was to say?"

"Not particularly. But I'm worried about you and your family. You don't just bring a bum in your house…"

"Don't call him names. He's not a bum."

"Fine, he's not a bum. He's still a stranger, and you've got to think about the safety of your family."

"He's not a stranger, and my family's not in danger."

I was going to respond when the old man started hollering for someone to help him out of that "goddamn kid's car."

"Listen," Tom said as he gently held my forearm, "I appreciate your concern, but I can take care of myself. I'm not worried about our Dad."

"Your Dad."

"Have it your way. If you're concerned, come in and talk to him for a bit. If you don't want to have a conversation, then just tell him what you think. Tell him that you're still mad about him leaving. Tell him whatever you want. You're not going to have another chance like this. He's dying, if you recall."

Tom went quickly around the car to the old man, who was now holding onto the edge of the roof as though this were the only thing keeping him from collapsing. I didn't immediately move, I wasn't going to get involved in this…whatever this was, and I stood listening with incredulity as Tom babied the old man while helping him out the car and onto his now unsteady feet. As I observed this comedic routine, I began to wonder if the reason that Tom insisted on taking my car was to get me back here at his house. If we had taken one of his cars, he knew that I might have bailed at the hospital instead of accompanying him on this absurd mission to his house. Tom also knew that by using my car, I wouldn't storm away and leave him at the hospital (what kind of scoundrel would let his brother take a cab when his car was available?).

Furthermore, Tom understood me well enough to know that after these curious little shows in the hospital and in the car, I was going to hang around long enough to find out why he wanted me to stay with him and the old man. And why did he want me to hang around? I did as he asked and went to the hospital with him, and yet I had a strong feeling that there was more, that he wanted me for something else. I suppose that I should have asked, but I can honestly say that I didn't think of it at the time. I didn't say a word. Instead, I watched with amazement as Tom became the old man's crutch, keeping him upright as he progressively became weaker, and then I followed them to the house, reminding myself along the way to get back my car keys. The charade, however, didn't end when we were at the door. Tom, heroically holding the old man with one arm and fishing his house keys out of his pocket with the other, unlocked the door and helped the old man inside and gingerly eased him down on a stool near the door. It was clear that Belinda wasn't home. The house was dark and quiet, and Tom didn't call out to her as he usually did when entering. After satisfying himself that the old man was safe from falling over, he rushed around turning on lights and making things comfortable for this pathetic old individual.

Tom lived in one of those ultramodern affairs in the ritzy part of town. It had two stories, a basement, and floor-to-ceiling windows on half the walls. Inside, where there weren't windows, there was art. Tom, as I said before, was a passionate buyer and selling of fine art, especially images of exotic animals either fighting or being killed (he told me one time that it would be interesting to buy several exotic "beasts" and put them into a cage where they could fight to the death while an artist recorded the scene). Throughout the place, there were also knickknacks of every kind, small sculptures, glassware, precious rocks, fine furniture, expensive carpets (some of the more valuable were hung on the walls), and, on the back wall of his study, knives. Tom was an ardent knife collector, and he often extolled their beauty and craftsmanship as well as the emotions they elicited when drawn. As Tom attentively walked the old man toward the living room, I noticed the old codger eyeing these and other things along the way as if he were prepping for a heist. Once we were in the living room and snuggled into our seats, the old man picked up a curio from the coffee table next to him and began examining it, as though he were assessing its value.

"Tom, tell him where you acquired that little piece," I said loudly so that if it came up missing, Tom would know where to look.

"Oh, that's nothing. Belinda spotted it at a thrift store and couldn't leave it alone. If you like it, Dad, you can have it."

I was shocked that Tom was so willing to give away his priceless possessions to the old man.

"Thanks, Tommy, but I don't have anywhere to keep things."

As if it weren't already fairly clear that things weren't exactly on the up-and-up, this momentary exchange fueled my suspicions even though I couldn't put my finger on what was wrong about it. What I did recognize, though, was that I had just been outsmarted. Determined not to let that happen again, I turned to the old man, who was sitting almost directly across from me, and asked him, "Let us know when you're ready to leave. I'll bet you're tired from all the tests and stuff from the hospital."

The old man glowered at me as if I had struck a nerve. Before he could say a word, though, Tom came to his rescue and told him to relax and stay as long as he liked. "We have plenty of room, as you can see."

Having won that round, too, the old man smiled and settled himself deeper into his chair. "I don't want to bother you, son, though I sure do like it here."

"I'm serious, Dad."

"I know you are, son. Say, this is a pretty nice spread. It must have cost you plenty of dough. But you were always an industrious boy, and I don't think anyone doubted you'd make it big someday."

"I just got lucky, that's all."

"No, son, you don't get this from luck." He opened his arms for the world to come in and admire Tom's possessions. "You get this by using your brains, skill, and hard work."

"Thanks, Dad, but you're making too much out of it. Belinda also worked hard so we could afford nice things."

"She'll be home soon, I hope. It'll be good to see her again."

It was a curious thing to say. Tom and Belinda met and married years after our father disappeared. "That's strange," I said, confident that I now had him where I wanted, "Our father ran away from our home when Tom and I were kids. If you're our father, how could you know Belinda?"

The old man tensed up. For a second, he looked like a wild animal in one of Tom's pictures. "I don't know what you're talking about," the old man grumbled. "I meant in person. I've heard so much about her."

"What kind of bull…," I began but Tom interrupted by handing the old man another object that he could examine.

"I got it in the Caymans last year. I don't really know what it is, but I think it's pretty cool."

"It sure is, Tommy. You always had a good eye for interesting things, even when you were little. You've come a long way since then. You're rich, you got a good family, you got it all, Tommy boy. I can't tell you how proud I am of you."

"Jimmy's done well for himself, too, Dad. He's a..."

"Don't sell yourself short, Tommy. You used to do that when you were a kid–giving credit to others, I mean–but it's time to stop letting others share your glory. You earned what you have, son, make no mistake."

"Thanks, Dad. I only wanted to point out that Jimmy has done well for himself, too. You should be proud of him as well."

The old man remained silent for a minute or so. "Yes, indeed, this place must have set you back a pretty penny," he said as he admiringly scanned the room. "But you got to junk the damn car, boy. It's for wannabes."

Tom pretended to laugh it off as though the old man were making a joke. I, however, had taken all I could about my car.

"That's my car, not Tom's," I said, a little more heatedly than I wanted to. "What are you driving these days?"

The man squinted at me as if this was the first time he had ever set eyes on me. "Who are you?"

"Dad, it's Jimmy, your other son."

He shook his head almost imperceptibly and then turned back to Tom. "Well, I can't tell you how glad I am that you came for me. I would have died in that place if it weren't for you, son."

"That's interesting," I said, trying to press what I thought was my advantage. "Tom said you were dying. Not true?"

The old man ignored me. "It was touch and go for a while," he said to Tom. "I wasn't positive I'd make it. But when you called...well, son, it meant the world to me and pulled me out of it. I'm not out of the woods yet, but I'm feeling better than I have in quite some time."

"What's the matter, Dad? Maybe I can get someone to help."

"Excuse me, who called whom?" I asked, as I watched what was now beginning to seem to be a farce of some kind performed for my benefit.

"No, it's too late for me. You got you own life to live. But I'd sure like to see your wife and that young daughter of yours before my time is up."

"They should be home in a few minutes. Hey, I've forgotten to offer you something to eat and drink."

"Don't go to any trouble on my account. I should be going soon. But I'll have a drink of whatever you're having."

Tom smiled and did his "sure-Dad" thing and ran into the other room. I sat silently, making a visual inventory of the valuables in the room. When I noticed the old man reaching for a small, valuable-looking object, I tried to distract him while at the same time attempting to get to the bottom of things. In a feigned, offhanded tone, I asked him where he had met Tom. He angled his round shoulders toward me and, with an irritated look on his hanging face, was about to respond when Tom came back in the room with a tray of drinks, each one a whiskey from the bottle on the tray.

"Here, Dad," Tom said, as he handed the old man one of the glasses. "If you're cold, this will warm you up." He gave me a glass, took one for himself, and sat down in a large, comfortable chair in front of us and placed the tray on the floor next to his chair.

"It looks good, Tommy. You sure know how to make them."

"Yeah, Tom, who taught you how to pour it in a glass?"

Tom didn't say anything, but the old man did. Without acknowledging my presence, he took a long, appreciative drink, and then asked Tom, "Why's he here?" He jerked his head in my direction.

Tom glanced at me. "Dad, it's Jimmy…"

"You know what he asked me while you were getting drinks? He wanted to know when I met you. That's an easy one, even for an old codger like me. It was the first time I held that little ball of crying flesh in my arms. Your mother had just handed you to me, Tommy, and it was the happiest day in my life."

"Thanks, Dad. I'll bet you remember Jimmy…"

"You know, son, I've said it before, but you make me proud. You always have, and I can't tell you how much I love you. Why, I…"

"A ball of flesh is one thing," I interjected, "but it might be more interesting to hear about your other memories of young Tom here. But first, maybe you could tell us a little about what you've been doing for the past thirty-five years and why you didn't utter a word to us during this entire time until you supposedly called Tom, your beloved son."

The old man placed his hands of the of the chair and, judging by his narrowed eyes and tight (though lopsided) lips, I thought he might leap up on all fours and charge at me. Luckily (for the old man), Tom verbally intervened and suggested that we table that discussion for another time and asked the old man to come with him to some other room in house to get a robe. "I forgot you were still wearing your hospital things." Tom gently helped him up and, as they left the living room, the man holding tightly to Tom's arm, Tom looked back at me. It wasn't a pleasant look.

He returned with the old man about ten minutes later. They were laughing about something when they entered the living room, and the smiles and chuckling continued as Tom helped the old man back into the chair. The old man was now in a clean robe and, from what I could tell from the open area underneath his chin, clean pajamas, too, red silky ones.

I should have taken off while they were out. For once, I didn't want to be in Tom's house, not with the old man there, but I couldn't leave because I was increasingly concerned that the old man might try to pull something behind Tom's back. Tom was tall, muscular, agile, and smart, but you never know what can happened when your back is turned and you're off guard. And I still wanted answers to my questions. It didn't matter to me whether or not the old man was the genuine article. Real or not, he had been gone for so many years that he couldn't be anything but a stranger. No, I wanted Tom to know what he was dealing with, especially because his wife and daughter would be home any minute.

Once they were settled into their chairs and basking in the warmth of family humor, I asked the old man who he was and why he reached out to Tom.

The old man snorted and then told me that I had "no goddamn business" asking him questions like that. Whiskey glass firmly in hand, he leaned back in his chair and glowered at me like an old, bald hyena.

"Do you remember my name?" I asked him.

"Come on, Jim…"

"Don't baby him, son," the old man said to my brother. "It's none of his business, but I'm happy to answer all questions. Just like always, right?"

"Okay, start with the questions I just asked you."

"Dad, it's not necessary. We have all we…"

"No, Tommy boy, I haven't kept any secrets from you–and I think you know that–and I don't intend to start now. Now, where was I?"

"Yes, where were you over the past thirty-five years?"

The old man took the final drop of his drink and asked Tom for another.

Since the bottle was practically empty, Tom ran out of the room and returned with another bottle, and refilled our glasses. Settled again in his chair, he looked at the old man as the latter took another big swallow and shook his head in satisfaction.

"Fine, fine, Tommy, really fine."

"And your answer?"

"You again? Answer to what?"

Tom looked at me and said that "dad" was a little tired and that this probably wasn't the best time to chat.

"Good idea, Tommy. Show me where I could take a load off for a few minutes, and then I'll be ready for your wife."

Tom led the old man back to one of the bedrooms. When he returned, I was on my feet and livid over his stupidity. "Why did you do that?" I demanded. "You told me this was my chance to ask about anything. Can't you see the old goat is pulling one over on you? I don't know why he was in the hospital, but he doesn't look sick. He looks old, but he doesn't look like he's dying. Look, Tom, if you really think he's our father, which I don't, we better get some answers about his whereabouts for the past three decades. Either way, he could be dangerous."

"Yes, this is our chance to talk to him, but not when he's so exhausted he can't think straight. I don't think he's pulling anything over on me, I don't think he's dangerous, and, yes, I think he's our father. I don't understand why you're behaving this way. What's the matter with you?"

"What's the matter with you?"

"Stop it."

"There's something wrong here, Tom, and I'm beginning to think you know what it is. This guy isn't our father, and you two have had conversations or interactions that you're not telling me about."

"What are you saying?"

"You just happen to have a robe and pajamas that fit him?"

"You better adjust your eyes. What I gave him fit me, and if you looked you should have been able to see that were way too big for him. It's what I had."

"Okay, okay, this is going nowhere. Tell me why this guy is here and why you're bringing me into it."

"What? He's here because he's our father, and I brought you into this so you could talk to him and maybe put the past behind you. Listen to me. I know what you're going through, but we can't be pissed all our lives. He could have changed. But you won't know unless you give him a half chance…"

"I have been trying to get answers from him, and you've either been covering for him or shuffling him out of reach."

"He's tired. Give him a chance to…"

"Give him a chance? I'll tell you what. Father or not, I'll give him the same chance our father gave us. God help you if you turn your back on him."

"Come on, Goofball."

I left the room before Tom could stop me and went to my car. Perhaps I was a little lightheaded from the whiskey, but I was confident that I understood the conditions on the road better than the conditions inside Tom's house. I loved and honored my brother, but something just wasn't right about the relationship between him and the old man, and I wasn't getting straight answers to anything. I was sure that Tom would claim that I was put off over the pajamas, which were obviously not his, but they were only the tip of the iceberg in terms of all the nonsense and subterfuge going on. Closing my eyes briefly, I sighed in disgust, and as I reached into my pocket for my keys, Tom came up to the driver's-side of the car.

"You're not going anywhere without these," he said as he dangled the keys on his index finger in front of the window. "Are you sure you can drive safely?"

I rolled down the window enough to grab them and then rolled it back up.

"Jim, this is no way to act. He's going to be gone soon, and this is…"

"Forget it," I shouted through the closed window and started the car. "You watch out for your wife and child and your other valuables." Putting the car into gear, I took off and left him standing in a shadow. I don't remember much after that, although I managed to make it home and put myself to bed.

6

I was standing at the kitchen counter the following morning staring at the cup of black coffee I had just poured. I couldn't quite bring myself to drink it. My head ached and my stomach was queasy over what had happened and was possibly happening at Tom's house. The old man was clearly a fraud, and my normally intelligent, discerning brother was letting this stranger lead him around by the nose. I couldn't tell what the old man was after (probably Tom's money), but it was clear that he was after something and that he intended to hang around until he got it. But there was something else beyond this simple fraudulent scheme. I couldn't quite believe that my brother, the one person whom I trusted above all others, wasn't entirely forthcoming about his relationship, if you could call it that, with the old man. Every time you turned around some non sequitur rose its ugly head. Who made the first call? How many calls had been made? Had the old man actually met Belinda and Chelsea? Whose silk pajamas were whose? I could go on and on. As I was going over these things and trying to make sense of what happened at Tom's house, Tara came into the kitchen and sat down at the kitchen table. She was dressed in loose slacks and a loose blouse, which suggested that she was going to be out of the house for a while.

"Pretty wild night, I hear," she said as she pulled the magazine on the table in front of her and opened it.

"What are you talking about?" I sniffed the coffee to make sure it was just right.

Although Tara was a year older than me, she looked as young and fresh as the first time I met her. Her features were still sculpturally perfect, and her eyes now seemed as luminous as those of a Persian cat. I couldn't resist her, especially when she smiled as she did now. "Tom called last night," she said in her calm, soothing voice, "and asked after you. He felt bad about letting you go home by yourself. He said he shouldn't have given you your keys in your condition, but you were belligerent and he didn't want another fight. He told me everything."

"In my condition? What do you mean belligerent? Either way, he's full of crap. I thought I was quite polite and reasonable under the circumstances. I hardly raised my voice once, and I only had a single drink, with maybe a couple refills."

"I see." She began turning the pages as she skimmed through the articles.

"I hope so. Did Tom tell you about the old man he invited inside his house for a drink?"

"Your father?"

"I don't know who this character is. He claims to be our father, but I can assure you he's not."

She looked at me. "Tom thinks he is. What makes you think he isn't?"

"Whose side are you on? I think I'd know our father as well as him. The man doesn't look like anything I remember."

"It's been a lot of years."

"He doesn't sound like him, either. He doesn't act like him. His mannerisms are unlike anything in our family. And he can't remember the very things he should remember if he's our father. He doesn't even know my name. None of this bothers Tom."

"Tom has had plenty of time to speak to him, am I right?"

"Oh, he's been speaking to him, all right, more than he's letting on. But that doesn't mean anything in terms of knowing who this guy is."

"It may be worth keeping in mind that Tom is older than you and that he had more years with your father than you did. It stands to reason that he has insights about your father that you lack. I'm not making a judgment, you understand. I'm only suggesting that Tom may be in a better position to determine if the gentleman is your father." Tara, if you couldn't guess, was always working, even during her off hours at home.

I carried my coffee to the table and sat down across from her. As Tara looked at me, I pulled her magazine toward me and glanced through the table of contents. Not finding anything of interest, I slid it back to her, leaving it at an angle. She straightened it and flipped through several pages until she found the one that she had been reading.

"Sure, but it doesn't mean that his judgement is better than mine or that he can see the truth when it's staring him in the face."

"No one's trying to downplay the value of your judgment. Perhaps for the short term, however, you might want to moderate the vehemence of your objections, at least in front of Tom. He believes the man is your father, and the situation is his to handle."

"Vehemence, my ass. Don't you get it? He's not handling it. Tom is practically the only family I have left, and so I have a right and an obligation to worry about him–vehemently, if necessary. Hold on. You're not getting it. Even if the old man were our father, he's been gone for so many years that we no longer know who or what he is. Or what he's capable of. But as I said before, he's not our father, and Tom let this dirt bag come into his house and mingle with his family. Can't you see how dangerous it is? If the old man hasn't already done what he plans to do, it's only a matter of time before he finishes his work and maybe Tom and his family at the same time."

"Calm down. You're losing control of yourself."

"I'm losing control? Don't you see? This kind of thing happens every day. Remember that case in Florida? We don't know a thing about that old man. We don't know why he's here. But, okay, maybe I'm wrong. Maybe I am losing control. Maybe I'm vehement. So, why don't you tell me what the old man's up to. You seem to have as much information as I do. Why's he ingratiating himself into Tom's family?"

She took a sip of her coffee and leaned back slightly in her chair (I say slightly, because she always kept her back straight when she was sitting). "I'm not claiming to have any particular insights. What I'm trying to say is that there's no reason to get so worked up over something you don't fully understand or have responsibility for."

"Did you hear what I just said?"

"Yes, I did, and I respect the fact that you're concerned about your brother. But since the man is not in our house, you should let Tom worry about him. Your brother's no dummy, and he's not going to let anyone take advantage of him."

"You didn't see him last night."

"No, but I know Tom. He also called again this morning. He's concerned about you. You should give him a ring back."

I tried to take a sip of my coffee but couldn't swallow. "Any aspirin around here?" While Tara was drinking hers, she motioned with her other hand to the cupboard over the sink. As soon as I was back in my chair, I asked, "Wait a minute. Why didn't you tell me sooner? Was anyone hurt? Did the old goat steal the family jewels?"

"You shouldn't have had so much to drink last night. Everything is fine at Tom's house. Your brother is, however, worried about your father. The man, I mean, at his house has a heart condition. I think you're aware of that."

"What are you talking about? The old man is still at his house? Is Tom out of his mind? That old fool didn't look like he had a health condition when we saw him at the hospital. He's a mean, cranky SOB, who didn't know my name. He's supposedly our father, and he didn't know his son's name. What a joke."

"Is that why you're upset? Your father didn't know or couldn't remember your name?"

I stared at her for a moment. "I have to get ready for work," I said matter-of-factly and went to the sink and poured my coffee down the drain.

"It's Sunday. You don't have to go into the office."

Tara was right, of course, but I insisted that she had misunderstood what I said. I explained that I needed to go into the office to catch up on a few things before tomorrow.

"Fine. Oh, I forgot to mention," she said as I was walking away. "Tom invited us to dinner tonight, and I accepted."

That stopped me in my tracks. I did an about face and said, "I wish you would have consulted me first."

"Since when do I have to consult you about going to Tom's?"

"We have other plans. We're not going."

"What plans? There's nothing on the calendar." She walked over to the pantry door and examined the calendar hanging on it. "I don't see anything for tonight."

I took a deep breath and reiterated the words "other plans."

"Unless these plans are a little more concrete, I'm going to go. I haven't seen Tom and Belinda in ages."

I didn't feel like arguing with her and so I agreed, with the proviso that we leave immediately if the old man was is there.

She shrugged vaguely and returned to her coffee and magazine.

7

I should have stayed home, but I didn't want Tara accusing me of making up a story. I know, I was being stubborn and childish, and I didn't want Tara accusing me of these things, either. Since my office was only a few minutes away, I made my way there with the intention of doing something for the week ahead.

Not surprisingly, it was dead quiet when I walked past the security guard, who merely nodded and didn't say anything. Once I was in my small cubbyhole of an office, I looked at all the papers spread across my desk. They were bits and pieces from various assignments either waiting for approval or waiting to be finished. I checked my computer for messages and then took a quick look at a poster that I was designing for a small client. It was boring, and the assignment wasn't very exciting, and at that moment I didn't feel like doing anything else to it, not even to change the colors that seemed off, and I leaned back in my chair and clasped my hands behind my head. I was killing some time before I went back home (I also didn't want Tara to think that, if I came home too early, I really didn't have anything important to do this day), and as I closed my eyes for a few seconds, I started to think about our father. I hadn't given him much thought for years, maybe decades, and I wondered what I could actually remember about him.

It wasn't much. He disappeared when I was eight, and so what I did remember was vague and maybe a little fanciful. For example, I remembered him as being tall and trim and very strong. But when I thought about it, I realized that his dimensions and strength were only in relation to me, a puny little boy, and that most boys grow up thinking that their fathers are big and strong. I am, however, positive that he wore gray suits and that he worked in a factory. I suppose that Tom might have told me this, and he might also have explained that the man worked not on the factory floor but in the factory office, hence the suits. But there were other things, things that I was positive I remembered, and they came back to me clearly, without an intermediary. One was that our father was rarely at home (our mother always said that he worked long hours), and, on those joyous occasions when he was present, he didn't like to be bothered, or at least he didn't like his two boys to bother him. He spent most of this time either in his bedroom (which he shared with our mother) or sitting silently in the living room in front of the TV. And, unlike other fathers, he didn't play with Tom and me (Tom disputed this), and he would get upset if we were noisy or if one of our toys got in his way as he moved around the house. There were other things, too–he had short hair (at the time, all the other fathers had short hair, too) and he favored plain, undecorated ties, mainly red and yellow–though none of the memories amounted to much, and none either singly or in aggregate helped me understand the man himself, which at that moment I wanted to do. For a few years after his disappearance, I sought to elicit more information from my brother who, as my wife indicated, was older than me and had a greater range of experiences with the man, but even he couldn't come up with more than a few details that made our father stand out from all the other men crossing our paths on a busy street. Our mother wasn't any help, either. She refused to talk about him, and, when the occasion moved her, she would cry incoherently about her loss and what he (and, by extension, the rest of the world) had done to her. However, there is one memory, or one set of memories, that I have of the man that stands out with absolute clarity, and the reason for this is that it concerns an emotionally charged event, quite possibly the most emotionally charged event of my life up to that point. It was the day our father disappeared.

It happened in the middle of summer, on a hot, cloudless day. By the time dinner rolled around, it was sweltering inside the house, even with all the windows open (we didn't own an air conditioner). I remember sitting at the dinner table with Tom and our father as we waited for our mother to set out the plates. Our father was at the head of the table, and I was centered at one of the sides directly across from my brother. (My brother and I never thought to ask why our mother cooked, served, and cleaned up while our father sat silently reading the newspaper, as he did this evening, or relaxing in front of the TV, as he did most evenings.) Like all the other times at the table, he snapped at Tom and me to sit up when the last plate (our mother's) was placed at the end of the table opposite him. Once she was seated, and after we all mumbled grace, everyone began eating–except him. I won't forget this moment, because he wasn't one to forego dinner at the table, even if he complained about the food.

Ignoring his plate, he carefully folded his newspaper, placed it on the table next to his plate, and with his right thumb smoothed the folds. Once he had completed this task to his satisfaction, he got up and, without taking the paper with him, announced that he was going out for a "smoke." That was his term for taking a cigarette break, which he did from time to time outside (our mother couldn't stand the smell of cigarettes) but never, as I recall, while we were supposed to be eating. Seconds later, I heard the clatter of the front screen door (it didn't close properly), and that was that. Our mother didn't say anything about his absence, though she had to have been angry that he hadn't touched something she had gone to a good deal of trouble to prepare, and she didn't give any indication that he wasn't coming back that evening. His dinner plate, I think, had remained on the table until long after Tom and I had gone to bed, and it wasn't until the following afternoon that Tom and I had any inkling that something might be out of the ordinary.

My brother and I didn't expect to see our father in the morning when we got ready for school and had our breakfast with our mother at the kitchen table. He left for work or whatever else he did before the sun came up and was usually home long after it went down. And so we went to school just like we always did. Even our mother didn't seem particularly distressed at the time. I think she was more quiet than usual during breakfast, but she still had enough strength to see to it that we were properly dressed and fed, and, as we left, she kissed us both on the top of the head and told us that she loved us. That was another thing–our father never to my knowledge told us that he loved us. If we assumed it, we probably assumed incorrectly.

I walked home that afternoon. As I approached our house, I saw a police car parked on the street in front of it. I guess that I was too young to connect the police with anything that happened to us or in our house. Tom, as I found out later, wasn't at home when the screen door clanged shut behind me. The lights were out in the house and, as I walked deeper into it, I spotted my mother's bare legs and the waist of her dress. In front of her, one on each side, were two gigantic policemen, dressed in blue uniforms and with large guns at their sides. Her head was down, and she was softly crying in her hands, and as I approached the policemen turned and squinted at me as if I were responsible for something.

I instinctively took a step back. The largest of the two officers, an older man with a bulbous nose, nodded to the other and came over to me, squatting down so that we were at eye level.

"You must be Tommy," he said with a smile that exposed his yellowish teeth.

I shook my head, and he looked up at my mother, who also shook her head. "Jimmy," she sobbed.

He turned back to me. "Yes, Jimmy, I should have known. Well, how are you, Jimmy? Did you have a good day at school? Quiet, huh?" Looking back at my mother, he asked her if he could take me into another room to have a private talk with me. She nodded. But before he could turn back to me, I skidded around his gigantic legs, sprinted upstairs to my bedroom, and slammed the door behind me. Glancing around the messy room in a panic, I squeezed under the bed next to an old stuffed tiger and a pair of dirty underwear. I think I fell asleep shortly afterwards. I don't know if the policeman came after me, and I don't recall how long I was under the bed. Later in the evening, I cautiously tiptoed downstairs into a quiet, empty house. The police car was gone and my mother, if she was home, was behind the closed door of the bedroom that she shared with our father. It's funny, but I don't have any memories of the rest of the day. I presume that my mother fed me and put me to bed, I'm sure that my brother came home at some point, but the rest, as I said, is all a blank.

The days immediately following the event were almost equally blank. I don't know if there were other calls and visits from the police, and I don't remember if our mother said anything to us during this time about our father's absence. Once, long after the event, I asked Tom about his recollections of the period, and he insisted that he couldn't remember any of it, at least nothing related to our father's absence. My memory is clearer about some of the things that happened a few days later.

Sometime during the following week (I don't remember the day), I came home from school to find another unknown person in the house. He was heavyset, though not as tall as our father, and he had a black mustache and wore a Hawaiian shirt that exposed his thick, hairy arms. He immediately came to the door when the screen rattled and, bending down slightly, he proffered his giant hand to me. As I instinctively took it, he announced that he was my mother's cousin, Mr. John Wellington, John for short. With a pleasant smile, he explained in a calm, confident voice that our mother wasn't feeling well and that he had been asked to stay a few days to help out while she got better. Standing upright with his hands on his sides, he gently asked if it was okay with me if he stayed a while. He made it seem that I had a choice in the matter and, when I agreed (what else could I say?), he laughed, patted me gently on the shoulder, and asked if I would like him to fix me something to eat.

Over the following days, weeks, and months, John established himself as another member of the family. Our mother during this time ceded control of the house to John and retreated to her bedroom, which she rarely left except on those rare occasions when she was "doing a little better." John cooked, cleaned, saw us off to school, and helped us with our homework. Unlike our father, he played and spent time with us. For one of my birthdays, he got me a trainset. He helped me set it up and spent considerable time sitting with me as I ran the engine and two cars around the oval track. Tom wasn't interested in trains, but I remember one day when he gave Tom a baseball bat, taught him the basics of baseball, and then went with him to every Little League game that Tom ever played. I admit that I was a little envious of Tom and his heroics on the baseball field, but I attended most of Tom's games and enjoyed them, too. One time, shortly before Tom went off to college, John coaxed our mother out of her room and we all went on a short vacation to the mountains somewhere. Tom and I had a good time, one that could have been better if our mother had come out of her motel room more often. I came to love John, and I loved him in a way that I could have loved our father. There were even moments when I wished he was our father.

There was something else that was coming to mind, though it quickly faded when I opened my eyes and looked at my watch. It was getting late, and I knew that Tara would have a snit if we didn't arrive at Tom's on time.

8

We were five minutes early. Tom met us at the door wearing an apron with the phrase "World's Greatest" emblazoned across the front. After the usual handshake and kisses, he waltzed us through the house to the back, glass-enclosed patio, where Belinda greeted us with more hugs and kisses. We chatted for a few minutes as we settled into the oversized, wicker chairs at one end, and then Tom went back inside to get drinks and check on dinner. While we waited for his return, Belinda casually informed us that Chelsea was sleeping in her room because she was a "little under the weather." There was a tinge of exasperation in her otherwise pleasant voice. "Maybe, if we're lucky, she'll make an appearance later if she feels any better."

Tom was back a few minutes later with a six-pack of beer and a plate of crackers with thin pieces of yellow cheese on them. As we stretched out while dinner simmered, Tom was unusually lively, chatting about this and that and jumping up whenever he thought that we might need something. I hadn't seen Tom this lively since he closed some "big deal" about four or five years ago. He was beside himself back then because of the "bundle" he made selling a certain property in the city, and, throughout the evening, he kept bouncing around and looking for every conversational opportunity to highlight his success and his business acumen. The cause of his excitement this time wasn't quite so clear, and so I attributed his behavior to another business success and, secondarily, to his happiness in seeing Tara and me. We were in the midst of an interesting conversation about problems Chelsea was having at school when Tara, of all people, asked Tom if the girl had met her grandfather. It was an innocent question, I'm sure, but it sent a ripple through my system and made Tom even more giddy.

"Belinda's father is a nice old gentleman," I began but was immediately cut off when Tom wholeheartedly said yes.

"She's thrilled. She now has two grandpas."

I guess I got a little hot under the collar. No one had yet ascertained who the old man was and, if there was a one in a trillion chance that he was our father, I couldn't understand why Tom would be so excited about introducing to his daughter the man who had deserted his family.

"Two? You don't know who this guy is, Tom. He could be a serial killer, for all you know."

"I know who he is, and I don't care if you accept it or not. Chelsea loved him right from the start."

"Wait a minute. How can you be so sure about the old man's claims? What exactly do you know that I don't? And why for God's sake did you introduce him to Chelsea?"

"Goofball, calm yourself. As I told you before, he told me things that only our father could know–things that no one could have guessed in a million years."

"Like what? Last time, you could only give me some vague nonsense about walking around the block. An idiot could have guessed that in three seconds."

"Let's not go over this again. I told you before what he said to me, and I'm satisfied."

"It doesn't satisfy me, Tom, and I was there when our father ran away from home. Admit it, you don't have a clue who this guy is."

There was a pause while Tom evidently worked to his check his anger. Taking a deep breath, he replied, "I know what I know, and if you don't want to accept it, that's your loss."

I couldn't help mumbling to myself, "I'm not the loser here." Tom's hearing was more acute that I thought, and he jumped up and looked around as if he was late for something. With the muscles in his jaws throbbing, he announced to everyone but me that he would be back in a minute. "I have to check dinner."

Belinda was silent while he was gone, but Tara wasn't. "What's the matter with you?" she demanded.

"What do you mean what's the matter with me? Belinda, what your husband's saying is ridiculous."

Tara wouldn't let it alone. "What makes you so sure you're right and he's wrong?"

"Because I was there. You weren't." Once again, I wasn't quite as dispassionate as I had intended. Tara and Belinda both turned away and pretended to look at something in the yard.

Tom reappeared a few seconds later with a tray overflowing with food and asked us to sit at the table. We sat down and, with forced smiles on our faces, managed small talk for the entire dinner. I didn't say much, though. I wasn't interested in the corruption of the American judicial system, or the strength of the US manufacturing center, or even the latest crime shows on TV. I was angry. I admit it. I was furious with Tara for having taken Tom's word over mine, and I was galled that Tom had revealed a character trait that until this time I didn't believe he had–gullibility. I was even pissed off with Belinda because of her refusal to weigh in on the issue and her smiling avoidance of what I thought was a legitimate line of inquiry–the old man. When dinner was mercifully over and we were all engaged in cleaning off the table, I wanted to ask Tom when the old man left the house (since he wasn't there this evening, I assumed that he was no longer staying with Tom, which of course didn't mean that he was gone) and then I began to feel a twinge of regret that I had argued with my brother. We rarely argued, and never with the vehemence that we had since the advent of the old man. When we were done and Tara and Belinda repaired to the living room for after dinner drinks (it was getting too cold to sit out on the patio), I went into the kitchen to help Tom with the dishes.

"Look," I said as I scraped food into the trashcan, "I'm sorry. I didn't mean to spoil things. I don't agree with you about the old man, and, yes, that's my opinion. It will always be my opinion."

Tom was at the sink rinsing dishes, and he stopped and looked at me. "That's okay, Goofball. We all have our differences."

I made a good effort to smile. "Would you stop calling me Goofball? I wrecked the dinner, didn't I?"

"You are a goofball, and that's why you wrecked part of the dinner. But that's okay. It wasn't the first time."

"There isn't anything more you want to share to convince me that he is…whatever he is? The old man, I mean."

"Maybe later."

While he was chuckling over my discomfort (I don't like apologizing), I asked him when Chelsea saw the old man. Did he wake up last night after I left?

"This morning before he went out."

I started putting dishes carefully into the dishwasher. "When did he go?" I asked a minute later.

Tom was now wiping off the counters. "This afternoon…"

"And you felt safe with him here at night. Sorry."

"Yes, I did. Very safe."

I stopped what I was doing and, still holding a dinner plate, looked right at Tom. "Okay, so did he tell you where he was going?"

"I thought you weren't interested. He didn't tell me everything, but he told me he had to go back to the shelter where was staying."

"I knew it. Makes sense. Okay, did he leave a contact number?" I didn't want to call the old man, but I was curious to know if he was planning to stay connected with my brother.

"Nope."

"Good, good. I think we're getting somewhere. He's gone, then. I mean, really gone. Is that a fair characterization?"

Tom stopped and eyed me skeptically. "Is what a fair characterization? What are you getting at? Are you asking me if I'm going to see him again? Of course, I am. In fact, I'm going to see him later this evening. You can, too, if you like."

"No, thanks. You're going to the shelter?"

"What are you babbling about?"

"The shelter he went to today. You're going to meet him there, right?"

"No. Why would I meet him there?"

"He lives there, right?"

"God, you sound like a prosecutor. He used to live there. He's coming back to stay with me."

"Here? Why?"

Tom ran the fingers of one hand through his thick, nearly black hair. There was a look of frustration on his face. "He went to the shelter to get his things. He's coming back here. I'm letting him stay here until he gets back on his feet. I was hoping that he would be back in time for dinner."

I was stunned, and the dish slipped from my hand and shattered on the floor. I started to apologize, but Tom didn't wait and reached down to pick up the large pieces. The wives, hearing the crash and fearing the worst, came rushing breathlessly into the kitchen. For a few seconds, I gave them every reason to believe the worst.

"Have you lost your marbles? Why would you do something like that when you don't have the slightest…"

He tossed the broken shards violently into the trashcan and turned to me. The muscles in his firm jaw were throbbing. "Get this through your thick skull," he practically shouted. "I don't care what you think, and I don't give a damn about the past. He made a mistake—everyone makes mistakes—and I'm going to give him a break. He deserves it. If you don't like it, too bad."

I didn't respond. When Tom yanked a whiskbroom out from underneath the counter and began sweeping up the small pieces on the floor, I walked away. It was becoming clear that when it came to the old man, he didn't give a damn about his own family or even me. It was pathetic, it was dangerous, and I wasn't going to listen to another crazy word about the old man and his supposed relationship with Tom. As I walked past Tara, who was standing wide-eyed next to the kitchen entrance, I asked without looking at her if she was coming with me. Without a word, she followed me to the car and got in as I started the engine. I was almost at the end of the driveway when a heavyset, shadowy figure approached the house on foot. I curved around the figure and continued home. Tara gave me silent treatment for the rest of the night.

9

I spent most of the following day at work struggling to make progress on two important assignments, a poster for an organization searching for missing children and a logo for a school offering adult education classes. I wasn't exactly thrilled by the work–there wasn't a lot I could do with the subjects from an artistic point of view–and so I was having trouble concentrating on what I needed to do and, on those rare occasions when my mind felt sharp, I couldn't draw a straight line without causing another line to curve or add a dash of pastoral color without turning the whole into a garish nightmare. My problem– my creative block, if you will–was exacerbated by my inability to set aside, if only for a few minutes, the ongoing argument with my brother. I just couldn't understand Tom's need to reconnect with our fugitive father, and I couldn't fathom why someone as smart and savvy as my brother couldn't see through that flabby old man. I still couldn't figure out what the old man's ultimate goal was, but it was quite clear that one of his sub- or ancillary goals was to drive a wedge between Tom and me. My God, it was evident in everything the old man did from the way he made Tom defend me when he supposedly couldn't recall my name to his absence at dinner, which he no doubt knew would encourage me to badmouth him behind his porcine back and force Tom to defend him against me. He knew that Tom would see me as the bad guy, the person who wanted to ruin everything for everyone else. Well, it was working, and it was becoming nearly impossible to have a rational, civilized conversation with my brother about the old man. Nevertheless, for the sake of our relationship, I needed to find a way around this roadblock so that I could help my brother and protect him, which I couldn't begin to do until we settled our differences about the past and came to a fraternal agreement about the future.

By the early afternoon, I had become so frustrated with my work and my brother that I shut off the computer as if I were going home and put my head down onto my desk. Shortly afterwards, a colleague, whose office was next to mine, came inside and offered me some surprising news about our firm.

"Hey, man, sorry for waking you," Jeff said as he sat down in the chair next to my desk. Jeff was in his early thirties, long and skinny, with a head of reddish hair that he forced behind his ears. He was a good friend, an inveterate gossip, and he frequently came across things long before management announced them. I often thought that he was having an affair with the corporate secretary, one of the few people in the firm who was in on all the corporate decisions, but he denied it and claimed that they were only good friends, coworkers.

"No, no, I was only relaxing my eyes. What's going on?"

"Maybe you know more about it than I do."

"About what?"

He ran both hands through his hair to make sure that it was firmly in place. "The reorganization."

I dropped the pencil that I wasn't holding. "What reorganization?"

He looked left and right as if someone might be hiding in my tiny office. "Don't tell anyone, but I have it on good authority that we haven't met our numbers for eight consecutive quarters, and there's going to be a reorganization to cut costs."

I reached for the computer but stopped before touching it. "I don't know what that means. What's going to be reorganized?"

"This. Me, you, the company, everything, man. I don't have the details, but it could mean job eliminations and salary cuts."

"They can't cut us. We do the work."

"I don't know what you're working on, but it would be easy to foist it on someone else and double their workload. Management is going to tell us to work harder for less money and fewer benefits."

"You serious?"

"Tell you what. I'm speaking with someone later this afternoon who knows something about it. This individual is on the inside, if you know what I mean. I'll let you know what she says."

Once Jeff was gone, I shrugged my shoulders and told myself that his claims were the product of someone's overheated imagination. We had good management, after all, and it seemed farfetched that they would do something like that to the very people who had been loyal to the firm and had help make it successful. I pulled out a sketchpad from beneath a stack of sketchpads on the floor next to my desk. I was going to jot down some ideas for my two assignments, but as I put colored pencil to paper, something else came to mind and I tossed the pad and pencil on top of the others on the floor. Finally switching my computer back on, I reviewed some of the work I had completed over the past year. There wasn't a lot, not as much as I had produced in prior years, and I couldn't exactly claim that any of it was particularly skillful (one of my junior colleagues might have done it all just well), and I started to wonder if I could be one of the employees on the chopping block. Despite my seniority at the firm, it didn't seem entirely unreasonable to replace me with someone who could produce the same amount of work at the same level of proficiency but at a lower rate of pay.

I massaged my temples with the heels of my hands. I couldn't imagine what I would do if the firm let me go. Unlike my brother, who was oozing dollar bills, I needed every cent I had, and Tara and I couldn't get by on her salary alone. And getting another job wouldn't be easy at my age and with my experience. Even in the best of economies, there weren't typically a lot of openings in my field, and I didn't know how to do anything else. In fact, this was the only real job I'd ever held in my entire life. Equally significant, if I was canned, I would have to tell Tom. Sure, he'd probably lend me some money, but I'd have to suffer the indignity of asking for handouts at my age. And I'm sure the old man would weigh in on my position somehow. Our father, as I vaguely recalled, wouldn't have been surprised if I lost my job, because he didn't think I'd ever amount to anything. Or was it the old man who said that?

"Damn him," I said aloud, "and that stupid brother of mine. He'd probably tell the old man everything. Why did Tom have to be so rich?"

I got up and started pacing my office. Since I had no windows, the bare, whitewashed walls made the small room more oppressive than usual. What was I going to do if I was laid off, and why did I have to think about the old man at this time of all times? Unable to stand my office, I went out into the hall and, with nothing better to do, went to see Jeff. Though it was unreasonable to expect him to have additional information since he left my office, I nevertheless wanted to speak to him about the situation and maybe ferret out some more details that he may have neglected to tell me. Maybe there was something he could offer that would lessen the significance of what he said.

He was working at his computer when I entered, and he turned toward me with a look of mild irritation, as if I were going to ask him to help me with my assignments.

"Jeff," I said, as I plopped into one of the two chairs in his office. "Got a few seconds?" I wasn't exactly sure what I wanted to speak to him about other than to get some reassurance that my position at the firm was secure. Rubbing my chin, I said, "God, I hope there isn't a layoff. You're in a better position to weather it than me."

"We're all vulnerable, man," he said and brightened a little. "No one's safer than anyone else. Well, I suppose upper management and maybe the secretary, but that's about it. No sense worrying about it until it happens."

"Sure, but…" I tried not to think about the old man and what he would say if he found out that I had been terminated, but I couldn't help myself. It was as if I was on the verge of suffering the same humiliation that I had endured as a child when people found out that our father was nowhere to be found. Now, I've always been a little reticent about exposing my childhood traumas to anyone, but looking at Jeff's arched eyebrows and knowing his willingness to take and share information, I wanted to ask him his opinion about the old man. I couldn't understand why everyone who met the old man took his claims at face value, and so I needed to speak to someone unconnected with the family to see what they thought. I needed someone like Jeff who would objectively evaluate the evidence I presented and confirm that the old man was an impostor and that I and everyone else had every right to be concerned. "Say, Jeff, I've got this big thing…"

"You're a lucky man."

"No, that's not what I mean. I've got something big that I'm worried about, and I guess I need a sanity check. Do you ever have such moments?"

"Yeah, I guess. Hold on a moment." His phone had come to life, and he put up his left palm to ask me to remain seated. Initially, I didn't pay much attention to what he was saying, but after a while he drew me into the conversation because parts of it were amusing, to him. He indicated as much through his wide eyes and his facial contortions, as well as the up-and-down motion he made with his right fist. Shortly before the end of the call, I decided not to tell him anything. If it wasn't clear before, it was clear now that I couldn't trust anyone with something so sensitive as my brother's unreserved acceptance of the old man. When he hung up, I apologized for intruding and got up to leave.

"Wait," he said, "The secretary doesn't yet know how things are going to shake out. It's all happening out of sight in the background, but she doesn't yet have enough information to make sense of it. She'll let me know when she has something. So what can I do for you, my man, I mean about your big thing?" He laughed and made another motion with his fist.

"Oh," I stammered, "That was it. I wanted to know how positive you were of the layoffs."

"Positive." As I left his office and quietly closed the door behind me, I heard him reiterate that he would let me know as soon as he got the details.

I returned to my office fearful for my job and furious that the old man had come into our lives. I went back to work and played around with the images that I had been collecting for the adult-education project. I took an image that I had of a smiling young adult and refashioned it into a bald, scrofulous old man with a scowling face. It the bottom of the image, I appended the caption, "Turn your back, and he'll teach you everything you didn't want to know."

It was late, my eyes were practically swimming, and I was ready to go home. I clicked the delete button to expunge the image and, I don't know how it happened, I accidently touched the forward button. When I realized my mistake, I panicked and blamed the old man for putting me in this position. Before I could do anything, the next person in my work flow chain sent a message back, saying that my creation was amusing but probably not what the client was looking for. I called him and apologized, letting him know that it was a mistake and that I would have an appropriate design for the client as soon as possible.

10

I obsessed over the layoffs for several days. I didn't panic. I was deeply concerned, naturally, and to keep my name low on the list of possible terminations, I did everything I could around the office to make myself indispensable. I asked my supervisor for extra work, I helped my colleagues where I could, and I volunteered for non-work-related activities in the office (for example, I helped arrange a going away party for a senior executive who was retiring). I told myself that I was doing these things because Tara and I needed the money, but there was in the back of my mind a fear that if I were to be terminated, I would be seen as a loser and compared negatively with my amazingly successful brother. One of the few things that I remember our father saying was that "Tom is the one person in this house who's going to be a superstar." I wouldn't dream of denying Tom's success (and he was successful by almost any measure), but it is worth noting that what constitutes success is a relative thing and not by any means universally agreed upon. For some, it's all about the shiny gold and the big houses and the pretentious cars and the expensive watches. I admire gold, too, but I admire it because of its extraordinary color and because of the wonderful things that can be made from it. I'm an artist, and what matters to me is creativity. Maybe I haven't set the world on fire, but I'm proud of what I've accomplished and I wouldn't trade places with Tom or anyone else even if I were desperate for the money.

My workplace situation, though, didn't force the old man from my thoughts. I continued to be deeply troubled by his existence, and over the succeeding days and weeks Tom and I had come no closer to an agreement regarding the bogus claims of paternity. I did my best to reach some sort of sort of middle ground with my brother over the old man, but our arguments became so intense that I had to step back for a while to give us both time and distance to reflect and revaluate. I still couldn't drop my suspicions regarding that first, precious phone call, and I couldn't cease worrying that, because of Tom's openness with this stranger, he was making himself and his family vulnerable to something the old man was going to do (rob them, torture them, kill them, and I don't know what else) and I was powerless to help. But after a period of relative stability at work (Jeff wasn't able to come up with any more information about the layoffs), and with no lurid details coming to light about the old man, my anxiety over what might be happening at Tom's house gradually subsided. I didn't for a moment believe that the old man's presence was harmless, but after a while I was nearly able to convince myself that if something extraordinarily dire had happened in Tom's house, Belinda or the police would have immediately reached out to me or to Tara, or to both.

This is not to suggest that I was beginning to adjust to Tom's absence in my daily life. On the contrary, I didn't feel quite right without the stability and the sanity he normally brought to my daily life. Tara was wonderful, I couldn't have asked for a better wife, and she had a wealth of academic information about human behavior that she gleefully trotted out whenever she encountered a superficially relevant situation. But while Tom lacked Tara's abstract knowledge, he had something immensely better–life experience, which he shared with me throughout our lives. I know that I've said this before, but it bears repeating–whatever I have become in life is due in large measure to my brother, to his advice and to his support. All this is another way of saying that I missed him, I missed our almost daily interactions, and, as the days of our separation stretched out, another feeling came over me. It was the fear that Tom's proximity to the old man was warping his ability to use his knowledge, experience, and wisdom–everything that he shared with me throughout the years–to evaluate the old man properly and to see what he was doing to all of us–such as erecting a barrier between Tom and me. I didn't know what Tom had on his mind during this time, but I earnestly hoped he would be using his smarts to step back from the old man and reevaluate the things that were happening to him and me. In other words, I wanted Tom to use this time to see the light and to do to the old man what he often suggested (humorously) doing to his competitors and those who wouldn't play ball with him.

The respite, separation, or whatever it was ended one warm, sunny Saturday afternoon after I pulled into a gas station located halfway between Tom's house and mine. I was running some errands when I noticed that I was low on fuel, and as I pulled up to one of the fuel pumps, I spotted my brother at a pump directly across from me. The fuel nozzle was pumping gas into the tank while he was leaning his back against the car and playing on his cell phone. I was hesitant to speak to him because of our last conversation, but after a moment's reflection I decided that, come what may, I wanted to see if I could tear down that invisible wall between us.

"Hey, sport, didn't you see the notice about not using cell phones while pumping gas?"

He glanced at a nearby sign, which said exactly what I just told him. He turned toward me ostensibly to respond, and when he recognized me, his frown rolled into a big smile and he stepped over to my car.

"You're sure it's going to stop on its own," I said, smiling and indicating with a nod the nozzle connected to his car.

"Goofball, how the hell are you," he said, barely resisting the impulse to hug me across a live fuel hose.

"I'm going to do better than you if you don't watch that thing." I motioned once more to the phone.

He slipped it into his pocket and then went back to his car and disconnected the hose and put in back into the pump. He came back over to me just as I was replacing my hose.

"It's good to see you, Goofball. It feels like it's been ages since you were at my house. I'm really sorry we argued. I guess it's mostly my fault."

"Mostly, especially the big parts."

"I'm sorry…"

"I'm kidding, brother. I'm sorry, too, and I missed you. We shouldn't have…I mean, we shouldn't have let the old man come between us."

"We shouldn't let anything come between us." He reached out to take my hand. I grabbed it and pulled him up to me for another hug.

"So how are things going?" he asked, barely suppressing his smile.

"Good and bad. All is well with Tara and me, but there's been some vague talk floating around at work about the firm losing money. The corporate officers haven't said anything, so I suppose it's nothing. Still, if it's true, I'd hate to be caught up in it, if you know what I mean."

"I'm sure you'll let me know if you need help."

"Thanks, brother. How's Belinda and the little girl."

"Little? It's not going to be long before we have to start think about college. Amazing how the time flies, isn't it? She's doing great. We're all doing great. Say, how about we try another dinner at my house. You game? I know it's short notice, but how about tonight?"

"Sure," I said, and we established the time and, after another brisk hug, went on our separate ways. I finished my errands and went home to tell Tara.

I could hardly contain myself as I went inside and called out to her. She was in the living room folding clothes, and before she had a chance to say hello I blurted out the good news and informed her of our plans for later in the evening.

"That's fine," she replied and continued her task.

"Aren't you excited?"

"I'm looking forward to it, but I can't say that I'm excited. But good for you. It's about time you and Tom made up. I can't believe…"

"You're acting odd. We haven't seen Tom and Belinda in how many weeks?"

She took a small stack of neatly folded clothes into the bedroom and put them away. I followed her, seeking to understand how she could be so calm about seeing my brother and his wife.

"You guys amaze me. You fight and pout…"

"Where'd you get the idea that we were pouting? We weren't doing anything of the kind. Tom can't get beyond this stupid fixation he has about that old man…"

"You don't need to rehash it." She sat down on the edge of the bed and looked at me. "We all know what happened, and Belinda and I think you're acting like children, especially…"

"Belinda? You've been talking to her?"

"Of course. I'm not going to stop talking to her just because you're fighting with Tom. Why would you think that?"

I sat down beside her. "I don't know. Maybe loyalty. You've been talking to Belinda all along?"

"Yes, and I've been talking to Tom, too."

I was irritated by this revelation, but I couldn't be too indignant because it was my brother, after all. "Why didn't you tell me? Since when do you keep secrets from me?"

"I don't. You didn't ask, and I didn't see the point of telling you when it was clear you were happy wallowing in your misery."

I got up. "Fine, but let's not keep secrets from one another. Okay?"

"Of course." She stood up and pulled me into her arms and kissed me. I felt warm from her touch, though I couldn't resist asking her about Tom and Belinda. How were they doing? Were there any problems at home?

"So, what's going on with them?" I began and gently put her at arm's length.

"The same as usual, I suppose. Tom's made some great investments, and they're building a small addition to their place."

"That's cool. That's very cool. I'm glad for him. What about the old man?"

The phone rang and, instead of responding to my questions, she picked it up. She exchanged a couple of short statements with the caller and then handed the phone to me, stating as she walked toward the front door that she was going out to get something to bring to dinner. I might have gone with her, but Jeff was on the line, and it rare to get a call outside the office from him.

"What's going on?" I asked as I watched the front door close behind Tara.

"Sorry to bother you, man, but I thought you'd like to know. I just had lunch with…it doesn't matter who. She told me that the firm is now shopping itself out to buyers. Nothing solid yet, but it's only a matter of time."

"What about our jobs?"

"Not a done deal yet, man, but who knows afterwards. I just thought you'd like to be the first to know. Jason was as shocked as I was." Jason was another graphics artist in the firm, and he had a pack of kids.

After the call, I sat back down on the bed and tried not to think about an acquisition and what might happen to me if the firm were acquired. But no matter how intensely I considered other matters (my wife, the TV news, a project for a client), I couldn't temper my anxiety over losing my job and being forced to ask Tom for a loan. And I couldn't help imagining what our father would say if he found out about my situation which, I reminded myself, would be the same thing that the old man would say. In other words, I wasn't my brother. I wasn't half the man Tom was. Later on, these thoughts were partially offset by Jeff's credibility. He was a great guy, and he often knew about things at the firm before anyone else did, and yet his gossip wasn't always one hundred percent accurate. Two years ago, he informed me (having heard it from an impeccable source) that I was going to be handed a large client and a promotion. The promotion part, he added, wasn't exactly solid, but the rest was "bedrock." Ultimately, neither one of them came through, and Jeff claimed that he was only speculating based on my work. But in the present case, while I had little reason to trust his information, I couldn't quite discount his statements (or, by extension, the secretary's), either. Shrugging my shoulders, I told myself that I was done worrying. Tara and I were going to have dinner at Tom's just like we always did and, since Tom hadn't mentioned the old man, I had every reason to believe that he was out of Tom's house and our respective lives.

11

The sun was low in the sky and the air unexpectedly cool when we arrived. Tom didn't answer the door this time, and so we went inside and began removing our coats while hollering his name. A few seconds later, he appeared and after the usual hugs and kisses, apologized for not opening the door. He took our coats and as he stuffed them into the coat closet, he shouted for Belinda to come because "we have very important guests." He didn't wait for Belinda, and as he walked us down the hallway to the living room, he informed us that it was too cold to eat out on the patio as planned and that we were going to enjoy our dinner in front of the fire. There was indeed a beautiful, crackling fire in the living room fireplace, and as we made ourselves comfortable in the large, cushiony chairs nearby, Tom offered us drinks from a rolling rack ladened with beer and his favorite rotgut that he pulled from around the corner. Belinda arrived seconds later. She had been detained by an important phone call, she said, and after more kisses and hugs, we all settled into the usual discussions of life, politics, business, and everything else. It was an enjoyable time, even though we all said more or less the same things we said whenever Tara and I visited.

"He should have acted more goddamn decisively," Tom bellowed at one point about a former colleague when the conversation floated back to business, his favorite topic. The individual in question had acquired a large share of a laundry-services company. The company had enormous potential, but this potential went unrealized for various reasons and posted increasing losses, or at least the company didn't post the returns that the colleague had anticipated. The colleague had a heart-to-heart with the CEO in which he explained that the company needed to restructure (he wanted different line managers to run the show), augment its client base, and expand its working hours in order to turn around the company. The CEO assured him that he understood and would get moving on some of the things that the colleague wanted to accomplish, but in the end he didn't accept the new managers and wouldn't open the doors at night. "My colleague is a great guy," Tom continued, "but he doesn't understand that you don't work with people like that. They either do what you want them to do or you cut them loose. Because he didn't act decisively at the outset, the CEO and everyone else walked all over him. It was a big con, and he fell for it." Tom took a drink and laughed in a derisive way. "If it were me, I'd have taken the CEO in hand and ripped his fucking heart out."

I wasn't in the least bit interested in business, and I generally found my brother's disquisitions on his own business dealings boring, to say the least. But this time was different. This time his words were profound. Tom's description of the interactions between his colleague and the CEO mirrored the interactions between himself and the old man. Tom was being conned, and if he didn't act quickly and decisively to rip out the old man's heart, the old man was going to rip out his heart. By the time that Tom had finished this touching little vignette about the colleague and the CEO, I realized that nothing had yet been said about the old man. Nothing, and so I began to feel a little more at ease that the old man was finally gone and that Tom had possibly done what he needed to do so that the old man wasn't walking all over him and all the rest of us. My confidence increased when Tom, switching to other colleagues, continued in the same vein, playing the tough, cold-hearted businessman who understood success as a process of winning and avoiding the con. As I was waiting for an opening to inquire obliquely about the old man and what it took "to cut his heart out," Belinda interrupted another of Tom's tirades about losers to inform us that dinner was ready and that we were all to "repair" to the dining room. Strolling through the kitchen on our way, I noticed some dishes in the kitchen sink (plate, silverware, wine glass, and a few other things), which made me wonder if Tom and Belinda were getting lax or had been rushed this evening for some reason. They had always been neat people, despite the fact that they had a young daughter, who was again upstairs in her room for the evening.

I forgot about the old man once we started eating and the conversation shifted to vacations (Tom and Belinda were planning at least three trips overseas later this year, one of them to their favorite vacation spot, the Cayman Islands), the challenges of traveling with children (Tom joked that we were lucky not to have this problem, though he asked with some seriousness why Tara and I hadn't put more effort into building a family), and then back to business. This time, Tom rattled on about the dynamics of the markets he played in. He noted how certain companies had "missed the boat" because they were either too passive or too afraid to play hardball with their competitors, or both. Company A, for instance, could easily have kicked Company B's "ass" and controlled the market, but it was afraid that a strong move, the kind that Tom would have made, might backfire and alert the authorities, and so, in the end, Company A not only lost its market position but had been forced into a niche where it was dying. "It was an embarrassment. You got to have jones if you're going to survive," he was insisting after dinner as we meandered, drinks in hand, back into the living room, "and sources on the inside."

I suppose it was an important business lesson, but the rest of us weren't business people and after a while Tom's talk about companies and what he would do in their corporate shoes was becoming tiresome and enervating. I could only imagine what Belinda felt, since she was probably hearing the same stuff, the same stories, night after night, after night. To mix things up a little, to keep everyone awake and give them a chance to weigh in on something a tad more interesting that Tom's heroics, I decided to change the topic of conversation, if you could call Tom's monologue a conversation. This was not, however, a simple thing to do. Since Tom was intoxicated by the sweet sound of his own voice, I had to proceed carefully so that I didn't hurt his feelings or turn a lovely albeit boring evening into something unpleasant. Because my head was by then mind-numbingly empty, I offered the first alternative topic that came to mind. As Tom paused to catch a breath, I mentioned the old man. I said that it was nice to see that he, Tom, had used his business acumen to send the old man packing. I had expected appreciative smiles and nods from Tara and Belinda, but after a quick glance at one another, they remained silent and stared blankly first at me and then at Tom.

Tom eyed me and, not picking up the baton, resumed rattling on about business. I gently pushed back, because I was confident that Tara and Belinda wanted something other than business to talk about and because I wanted more details about what prompted Tom to rush the old bum from the premises. Was it unreasonable to assume that because the old man was absent from the conversation, he was also absent from the house, permanently?

"Was it hard?" I interjected. "I mean, what did it take? Did you cut out his heart? Or maybe you used a baseball bat."

I was trying to be funny, but Tom eyed me as if I were talking gibberish. "Heart? Baseball bat? I don't know what you're talking about."

My initial sense was that Tom was reluctant to tell me what had happened. His naive acceptance of the old man probably embarrassed him–it was, after all, contrary to the tough-guy business persona that he like to don on occasions like these–and so I stretched out and mentally prepared myself to savor the moment when Tom finally came clean, about everything.

"Yeah, he's got some things going on…"

"Things? Yes, things. What kind of things does he have going on, if I might ask?"

"He's with some business associates he reconnected with recently. I don't know the back story, but I'm sure he'll tell everyone when something's finalized."

I was almost certain that this was one of those rare instances in which Tom tried to say something funny. My brother, if you didn't know, wasn't by nature a funny person. He liked to tell jokes and funny stories, but only if they showed his rivals in a degrading or humiliating light. This wasn't that kind of joke, of course, but what else could I think when he coupled business associates and business deals with the old man. Look, I don't have to tell you that the old man was a bum. He looked like a bum, he walked like a bum, he quacked like a bum. He was a goddamn bum. And what kind of business acquaintances…no, what kind of business could a duck like that have that required finalization (meaning, in Tom's parlance, something that made money)? No, it was ridiculous. It had to be a joke. I looked at Tom intently for a moment and then laughed loudly. I was surprised that neither Belinda nor Tara found any humor in what Tom said.

"What's so funny?" Tom asked.

"What you said. There's no way that old bum could have business acquaintances unless they were all standing around the same fire barrel."

"What the hell are you talking about? And don't call him a bum."

"You know what I'm talking about, and he is a bum. What business could he possibly have apart from monkey business?"

Belinda quickly interrupted to see if we needed refills and to find out if we were ready for "treats." While Tom handed out beer and refills and Belinda passed out plates with cookies on them, everyone was silent, although I ruminated on Tom's inexplicable statements. Once everything was in order and everybody was again relaxed, I asked Tom why he thought that the old man was doing something constructive. "If he's not industrious enough to be in a shelter right now, he's probably face down in the gutter somewhere."

"Are you snorting something behind my back?"

Belinda became more assertive this time. She demanded to know if we wanted an additional drink and, when no one took the bait, insisted that we listen to some music. "I have a new CD. I spotted it at the store the other day. It was on sale. I'd never heard of the artist before and, judging by the way he looked, I knew I wouldn't like his music. But it was a sale, and I bought it, anyway. You know, I just melted the second time I listened to it. I guess it happens that way with good music. Do you know what I mean? Tara, do you know what I mean?"

Tara didn't respond. She sat stolidly, her eyes moving from me to something else in the room.

"You bought a CD that you thought you wouldn't like?" I asked, momentarily distracted by the inanity of her statement. "Wait a minute. Wait a minute. What do you mean, am I snorting something behind your back?"

Belinda again inserted herself to prevent our happy little gathering from unraveling. "Tara, darling, do you suppose we could get one of the men to help us with the CD?"

Tara didn't respond. She acted as if she were watching a play or a dramatic TV show. Maybe she was. Seconds later, as if on cue, there was the sound of a door closing in another part of the house. I didn't think too much of it, because Chelsea was around somewhere.

Tom had a puzzled look on his face. "You act as if you didn't know Dad was living with us. Didn't Tara tell you?"

I glowered at my wife.

"I thought I did," she said with a fatuous smile on her lips. "It might have slipped my mind. You know how it is…"

I glowered at Tom. "The old man is living with you?"

"Yes, Dad is living with us."

"He's here right now?"

"Somewhere. He's getting back on his feet, and I'm helping him out. Why do you care?"

"Why do I care? Are you out of your mind? How many times do I have to say this? You don't know who this person is. It doesn't matter whether or not you think he's our father. You don't know a thing about him. Have you done any background checks? This is insane."

Tom hesitated before slamming his fist down onto the arm of his chair. Leaning toward me as if he was ready to jump out of his chair, he shouted, "Enough. I'm sick of all your nonsense. It's the same every time. I will do what I want to do, and, if you don't like it, that's your problem. And you know what else? I'm tired of your lack of respect for me and my decisions. Do you understand?"

I'd heard him yell before, many times, in fact, and so I wasn't intimidated. "I understand plenty," I replied, speaking carefully so that Belinda and Tara would see that I wasn't the one who was out of control. "But I wouldn't be your brother if I didn't speak up when something's wrong."

Tom must have had second thoughts about his unfortunate outburst. He took a deep breath to calm himself and leaned back casually in his chair. "Goofball," he said quietly and coolly, "I heard everything you said the first time. I appreciate your concern. I'm not changing my mind, however, so maybe it's time to drop it. You're beginning to sound like a broken record."

"I don't need clichés..."

"And I don't need your help. Let me handle my business my way, okay? Now, how about another drink? I think you spilled most of yours on your lap."

Everyone laughed as if he had said something amusing. Moments later I thought he winked at Tara, but since this didn't make any sense, I shrugged it off.

I refused to let Tom's lordly serenity distract me. It was one thing for Tom to put himself, his wife, and his daughter in danger, and quite another to put others outside of his immediate household in jeopardy. I was concerned that once the old man had established himself in Tom's house, he could use that as a convenient base from which to launch his machinations elsewhere. He was supposedly my father, too, right?

"Okay, fine, but why didn't you tell me that he was staying with you? Why didn't you tell me before I came here this evening?"

"Don't you and your wife talk to each other? Maybe not. My apologies."

I couldn't look at Tara. I was certain that she was pantomiming some silly mea culpa which, at that moment, would have set me off.

"But I have to tell you, Goofball," he continued, "You'll have a different impression of him if you get to know him."

"Would you please stop calling me Goofball? How long is he going to stay?"

"That's up to him. He can stay as long as he wants."

"Wait a minute. Tara said that you were adding an addition to your house."

"Yeah," he replied, hoping that I was changing the discussion. "Would you like to see the plans. We haven't started demolition yet..."

"I don't give a damn about the demolition. You're building an addition to your house for the old man?"

"Belinda, darling, that music of yours..."

"Stop with the music. Is that what the addition's for?"

Tom's amused expression took on a momentary warmth as he looked at something behind me or over my head. "Yes, that's what the addition's for."

I was tempted to leave at this point. The old man was somewhere in the house, and neither Tom nor my own wife had been honest with me regarding this seemingly permanent fixture in Tom's life. I didn't move, though, because I had more questions for which I needed answers. "Is he here now? He's not upstairs with Chelsea, is he?"

"He's here, but not with Chelsea."

"Okay, let's stop playing games. Where is he?"

"He just came in. He's right behind you."

I whipped around, and there he was, a few feet behind me and leaning against the wall with his arms crossed. He looked different than I might have expected. He wasn't in his dirty bathrobe but dressed normally, casually, in oversized khakis and an open business shirt. The remnants of his hair had been trimmed, and, if it weren't for the scowl across his craggy lips, I might not have recognized him had we passed each other on the street.

12

"Dad, come have a seat. We're just relaxing and having a beer."

"I'll get you one," Belinda chirped, and quickly ran out of the room and seconds later returned with a beer and handed it to the old man. "I think you like it slightly warm." The old man smiled, or pretended to smile, and kissed her lightly on the cheek. Beer in hand, he walked over to a chair next to Tom (as he crossed in front of me, I had to resist the temptation to trip him) and made himself obscenely comfortable. Did he and Tom touch bottles?

We were all waiting for someone to begin the conversation when Tara smiled knowingly at the old man and, as if she knew the answer beforehand, asked him to tell us about his activities. "Tell me, Mr. Reid, how did it go today?"

The old man didn't even glance in my direction. Again doing his approximation of a smile, he said to my wife, "Tara, you know you don't have to stand on formality with me. Please, call me Bill."

Tara laughed and so did Tom and Belinda. Everybody seemed to find something amusing and charming either in his words or in the manner in which he gently chided my wife–everybody, that is, except me. I didn't see anything funny, and I was troubled by the familiarity of their words and gestures. It was as if I had interrupted a conversation already in progress.

"Okay, Bill," she began, again to my consternation. "Any luck today?"

He slowly adjusted himself in his chair and took a long, appreciative drink from his bottle. Things were promising, he said, and he emphasized that he would soon be in a position where he could choose between several, equally viable options. "I've been in contact with certain well-placed individuals, and I am relatively optimistic."

I was furious with this familiarity between him and my wife (and when did she give him her name?) and with his assumption that he was at home and could speak as freely as he liked. Had I been a little more reasonable, I might have graciously left Tom's house before things got out of hand, but I was determined to find out what this scoundrel was up to and to expose him to Tom, Belinda, and of course my beloved wife.

"So, tell me, Mr....," I began, pretending to sound like some inoffensive detective in a third-rate novel, "I'm sorry, what name are you using these days?"

The old man seemed far more capable than he did when we met at the hospital. Glancing around as if he were letting everyone in on a pleasant joke, he replied, "You can call me Mr. Reid."

Naturally, there were some approving chuckles.

"Okay," I said, feeling a little stupid and unwilling to use any name when addressing him, "Okay, have it your way. So why don't you tell us about these promising options, as you call them. They sound interesting. Are you investing in a high-tech startup or looking to land a solid position in the business world, say, as a corporate janitor?"

I thought that I might get some laughs out of my question, but everyone remained silent.

The old man didn't miss a beat. He replied pleasantly, engagingly, as though he were humoring a headstrong child. "We shouldn't make fun of corporate janitors. They are hardworking people doing a necessary job, and they should be given more respect and higher wages than they presently get. Now, as for the promising options Tara so kindly inquired about, they are indeed employment-related though not for janitorial work." He winked at Tom, who nodded with a smile in return as if to suggest that he was in the know and that he, like the old man, was laughing at my expense. "I don't want to get ahead of myself right now. I don't want to suggest something only to have it fail to materialize. Maybe I'm a little superstitious. But if and when I actually make a choice, I'll let you know. I'll let everyone know." The old man finished off his beer and asked Belinda for another.

"Absolutely." She ran into the other room and returned with another bottle.

I looked at Tom, Belinda, and then Tara. They all turned away. I could have sworn that they were afraid I might find out what was going on if I examined their eyes. Looking now at the old man, I said, "Surely, you can tell us. Aren't we all family?"

He leaned forward slightly and squinted as though he were trying to identify me from a line up. "Why are you here?"

Tom appeared momentarily uncomfortable. "Dad, Jim and Tara are here for dinner and drinks. Now we're all just relaxing and having a nice conversation.

"I was just joking, son," he replied to Tom. "Can't you take a joke? I may be an old man, but I'm not senile, not yet." For some reason, the last statement got a burst of goodhearted laughter.

"No, Dad, you sure aren't."

The old man gave a half shake of his bald head. "John," he said, turning to me, "I don't quite know what to say to you."

"The name is James, and you can start by calling me Mr. Reid." I was a little put off that my response didn't engender a few laughs.

"Whatever you say, boy, but you still ain't getting nothing out of me before it's time." That statement, too, inexplicably got some pleasant laughs.

I didn't laugh. I didn't find anything amusing about the old man's avoidance of questions. As I was pondering over some way of exposing him without upsetting everyone, Tom figuratively stepped in and closed down what could have been an interesting discussion.

"Yes, Dad, when you're ready, you can tell us. You can tell the family, as Jimmy said."

"That wasn't what I meant." I glanced at Tara before saying loudly to Tom, "Do you have any clue what this guy is up to?"

The wives gasped and the old man immediately stood up (far too quickly, I thought, for somebody supposedly at death's door), while Tom is his serene fashion told everyone to calm down. As soon as the old man eased back into his chair, Tom leaned forward and practically whispered, "Yes, I do, and it's all good. If I were you, Goofball, I would take this opportunity to speak to him. I guarantee you that all your doubts will evaporate within five minutes. If you're not willing to do that, then sit back and have another beer."

"I'm not going to speak to him. I don't care who he is…" I lost my train of thought and, when I looked to Tara for support, she and the old man were talking about something that seemed to amuse them. "Quit calling me Goofball," I said to Tom.

I must have spoken too loudly, for the old man stopped speaking to Tara and gazed at me with broad smile and said, "Goofball? I love it." He burst out with a loud, raucous laugh, which of course infected the others. "I'll call you Mr. Goofball."

"Come on, Jim," Tom said, turning to me only after the laughter had momentarily subsided. "He doesn't mean anything by it. He's just having a little fun. He hasn't had much to laugh at in his life. Let me get you another beer or whiskey?"

That was the last straw. I had done everything I could to remain calm and civilized, but I couldn't take it anymore, not with the old jackass bellowing "Goofball" in the background. I stood up and, observing everyone laughing at me, angled my head toward my brother and said, "Yeah, I can see the sorrow in his eyes. But it's getting a little late for us." Ignoring my laughing wife, I said to Belinda, "As always, it was good getting together."

"Wait a minute, Jim," Tom said as he stood up and faced me. "It's early, and Tara doesn't look like she wants to leave."

"You don't know my wife as well as I do," I replied without including her in the conversation. "It's time for us to go."

"It's not time for me…Goofball," Tara hollered, squealing with laughter and tapping the tips of her shoes on the floor.

"Of course, not. Say, Jim, you're not having a good time, so why don't you go. I'll drive Tara home later."

It was a neat way of getting rid of me. However, I wasn't going to make a fool of myself by declining his offer, since I didn't think that Tara would come with me, not with all the fun she seemed to be having at my expense. But, as I reconsidered the situation, I thought it might be nice to be home by myself for a little bit to reflect on what was happening and to figure out why everyone was so friendly with the old man, especially my own wife.

"Fine," I replied without looking at Tara.

Once I was home, I didn't have a lot of time for reflection. I started putting away some work papers spread across the kitchen table when I remembered a conference call that I was supposed to have attended earlier in the day. It was too late now to contact anyone about it, and I worried a little that I might have done something else that made me more vulnerable if the firm was actually reorganized or acquired. Tara came home about an hour later. I was pleased that she hadn't stayed late, though I was still upset with her for laughing at me and calling me Goofball. It was hardly the first time that Tom had used the term. I might have mentioned it, but she seemed put off about something, probably for feeling compelled to leave the festivities earlier than she wanted, and so we went about what was left of the evening as if we were strangers. I made some sketches for work and then prepared for bed, while she cleaned up the kitchen before taking her turn in the bathroom. When the lights were out and we were lying next to one another under the covers, I felt that it was time to break the silence and get some answers. I wanted to know, for example, when she first met the old man? Why didn't she tell me about this meeting? How many times had she spoken to him, and why didn't she tell me about these interactions? And, since the issue was critical, on what basis did she form her opinion about the old man's legitimacy? Rolling to my side and facing her, I asked my first question serenely and without judgement.

"Tara, sweetheart, did you have to call me Goofball in front of the old man?" She didn't answer. I repeated the question in case she hadn't heard me or, I hoped, in case she was too ashamed to reply immediately. When she didn't respond this time, I waited for a few seconds before leaning over and in the nearly impenetrable darkness peering into her face. I wanted to know what she was feeling and whether or not I needed to explain the question. But it was too dark to see clearly. As I rolled back onto my side of the bed to regroup and possibly repeat the question, I caught a faint sound that resembled a half breath. Seconds later, I heard a sputter followed by deep, rhythmic breathing. Maybe it was for the best, I told myself. I could always ask her in the morning. In the meantime, I needed sleep. I was extremely tired, and I told myself that I was going to forget about this evening for the time being and get a good night's sleep for once.

But if I thought it possible to get a peaceful night's sleep, I was mistaken. I couldn't tell if my eyes were open or closed, and as I remained stretched out on my back like a helpless beetle, I couldn't stop thinking about the evening and wondering what Tom and the others saw in the old man. He was repulsively ugly and had shifty eyes, and these facts alone should have been enough to prove that he was a fake and couldn't be trusted. Even if he were our father, even if he apologized for the crimes he committed against Tom and me and our mother, why should we care? Why should anyone care? How could an apology make up for all the years we lived without a father or erase from our memories the stigma of being fatherless–how could it make up for the jokes and ridicule of our peers ("You weren't born a bastard like normal people. You're father made you one.") and the condescending glances of our supposedly well-meaning neighbors–or even the constant weeping of our mother, who had difficulty reconciling herself to the fact that her lousy husband deserted her and her two boys? How could a few pointless words make up for all the pain and suffering that we had endured? Later, as the night dragged on, I felt a momentary elation for having had the sense not to kiss the old man's fat ass over his spurious business associates, although I was also angry that I hadn't stayed longer to find something that would expose the old impostor for what he was. When I finally rose the following morning, Tara was gone and I felt like I had run a marathon.

13

Tara left a note on the microwave to let me know that she was going to be out for the day seeing patients. It wasn't surprising. Strange people often have strange needs, and she spent a fair amount of time away from home catering to the strange needs of these strange people. Still, I was a little put out that she was gone. I wanted to spend my Sunday with her, I wanted us to relax and maybe go for a walk, and I also wanted to find out more about her relationship to the old man. I wasn't going to press the issue, though, and possibly spoil what was left of our Sunday. She, like everyone else, seemed to be overly protective of the old man, and so I didn't want to say anything about the old goat that might be perceived as insensitive or off-putting. I also didn't want her to think that after all our years together, I was now insisting that we had to agree on everything in order to be happy. Loyalty was another matter, but opinions were opinions, and I didn't have a problem if her opinion about the old man differed from mine, even if her opinion was biased and unsupported by the facts. Well, when she was back home and had a few spare minutes, I told myself, we could sit down and have a fine conversation about any number of things, as long as she came clean about her relationship to the old man.

I spent most of the morning developing ideas and drawing sketches for some possible accounts, and shortly after lunch I called Tom. I loved him, and regardless of our respective differences, I didn't want the old man to come between us. It was also the case that I was still a little apprehensive about the old man living in Tom's house. Tom was generally more than capable of defending himself and his family in adverse situations. But I was troubled that he was now up against something that he hadn't encountered before and didn't know how to handle. Realistically, how could anyone have prepared for something like the old man?

I reached out to him at what I thought was a good time. It was, he picked up, and for a few minutes we chatted about all kinds of things (business, weather, sports, business) as if the old man had never existed. At one point, though, I could have sworn that I heard Tara's voice in the background, but when I asked if she were there, he assured me that she wasn't.

"Belinda and Chelsea are talking about something in the other room, and you probably heard one of them."

"Sure," I replied. "Tara is meeting with patients today, and…well, you know how that goes."

We continued talking for a few more minutes about something else when, out of the blue, I asked if he, Tom, had considered having the old man investigated. "Your company, I would bet, has the kind of resources needed to do a thorough investigation of just about anybody," I said as if I knew something about how these things were done. "It shouldn't be a big deal, and it wouldn't take very long."

"Are you starting up again? No, I'm not going to do that."

"Why?"

"Why? Because I have all I needed to know about him. It's too bad you can't make more of an effort to meet him halfway to judge for yourself. As I said before, I know you guys would hit it off."

"You're out of your gourd," I said perhaps a little too vehemently. "Have you ever met a con man you didn't like?"

"Forget it, Goofball. He's a decent guy, and, like it or not, he's our father. He's changed, and he's trying to make amends for the past. He understands everything we went through, and he's not trying to downplay it or diminish his role in it. He's sincerely contrite, and therefore I think he deserves a second chance. If you knew what he went through during those years, you might yield a little."

"What about what we went through? Father or not–and I don't believe he is our father–I don't give a damn what he's been through. But let me ask you this. Did you ever invest in a company without doing due diligence? Official or unofficial, it doesn't matter. No? There's no difference between business and people. It's simply a matter of knowing what you're investing in. The old man may be worth his weight in gold somewhere, but you can't assume that without some kind of records check. If he turns out to be our father, so what? All you've lost is a few dollars, and you've gained some valuable peace of mind. Now, what if he turns out not to be our father? What if the investigation turns up troublesome things? What would that be worth to you?"

"Give it up. It ain't going to happen. And I recommend you stay away from it, too. Understand?"

"Do you know how crazy this is? How can you be so confident…"

"Because I am, and so let's drop it. Listen, Chelsea's going to have a sleepover with one of her friends next week, and Belinda thought it would be fun to go out to dinner for a change. Why don't you and Tara meet us at the restaurant. We'll have a great time. My treat." Tom named the eatery, which was one of those expensive, high-class places that would have cost me a month's salary if I were paying.

"Is the old man going to be there?"

"No. He'll be out on a business deal of some kind."

"You buy that? He was dying and didn't have anything when we picked him up, and now he's alive, he's got prospects, he's doing deals, and he's got money. Does this make sense to you?"

"He has a heart problem. And, for your information, I loaned him money to get started."

"Are you out of your mind?"

"Stop saying that."

"Why would you give a stranger money?"

"It's my business, it's my money, and you stay out of it."

"I can't believe…"

"Belief has nothing to do with it. I'll see you next Saturday. Oh, and one more thing. Wear a tie, and look like a grownup for a change."

"Very funny."

Tara came home shortly after our call ended. I met her at the door and, while she was taking off her shoes, I told her about my call with Tom. I mentioned several times how stupid it was for Tom to give the old man a loan, even if it was only pennies, and I emphasized that it was only a matter of time before things go wrong and Tom regrets his decisions.

"Those are his decisions," she replied as she went into the living room and sat down on the couch, "and we should respect both them and him. Tom can handle himself. But I have to tell you, your father seemed like a nice man when I spoke to him."

"He's not my father," I insisted.

"Tommy and…"

"I don't give a damn what anyone says. I should know. The old man's a fraud, and he's up to something."

"Why would he be up to something?"

"And why did you have to call me Goofball? That wasn't very nice. You know I hate it when Tom calls me that."

"I'm sorry. It just seemed funny at the time, and I was tired of the fighting."

I was still indignant about it, but I let it pass. "Why would he be up to something? Maybe because Tom has money, and he pegged Tom for being the fool who's easily parted from it. I just don't understand why Tom's so desperate to have our father back, especially after everything he did to us."

When Tara started giving me her psychological mumbo-jumbo about people in general and me in particular, I nearly exploded. I'd had enough of the 'infantile' and 'narcissist' routine, and I was ready to insist that she tell me everything she knew about the old man, including her relationship with him, and then demand that she cease seeing him behind my back...no, that she cease seeing him, period. Somehow, though, I managed to hold my tongue. I knew that if I reacted this way, it would not only create a backlash but also do nothing to end Tara's relationship with him. I also realized, or I was beginning to realize, that there was no getting rid of the old man unless I was able to prove that he was a fraud. It was obvious that my knowledge, my feelings, my intuition were not enough. Of course, I didn't have a clue about the kind of proof that would be acceptable, though I was confident that this wouldn't be the time to ask Tara. I also felt that this wasn't the best time to grill her about the old man's questionable business activities or the change he pocketed from Tom. I wasn't entirely confident that, if she did know about these things (remember, she was always talking to Tom and Belinda, and I guess the old man), she wouldn't voice her confidence in the old man's unique business acumen, and I wouldn't as a result lose the temper that I was trying hard to keep. Instead of asking her about anything having to do with the old man, I informed her about Saturday's dinner at a chichi restaurant. She seemed pleased, even when I mentioned as an afterthought that the old man wasn't going to be joining us.

"Business, you know," I added. It annoyed me that she didn't ask for details. Had Tom told her?

The rest of the day went relatively well. By an unspoken mutual agreement, we refrained from speaking about the old man, though I have to say that I struggled to keep from asking Tara directly about her relationship with him. I inquired about her crazy patients multiple times, and I made any number of suggestive remarks that, I hoped, would elicit something about him (I asked, for example, in a variety of ways about the increasing likelihood of psychosis as the body ages and flattens out), but she always seemed oblivious to what I was looking for. It could also have been the case that she understood me very well and was doing her professional best to dodge the issue. I also left Tom several phone messages and e-mails to tell him that he needed to be cautious and on his guard while the old man was around. (To prevent arguments with him, I called at times when I knew that he and Belinda were out of the house.) On Friday, I left him one final e-mail to say that something had come up at the last moment and that Tara and I wouldn't be available for dinner, after all. It was a lie, but it was based on the fact that I wasn't ready to spend time with Tom and Belinda while the old man was hovering somewhere in the background, perhaps coaxing them to get information about me. My behavior wasn't entirely rational, I suppose, but then the whole situation with the old man wasn't entirely rational, either, and so I responded in a way that at the time seemed reasonable. Tara, of course, was upset, and, though she threated to go without me, she stayed home silently with me.

The following Monday, I had to mail some drawings to a longstanding client. Packet under arm, I left my building, rounded the corner, and headed straight to a post-office box a block away. I dropped the packet into the box and, as I started back for the office, I thought I saw Tara walking quickly around the opposite corner. I didn't have a clear view of her face, but I recognized her hair, her coat, and the manner in which she practically glided on her toes. Since her office was on the other side of town, I hurried after her to see what she was doing out here, if she needed a ride, and so forth. But as I reached the opposite corner and turned, I lost sight of her. She was nowhere to be seen on either side of the street. 'How odd,' I told myself and waited around, hoping to catch her as she came out of a building. When she didn't reappear, I went back to the office and continued working. 'I must have been hallucinating,' I told myself, though I meant to ask her that evening if she had been near my office. Later that evening, Tara assured me that she hadn't left home the entire day.

I mention this because an odd thing happened after work a few days later. I was heading toward the parking lot to get my car and, as I started to cross the street, one of Tom's sparkling, luxury cars passed right in front of me and forced me back onto the sidewalk. The old man was driving, or so it appeared, not Tom. The car immediately angled away from the curb as though the desired effect had been achieved and disappeared on the freeway. Before it was gone, however; I managed to catch a glimpse of the occupant on the side nearest me– it was Tara, or at least it looked like my wife. It was the same profile, the same hairstyle, and, unless I was mistaken, the same color blouse that she was wearing at home this morning. Initially, I was stunned, though seconds later I nearly convinced myself that the car had been moving too quickly for me to have made an accurate identification of either the driver or the passenger–or even the car. It looked like one of Tom's, but then most of Tom's cars look like all the other cars on the road. Could I have been delusional? I called Tara's cell a couple of times on the way home. I wanted her assurance that my eyes had been playing tricks on me. There was no answer. I was uneasy by the time I arrived home and found her cooking dinner. I didn't question her about her day, since she seemed quite preoccupied with fixing dinner, and it would have been logistically difficult, though not impossible, to get home and cook half the food before I arrived. Nevertheless, I did ask her why she hadn't answered her phone when I called. Somewhat plausibly, she explained that she hadn't heard it ring because the noise of cooking masked all the other sounds.

After a few days, Tara and I had both softened our attitudes and, with her approval, I called Tom on Thursday and left an additional message, saying that we would be happy to accept another invitation to dinner (I added, without Tara's notice, as long as the old man wasn't there). An hour later, my brother returned my call and said that we were on for the Saturday night. "No excuses," he insisted and then said that we would have dinner out, which was fine by me because he was paying.

The following day, it was business as usual at work. Sometime shortly before lunch, I managed to corral Jeff to chat about the pending reorganization and acquisition. He still appeared confident that it would happen (he said as much), though he was less certain about the timing. "Today, tomorrow, next year, it's anyone's guess, but it will happen." I guess he wasn't getting anything more definitive from his source, or maybe she was backing off a little from her early conviction. Since nothing seemed unusual around the office (no one that I saw or spoke to seemed unduly anxious or wanted to share a confidence with me), I went back to work and spent most of my time either on the computer or at my drawing board making sketches. Shortly after two, I left to get something at the vending machine down the hall, and when I returned the old man was sitting comfortably in the chair next to my desk.

"What the hell are you doing here?" I gasped, barely able to believe my eyes.

The old man looked surprisingly clean and fresh. He was dressed in a dark, blue business suit, with a white shirt, a black vest, and a red-striped power tie. He was also wearing tortoiseshell corporate glasses. If I hadn't known better, I would have pegged him for a Fortune 500 executive, not some dirt bag who used to go around in a filthy bathrobe. He didn't immediately respond as I went to my desk and sat down. I didn't know what else to do, but since I was the closest to the door, I was somewhat relieved that I could easily holler down the hallway for help, if needed.

"This is a nice business," he began, casually scanning my office as if he were looking for clues about the business. "What's the monthly burn rate?"

"None of your business. Why are you here?"

"Why do you think I'm here?"

"I don't know who let you in."

He picked up my large, pink eraser from my desk and twirled it around in his hand.

"Put that back," I demanded. I wanted to shout at him, but I was so unnerved by his unexpected visit that I was afraid my voice would quaver if I became more demonstrative.

He casually placed the eraser back onto my desk and once more examined me with his large, sagging eyes. "Listen, boy, you can think what you want about me. I can't change that. I made some mistakes in my life, sure, but I can't change those, either. Do you know what I'd do if I could change one thing? I'd make sure this meeting never happened. It's distasteful to me."

I breathed deeply to keep myself under control. "If it's distasteful, then why don't you get lost?"

"It's the cost of doing business."

"Fine. Tell me what your business is and get out, and don't come back."

"God, you sound like someone I used to know. Listen, Tommy seems to like you, and I'm fine with that. But Tommy has some things going on right now that I don't want you getting involved in. It's none of your business. You steer clear, got it? Have fun, see him from time to time, but don't let it go any farther than that. You stick your nose in where it don't belong, and I'm going to end things right then and there. Do you understand what I'm saying?"

"Sure," I replied and nodded my head slowly. I kept my eyes locked on his to show him that he couldn't intimidate me.

"One more thing. Don't you say a word about this conversation to Tommy. You got it?"

"Or you'll end things right then and there?"

"You're a funny guy, but I don't got a sense of humor."

"Hey," I said, feeling my fortitude coming back. "Let me ask you a question. Do you know my name?"

The old man looked at me as though my question didn't make any sense. Seconds later, he laughed as if he had just got the joke. "You better know mine," he said.

He got up and, as he walked past my desk to the door, I was taken aback by how powerful he looked. It wasn't just the clothes. His arms and hands and his whole bearing suggested force and danger. When he was at the door, he looked back, laughed again, and then shut the door behind him. I waited a few seconds before opening the door again and craning my neck into the hallway. He was gone and so was my eraser.

14

I wasn't afraid of the old man or intimidated by what he said. He was an old man, after all, and he could huff and puff all he wanted, but I wasn't going to back off from warning my brother. Nevertheless, I didn't immediately let Tom know about the conversation. I can't explain it, but I wanted to wait until the old man did something else that would justify another, more serious warning to my brother.

On Saturday before heading out to the restaurant, I called Tom to make sure that the old man wasn't going to join us. Tom, smooth as ever, reassured me that the old man had other plans and that he had made reservations for four.

"You're being stupid," he added with exasperation. "You're letting your feelings for the man hurt your relationships with me and Belinda."

"Maybe," I responded, "and maybe someday you'll thank me."

"I doubt it."

The restaurant was, as I noted earlier, one of those overpriced places that Tom and Belinda enjoyed. The dining area was covered with a thick, ornate carpet, and there were large, off-white pillars stationed throughout, as though the ceiling were extraordinarily heavy and needed the extra support. Tom and Belinda were already at our table, a half circle covered with white linen table cloth, enjoying a drink while waiting for us. They both stood up (as well as they could, since the table was fairly snug against them) and shook hands and blew kisses in lieu of the usual hugs. Before sitting at the end of the long, curved and cushioned bench, I counted the table settings to make sure that there would only be four people this evening and that no one else had been sitting at the table since Tom and Belinda arrived.

"We're by ourselves for a change," I said once we were comfortable and Tom had ordered drinks for Tara and me. I never knew why he felt that he had to order for us when we were out together, but I didn't object as long as it was on his dime.

"What are you talking about?"

"Good God, you know what I'm talking about. The old man. It's nice that he isn't hovering around for a change.

"Are you onto this again? Look, we have a reservation for four tonight–count it yourself, if you don't believe me–and he has made his own arrangements for dinner. Not here, I should say. Does that satisfy you, my wacky brother?"

"You mean Goofball?"

"You are a goofball."

"Fine. Let me say that if you looked at the situation a little more dispassionately, you'd probably come to the conclusion that I'm not the wacky one in this family."

"Maybe so."

The waitress unexpectedly appeared with our drinks and passed them to us without error. As soon as she left our table, Belinda peered around Tom's chest (she was sitting on the other side of him from me) and said, "Can we all stop this? If you two can leave it alone for once, we might actually have a good time."

"Me?" I asked, resenting the implication that I was responsible for whatever the old man was doing in their household. "Talk to your husband. I'm not in control of the old man."

It was a stupid thing to say. I would have corrected myself, but just then Tara chimed in to offer her two cents.

"Belinda's right. Let's just forget about Bill for a while so we can have a pleasant dinner. Tom, this is a wonderful place."

I found it grating that she should play up her relationship with the old man by using the name he was using to pull the wool over everyone's eyes, but I let it drop and, like the others, tacitly agreed to forget the old man for the evening. For the next few minutes, we silently sipped out drinks and tried to appear nonchalant and preoccupied with pleasant thoughts. As I casually looked around to find something to occupy the time until we could agree on another topic, I noticed on the far wall a large painting of a matador dispatching a bull. It was exactly like the one in Tom's living room–the same composition, the same colors, the same black velvet–and I was tempted to ask him as a joke if he had acquired it here or merely had it copied so that his home would feel more like a restaurant. But before I could lighten the mood, Tara cheerfully mentioned something about the weather, which spurred Tom and Belinda to chime about the rain and how much we needed it but didn't want it. Once this fascinating line of discussion petered out, we again sat silently until the waitress and her two assistants started laying out our dinners. When they were finished and Tom confirmed that we as a group didn't need anything for the time being, another conversation spontaneously sprang about the food and the beautiful decorations throughout the place. Once again, I was going to bring up the bull fight, but Tara and Belinda started chattering about Tom's good taste and excellent choice of establishments, and so I dropped it and chimed in like the others. Tom, always on his toes to bring attention to himself, mentioned another restaurant not too far from this one that he considered acquiring a few years ago. He didn't, he said, the fundamentals were weak, and then he launched into a rather baroque tale about another place that he or someone either did or didn't buy that caused all kinds of troubles.

"I made a bundle betting against it, and got sick in the process," he said, and we all laughed as though we knew what he was referring to.

We continued listening spellbound to Tom's tales of skinning the culinary-world cat when the conversation slipped out from under his feet and centered on a broad array of general topics that everyone including my brother was interested in. I don't exactly recall all of the topics, but I remember something about malls, stores, sales, the weather (in reference to outdoor shopping?), news (by an unspoken agreement, we all steered away from business news), music (Belinda's special CD wasn't mentioned), and so on. Everyone was having a good time. What was even more interesting (from my current perspective) was that the old man as a topic of interest didn't come up one more time throughout dinner. Tom didn't mention him, Belinda was silent about him, Tara didn't inquire after him, and I...I guess for a while he was as good as dead to me. Admittedly, early on I expected him to appear out of thin air and squeeze in between Tom and me, but once the conversation became lively and we were all chattering like school kids, I completely forgot about him and, on the few occasions that someone bearing a slight resemblance to him passed in front of our table, I turned away and kept silent so that I wasn't responsible for derailing the good time we were all having. We continued this way practically nonstop until we were finished with dinner and the check was paid. As we were saying our goodbyes just outside the entrance, Belinda suggested that we all come back to their house for drinks. I must have looked like I was going to object, for Tara wrapped her arm around mine and said that it was a "lovely idea," and Tom, now considering it a done deal, said in an expansive tone that Tara and I should follow him back to his house. (I don't know why he felt that we needed to follow Tom back to his house, unless he was concerned that I might change my mind and head home.) Before I could agree, or put forth the expected objection regarding the old man, Tom said casually that he didn't expect "Dad" to come home until much later in the evening. Even though the statement was directed as much at Belinda as it was at me, everyone looked at me, including Tara, as though I was going to be the one who would spoil the rest of a lovely ending.

"Goofball, are you coming or is Tara going to ride with us?" Tom asked good-naturedly, though it was clear that he was trying to pressure me into coming.

Since I didn't want to be the spoilsport of the evening, and I didn't want Tara doing something else without me, I smiled agreeably as though I was in on the joke and said that it sounded like great fun. "I'm in," I reiterated, "But only if you stop calling me Goofball." I smiled and chuckled a little to show that I was as good natured as everyone else, but no one appeared to find anything funny in my retort and without another word we walked to our respective cars in the lot.

I was silent on the drive to Tom's house. Tara, on the contrary, was chattering up a storm about the food, the restaurant, and the good time she had. Just as we pulled up in front of Tom's house, she mentioned almost in passing that she was glad that I hadn't ruined then evening with my "nonsense" about "Bill." I didn't respond. I didn't appreciate her choice of words to describe my concerns about the old man and what he might be doing while he was staying with Tom (remember, what affected Tom often affected me, too, directly or indirectly), but I let it go. I didn't even remonstrate with her about the choice of names. I, too, had had a good time, and I was looking forward to a continuation of the evening at Tom's, just like old times, just like all the times before the pseudo-Bill showed up and systematically poisoned everything.

Once we had convened in Tom's driveway, we immediately picked up where we had left off in terms of conversation. Tom tried to guide the talk to business, but Belinda artfully outflanked him and maneuvered it to the weather, which then opened up a wealth of considered analysis about the heat and the annual rainfall. Not to be outdone, Tom chimed in with some pearls about climate change (fortunately, no one bit when he mentioned how it was negatively affecting business). The lights in the house were on when we came inside. Neither Tom nor Belinda seemed concerned or surprised. Chelsea might have left them on, and the three of them often left the lights on when they were out as a security measure (a bright, occupied house, the theory went, is less likely to be burglarized than a dark, seemingly unoccupied place). Anyway, after we took off our coats and began slowly chatting our way toward the living room, I could see the glow of the living room lights from down the hallway, and I couldn't help wondering why these particular lights were on. Sure, a well-lit house equaled a secure house, and yet these lights couldn't be seen from the front of the house and therefore it was simply a waste of energy to keep them on when the house was, as I assumed it was this evening, unoccupied. I should emphasize that I was only curious and that I had no intention of asking Tom or Belinda about it. If they wanted to use more electricity than necessary, that was their business, and I didn't want my innocent inquiry to be misconstrued. ('Oh no, he's going to wreck everything with another argument about their father.')

Tom was telling us as we approached the living room to make ourselves comfortable while he got our drinks. But as we entered, we all immediately stopped and stared, mouths open, in the direction of the fireplace. The old man was there. He was dressed in his business-casual getup and leaning against the mantle as though he was posing for a photograph in an executive business publication.

"Dad," Tom said with feigned surprise, "I thought you were going to be out for the night. I'm glad you're here, though."

"Tommy, I had a change of..." he started to say but didn't finish. When he was sure that all eyes were on him, he pretended to notice me for the first time and appeared to faint. Not a complete faint, however. He dropped to his hands and knees and then scampered like a fat rat toward the couch and hid behind it. It was obviously an act. But unlike the others, I saw through his game and remained standing nonchalantly while they rushed over to him to find out what was going on. Once Tom, Belinda, and Tara had surrounded him and were solicitously asking him if he was hurt, how they could help, and if he wanted a drink of water, he started howling–yes, howling–about how I had promised to do bad things to him if we ever came face-to-face again. I would have laughed off this grotesque charade–for a few seconds, I thought that the old man was actually trying to be funny–though I quickly realized that there was nothing intentionally amusing about his behavior and that, if there were indeed a joke somewhere, it was on me. After spending several minutes on the floor ministering to the blubbering old fool and assuring him that I couldn't have been serious, all four of them–Tom, Belinda, Tara, and the old man–in unison looked over the couch at me, each one silently demanding an explanation for my egregious behavior.

I did my best to laugh as their expressions intensified. "Hey, he's not serious. I said nothing of the kind. The only time I've spoken to him was here and, a couple of days ago, at my office. Did you know he did that? He came inside and sat down on my chair without being invited. He told me that if I knew what's good for me, I would have to stop coming between him and Tom. If I didn't, he said he'd end things pretty quickly–and I don't think he was suggesting that he'd walk away. Ask him yourself. Ask him what he meant if I didn't stay away from Tom. And, while you're at it, ask him what he did with my eraser."

Tara was the first to respond, and she proved to be the most vociferous in his defense. "Oh, for God's sake, he's an old man. Even if he said what you claim he said, what could he do to you?"

"What? I don't know. Maybe he's got a gun. I don't know. He said it, though, and he's not as feeble as he pretends to be. Did you see how quickly he crawled behind the couch?"

"I would, too, if I were that afraid of you."

"Afraid? What are you talking about? He threatened me. I didn't say a word to him."

"Not even during this supposed meeting at your office?"

"What are you saying, Tara?" I demanded and instinctively took a step forward. That, of course, was a big mistake, because the old man and the two women leaned back as if I were going to charge at them.

Tom graciously came to rescue. "I think there's been some miscommunication," he said authoritatively. "Let's chill out and get comfy. We'll have some drinks, and I'm sure everything will be fine after that."

While Tom helped the old man to his feet and walked him slowly to a nearby chair, Belinda and Tara silently looked on. Once the old man had been meticulously eased into the chair, Belinda handed Tom a bottle of beer and a glass. He carefully poured a small draft into the glass and equally carefully handed it to the old man, acting as if the old man was as fragile, if not more so, as the glass. When the old man had finally secured the drink in his still trembling hands, Tom stepped back and waited while he sipped it and pronounced his complete satisfaction. Belinda and Tara, who had been watching this touching scene, practically applauded, and they, along with the old man, insisted that Tom was a kind and thoughtful individual. I sat down after that, as did Belinda and Tara, and as Tom began pouring drinks for everyone else, the old man added, "I don't think I've ever known a wiser or more thoughtful individual than Tommy here." Like bobbleheads, Belinda and Tara nodded in agreement while I did my best to refrain from laughing over this statement. Tom was indeed a wise individual, but the old man was patently sucking up to him and trying (successfully, it seemed) to manipulate him and Belinda and Tara. Look, how much wisdom did it take to pull the old man's flabby ass off the living-room floor and drop it into a nearby chair? And the fact that Tom told us all to have a drink, relax, and enjoy ourselves…well, was that an act of exceptional wisdom or banal courtesy? The problem, though, was that in Belinda's and Tara's eyes, Tom was showing himself an example to which we should all aspire.

Well, that was enough for me. I had made it clear earlier that I didn't want to spend a second with the old man, unless it was to help remove him from the premises, and so I decided to leave, with or without Tara. This time, though, I was going to inform Tom that I would never return until the old man was gone, for good. I was going to inform him that the time was over for a middle ground—you can't have a brother and a fake father—and therefore it was time to choose me or the old man. It was stupid, I know, particularly because I wasn't absolutely certain that he would choose me over the old man. Fortunately, everything changed before I was able to utter my ultimatum. Just before I opened my mouth, I glanced over to Belinda and Tara for support, however tenuous, and saw to my surprise that neither one of them would look at me, not even to acknowledge my presence. My own wife turned away from me, and I could tell by the way she squinted and tightened her lips that she wasn't happy with me, either. Maybe it was the way Tara refused to engage me that brought to life my earlier regrets at not having stayed long enough to expose the old man's trickery. I don't know, but this time instead of making demands or leaving, I decided to sit back and stay a while. I was going to show everyone that I could be wise, too, and I was going to find something that would end this farce once and for all—I was going to prove to the others that the old man had been faking everything, including the touching scene behind the couch.

"Yes, yes, Tom's exactly right, and I applaud his effort to help the...him to a chair," I said to show that I was a good sport and as enthusiastic as everyone else. Without looking at the old man, I angled my thumb toward him. "I would have helped, too, but Tom was there first. Yes, he was, and it's his house, after all." I was careful to sound pleasant and supportive, but I'm not sure I came across that way.

As if on cue, Tara and Belinda angled their chairs a little toward the old man and away from me. While I sipped my drink and wished I had a cigar (even though I don't smoke), Tom, Belinda, and my wife opened up a lively conversation with the old man. They asked him how he was doing today, and Belinda and Tara pleaded with him to tell them more about the prospects he was considering—but only if he was ready to talk about them. The old man soaked up all this attention, and I watched his personality change from the seemingly frightened old man to the bombastic old fool who felt that he could get away with anything.

"Brenda," he intoned in a pompous baritone, "Things are moving along quite nicely. With a little help from your wonderful husband, I hope to be able to finalize certain of these prospects fairly soon. If that's the case, I will be able to share with you and your lovely family the fruits of my success."

Had I been holding the cigar I wanted, it would have slipped through my fingers and dropped onto Tom's expensive rug. Forget about these phantom prospects. The old man had been staying at Tom's house for how long and still didn't know that name of Tom's wife?

"Her name's Belinda, you…," I started to say when he interrupted me as if I weren't there.

"Tommy, you know me, and you know that family means everything to me. My success means nothing unless I can share it with you and yours."

"It means everything to me, too, Dad. Let's not forget Jim and Tara. Jim is her husband and your other…, Tom began, winking at me as if we were now on a line of conversation that could win me over.

"Yes, yes, son, Tara…and did you say her husband?"

It was laughable. The old man couldn't string together two sentences without tripping over the facts and making statements that only someone completely ignorant of the truth would have believed. What surprised me even more was that Tom knew better, and yet he sat back with a loving smile on his lips and let the old man pull the wool over his eyes. I took a quick breath to remain calm and collected, though I wasn't sure how long I could hold out if everyone continued to eat this dog food.

"Excuse me," I interrupted at last, unable to let these statements go unchallenged. "If you're our father, as you claim," I began, "I don't understand how you could be so enamored of family when you deserted yours thirty-five years ago and not once until recently did you reach out and say a word. Our father allowed our family to disintegrate, our mother to lose her mind, and his two boys to grow up like orphans. Can you reconcile your claims with the facts?"

I sat back, pleased with what I said. I was confident that because the issue of desertion was now out in the open, everyone would want an answer. But when I looked around expecting to see agreement on everyone's faces, I was met with glacial stares, suggesting that I had done something wrong, that I had become once more the villain in the room.

Tom, the wise one, was the first to break the silence. "That was a long time ago. We all make mistakes, and I think the quality of our character is shown by our ability to forgive and by our recognition that no one's perfect."

There was a general murmur that Tom had said something else that was extremely wise and that we would be better people if we listened to him.

"I know I made a lot of mistakes," Tara chimed in to the approbation of the others.

"Me, too," Belinda added. There were tears in her eyes, and for a moment I thought that she and Tara were going to reach over and hug each other. We were spared that spectacle when Tom piped in with another gem.

Smiling sagely, he looked at me and said, "How about you, Goofball? Have you ever made any mistakes?"

With all eyes on me, especially the old man's rheumy eyes, I was about to explode. I had been hopeful that we were at last going to get to the heart of the matter (the identity of the old man and why he was here), but now I was beginning to feel as though I were the object of the conversation—as if this were an intervention designed to force me to accept the old man. Maybe it was.

I cleared my throat in an attempt to show everyone that I was just as rational as my brother. "Tom," I began, "Would you please stop calling me Goofball." Out of the corner of my eyes, I could see the old man's lumpen shoulders shake as he again giggled over the nickname.

"Okay, let's everybody stay calm."

"I am calm, but it's demeaning…okay, it doesn't matter. Sure, I've made mistakes. We've all made mistakes, even you. But there are mistakes, and there are mistakes. I'm willing to forgive a mistake given the context in which it was made. But there has to be a recognition of the wrong and an apology, a sincere apology. In this case, however…"

"I think your Dad's apology is sincere," Belinda chimed in. "I've been around him enough to see just how sincere he is. Let's not forget that he, too, has suffered horribly throughout the years."

"I agree," Tara added.

"Then it's settled," Tom added, as if he were making a sapient proclamation. "Dad," he said pompously addressing the old man, "You are forgiven and welcomed back into this family."

I was flabbergasted. What had started as a way of getting to the truth was quickly morphing into a lovefest for the old man. Our father had suffered horribly? What about the suffering the rest of us endured because of his actions? It was a ridiculous comparison, and I couldn't imagine forgiveness coming this easily on the day of judgment, at least not without an acknowledgement of sins. But there had to be a day of judgment, and I was now more determined than ever that it had to be this evening. Postponing it, I was certain, would only enable the old man, like a tick, to burrow deeper into our lives

"Wait a minute," I said, perhaps a little more assertively than I had intended. "Wait a minute. Just because he says sorry now doesn't mean a damn thing. It's easy to apologize long after the fact, assuming of course that this individual over there is actually who he says he is." I indicated the old man with a sideways movement of my head. "Listen, if he is our father, I'm not forgiving him this easily. Our young lives were ruined because of him, and a simple sorry isn't going to fix things."

"My early life wasn't so bad," Tom interjected. "What do you want him to do to receive your forgiveness?" He placed emphasis on the pronoun 'your,' which made it appear as if I were acting as judge, jury, and God.

"Mine wasn't so great," I responded. "I love you, Tom, but I needed a father. I needed someone to help me grow up, someone who would play with me and give me advice on all kinds of things. I also needed someone to protect me from all those kind people who ridiculed me because our father ran away from home. A simple sorry and a phony story about dying doesn't cut it is my—yes, my—book. But you're all missing the bigger picture."

"Seems like a pretty big picture to me," Tara said, speaking like she was saying something to herself. I was beginning to suspect that she might have had one too many.

"No, for once listen to me. Nobody seems concerned that he might not be the person he claims to be. Did anyone think to check out his story?"

We were all speaking as if the old man weren't in the room. I glanced at him, and I thought that he had a slight smirk on his lips, as if he were confident that he was getting closer to the family while I was moving farther away.

"He told us who he is," Belinda said. "Tommy said he told him things. What more do we need?"

"Are you kidding? Tom told me what he said. It's the same experience that every boy has growing up. Why doesn't he tell me something about my life, so I can judge for myself?" I glowered at the old man and then at Tom.

"He liked baseball," the old man burst out to no one in particular.

"Give me a break," I said. "Every kid…"

"I'm satisfied," Tom said, and I could see Belinda and Tara nodding in agreement. "You do like baseball. Listen, I don't need any more convincing. Got anything else?" Tom's sagacity and brotherliness seemed to be fading, and it was becoming clear that he was tired of the discussion and wanted it to end.

"All right," I said, standing up and looking at Tom, Tara, and Belinda in turn. "He came in here tonight telling you all that I had threatened him. You've all known me for how many years? Do you really think I'd do something like that? Do you think I'd make up a story about him coming to my office when it could easily be checked? There are guards where I work, and I'm sure they have records of everyone coming into the building. Either he's lying or I'm lying. Which is it?"

"Goofball…"

"Jesus Christ, shut up with the Goofball shit."

"All right, James," Tom said as he, too, stood up. "You've been a little hotheaded lately, but then you've always been hotheaded. You're turning this against me. You're asking Belinda and Tara to discount what I said, and you're telling them that my judgment is questionable. Is that how you want to play this game?"

"Have it your way," I said and, against my determination to stay and see this thing to its end, walked out of the room.

This time, surprisingly, Tara followed me, and I could hear her thanking Tom and Belinda for dinner and apologizing for something else. She was silent on the way home, but once inside our place, she scolded me for my behavior, lecturing me as if I were the one who had made a scene. Maybe I had.

"You were disgraceful. It was the same thing the last time we were at his house, and the time before that and the time before that. When is it going to end?"

"Did you hear what that old goat was saying? Family? Are you kidding me, family? He's either a fraud or the greatest scoundrel to ever walk the face of this crummy earth."

"I can't believe you threatened him."

"I threatened him? Do you really believe that? He was acting. He was working to get everyone's sympathy and turn them against me."

"Why would he want to do that?"

"Why? Isn't it obvious? He's up to something. I'm the only one standing in his way. He's learned enough about us to know that he can separate us, pit us against each other, or against me, by acting out these simple games."

"Come on, he's a harmless old man. He's not doing anything of the kind."

I could feel myself losing control. "How would you know? Come to think of it, you seem to know him fairly well. How is that? Have you spoken to him without telling me? Were you driving around with him the other day?"

Tara didn't respond. The cool, taut expression on her face resembled my mother's when, as a child, I defied her instructions.

"Why don't you answer? Why are you and everyone else so intent on defending him? You don't know the slightest..."

"Maybe you're the one who doesn't know. For God's sake, he's your father..."

That was it. I had reached my breaking point. I raised my voice and informed Tara that she was not only wrong about the old man but also that she had no business deciding who was or wasn't our father. When she stubbornly pushed back and reminded me for the nth time that Tom was convinced, I informed her that Tom was a fool. He was so desperate to have a father, I said, that he would have accepted Rasputin as his father if that august individual had made the same gratuitous claim. Even at that point, we might have been able to step back from the brink, but I added some ill-advised statements questioning both her psychological acumen and her intelligence. Shortly afterwards, we went to be in separate rooms.

15

In the morning, before she left for work, I apologized to Tara and explained that I had let my emotions get the better of me and had said some things that I didn't mean or believe. She seemed guardedly satisfied. To help my situation, I also appealed to her psychological discernment with respect to my judgment about the old man. I said that it was my understanding that the memory can be easily tricked into believing something that isn't true (as an illustration, I mentioned false memories and the ease with which researchers could implant fictive memories into test subjects) and, therefore, without a fact-based study of some kind, I didn't think that I was out of line contradicting Tom and questioning the old man's veracity.

"What kind of study are you talking about?" she asked.

"I would defer to you, but I don't think there is any objective study that can determine whether someone was actually a father–these days, a woman can serve that role quite nicely–but I do think that a simple investigation of some kind can easily determine if that someone is who he or she claims to be."

Tara was thoughtful for a minute. "Where could you get that done?" she asked as if this were something that you bought at the local strip mall.

"I don't think you have to go somewhere to get it done. We hire a private investigator, and he does everything."

"I don't believe it."

"Look, these guys are careful. They operate in stealth mode. The old man won't know it happened until we present the results."

"No, we're not going to do that."

"Why not?"

"It would be a violation of his trust. It would be like stabbing him in the back. Plus, it's expensive."

I smiled weakly and pretended that we were having a reasonable discussion. "It wouldn't be stabbing anybody. If the results are favorable, don't you think he'd want to know? Don't you think everyone would want to know? We wouldn't have a reason to doubt anything he said after that."

"I'm not so sure about that."

"Let's be very clear here. At this moment, there's absolutely no reason to believe the old man is who he claims to be."

"Who else could he be?"

"A lot of people."

"I'm not ready to…"

"For the sake of argument, let's consider the possibility that he's a sharper after Tom's money."

"Okay, but how would he know what Tom's financial situation is?"

"Tom's house, his cars, his job are dead giveaways. The old man may have spotted him one day, found out his name, and done some research. Once inside Tom's house, he would have access to all kinds of information that he could use to hack into Tom's computer system, his accounts, and even some of those companies he's doing business with. I'm sure he can do a lot of other things with the information he's already gathered."

"But he hasn't touched Tom's bank accounts or…"

"Maybe, and Tom might not know it until long after the fact. The old man's careful, and he's not likely to strike until he's ready–until he's sure he can get away with things. It's the same with any psychopath."

Tara winced at the psychopath characterization, but an instant later she seemed to be seriously weighing my statements and considering my proposal. When she finally spoke, her words were measured and her movements were slow and deliberate. "Throughout my conversations with him," she began, using her considered, professional voice, "I studied his speech and mannerisms very carefully. He was generally clearheaded, though there were moments when he was nervous as well as confused and forgetful. These attributes could suggest deception, or they might simply be a reflection of advanced age and possibly illness. If you want my considered opinion, I would have to say that Mr. Reid is the genuine article. Please, let me finish. It is also my opinion that if we hire a private investigator, as you suggest, we would be flushing good money down the toilet at a time when we can ill afford to lose a single penny. Your job situation is tenuous, am I right?"

"No, no, everything's fine jobwise," I insisted. "I spoke to Jeff, and he agrees that the acquiring company isn't going to do away with the very reason that makes our firm an attractive target. As for a detective, I don't think it's as expensive as you think. I don't know how much, but out of curiosity I can find out."

"No," she replied adamantly. "We're not going to do it. We're not going insult your father with something like this. We could be damaging our relationships in a way that won't fully heal for quite some time."

Before I could reply to this nonsense, Tara informed me that she had an appointment and would return later.

"What? Okay, sure, let's discuss it later this evening," I replied as the front door closed behind her.

I sat down and mulled over the idea of contracting a private investigator on my own and letting him go to town on the old man. Fifteen or twenty minutes later, I made a decision and called in sick at the office so that I could contact one of them. It didn't take long after this, though, before I began to have doubts and second thoughts. The money was a problem. No matter how much it cost, I couldn't hide the fact from Tara that I had engaged the services of one of these people. And even if I did hire someone, I felt certain that no matter what the individual dredged up about the old man, Tom would dismiss it as being of little importance or completely irrelevant. That he could dismiss facts and figures was extraordinary (I had witnessed him doing it on numerous occasions that had nothing to do with the old man), since his success in business depended on facts and figures, along with a little bit of leverage. It wasn't until later in the day after I woke up from a short nap that something inside me seemed to have changed. I was fatigued, but this had nothing to do with my physical state. I was simply tired of worrying about the old man and what he might do. I even considered the possibility that I had been getting worked up over nothing, or very little. There was no doubt in my mind that the old man was a fraud, and yet apart from his feckless threats and his ridiculous posturing and psychodramas, he wasn't exactly hurting me and, since I had no intention of getting to know him much less opening my door to him, I probably had little to fear from his presence. I couldn't help feeling sorry for Tom, though. If the old man eventually did something heinous, Belinda and Chelsea would bear the brunt of my brother's folly. But the old man was a problem that he created, a problem that he was fully capable of solving without my help, and so I came to the conclusion that I had to stop destroying my peace of mind over something that was essentially beyond my control.

Nevertheless, I was still interested in finding out how many times Tara had seen the old man behind my back and in knowing why she kept these meetings, or whatever you call them, a secret from me. Was that really her in the car with the old man? Could he have been a patient of hers and therefore her failure to inform me had something to do with patient confidentiality? I would have thought that with her professional skills, she might have deduced that I was angry about the meetings mainly because they had been hidden and that I might have been a little more amenable to things had she kept me informed from the outset. No, this is not exactly right. I still would have been furious that she was meeting the old man, but my anger would have been tempered somewhat had I known about the meetings and had I been able to get my feelings off my chest before she ventured out on something so manifestly pointless and ridiculous. But while all this was simmering in the back of my mind (how many times had she met the old man?), I was determined to temper my curiosity in the interests of world peace and the comity between men.

Jeff called later in the afternoon. After asking me how I was doing (he heard that I was out sick), he told me that I should extend my time off. "Relax and have a good time. It's a done deal. Our firm's been acquired. No one's saying anything, but there's lots of closed-door meetings with the C-suite, and it's obvious that some of them aren't happy about things."

"Why should I stay home another day? It's not going to affect us. We'll do our jobs and let our superiors deal with the bigger issues."

I think Jeff was expecting me to get as worked up over the information as he was. As long as I've known him, he always seemed to appreciate a companion in troubles. I remember once when…but it doesn't matter. At this moment, I didn't want to get worked up over anything, and so I downplayed the issue and advised him to "chill out" for a while until we had more details. He ended the call quickly after that. I have to admit that I regretted speaking to him this way. Jeff was a good friend and, with the way things had been playing out with respect to the old man, I needed good friends like him. Well, as I noted, I was determined to remain at peace with myself, and if Tom succeeded in dealing effectively with the old man, I could handle anything, even being laid off by new management.

When Tara came home that evening, she seemed tired and a little distant, as if she'd had problems with one of her patients. She insisted that nothing was wrong and that her day had been just fine, and so I let it drop. Later in the evening, as I was beginning to suspect that she was still sore with me, it occurred to me that we might be able to put aside our problems for a while and refresh our mental processes if we got away for the weekend. I thought that one of those quaint bed-and-breakfasts on the coast would do the trick. I presented the idea to Tara and, to my delight, she immediately accepted. There was no considering, no dithering, no worries about patients, no whatever, and, to my surprise, she knew the very place where we could stay. One hour later, reservations in hand, my workplace duly informed of my continuing absence, we made the two-hour trek to a lovely little house only a block from the ocean.

We were exhausted by the time we checked into the quaint, Victorian-style house. But rather than heading to the beach as we had planned, we went directly to our room and practically flopped onto the huge, overstuffed bed and went to sleep, listening to the muffled booms of the ocean waves. We were up early the following morning and, after a leisurely breakfast and a pleasant conversation with one of the other guests, we made the short trek to the beach. The air was thick and salty, and, except for a few wispy clouds overhead, the sky was clear. There was a brisk wind that pushed against us as we strolled across the cool, wet sand and did our best to avoid the cold ocean water as it hissed ashore and licked our toes and ankles. Not once, throughout this time, did I think about Tom, the old man, or our arguments. To me, it felt like Tara and I were back on our honeymoon, where we enjoyed the beach on the other side of the country and didn't think about the past or the future. Since we hadn't brought our bathing suits (the water was too cold this time of year for swimming), we found a lovely rise of sand just outside the water's reach and stretched out to take in the sound of the ocean and to watch the heavy clouds roll in from the other side of the world. Less than an hour later, I voiced my concern about an approaching storm, and it was practically at this moment that Tara's phone pinged.

"I thought you weren't bringing that thing," I said as I rolled over onto my side to face her.

"I have to," she replied while fishing it out of her blouse pocket. "I need to be available to patients." She took two or three minutes to read and respond to a text before leaning back with me. She was quiet for several minutes afterward and then chuckled gently, as if something amusing came to mind.

"Who was it?" I asked, connecting the chuckling to the texter.

"No one, just a patient."

"Amusing, huh?"

As the dark, nearly black clouds were now practically overhead, we got up and strolled over to the shopping district of the seaside community. We went into several shops (Tara bought a lovely, out-of-season blouse and I acquired a brass, ship's compass) and then had lunch at a little café practically on the beach. It was raining heavily by then, and so we remained inside nursing our lattes while waiting for the weather to clear. Once the shimmering rain stopped and the bright light reflected off the sidewalks, we started to leave when Tara's phone beeped again. This time, though, she merely glanced at it and then slipped it back into her pocket. Back outside, we spent a little more time wandering among the shops before heading back to the beach, where we rolled up our pantlegs and ventured a little into the waves as they rushed ashore. When the sun went down, we stopped for a while and listened to the plaintive cries of the seagulls as they glided effortlessly over the waves and the distant moans of the ships as they slowly plowed through the waves. Back in our room, as we snuggled under the covers in the darkness, I was about to tell Tara that this had been one of the best days of my life when her blasted phone beeped several more times. Since it was within arm's reach on a small table on her side of the bed, she rolled over and checked it each time, putting it away in the table's drawer sometime after I fell asleep. We were up with the sun. We made a quick visit to the beach and then returned to our room to pack our bags, which we brought with us as we sat down for breakfast. While we were eating, I remembered the shirt that I had left hanging in the bathroom and went back to the room to retrieve it. Tara was slipping her phone back into her pocket when I came back, and shortly afterward we left the place and headed home. Once we were back on the highway, Tara's phone beeped and she read the message for what seemed to be an inordinate amount of time. After this, she stared me for several seconds with a heated expression on her gentle face.

"Anything wrong?" I asked in a pleasant voice.

She silently shook her head as though she were forcing the tangles out of her hair. I let it go. Tara always had a troublesome patient of some kind, and her interactions with these individuals sometimes left her in a less than upbeat frame of mind. 'I wonder if it's somebody at Tom's company,' I asked myself as I went around a slower car and merged back into my lane.

This moment was the only blight on what otherwise was a wonderful experience. Shortly before breakfast as we were packing, we talked about coming back, maybe in a few weeks, and promised ourselves that we would stay longer, if possible. I was confident that during this short period, we had put our marriage back on track. Our marriage wasn't in serious trouble despite the hovering presence of the old man, and we certainly didn't have the kind of issues that required outside help. The main problem, it seemed to me, was that we had focused too much on our careers and other distractions and hadn't taken enough time to keep our life together fresh and alive, as Tara might have said. This is not to say that the old man wasn't part of the problem, and I felt that until he was gone for good, Tara and I couldn't be fully free to enjoy our life together to its fullest. Regardless, I didn't think again about the interruptions, the so-called patients, until later in the evening when we were home. We were in the bedroom changing out of our vacation clothes when, as I pulled off my windbreaker over my head, my cell phone fell out of the side pocket and bounced on the small rug next to the bed. Tara stopped undressing and angled her head toward me. It was another one of her strange looks, only this time it seemed to suggest that we both knew the answer to some unspoken question.

"It's okay," I said and held the phone up so that she could see it. "The cover's like steel."

"You told me you didn't bring your phone to the beach. You scolded me for bringing mine."

"I didn't scold you. And I thought I had left mine at home. I didn't know it was in my pocket."

"Couldn't you feel the weight? Didn't you feel something hard in your side pocket? Wait a minute, didn't you have your hands in your pockets while we were actually on the beach?"

"I just didn't notice it. If I touched it while we were there, I didn't think anything of it. Maybe I thought that it was a wad of papers."

"What kind of papers?"

"What are you talking about?"

"You said that you felt papers in your pocket. What kind of papers would those be?"

"I honestly don't understand what you're getting at."

"You brought your phone, didn't you?"

"What? Yes, by accident. Why the third degree?"

"May I see it?"

"There's nothing to see. It's just a phone. You've seen it before." I held it up again and then shoved it deeply into my back pocket. It didn't occur to me at the moment that Tara might get the wrong idea if I didn't hand it over to her. I was positive that there wasn't anything wrong with the phone, and I didn't want to get into a protracted discussion over virus prevention or apps I should have downloaded.

She tightened her sun-touched face and silently went away.

"I don't know what's bugging you," I said, following her into the living room as she sat down on the couch and pulled out the black notebook from under it and began writing something. "At least it wasn't going off all the time like yours."

She kept the notebook there for those odd moments when she had a fleeting thought about one of her patients and didn't want to run into the other room and unlock her desk. I never looked at the contents (it wasn't my business), and I shrugged my shoulders and went back into the bedroom. The phone probably jogged something in her memory that she wanted to record for an upcoming patient meeting, I concluded, and gave no more thought to the matter for the rest of the evening.

Tara was preoccupied with her notebook until it was time for dinner. Normally, we both would have prepared the meal and sat down together for a pleasant conversation. This time, however, she begged off because she had to see a patient and informed me that she would be back later.

"You're going to see a patient now, when we haven't had dinner?" I asked. It was a strange time to leave even for her, and I felt slightly troubled by the seriousness of her attitude and the sculptural hardness that came over her face and body.

She stopped, looked at me with her eyebrows raised as if she couldn't understand something about me, and left.

I didn't know what to say, and, when I thought to ask her to be a little more specific about when she would return, it was too late. She was already out the door. 'I'll text her later,' I told myself as I went into the kitchen for something to drink. I went to my computer after this to catch up on some work that was coming due.

16

Tara didn't come home until much later at night. I had meant to text her earlier in the evening, but I had become so engrossed in my work that it simply slipped my mind. By the time she came into the bedroom, I was undressing and getting ready for bed.

She glowered at me for a moment before inhaling deeply to ease her rising emotions. "What did you say to your father?" she asked. It was clear that she already had an answer and was only giving me an opportunity to confirm it.

I wasn't going to fall for the game of calling the old man my father, and so I remained unruffled and replied to the literal meaning of her question. "What did I say to my father? A lot of things, I guess. The most important things were those that I said when he was no longer around. Like, 'Why did you leave?' 'Did you leave because of me? and 'When are you coming back?' 'Do you hate me?' was probably the one I asked the most. There were others."

She wasn't biting. "You know what I mean."

I finished putting on my pajamas and looked directly at her. "No, I don't. Would you like to tell me what you mean?"

Tara walked around to her side of the bed and positioned herself so that the bed was between us. "Your father says…"

"If you're referring to that old man, don't call him my father. He's not my father. In fact, I'd bet a thousand dollars he wasn't anyone's father."

"Remember when we were at your brother's and he said you threatened him? I had some reservations then, but it was obvious that he was genuinely scared. Now he says that you sent him several texts yesterday, saying that you were coming after him."

The absurdity of the idea made me laugh, and I thought for a moment that Tara might be joking.

"You're laughing because you sent the texts?"

"Are you serious? Did he tell you that?"

"You're not denying it?"

"Denying what?" I sat down on the edge of the bed and angled the upper half of my body toward her. "What's the matter with you. I can't believe you take this stuff seriously. Of course, I'm denying it, and I deny having made any previous threats to him, too."

"You don't like him, do you?"

"What does that have to do with anything? No, I don't like him, and I wish he'd crawl back into whatever hole he crawled out of. But I wouldn't threaten anyone except threaten to call the police. Maybe that's what we should do in this case."

I angled my shoulders a little more in her direction, and she reciprocated by taking a step back. Was she expecting me to spring from the bed like a wild tiger?

"The texts were sent yesterday morning just before we got onto the road."

"How would he know when we got onto the road?"

"He didn't. He gave me the time of the texts."

"Okay, and that's significant because…"

"Before we left, you went back to the room, and you were there for quite some time while you ostensibly searched for the shirt that you left hanging in the bathroom. You could have texted him then with the phone you had conveniently forgotten."

"Are you the prosecution? Yes, I suppose that I could have texted him then if I had his number, which I don't. But, for your information, I was going to the bathroom and, believe me, writing texts wasn't high on my list of priorities right then. What's the matter with you? How can you ask me such questions?"

"Because I've seen the texts."

"When? Did he send them to you?"

"Yes."

"May I see them?"

Something seemed to be on her mind before she spoke. "Let me see your phone first."

"Why do you need to see my phone?" It didn't matter to me whether or not she examined my phone. What did bother me was that my wife of many years wanted proof of my innocence before she would believe me.

"If you have nothing to hide…"

"Of course, I have nothing to hide. But I don't understand why I have to prove anything to you. Don't you trust me? How can you take his word over mine?"

"I saw the texts."

"And you know they were from me and my phone?"

"You won't show me your phone to verify…"

I stomped to the closet. I yanked the pants I had been wearing off a hook and pulled the phone out of the back pocket. "Maybe I erased them," I practically hollered as I reached toward her with the phone. I was outraged.

And why shouldn't I have been? She didn't believe her own husband. Worse, she took that old scoundrel's word over mine—and she wasn't subtle about it, either, as she might have been with one of those crazy patients of hers. Okay, so maybe I tossed the phone to her a little harder than I had intended. It slipped through her fingers, bounced off the wall, and shattered on a section of the floor not covered with carpet. I cursed (not at her but at the situation) and, when I went over to the shattered remains, she backed away and glowered at me as if I had done it on purpose. In fact, the next word out of her mouth was "convenient."

Tara was standing behind me as I picked up the pieces. I was a little more relaxed after I had recovered the last piece, and, as I looked up at her over my shoulder, I asked her in a reasonable voice if my name or phone number had been associated with those texts.

She didn't immediately respond and, as I stood up, she backed away from me.

"You don't need my phone for this. If my name or phone number isn't attached to the texts, then you can't accuse me. Let me repeat—I didn't send him anything. I told you, I don't know his number. I didn't even know he had a number."

"All right, I'll doublecheck the name and number of the sender," she replied. She was glacial but composed, and it was obvious that this simple statement was a threat that would be hanging over my head until she had a chance to verify the signature of the texts.

"Fine, you do that," I replied, barely able to control myself. "But let me just say that I can't fathom why everyone automatically accepts everything the old man says. I especially can't understand why you, of all people, discount everything I say if it contradicts anything he says. You've known him for how long?"

"I've studied…"

I sat back down on the bed. "I know, I know. But let me tell you something else," I began as I stretched across the bed to toss the pieces into the small, plastic trashcan near the headboard, "If I were violent and wanted to do something to him, I wouldn't threaten him. Did you ever think of that?"

Tara opened wide her sensuous green eyes and stared at me. "What are you saying," she asked as if I had just revealed my plans for the old man.

"Good God," I responded, gritting my teeth and shaking my head. "For the last time, I didn't threaten the old man. I didn't text him or communicate with him in any fashion. I can't believe that no one is willing to question his statements or look into his background. A year ago, I wouldn't in my wildest dreams have believed that Tom and especially you would have taken a stranger's side over mine."

"This isn't about taking anyone's side, and you know it. It's about…"

"It's exactly about taking sides. The old man evidently knows how to divide people, and he's divided you all between his camp and mine. To be in his, where you all want to be, you have to be against me. You have to believe everything he says and deny everything I say. You think you know what our father was like, but you don't know a thing about him because you haven't walked in my shoes. But that doesn't stop you from making judgments. And don't give me this crap about Tom's experience. He's overlooking everything because he's desperate to have a father, any father. If you want to use your psychological powers on someone, use them on him and the old man."

I got up and left the room before she could pretend to be the cool, collected, rational psychologist and went into the spare bedroom and slammed the door. No, I didn't slam the door. I closed it firmly enough to let her know that I wasn't coming back to our bedroom until she put her thinking cap squarely on her head.

Later that night, as I relaxed in the silent, impenetrable darkness that covered me like a blanket, I mentally rehashed our argument to understand why she would take the old man's word over mine. She knew me better than she knew anyone else, and therefore she had no reason to question my statements even when they contradicted the old man's. What, after all, did she honestly know about that stranger? Why was she so eager, like everyone else, to accept his word even when it blatantly contradicted the facts? "For Christ's sake," I said out loud, "Would any reasonable person think his claim that I liked baseball as a child was enough to prove anything, much less kinship?" For Tom it was, but then his entire acceptance of the old man as our father was based on vapor, the old man's word. Since the old man was the last thing I wanted on my mind as I fell asleep, I put him out of my thoughts, as I did my argument with Tara.

At least I tried to put him and everything else out of my mind, but it didn't work. I couldn't sleep, and so I rolled over to one side and tried to force myself into unconsciousness or whatever it is that happens as we fall into oblivion. This didn't work, either, nor did my desire to leave the old man to Tom, and I flopped over onto my back and, as I stared into the nothingness overhead, the old man began creeping back into my mind–his accusations to Tara, his puerile behavior at Tom's house, and then the fact that I had, again, let him slip through my fingers. I should have forced myself to stay long enough to demonstrate that he was playing a vile game and, whatever the rules for this game were, they didn't favor the house, not Tom's house. If only I had come equipped with some indisputable facts about our father that I could have presented at the party to dispose of the old man and get my family back. If only, but the problem was that a lot of what I knew about our father was vague and possibly not true (our last supper with him was practically the only hard fact I possessed). Tom had undeniably known our father for more years than I had, and he often claimed that because he had known him longer, he knew him better and could remember more things about him, including the love he supposedly showed us (Tom liked to highlight a game of chess or checkers that he once played with him as evidence of this knowledge and these feelings). But the kind of intimacy that Tom pretended to remember didn't jive with my experiences with our father. On the occasions when he was home and visible, our father either acted like a hard-bitten army officer–'Do this, do that, why haven't you done the other thing?'–or didn't say anything to us at all. Still, there had to be something, some memory worth recalling that would make sense of what was happening around me and, maybe, force the old man out of our lives and bring Tom and my wife back into mine.

I don't know how long I had been searching in the depths of my memory for facts, facts other than those describing the day our father disappeared, when my eyes began to droop and my thoughts began to cloud over. I woke up with a start, it was if I had stepped into a deep hole, and I remembered the day that our father had taken me to work with him. I think he had taken Tom the year before, and it was my turn to see where "Dad" worked and to be impressed with his importance.

Vague at first, my memory became clearer as more details of the event came to life. I was around six at the time. It was early morning. The sun was out, and there was a slight breeze throwing up leaves and dirt. I had just come inside from playing in the backyard when our father unexpectedly appeared, towering over me in a gray business suit and casting a giant shadow across my entire being. He hollered something to my mother, who was in another room, and then silently took me by the hand, led me to the family car, and ordered me to get into the back seat. The car took off with a shudder and traveled for what seemed like hours. Throughout this time, he said nothing to me, not even in response to my questions. When we arrived at our destination, he got out and came around to the side and let me out. I took three steps away from the vehicle, but he grabbed my hand and held it firmly (not painfully) in his as we walked toward the towering glass entry doors where he worked (he informed me of this salient fact as we approached).

Once inside, we passed by a solitary desk in the lobby and then traveled down a long empty hallway that ended in front of a large, gray metal door (it looked like metal to me). We didn't go through that door, however. Just before we reached it, we turned abruptly to the left and approached another door, a much smaller one with a glazed window occupying most of the upper half. My father, after clearing his throat with a loud explosion, knocked on the door beneath the window. A shadow from the other side floated toward the window and the door mysteriously opened. Standing in the doorway was another tall man in a gray business suit. His hands were holding onto the sides of his wide hips.

"What do we have here?" the man asked to no one in particular. His voice was gravely and unpleasant, and he had a wide, oval and roseate face. After a short interval, my father pulled me in front between him and the man and commanded, "Jimmy, shake hands with Mr. Smith. Mr. Smith is the president of our company."

Mr. Smith, if I remember his name correctly, grasped my puny hand in his giant, hairy paw and gave it a violent downward yank. "Glad to meet you, young man," he said and patted me firmly on the top of the head. He didn't say anything else to me. He looked at my father and said something to him that I didn't understand, after which my father yanked me away and continued down the hallway to the large gray door. Still grasping my small hand, he pulled the door with his other hand and we were hit with an earsplitting blast of thumping and scraping metal and, shortly afterwards, the foul smells of oil, grease, and sweat. The second we stepped inside, the door slammed behind us with a thunderous boom.

We didn't move for a few moments as my father said something about this being the factory and that, because it was filled with dangerous equipment, I was supposed to do something if I knew what was good for me. Whatever that something was, it was lost in all the loud noises filling my ears and the pandemonium that stretched out in front of us. Once he had his say, he pulled me after him as we walked toward a seemingly limitless expanse of towering, black machines furiously pounding and thumping, each one surrounded by men in black overalls hurrying back and forth to satiate the needs of these metallic demons. But no sooner had we started walking into this this menagerie than we came up to a man who was standing near one of the machines. He was covered head to foot with dark grease and soot, and he was wearing a hard, black hat that at one time must have been white. The man smiled politely at our approach, and my father said something to him as he pulled me past the man toward other parts of the factory. We stopped several times along our way, and each time my father said something to similarly dressed men about matters that were either lost in the noise or simply beyond my comprehension. After about an hour of this incomprehensible tour, we arrived at the largest, smelliest cluster of black machines I had yet seen.

Then as now, I had no idea what the clanging machinery in this area did, but seconds later a hatless man covered in soot and grease magically appeared from the shadows between two large metallic beasts and came over to my father. He was as tall as my father, but he looked bigger, thicker, and he had a smile on his grease-covered, pock-marked face that continued for the entire time we were there. He also had deep, growing red eyes that seemed to sink in the recesses of his face. Unlike the other factory men we met, he didn't offer his hand to my father or me. My father, for some reason, pushed me in front of him and directed me to hold my hand out so that the man could shake it. I don't know what else my father said to me, but there was nothing that he could say or do to make me reach out to this strange, frightening creature, even when he slowly bent down and, smiling broadly, held out two bent fingers of his gloved appendage for me to grasp. I couldn't do it, I couldn't touch what looked like a claw reaching out for me, and I retreated with all my might behind my father and, clutching one of his strong legs, refused to come forward even to see the man. The man laughed loudly, raucously, the sound rising above the screaming shrieks of the surrounding machines, while my father groused a response that I couldn't hear. I knew that my father was displeased with me, but I would rather have faced the worst of his displeasure than to have fallen into the clutch of the towering, sneering monster with the black claw.

"Mr. R.," the man howled shortly afterwards. "You brought me another one? That makes two, if my addition's correct. But, hell, this one don't look like much." The smile didn't leave his face.

My father growled sullenly.

"I understand, Mr. R. We all get what we get. But, I have to be honest with you, you didn't get much. A gizzard first and now the liver. Where's the rest of the bird?" His laughter sounded like a peal of thunder. My father said something in return, and the man took a step back and raised his hands as if he were under arrest.

"Whoa, Mr. R., no reason to burn on this one. It's hot enough in here already. Like I always say, I'm only here to do a job. I'm here for you, if you want my help. Do you, Mr. R? Do you want my help?"

The man laughed again, and my father yanked me out from behind him and together we walked swiftly away. This didn't stop the man, however. "Mr. R.," he called out a few seconds after we left, "There's no hard feelings, is there? I'm only here to help. Are you sure you don't want my considered and considerate help?" The man continued shouting and laughing until the factory gradually absorbed both him and his words.

Shortly afterwards, we came up to another gray door, which looked exactly like the first. Instead of opening into another part of the factory, this one revealed a large room filled with desks and people pounding on keyboards in front of their computer monitors. Several of the people looked up as he dragged me silently past them toward a wall of doors with glazed windows. He opened one of these doors, yanked me inside a small room, and sat me in an oversized chair next to a desk that seemed as wide as a car. Once he was seated behind the desk, he opened a drawer and pulled out several sheets of paper along with a handful of pencils and directed me to occupy myself while he worked. He pulled out from another drawer what I now think was a green ledger-book and proceeded to fill its pages with what I can only assume were numbers. I don't remember much after that. I fell asleep at some point in time and woke up in my own bed.

A loud, insistent buzzing filled my ears, and I blindly slammed my fist on the offending object and sat up. Looking around the dimly lit room, I slowly recalled bits and pieces of the memory, or what was left of it, for certain parts of it were fading rapidly. Had it actually been a memory or merely a dream-soaked figment of my imagination? Parts of it were certainly true. Our father, for example, worked in an office connected to a factory, though I don't think I ever knew anything about what he did. Tom once said that he was the payroll manager, but at another time he stated with equal assurance that he managed payables. Most recently, he said that he wasn't sure. "He had an office," Tom noted confidently, but what he did in that office was anyone's guess. On the contrary, Tom never doubted his visit to the factory. It was an absolute fact, he insisted, and he also insisted that our father never took me there. My recollections, he asserted every time I mentioned them, derive from his experiences. "I told you all about my visit, many times, in fact," he once said to me. I don't know. But I have to say that this particular version of the event was extraordinarily vivid and dramatic. The hellish factory, and the devilish machinist wanting the rest of the bird and offering to help only if he got the request? Then again, our father's reticence makes sense, as does the difficulty I had in hearing him amid all the clatter of the towering, monstrous machines. There also wasn't anything odd or contradictory about dragging me from place to place. I was a typical six year old. I got into things, and I was shy in front of strangers, especially gigantic adults. As for sitting at our father's desk and drawing pictures, unclear. I can't recall a single time when he was working at home that he allowed me or Tom to be near him, or even within earshot. And, like any child that age, I had to have been making noise when I sat his desk in his office. So, was it a true memory or just a dream? God, I wish I knew.

17

Tara had left some time before I ventured out of the room. She generally liked to get into the office early to prep for the day's sessions, but I was almost positive that she had left early this time to avoid me. I couldn't blame her. I had said some things, she had said some things, and I had ended up sleeping in the guest room. Well, I was determined not to let this sort of thing happen again, and I promised myself that I would smooth out things with Tara this evening and explain, in a considered, rational way, my feelings about our father and share my analysis of the old man. Sure, we had talked about this before (or tried to, at any rate), but I felt more strongly than ever that if we didn't come to an understanding–and soon–then we'd end up in a downward spiral of anger, accusations, recriminations, and so forth. In other words, we'd fall into the old man's bloated, greasy hands. In the meantime, I was running late, and I rushed out of the house and drove like a madman to the highway, only to find traffic moving at a snail's pace, if that. There was an accident ahead, and as I inched past the tangled globs of metal, the shattered glass, and the flashing red lights, I did my best to avoid looking at the occupied stretcher being loaded into the back of an ambulance. I was in a somber mood when I entered the lobby of the building, rode the rickety elevator to the third floor, and walked into the firm's reception area. I'm not prescient, but I immediately had a feeling that something wasn't right.

The receptionist, an almost transparent older woman with large, sad eyes, didn't look up as she usually did when I passed her desk on the way to my office. The noise and chatter around the various other offices and open areas seemed a little louder than normal. Just before I reached my office, I ran into Jeff. He had a strange look on his unshaven face. Shrugging his shoulders as if he didn't have an answer for the question I didn't ask, he told me that I should have taken more sick leave.

"Why, what's happening?"

"Just what I told you was going to happen."

"You mean the…?"

"Yep, the acquisition. Somebody bought the firm. You haven't seen your e-mail, huh?"

"No, I'm just getting in."

"Not a lot of details, except that someone else now owns the company. The e-mail assures us that it will be business as usual, but my source tells me that there are going to be layoffs and a reorganization of our lines of business. What that tells me is that you and I and all the rest of us had better start polishing our resumes."

I opened my door and stepped in. Jeff followed.

"I can't believe it's going to be this bad. Why would anyone buy the company if they didn't want our lines of business and the employees working here?" I sat down and switched on my computer.

Jeff remained standing. "A lot of reasons, my friend. One is that the acquirer is going to shut us down to weed out the competition. Happens all the time."

"Get out of here," I replied with a smile. "I'll read the e-mail, and we can swap assumptions later."

Despite my bravado, I was deeply troubled, and I couldn't dismiss Jeff's statements as mere nonsense or unsubstantiated rumor (he had an impeccable source, after all). While I assured myself that the acquisition was benign and that it would do nothing more than bring us under the umbrella of a better funded, more competitive organization, I still couldn't get Jeff's worst-case scenario out of my mind. Such things did happen. Tom often mused about the possibility of buying this or that company and selling it for scrap (and the way he sometimes talked, I had the feeling that he had done this very thing to companies that wouldn't play ball with him). Although I had never questioned my brother's judgment in business matters, I now saw that this kind of business action was unconscionable and, for me, a terrible thing to contemplate. Companies weren't just bricks and mortar or electrons floating across the Internet. They were people, too, and I was one of those people, someone who couldn't easily jump from one position to another without losing something in the process—assuming that I could even find another job in a timely manner. Nevertheless, I'm proud to say that I didn't fall apart. I dusted off my resume, which required only a few minor modifications, and then turned my attention to a couple of projects that were on the verge of being late. I also kept my ears open for anything that might clarify the firm's position. Apart from Jeff's information, the only thing that I knew for sure, and this happened later in the morning, was that one of our corporate VPs was terminated. No one seemed to be talking about it, though Jeff insisted that it was merely the beginning of a series of terminations that the acquirer was going to make.

"Tip of the iceberg, my friend," Jeff said as he poked his head into my office shortly after lunch. "There'll be more, lots more."

I got up and stood next to him in my doorway. Looking up and down the hallway, I tried to gauge the sentiment among the workforce, but couldn't come up with anything more than what Jeff was telling me right then.

He, too, looked up and down the hallway before whispering, "I'm told there'll be more later this week and new management will be coming in shortly thereafter."

"Your source?"

"The best."

"Okay, but maybe this is a good thing. I mean, we have some managers that need to go. You said so yourself. So, maybe the new managers will be better and, while we'll have to make some adjustments, we'll at least be here to make them."

"You're dreaming, man. There's going to be more terminations, and they're not going to be confined to management. There's going to be carnage, and it's going to happen in a few days, if not sooner."

"How can you be so sure? Come on, how can your source be so sure? Tell me again who your source is."

"No can do, man. Gave my word. Besides, if it got out who the person is, that would be the end of my information."

"All right, but let me know if you hear anything else."

"You'll be the first. Hey, did you read the e-mail?"

I had forgotten. When I was back at my computer, I skimmed through my inbox but couldn't find it. Seconds later, as if it had been timed, it appeared. As Jeff said, it was a message from the president of our firm. The president stated, in a short preface, that he appreciated all the hard work that we (the employees) had done in recent months to finish our work on time and to acquire new contracts. After this, he detailed the "exciting news," the purpose of the message. Our firm had recently received funding from a major source (unnamed), and "together" (it wasn't clear if this meant our employees or our respective firms) we were going to do some exciting things in the near future. He didn't detail what these exciting things were, but he did emphasize that we shouldn't be alarmed. Our jobs were safe, he assured us, and he expected all of us to work hard and show our "new corporate officers" (whoever they were) what "we are capable of doing."

The e-mail wasn't quite as clear as Jeff suggested, though it did succinctly (I thought) suggest that organizational changes were afoot. Since I couldn't tell what these changes might be (layoffs, lines of business discontinued, etc.), I was going to shrug off the whole thing until we heard something more concrete–something that wasn't dependent on Jeff's squeeze. I went back to work and fiddled with a project that I had been putting off for quite some time and when I tired of that, I turned to a new assignment that promised to be more interesting. I didn't manage to connect with Jeff again that afternoon, but as I walked between desks and past offices on my way out for the day, I detected some anxiety about the future of the firm. Since I was in a hurry to leave, I didn't stop to ask questions or stand aside to listen to what was actually being said. As I was waiting for the elevator, I overheard two of the accounting clerks, who were standing on the other side of the elevator, whispering something about the new source of funding. They became silent when they noticed that I was looking at them. I let it go, I didn't want to worry at home about what may or may not happen in the coming days and weeks, and I promised myself to ask Jeff in the morning if he got anything additional about the funding source–in other words, the firm's new owners.

I was home before Tara. The morning wreck on the highway had been cleared, and so the traffic was flowing smoothly and quickly. I had planned to tell her about my situation at work, but when I entered the house I had second thoughts and considered the very real possibility that she might not want to speak to me about anything. Because of my potential problems at work, I had completely forgotten until this moment our quarrel and my promise to fix things or face another night in the guest room. Fortunately, Tara was ready to talk the moment she came through the door. Maybe a day of counseling others helped her understand the pointlessness of our fighting, but whatever it was that changed her mind, we quickly got over the issues of the phone, the old man, and I thought all the rest. I assured her that she could read my phone texts to her heart's content as soon as I got a new phone (and I promised not to erase any before she had a chance to look at them), and I also emphasized that I wanted to get one as soon as possible. Regarding our father, I explained that Tom and I didn't always see eye-to-eye on the subject because of our respective experiences with him. I went on to say (as I noted previously) that our young lives had been scarred because of his disappearance–our mother, of all people, couldn't handle the loss and had become a drunkard–and that without John, our mother's cousin, we might have come through the experience broken people. Tara agreed that it had been a difficult situation. She also said it was understandable that I had a lot of baggage I needed to offload before I could "objectively" accept or reject the old man as our father. I demurred, of course, and when I politely inquired about the times that she had met with him behind my back, she was forced to admit that she had met with him–several times, in

107

fact–but that this wasn't the right moment to talk about these meetings. We (she and I) still had a lot to process before moving on to other issues. All was now good, she assured me, and she added that she had felt lonely last night without me and that she didn't think another night of separation was constructive.

"It doesn't promote a healthy relationship," she said in her best professional voice.

Once I got her tentative agreement not to refer to the old man as our father in front of me, our home life again assumed a degree of normalcy.

Later that evening, Tara and I had a lovely dinner and, instead of the usual talk about her patients and my design challenges, we joked and laughed about all kinds of unrelated matters. Tara at one point mentioned a local politician who had been caught, literally, with his pants down (he had fallen out of a first floor bathroom onto a canopy covering a street-bazaar stand), and I followed that with a series of jokes and puns about the position the unfortunate politician found himself in. There were moments throughout dinner in which I had tears in my eyes from laughing so hard, and I couldn't help thinking about all the great times and all the fabulous dinners we had enjoyed when we were first married. Sure, we were younger and lacked the experiences and responsibilities that we had gained over the years, and yet it was a good feeling and I hoped, without saying as much, that we could have more of these days. Later, as we were cleaning the dishes in the kitchen, our current life came back to me and I couldn't help ruminating over what was happening at work. Was Jeff right? Were the rumors justified? What would happen to me if my fears came true and I lost my job?

"You seem troubled," Tara said as she handed me a dish to dry. "What's on your mind?"

"Nothing much," I began tentatively and then all the words leaped from my mouth, and I told her in general terms about the CEO's e-mail and what might happen to me as the result of an acquisition.

"I'm sorry," I continued, "I should have kept you informed about the rumors, and I could have called you yesterday about the CEO's e-mail. It's got me so unnerved that I wasn't thinking straight. But we're in this together, right? That worthless old..."

"Worthless?"

I was getting heated over my situation, and I knew what the old man would say if he found out that I was one of the terminated employees. "I mean, our CEO. I can't believe that he would sell everyone out like this. He'll have a golden parachute, but the rest of us...what about me?"

"I see," she replied evenly as she put the last dish in the cupboard and hung up the drying towel. Without another word, she headed for the living room.

"Despite the economy, it's still a tight market for graphic artists," I continued, following her into the other room. "It could take months, even a year or more, to find another position, and it's highly unlikely that it would be at the same much less a higher salary. If I'm lucky to land something in my field, I would still lose all the seniority I currently have, which basically means that I would be starting all over again."

Tara sat down on the couch and folded her arms. The warm, smiling expression that had graced her gentle face over dinner was gone and in its place was the cold, scientific look that she probably offered to all her patients. I started to sit down next to her, but she grunted me away and so I sat down on the carpet, practically at her feet.

"Yes," she began, lightly tapping her forearm with her red-nailed index finger, "You should have informed me much sooner. It would have given us more time to formulate a considered response, if necessary. But while the situation looks serious…"

"You're damn right it's serious, but it didn't make sense to worry you until I had more to go on."

"But now you have something substantive."

"Yes."

She stared at me for a few more seconds and then reached under the couch for her notebook and pen. After placing both on her lap, she glanced at something on the ceiling and said, "All right, tell me again exactly what you know. And this time, please don't leave out any of the details."

"You're not going to write this down, are you?"

"We'll see. I tend to think better after I have after I've put my thoughts to paper."

"Okay, then," I began and proceeded to give her all the details that I had initially left out. I told her everything that Jeff told me, I noted all the rumors that were floating around the office, and I even mentioned the unusual behavior of the receptionist. When I was done, I hesitated and then explained that everything Jeff said had come from an impeccable source, one that neither I nor anyone else had reason to doubt.

"The secretary?"

"She works directly for the C-suite, and if anyone is in the know, it's her."

"It's she."

"Yes."

"I see." She paused, opened her notebook, clicked the button at the end of her pen several times, and then began writing. I understood the business about thinking and writing, but I nevertheless felt slightly uncomfortable watching her as she wrote I don't know what about me. I could only imagine what her patients felt.

"Well, I guess there was something else," I said to break up a silence in which the only noise was the scratching sound of her pen.

She stopped writing and looked up briefly as though I had said something potentially interesting.

"I don't know if it's important, but I overheard our accounting clerks talking about the money that the buyer was dumping into the firm."

"That might be an important detail. Did they mention the name of the buyer?" Tara raised an eyebrow, and then shifted her position and crossed her legs, angling the pointed toe of her free shoe only inches from my right eye. "Tell me what you know about the buyer."

"Nothing really," I said and explained that our CEO didn't exactly say that the firm was being acquired, only that there was a big infusion of money that had come into the firm and that this would change our business. "But big money means the acquisition of stock, and this means the control of the firm, which is tantamount to an acquisition however you say it. Ask Tom. He's said something like this before."

Tara nodded noncommittally and became silent for quite some time. She started writing again and, from time to time, would glance at me before writing some more. I moved to the side to prevent an accidental movement or muscle spasm from blinding me, and waited patiently until she was finished with what was beginning to seem a novel. When she was done for the moment, she inserted her pen into the spine of her book and slipped them back under the couch. Folding her arms again, she stared at me as though she expected me to do or say something.

"Well?" I asked, tired of waiting for her to break the uncomfortable silence.

"Well?"

"Did you understand what I was saying about possibly being laid off? What do you think?"

"I'm sorry, I had something else on my mind. Okay, I don't think there's much to worry about at the present. The CEO's e-mail, the most important piece of information you have, doesn't seem to be very explicit, at least not enough to base decisions on. Jeff, as I don't need to tell you, isn't the most reliable of sources, and I wouldn't know what to do with the secretary's insights, assuming that Jeff adequately conveyed her information. As for the rest, I agree with you about the acquisition of stock, even though your firm is private, but this tells us nothing about possible changes in the firm or, if there are going to be changes, how they'll affect you and your position there. Right now, the only sensible position to take is to have positive thoughts and wait and see what, if anything, changes."

"And the accountants?"

"As you already know, accountants like to talk about money, and since you don't know exactly what they had in mind, I think you have to assume that they were merely chatting about routine business matters."

"No way it was a routine business matter. When they saw me, they immediately closed their mouths as though I had caught them discussing a special, confidential...a big thing. An important matter that they weren't supposed to discuss in front of anyone. You should have seen the way they acted."

"I wish I had. But that still doesn't give us anything upon which to base our fears, much less to act. Do you see what I'm getting at?"

"I've seen these guys before, and they weren't talking about routine things. They were concerned about something big, and they were afraid that I might have heard too much."

"I do wish accountants would keep a tighter lip on business matters no matter how routine. But it doesn't matter. Until you have something more specific, we have no actions to take in response. However, you should, as a courtesy, inform Tom..."

"Sure, but what good's that going to do? What if the worst happens, and I'm out of work for quite a while?"

"Let's not go off the deep end. Your brother might be of use..."

"I don't want to borrow money from him."

Tara looked at me as though she were reaching a limit in terms of my objections. "All right, but I'm not talking about money. I was going to say that he might of use in terms of helping you understand the situation. As it stands, I don't think there's anything we should do until we have a solid set of facts about what may or may not transpire because of the company's new funds."

"Fine, but one more thing. I don't want the old man to know about this. I'll speak to Tom about it when I have a chance, but I don't want you or anyone else to let the old man know what's happening."

"Don't you think that..."

"It's completely off the table."

"You are going to speak to your brother, or did you have another fight with him?"

"No, and whatever we spoke about had very little to do with the old man."

"Don't you think you're overreacting to a problem that hasn't yet occurred. Do you know what we call this?"

"I don't care what we call this. We're not required to tell the world about what's happening to me."

Tara placed her hands in her lap and for a moment smiled serenely. "We'll do as you say. But after everything you said, I'm not convinced that your concern is warranted. I'm confident you and your job are safe. Should the worst happen and there are layoffs, I'm also confident you won't be among them."

"How can you say that?"

"Where's your evidence to contradict this? There may be things, if there are things, going on that you're not aware of or don't yet understand. Right now, I think the smartest thing to do is to wait and see what happens. Do you think you can do that?"

I got up, stretched, and started for the kitchen. "I wish I had your confidence. I'm hungry."

"You could, if you wait for all the facts and cease giving credence to Jeff and his impeccable source."

I didn't respond. I thought that she might be right about waiting for more facts, though I couldn't help being more than a little concerned given the factual e-mail, the accountants' hushed-up chatter, and, yes, Jeff's impeccable source. For God's sake, all of this should have been more than enough for Tara to see the bind I was in–for her to see the bind that we were both in if I lost my job. 'I must not have explained things well enough,' I told myself as I poured a drink from the faucet. When I was done, I went back to the living room to clarify things with her, but she was gone. Seconds later, I heard the sound of the shower. Out of curiosity, I reached under the couch for her book. I wasn't interested in what she said about her patients. I just wanted to know if she was writing about me. But as I touched one hard corner, I pulled back. I couldn't do it. It was her private property, and I had no business snooping.

18

I let the matter drop. Work over the following two weeks went on as normal. There were still rumors concerning the acquisition, and Jeff sometimes talked as if he had information that he couldn't yet share, but there were no layoffs and management, save for the one individual, stayed intact. Perhaps because things were going well and I had fewer and fewer things to worry about, I started thinking more and more about my brother. I couldn't stand his mindlessness regarding the old man, but I still missed him and was willing to concede a little about the old man if Tom and I got together or talked like we used to. I can't emphasize this enough—Tom had always been an integral part of my life. No, ever since I was child and especially after our father vanished, he had been my hero and the rock on which I have been able to keep my own life steady. Even more than our mother's cousin John, my brother was a father-like figure for me when I no longer had a father, and he advised and guided me throughout school to college graduation. He had a knack for success, and he used his success to help me get along in my life. Did I mention that I wouldn't have married Tara had Tom not approved? Luckily, he approved immediately, told us to have a lot of kids, and the rest is, as they say, history. Well, we didn't have the kids—too many complications—but we have a happy life together, for the most part.

One afternoon, I set aside Tom's pettiness in refusing to reach out to me and called him at his office, just like I used to do before he welcomed the old man into our lives. Tara at that time had become inexplicably distant, and I yearned for the affection and companionship that only my brother could provide.

The phone rang several times before Tom picked up. When he did, I sensed that the phone had been ripped off the set. "What do you want?" Tom asked, his voice stern and uncompromising.

This wasn't the Tom that I knew and loved, and I immediately assumed that he thought I was someone else, maybe a financial consultant who had advised him incorrectly.

"It's me, Tommy. What's with the attitude?"

There was a long pause before he spoke. "There's no attitude here, James, at least not on my part."

"What's the matter, then?"

"Don't play with me," he practically spit.

"What are you talking about? What are you mad about?"

"You know."

"Know what?"

"You know what you did to our father."

"Is the old goat finally gone?"

"Shut up, James, I'm warning you."

"Tommy, please. I don't know what you're getting at. Is he gone? What's the matter?"

There was another long pause. "I knew you didn't like him, but I hoped that over time you'd come to accept him. He made mistakes, but he asked for forgiveness, and I don't mind giving it to him."

"Fine, he's not getting it from me, because I don't believe he's our father. He's a fraud…"

"No more warnings. If you come near him again…"

I waited for him to finish his sentence. When he didn't, I sought to get to the bottom of this strange statement. "Tom, I honestly don't know what you're talking about. Is it about those texts that I supposedly sent him? I didn't send anything to him, and I haven't seen or talked to him since that night at your house."

He seemed to be gathering his thoughts. "You know," he began, "I wasn't entirely convinced you were serious when you threatened Dad. I thought for a moment that we had all misunderstood your intent. This business with the texts…well, those were pretty clear."

"I told you I didn't send him any texts."

"I know, and I know how you get sometimes. I was willing to blow it off–you're a hothead, after all–but I was forced to rethink everything."

"What are you trying to say?"

"I'm not trying to say anything. I'm saying that words are one thing, and actions are another. You took it out on him the other night, didn't you?"

"What? Took it out on who? Are you crazy? I never touched him. I'll admit that I wouldn't give a crap if somebody else did, but I'm not the violent type. You know that."

"He has a witness."

"I don't care what he has. He could have a sack of shit for all I care. I didn't touch him."

"I don't know you anymore. I didn't expect you to react this way to him. Two days ago, he told me that you caught him and a friend of his downtown and slapped them around. He has bruises on his face and arms. I suspect his friend's not looking so good, either."

"He said I did what? He's a liar."

"He's an old man. You stay away from him, James. Do you understand me? If you lay one finger on him…"

"You believe him and not me?"

"You heard me."

"Wait a minute. I can prove it wasn't me. What time did he say this happened? What time?" I don't think he heard the last part. He hung up. I wanted to call him back, but I didn't think he'd pick up, not right then. Even if he did, I was too frustrated to speak clearly and coherently.

In fact, I don't think I had ever been as frustrated and furious as I was at that moment. My brother, the person who mattered more to me than anyone else in the world (including Tara), my beloved brother believed the old man's silly lies and turned against me. Once again, Tom had succumbed to the old man's con job, and this time he was apparently willing to believe without proof that I had done something that I had never done in all my life. There have been times when I have been frustrated and angry, when I have been what Tom aptly called a goofball, but never once have I committed an act of violence, not even as a child being bullied because I lacked a father. Tom knew this, he knew me inside and out, and yet he fell for a story that was so unbelievable that it was…I don't know, it was mind boggling. So what if the old man had bruises on his arms? So what if he had a witness? Let the witness come forward to identify me before betting the farm on some nonsensical tale. If it wasn't clear before, it was crystal-clear now that the old man could have sold Tom the Brooklyn bridge. Yes, I was frustrated and furious, but not simply because I was losing my brother to the old man. It was also because I understood what the old man was doing, I could see through his conniving, and I still didn't know what to do stop him and fix this broken world. Do you know why the old man was trying to make me disappear? It wasn't because I was close to my brother and therefore getting in the way of something. It was because I was the only one who knew that he was a complete fraud, and as long as I was close to Tom I was the only one who could foil his plans. It was only my complete elimination that could ensure both the success of the old man's game and his survival.

I met Tara at the front door when she came home after work. Before she had a chance to say a single word, I told her everything that Tom told me, and I emphasized my innocence. I even showed her my knuckles to support my claim. Now, I knew Tara would be a little reluctant to accept the worst about someone (her profession taught her to see something positive in everyone), even her husband of many years, but I was totally unprepared for her response. When I paused in my speaking, she looked at me silently for several moments, and then went into the kitchen and poured a glass of white wine. Having finished it, she carefully placed the empty glass on the counter next to the sink and, turning to me and looking directly into my face, she stated in her cool, professional tone that I ought to see someone about my "issues."

"What issues?" I asked. I didn't quite know what she was getting at.

"Anger, violence. What you did was unthinkable. You don't care in the least for everything your father has been trying to do for you. Well, I can't help you. We're too close. I'm going to connect you with someone who can. It won't be anyone from my office, though, because I don't want this getting out."

I was floored. She, like Tom, had fallen for the old man's story. Perhaps there was something about age and decrepitude that lent such fabrications a ring of truth. I don't know. But Tara knew me almost as well as Tom knew me, and it shook me to the core that she would think that after all the years we had been together, I would do something that... Look, I'm the kind of person who would hire a private investigator, not a professional hit man. It was also troubling that she, a psychologist, would counsel me to get professional help. She was becoming as crazy as her patients.

"You spoke to Tom, or was it to the old man? Both? And you believed them? Did they tell you when this was supposed to have happened? While we were eating dinner? Or maybe while I was in the bathroom? Did you think about the timeframe? Do you honestly believe them instead of me? After all the years we've been together, you're not even willing to give me the benefit of the doubt?"

She hesitated before speaking. "It's because of all the years we've been together that I'm trying to get you help."

"I need help, huh?" I raised my voice. "Tell me, if you believe this crap, why are you still here? Aren't you afraid I'm going to do to you what I supposedly did to the old man and his buddy?"

Tara didn't respond. Her beautiful eyes were glistening and her delicate face was practically drooping as she silently gazed at me. For a moment, I felt as though I were the family pet that was waiting to be put down. It was when a tear from her left eye rolled down her soft cheek that I had my answer.

"God, of all the people not to believe me. I thought, when we got married...well, if you love that goddamn old man so much, you should marry him."

I didn't let her respond. She didn't look like she was wanted to say something. I again stormed into the bedroom and slammed the door behind me, several times, in fact. I didn't speak to Tara again that evening.

The following day, I didn't go to work. I couldn't bear to listen to their petty concerns with layoffs and whatever when my life was falling apart. I needed to be alone for a while. I needed time to come to some conclusions about what had happened the night before. I was also exhausted. I hadn't been able to sleep during night, and I didn't think I had the stamina to do a decent day's work. Tara went to work, though. She didn't let anything come between her and her goddamn patients.

Around lunchtime, I ventured out of the room to get some fresh air and scrounge about for something to eat. From the time I entered the bedroom until the time I exited, I was being eaten from within by all the insanity swirling around me–the stupidity, the lies, and, of course, the old man–and I could feel my ability to remain in control of my life quickly slipping away from me. I needed help–there was no question about that–but not the kind of help that a psychologist or social worker provided. I needed real help. I needed someone to come in and take charge and, after setting everything straight, help me get back on my feet so that I could resume living like I did before the old man appeared. I needed John to come back and reset everything to the time before our father disappeared. But John died twenty years ago, and I was forced to accept the ugly truth that I had no one to depend on except myself.

I staggered into the kitchen. I felt as if I were starving, and, as I pulled out something indistinct from the refrigerator, the cool air that washed over my hands and the smells that accompanied the food filled my senses and loosened the lugubrious straps that had entangled me since our argument and enabled me to think clearly and rationally in a way that I hadn't been able to think for quite some time. I was beginning to see that Tara wasn't actually siding with the old man against me. She was a psychologist, a scientist, and she was compelled to go wherever her scientific rationale took her. I must have said something or behaved in a way that ran counter to my normal way of behaving, and she reluctantly latched onto that as proof that I needed help before I broke down completely. Or maybe she had actually seen through the old man's vaudeville and was using a form of therapy on me as a way to prevent me from ending up like him, a pathetic old goat whose criminal tendencies were threatening everyone's lives. I don't know exactly what she thought, but it was clear from her tears that she still loved me and didn't want me to end up like her demented patients. After I had eaten the unappetizing slop, I went into the living room and sat down on the couch. I didn't know what to do at that moment other than puzzle over how the old man had been able to bamboozle so many people so easily.

The house's foundation groaned as it briefly settled, and I leaned forward and reached under the couch for Tara's book. I really wasn't interested in her book. I was never interested in the damned thing. I just wanted to find out if she had written anything about the old man and, in particular, her clandestine meetings with him. If there were other insights about the old man and his criminal behavior, I might have been interested in those as well. But after blindly fishing with both hands under the couch, I came up empty. I refused to give up, however. I cursed several times, got down on my hands and knees, and, after fruitlessly peering into the nearly impenetrable darkness underneath, I inserted both arms into the darkness and swept them back and forth across the carpet to find something other than dirt. When, as before, I came up emptyhanded, I grabbed a corner of the couch and pulled it halfway across the room to expose a darkened, reticular patch of carpet. Nothing was there except an amazing variety of dust balls, a scattering of tiny flakes of black dirt, and the top of one of Tara's pens.

Cursing again and more determined than ever to find out what she was hiding from me, I charged into one of the two spare bedrooms, the one that served as her home office, and checked the drawers of her desk and then rifled through the folders in the large file cabinet on the far wall. Luckily, it was unlocked, and unfortunately it didn't have what I wanted or even the other books that she had been filling for years. I made a quick check through the files to see if there was something on me or Tom or the old man, and I drew a blank here as well. There was nothing except a bewildering array of what appeared to be statements of some kind. I didn't look carefully at them, I assumed that they were related to her clients, and instead I ran into our bedroom and searched through her dresser drawers, under her dresser, and her side of the closet. After that, I rummaged through all the closets in the house as well as through the cupboards in the kitchen. Nothing. She had taken it with her. It was evidently too sensitive to leave at home with me in the house. Nervously rubbing my hands together, I went outside and walked a couple of blocks to the neighborhood park to cool down.

It was the perfect time to be there, almost. The air was still, and though the gray sky was covered with wisps and masses of pale clouds, the wisps and masses blocked the sun's harshest light, making it comfortable to be outside without either a coat or a hat. Tara and I had been to the park many times. We enjoyed strolling through the grass and watching other couples, often with children, relaxing on multi-colored blankets and sharing sandwiches and soft drinks from a picnic basket. But even though the park had always seemed a magical place to us, it seemed even more so at that moment than I could recall. The green, sparkling lawn that all but blanketed the park from end to end seemed to be reaching out of the ground and tugging me downward to sit down on its moist blades and roll around like I used to do as a young child. Near the center of the park, the only place not covered with grass, was a large, sand-covered playground, replete with swings, slides, monkey bars, climbing walls, and virtually everything else that a young child would want to play on or crawl over. It was a wonderful complement to the park, because it symbolized the love of the neighborhood for its children and also the carefree days of childhood, where a six-year-old could while away a summer afternoon playing on the equipment or lounging at the bottom of a slide and staring at the indeterminate sky and following the progression of a few fluffy, white clouds as they floated from one end to the other, or faded away before they were even halfway across. But instead of yielding, I turned my attention to a momentary sliver of pain that knifed through my shoulders as I noticed that there were no picnic baskets in the park and not a single child was frolicking in the playground. Saddened, I sat in one of the swings and slowly rocked myself back and forth, attempting to recall the joys of the children that I had once seen here as well as my own happiness in the days before our father disappeared–the days before the neighborhood kids started taunting me for being a fatherless child and abandoning me for others whose households were more or less normal and intact–in the days when life seemed joyful and worth living. I couldn't. No matter how hard I tried, no matter how many ways I sought to divert my thoughts to pleasanter things, I couldn't forget those days or the pain I endured because I was certain that I had chased our father away. At the same time, I couldn't stop ruminating on the loss of my brother and wife to a man who was even more of a fraud than our temporary father. An hour later, I walked home with a new resolve.

19

I was going to identify the old man and throw his identity into everyone's faces. I was going to teach my brother a lesson about gullibility, I was going to teach my wife a lesson about trust, and I was going get the old man out of our lives once and for all. But as I approached my house, I realized that this wasn't going to be an easy task. I didn't have the old man's real name, and I didn't know how to go about getting it–and without his name, it would be practically impossible to find out anything about him. I could search the Internet (everything is on the Internet, isn't it?), but it didn't seem likely that searching "old man" would come up with anything particularly useful. But, as I considered the matter more, I thought that I could give the police a picture of him to run through their database of criminals and degenerates. It was a great idea (I was positive that he was on file somewhere) and perhaps the simplest solution. The catch, as I realized seconds later, was that I didn't have a picture of him, and the odds of getting one, now that I was practically persona non grata with everyone, was slim to none. The house was empty when I came back inside, and in frustration I began considering Plan B. I was still trying to figure out what Plan B was when it occurred to me that I didn't need to know the old man's identity to teach my lessons and to get him out of our lives. I only needed to prove that he wasn't our father. Perhaps that was Plan B.

Excellent, Plan B. My work seemed practically done. And yet, as I thought more about my plan, I couldn't figure out how I would go about proving anything, much less that the old man wasn't our father. I walked around the living room for several minutes wondering how I could get Plan B off the ground, but nothing came to me–nothing, that is, until I remembered the private investigator that I had threatened to hire. This time, however, I wasn't afraid of what Tara would think. I didn't have to hide anything from her, either, not after her threat to have me examined. But who? Which private investigator? I hadn't done any research. I ran to the kitchen and pulled a large, floppy phone book from a shelf in the pantry and flipped through the yellow pages until I came to a surprisingly large section on private detectives. Since I couldn't tell one from the other from their splashy ads, I picked out a name (the ad guaranteed results) and asked the detective if he could help me. The man had a raspy voice (I felt certain that he had been a chain smoker for decades) and, after a short discussion, informed me between coughs that I would have to come to his office and pay a fee before he could assess the feasibility of taking on my case. I hung up and called another. A woman answered. She sounded young and charming, and she was definitely more helpful than the man, but she insisted that I would have to provide several items of identification on either the old man or our father (preferably both) before any reasonable investigation could be undertaken. Unfortunately, I didn't have anything that would constitute an identification for either the old man or our father (all the artifacts defining our father had disappeared or had been trashed years ago), and so the only thing I could offer was my statement. It was the same thing with all the others I called and, after three hours of fruitlessly pleading my case to strangers, I gave up. Plan B was over. There was no way that I was going to find anything to prove either my innocence or my contentions.

I went back to the living room, put the couch back where it had been resting, and plopped onto it. After a quick, reflexive reach under it, I remained there in a state of mindlessness for quite some time before I again started considering the possible means to getting the information I needed. To say that I was considering the means is perhaps an overstatement. I couldn't come up with anything. My mind was practically blank on the issue. It was beginning to seem as if there was nothing that I could do. Slapping the seat cushion in frustration, I jumped up and went into the other spare room to check my work e-mail and do a little work on another project that might have been overdue. As I sat in front of the faceless screen waiting for it to come to life, another idea came to mind, a splendid idea, one that would help me achieve everything I wanted to achieve and would do so at little or no cost. It was Plan C. Instead of logging into my work account, I pulled up a browser and began to search. It goes without saying that it was pointless to search for the old man, but not so for our father. I knew his name, and, if what everyone said about the Internet was even half true, then there was bound to be information on him, especially if he was still alive.

Was our father still alive? I entered his name and then waited before hitting the search icon. It seemed odd that not once in over three decades had I entertained the idea that he might still be living. Early on, for a few years after he disappeared, I often wondered where he was and if he was thinking about me. Did he ever think about me? Did he ever wonder what his absence was doing to me? As the years went by and there was no word from him or about him, I gradually stopped wondering if he thought about me and started to suspect that he was dead. I hoped he was dead, because for him to be alive and perpetuating his initial crime was too vile a thing to accept. Long after this, I wanted him dead for what he had done to me and to Tom and to our mother.

She was a wreck and couldn't get beyond the loss of her husband. After our father left us, our mother left us in another way. She fell apart and couldn't "handle" life without him and so spent the greater part of her time each day in her room drinking. During those rare times when she actually did step out of the bedroom, she was either crying or on the verge of crying, and it didn't stop until ten years later when she passed away. Our father was responsible for all that, and I wasn't ready to forgive him if, by some aberration of nature, he was still alive.

I tapped the icon. I wasn't entirely surprised that it returned a lot of results. I half-expected it, since I knew that William Reid was a fairly common name. But what I didn't expect was that nearly one quarter of the known universe was populated with people with the same name as our father. How was I going to page through all these results and glean something relevant to my search? Compounding the problem, I couldn't remember what our father looked like. There were lots of images of individuals named William Reid, but I had no way of determining if any of these were of our father, either young or old. I tried narrowing the search by adding Bill and some of the particulars of our early life (town, street, etc.), but these didn't seem to help all that much. There was still too much stuff to search through in this lifetime (especially with all the irrelevant garbage that came up—hair salons, sex ads and services, and a wide range of other unrelated nonsense, some of which was…unbelievable). I undertook various other searches, including some with the names of various members of our family, but nothing came up about anyone who might possibly be our father. What was troubling was that if such information arose from the flotsam of irrelevant details, I'm not sure I'd recognize it. I gave up. I was going nowhere, and I didn't feel like wasting my time on it anymore. Fearing that there would be no way of finding what I needed, I left the house again to clear my head and get back to my life such as it was.

This time, I drove out to a local café for dinner. I didn't know when Tara would return, and, frankly, I didn't care, not right then. I didn't have the stomach to sit down to dinner with her and pretend that everything would be fine and dandy as long as I met with some fool and told him exactly what he wanted to hear. As I sat over a plate of fried eggs and hash browns, I tried to forget all the unpleasant things that were tearing my life apart and concentrate only on stuff that made sense and that, to an extent, I could control. Toward the end of my meal, I had been halfheartedly inscribing the faces of my fellow diners in the remnants of my eggs and potatoes when a brilliant idea came to me, and I asked the waitress for extra napkins and a pen. The faces that I had been drawing suggested a new direction for an advertising campaign that I was supposed to create for a minor client, a manufacturer of specialized bathroom fixtures. Now, it can be challenging to sex up something as banal as a towel bar or a toilet paper holder, but as an artist I've always loved a challenge, and the more difficult the challenge (from an artistic point of view), the better. I should note that in my work, I've always strived to force my clients and their customers out of their comfort zones in order to help them see and appreciate things as pedestrian as a drainplug in a radically new and different ways. For example, by placing a lowly drainplug in an unexpected context–say, in the middle of a busy intersection–I can get people to savor an object that under normal circumstances they wouldn't have given a second thought to. The drainplug, in this case, can be viewed not simply as a tool to stop up sinks and bathtubs but as an essential part of life in the same way that the family car is and, if I've been especially effective, as desirable as a high-end sports car can be. Either way, the result is a profound revelation to the buyer and a powerful sales gimmick for the seller. Regardless, I had been working out a wide range of creative possibilities, covering napkin after napkin with people balancing toilet-roll holders on their head and towel bars on their upper lips, before it occurred to me that I might be headed down a dead end from an artistic perspective. This happens sometimes, especially when the subject of the exercise is as obdurate to perfection as these products are, and so while the effort was useful and helped me work out some good ideas, I was coming to the realization that it might be easier to sell the fixtures if I focused more on the customer of the products than on the fixtures themselves. The customers, in this case, were the elderly and the infirm, and, after a fresh infusion of napkins, I drew them in every shape and size to see if there was any particular type of individual or infirmity that would make the fixtures appealing enough to increase sales. I had been working for several minutes on one particular drawing of an elderly woman when something about the image–the sag of the face, perhaps, or the hump at the back of the neck, or even the heavily painted eyebrows–looked familiar, looked as though I had seen this person in real life. Instead of developing the image for the assignment, I began working on it for its own sake, sharpening the bridge of the nose, engorging the flesh beneath the tiny chin, and darkening the troughs beneath the eyes, until the subject flowered into a recognizable image of who might be able to solve a problem that had nothing to do with this boring advertising campaign. By a quirk of fate or luck, the person that I had been drawing turned out to be Aunt Betty.

Aunt Betty was an elderly aunt of ours on our mother's side. She knew our father very well, and she was the only one of our extended family (apart from John) who had kept in touch with us after our father ran away. If anyone had information that I could use to locate our father and discredit the old man, it was she. I thanked my lucky stars that I had kept in touch with her over the years, mainly through greeting cards, and I thanked them again, because she lived in a retirement community not more that forty-five minutes from the café. 'Dear Aunt Betty,' I said to myself as I pocketed the napkin, gently patted my pocket twice, and called for the check.

Sensing that I had little time to lose (the sun was going down, and I didn't think that she would be awake late at night) and knowing that I had to speak to her in person rather than hazard a phone call, I paid the check and rushed out of the café. One hour later, I pulled into the Sunnydale Retirement Community parking lot, went through the main doors, and asked the concierge if I could speak to my beloved Aunt Betty Armitage. The concierge, a charming young woman dressed in jeans with a gold ring in her left nostril and a black, knitted cap on the back of her head, dutifully dialed my aunt and, after a short conversation between the three of us about what I wanted at that time of night, nodded her approval (my aunt would see me) and led me upstairs to her apartment. After a wait of fifteen minutes while she made herself "presentable," my aunt timidly opened her door and, when she saw the concierge through the crack, allowed me in and slowly led me to her small living room.

The place looked like a tiny museum with all the old furniture and the framed, black-and-white photographs on the walls. And my aunt looked as if she were one of the exhibits. Her silver hair was neatly and elegantly done up in tall bun, and she wore a floor-length, shimmering gray bathrobe that reminded me of the splendid gowns worn in the old, black-and-white movies. She looked like someone from an old, black-and-white movie. Aunt Betty graciously offered me her wrinkled cheek and then sat down in a large Queen Anne chair and waved me to a less imperial throne directly opposite. She was visibly pleased to have a visitor from outside the retirement community even at this time of night.

I hadn't actually seen Aunt Betty in years, and I couldn't remember much about her apart from the cards she sent. I didn't know, for example, if she had even been married and, if so, what happened to her husband (if she had been, the man probably wasn't alive, since she was living alone at the community). But I still retained vivid memories of the of the visits she made to our house. Though these visits were infrequent and always of short duration, I will always recall playing in the backyard sandbox with her and watching her toss a baseball back and forth with Tom. I don't recall anyone accompanying her on these visits, and so I suspect that most of her traveling was done solo. Years later, long after our father disappeared and she had settled down in this community, I came to have a more faceted image of her. In addition to her playfulness, she displayed the kind of thoughtful elegance that comes from education and cultural sensitivity. (At least, that's how she came across in her cards, especially the ones featuring great works of art or ancient cathedrals.) But even if I didn't immediately recognize her worn, sagging face and tiny, frail body, I could still sense the charm and the zest for life that radiated from her whole person and that encouraged me, when younger, to live joyously and savor life to its fullest. When we were finally comfortable, I looked across to my aunt and I was a little amazed that she seemed so small, smaller than I had expected when I met her at the door. Her words made up for any deficits in her physical stature.

"Darling," she began, as I readjusted myself in her unyielding chair. "I'm so glad you were able to take time away from your busy schedule to visit me. It's been quite a while, I must say." She smiled coquettishly, and it appeared as though the upper and lower halves of her head were fighting each other for control of a line across the center of her face.

"I'm glad to see you, too, Aunt Betty, and I'm really sorry that I haven't visited in some time. It's very easy to get caught up in the daily grind of work and living."

"Sweetheart, I know exactly what you're talking about. It's the same with me, although when I'm here, I have to deal with so many difficult personalities. It occupies one's time terribly. But, then, I guess you know what I mean. Tell me, you are doing well, am I right? I always expected great things from you."

"I'm doing fine, Aunt Betty. Thanks for ask…"

"And that lovely wife of yours? She's still living, I presume?"

"Yes, and she's doing great, too, and as healthy as ever."

"And your brother? He's not in jail, is he? He was always such a scamp, you know. God knows, I tried to love him like I loved all my relations."

"He's good. He's doing quite well for himself."

"I'm happy for him. He doesn't visit. But you, you were always the apple of my eye. I think you always knew it."

I remember thinking that if I came away from my visit with only this, it would have been well worth the time. I also wondered what she would say to Tom, if he ever visited her.

"Now, my love, it's getting late, and I don't have the strength I used to have. You didn't come to speak about good times. What can I do for you? You want to discuss an important matter with me?"

I leaned forward. "I'm sorry for visiting so late, Aunt Betty, and I won't stay very long."

"Suit yourself, my dear."

I cleared my throat. "Well, the thing is…I mean, what I want to speak to you about is a little complicated, Aunt Betty. I want to know something about my father. It's been a long time since he disappeared, and I don't remember much about him. I'm looking for something concrete about him–his hobbies, his friends, the name of his workplace, his relationship with my mother, anything. You see, there's an old man claiming to be…"

"Ah, my true love, I understand. I understand completely." She sighed histrionically and settled deeper into the chair. For a second, I thought she might disappear. "He was a wonderful man. Big, tall, and brave, and he had a way of holding me in his muscular arms…but a child like you doesn't need to know this."

I was a little perplexed by what she said. "I suppose not. What I'm really looking for is information that I can use to find him. Let me backtrack. I'm not really trying to find him, though I suppose that would be useful, too. I'm looking for information that will help me find out what happened to him. Like I said, it's a little complicated. There's an old man…"

"Darling, I know exactly what you're saying. I used to think it was only the young men, but over the years I've come to see that the old men are the same way."

"Sure, but what I need…"

"I know exactly what you need. Now, where do I start?" She lowered her head slightly and appeared to be thinking about something. A few moments later, I thought that she had fallen asleep, but she lifted her head and stared at me with a questioning look on her wrinkled face. "Were you going to tell me something, my dear?"

"I'm sorry. I was hoping you could tell me what you knew about our father? I'm looking for the kinds of things that…"

"Yes, yes, of course. I know what you're asking. I knew him almost as well as I knew myself. Oh, but he was a large man, and he loved deeply, intensely, as if there was no tomorrow. I could tell you things that would shock someone as young as you."

"Are we talking about my father, the man who deserted his wife and two children?"

She sat up as if I had said something offensive. "What are you saying? I cannot allow you to…to…" She lapsed back into deep thought.

"Aunt Betty, I think you have things confused here. I'm not asking about your…"

Once again, she sat upright. "I'm not the one who's confused." Gripping the arms of the chair with her cadaverous hands, she painfully struggled up onto her feet. For a second, I couldn't tell if she was sitting erect or standing. "I must ask you to leave now. I am very tired, and I don't want to hear any more of your jealous nonsense."

"I'm sorry, Aunt Betty. I didn't mean to…I wasn't trying to…I, I just want information about my father, not your…"

She closed her eyes and took a deep breath. I thought that she might be having a problem, but before I could step over and help her, she sat back down and closed her eyes. Opening her eyes and expressing surprise that anyone was in her apartment, she again asked me to leave. I made another attempt to apologize, but she wouldn't hear of it.

"Tim, I will pretend this day never happened. Now, if you please," she said with a surprising firmness and waved me off with an elegant backhanded movement of her left hand. She didn't offer her cheek this time.

It was a major blow. Everything hinged on what I was beginning to call her testimony (and why not call it testimony? The old man was a criminal, after all.), and in one fell swoop it all fell apart. It was as if I were a prosecuting attorney watching my case crumble in front of the jury. Regardless, it was late at night when I arrived at home. Tara was already asleep and, since I didn't want to wake her, I went back to the spare room for the night.

20

I have to say that I couldn't fathom why Tara thought I was a dangerous man. Never once had she seen me commit what could even remotely be considered a violent act. Equally troubling was the fact that she was led to this nonsensical and unwarranted assumption by her indiscriminate acceptance of every lie and obfuscation the old man peddled—and she believed the old man in spite of my personal, firsthand experience of our father. Tom could contradict me until the cows came home, but I knew our father, too, and I knew that my experiences with him were every bit as valid as my brother's. You would think that a psychologist like Tara would have had the sense to know that even if Tom and I differed about our early years, we could both be right and our personal experiences equally valid. It's clear that I was wrong about her. Have I said all this before? Am I repeating myself? You know, what truly mattered wasn't simply her stubbornness in refusing to believe me. That was unconscionable, certainly, but what was even worse was that she was allowing the old man to come between us. Our marriage was crumbling because of what she and the old man were doing to me. Well, the following morning as I exited the highway and made my way toward the firm, I told myself that I was going to reconsider things and consider whatever steps I needed to take in order to keep my life and my marriage from falling apart. I also toyed with the idea of running things by a neutral third-party, Jeff, who I knew would be happy to give me his two cents on the matter. As I was thinking about Jeff, I pulled into parking lot and noticed, even before I headed toward my usual space, that the lot seemed practically empty. Over half the spaces were open. It didn't make sense. Had I missed something? Was it a holiday?

Inside, the atmosphere didn't feel particularly festive. The receptionist glanced up at me from her desk and, with a scowl on her normally smiling face, turned away and pretended to be preoccupied with something important. I shrugged it off and was going to continue to my office, but I decided to stop and ask her about the parking lot. Surely, she would know what was going on or at least have a sense that things weren't entirely normal. Before I could speak to her, though, two men in suits came through the outside door and instructed her to inform our president that they had arrived. They gave their names, which meant nothing to me. I decided not to wait and continued down the hallway. Halfway to my office, I saw several people heading toward the front door carrying cardboard boxes containing what appeared to be their personal effects.

I didn't know what to think about their situations until a young man in jeans and a pony tail carrying a similar box appeared. He was one of the IT people and, as he approached me, he stopped and blocked my way. He glowered at me and said, "Thanks, bro."

I smiled stupidly. "Sure. For what?"

"For this." He pushed his box against my chest and forced me to take a step backwards. "If you ever see me on the street, you better keep clear." He pushed me against the wall with his box to get past and then left through the front door like the others.

I wanted to follow him and find out what he meant, but I didn't. I didn't have time. When I got to my office, I noticed the word 'pig' penciled across the face of the door. Was it a joke? I went inside and sat down.

'What the hell is going on?' I asked myself. 'Why are all these people leaving?'

It was obvious that they were being terminated. But why were they being let go, and why now of all times? It occurred to me that Jeff might be right and that these people were the first in a series of layoffs that might eventually include me. The takeover would also explain why the two men wanted to speak to the president. They were probably representatives of the acquiring firm, whatever that was, and either wanted to finalize some details or ask him to vacate his office. However, none of this explained why the IT guy was angry with me or why someone had scrawled "pig" on the outside of my door. A few minutes later, I got a call from someone inside the firm who, when I picked up, began ranting about something and telling me that he held me responsible for something else. It didn't make sense, a lot of what he said was incoherent, and, when I demanded the caller's name, he hung up. Determined to find out what was going on, I called the corporate secretary, Jeff's secret source, but she didn't pick up. Neither did the two other people I called. I was dialing Jeff's number, when he magically appeared in my doorway, sullenly glowering at me.

"Thank God, you're here," I said and asked him to sit down. He didn't budge. "What the hell's going on? The parking lot is empty, people are apparently being terminated, and for some reason a lot of people seem mad at me."

Jeff sighed and shook his head. "You're amazing, man," he said. He sounded tired. He sounded as if he had been up all night.

"I called the secretary to find out what was happening, and she didn't pick up. Maybe she knew it was me on the line."

"She's gone."

"Gone? What do you mean? Where did she go?"

"Gone."

"Terminated? God, are you serious? Canned? What did she do?"

"Not a goddamned thing."

"I don't understand."

"Oh, I'm sure you do. Got to tell you, man, I used to think you were one of the good guys. That's why I talked to you and let you in on my sources. And now you pull this. I can't believe you. I can't believe I fell for it."

He was about to leave my office when I jumped up and grabbed his sleeve to stop him. Pivoting to face me, Jeff warned me not to touch him again.

"Jeff, what's the matter with you? Why are you acting this way? What have I done to you?"

I could see the muscles tightening in his jaws as he gritted his teeth. "Do you think I'm an idiot? Who knows? Maybe I am one for coming here."

"Honestly, Jeff, I don't know what you're talking about. I just got in. I was out yesterday. Please, don't go away. Tell me what's going on."

He stood there as if he was churning something around in his mind. Should he tell me or should he just keep his mouth closed? "Okay, buddy, old pal, your father is letting everyone go. To be more precise, he's firing everyone that, according to you, doesn't work hard enough and is a drag on the proverbial bottom line."

I was momentarily speechless. It was like a bad dream in which our father reached out of the mist of the past and does something to change my world for the worse. "What? I didn't have anything to do with this. What's this about my father? I haven't seen him since I was eight. He's dead for all I know. Is this a joke?"

"Not from where I sit. I have a meeting with management later today to discuss my tenure with the firm. I was told that your father called for the meeting."

"My father, my father, why do you keep saying my father? My father isn't doing this. I don't even have a father. You have the names mixed up. Who the hell is this father person?"

"This father person is the new owner of the company. I didn't know his name until yesterday. Is it getting a little clearer now?"

I demanded the name and description of the person calling himself my father. It was the old man. There was no doubt about it. I started to feel sick, and my knees buckled slightly. Steadying myself against my desk, I wondered how the old man could have come up with so much money. The firm wasn't large, but it was successful and should have commanded more than the old man could have raised in a thousand lifetimes. An instant later, I knew the answer. Tom had given him the money. Tom could afford to buy the company, and I could only assume that his desire to turn the old man into our father was so compelling that he was willing to sacrifice anything, including me, to make it happen. The firm, I suppose, was a place where the old man could have father-like authority and stature.

"A meeting yesterday?" I asked in a voice that was little more than a whimper.

"Don't mess with me, man. The staff meeting, the big meeting, the one held every week in the large conference room. Your father…"

"Please stop calling him my father. I don't have a father, and I had nothing to do with this."

"Okay, so this guy with your last name stood next to our president and, in front of everyone, announced that he had acquired our firm. He said that the firm still had life in it, but to keep that life some major changes would have to be made. He was going to install a new management team, and there was going to be some belt tightening. In other words, there were going to be layoffs and other personnel actions, in addition to benefit changes. We apparently have too many employees who aren't working hard enough. They're holding the firm back. He said–and you'll appreciate this–he said that in consultation with you, man, the deadwood have been identified, and they will be getting their notices throughout the week. Now do you understand why everyone's pissed off at you?"

Jeff again started to leave, and I stepped over to him. "Please, you have to believe me."

"You knew what was going on all the time I was talking to you about the acquisition. You knew about it even before. I feel like an idiot. I'm probably going to lose my job, because I was talking to you instead of working hard at my desk."

"No, no, listen. I'm not involved in any of this. The old man isn't my father. He's an imposter. I didn't talk to him about anything. I didn't know he or anyone else was buying the firm. I got that from you. As far as the money is concerned, I don't know where he got it unless it was from my brother."

"So you do know him."

"No, yes, no. Look, he's just an old bum that appeared in our lives a few months ago. I can't stand him, and he can't stand me. In fact, he threatened me if I ever came between him and Tom, my brother. I don't know what's wrong with Tom, but for some reason he thinks this old guy is our long, lost father and…and he's willing to do anything to help him out. Giving him money to buy the firm, for example. I don't care what the old man calls himself or what he says about me, but he's not my father. He's a fraud and I'm going to prove it to everybody and have him locked up."

Jeff sniffed and jerked his head. "Hard to believe, man. Hard to believe someone could do all this in your name, and you don't know a thing it."

"I swear to God I didn't know anything about this. He's doing this to ruin me and keep me from Tom. I know it's difficult to understand, but it's the honest-to-God truth. Jeff, you're one of the few people here I trust. Don't turn away from me. Help me expose this fraud and then maybe we'll all get our jobs back."

"I'll think about it. But, right now, it looks like you're the only one who doesn't have to worry about his job."

Jeff left my office, and I ran over to the management offices. I wanted to find the old man and drag him off the premises. Since the secretary was gone, I went directly to the president's office and pounded on his door. He didn't answer, nor did any of the other executives when I pounded on their doors. Frustrated, I shouted the old man's first name (the name he was using, and not the last name, not my name), but there was no response. A few seconds later, a young woman came up to me holding a box in her hands. I didn't know her (she was probably in sales), but she was kind enough to tell me that most of them (the C-suite) were in an offsite meeting and wouldn't be available for the rest of the day. I asked her about the old man, and she told me that he wasn't expected back until next week. I thanked her and let her know that I didn't have anything to do with this. She had a curious look on her adolescent features when she glanced back at me as she presumably headed for the exit.

21

Tara wasn't home when I returned. I was overwrought and needed something to sooth my nerves, and so I had a couple of beers, maybe three. Mind you, I didn't get drunk, but I did feel more relaxed and ready to explain cogently what was going on at the firm. Bottle in hand, I sat down on the couch and waited, like a dog expecting its master, for Tara to come through the front door. I was confident that once I explained what was happening at my office, Tara would be forced to accept the fact that I had been right all along and that the old man wasn't our father, not by a longshot. It was a long wait, and I might have dozed off at some point, for the next thing I knew was Tara standing at the foot of the couch staring at me, her lips firm and compressed.

"You're home," I said as I sat up and smiled.

Tara silently narrowed her eyes at me.

Without rising, I asked her to sit down next to me, patting the place where I wanted her to sit. I told her that I had some very important news to tell her, something that would end our ongoing disagreement over the old man. I couldn't tell what was on her mind, but she refused to sit where I indicated and took the chair opposite me, positioning herself rigidly upright with her arms and legs crossed.

"I know you don't want to believe me," I began, pretending to be as cool and rational as she often pretended to be, "but the old man isn't who you think he is. He isn't who Tom thinks he is, either. Please don't leave. Listen to me. Did you know that he's been interacting with people at my office? No answer? Well, he has, and do you know why? Still silent? Okay, sit still for this–he bought the firm. Yes, he acquired the firm that I work for. I can't fathom how he came up with the money unless Tom gave it to him. He probably robbed a convenience store. But the point is…"

She arched her left, perfect eyebrow. "He didn't rob a convenience store, and I know all about it."

For a few seconds, I didn't know what to say. "You know all about what?"

"I know he's been working with people at your firm. I also know Tom loaned him some money so that he could acquire the firm."

I could feel my rational equanimity ebbing away. "You knew this? Since when? Why didn't you tell me? I suppose you also know what's going on at my office."

"One question at a time." Tara was once again the calm one, and she slipped off her shoes without touching them with her hands. "Your father–and I'm going to call him that whether you like it or not–your father was looking for something he could do that would be useful and help the family. He's been in business most of his life, and he thought that it might be worthwhile to invest in a business of some kind. Your brother, as you well know, has also been investing in companies for quite some time, and he encouraged your father to go ahead with his idea. I'm not sure how far Tom thought he would run with it, but a week later your father came back with a fully fleshed-out plan to buy a small firm in the advertising business and grow it. Tom was impressed, and he invested in the plan like he often invests in other promising plans."

"He's been in business all his life and he didn't have the money…wait a minute, how much are we talking about?" She stated a figure that she said was a ballpark number. I practically jumped up. "Is he insane? My God, Tom's giving this fool the keys to the kingdom."

"Your brother's not insane. Your father has a solid plan–Tom told me all about it–and he has the right skills and background to execute on it."

"Background? Tom did a background check on the old man?"

"You'll have to ask him. Your brother's confident your father can do the job, and so am I."

"What do you have to do with it? Are you some kind of business expert?"

"I didn't have anything to do with it. Tom laid it all out for me and asked me for my advice. I have to say that your father's plan is well thought-out. The budget is reasonable, particularly with respect to the long-term earned value, and he thoroughly understands the risks."

I grabbed my head in desperation. "Since when are you a business expert?"

"Please sit back. You're starting to lose control over yourself."

I leaned back as if I were one of her patients, and did my best to appear relaxed and in command of myself.

"Let me explain something to you. Over the years, Tom has often solicited my advice on any number of issues. This time wasn't any different. Besides the business fundamentals, I thought this venture was an extraordinarily generous thing to do–on both their parts–given everything else that's happened recently."

"What are you talking about?"

"What am I talking about? I can't believe you're asking me such a question. You threatened him multiple times…"

"I didn't threaten anyone. The old man was making up stories. He was telling lies to make me look bad."

There was an expression of impatience of her otherwise gentle facial features. She reminded me of my mother, in her better days, when she was unhappy with me for something. "You seem to forget that I've seen the ten or fifteen texts you sent him. They're horrible…"

"I'm sure they are horrible, but I didn't send them. I told you that before. I didn't know his number. Wait a minute. Ten or fifteen? What are you talking about. There were only two…"

"How do you know the number if you didn't send them?"

Tara had me cornered. I didn't know how many texts that the old man claimed to have received from me, but I only sent two, both of them from the bathroom of our hotel room at the beach. I wasn't lying earlier when I claimed that I had gone back to the room to retrieve a shirt, I wasn't lying when I said that I had forgotten that my phone was in my pocket, and I wasn't lying when I said that I had been delayed because I had to use the toilet. The fact is that I had first noticed I had my phone with me when I was in the bathroom pulling my shirt from the towel bar (it was a small, light phone that anyone in my circumstances could have missed). But once I noticed it and pulled it from my pocket, something happened inside me and, despite my determination to let Tom deal with the old man, I couldn't resist playing his own game with him, showing him that he wasn't going to get away with his subterfuge. I had his number (I think I overheard Tom mentioning it to Belinda soon after it was set up), and so I told him in two, brief texts that if he didn't leave, I was going to make him leave. I was surprised that he shared them with Tara. Look, it was a moment of irrationality that I deeply regret, but I would never have followed through with my threats (and I didn't touch him or his buddy. They did that to themselves.). Sure, I lied to Tara about the texts. Had I told her the truth, she would have abandoned her psychological training and used my statements to support all the other crap that the old man had been feeding her. Now, with my back against the wall, my anger started getting the best of me, and I again lied about the texts.

"You told me the number, and I'm beginning to think that there's something else that the old man is doing to pull the wool over your professional eyes. Exactly how many texts did he say he had from me?"

It's absurd, but the audacity of my lie actually worked. I guess that Tara didn't think that I could be so brazen in lying to her. She hesitated for just a moment before renewing her attack. "You can say all you want about those texts, but there's no denying what you did to your father and his friend. Let me finish. I'd like to say your behavior was an aberration, but I can't. It's part of a long-running pattern with you. Do you want to know something else that's part of a long-running pattern?"

I could feel my back tensing up as I inched closer to the edge of the couch. I kept myself under control, though. I didn't want to be accused of being infantile or narcissistic, and I didn't want her to storm off before she told me what else about my personality fit an undesirable pattern.

"What's also part of a pattern is that despite your criminal behavior–yes, your criminal behavior–your father is still trying to show his love for you. Despite what you did to him, he still wanted to move forward with the acquisition. He was determined to make sure that you had a job as long as you wanted, a job that paid a substantial wage for your efforts. That's an unbelievable pattern. I can't imagine anyone else doing such a thing. You should thank your lucky stars that you have such a loving and forgiving father."

That was it. I couldn't take this lunacy anymore, especially when Tara leaned back and, with her arms folded across her breasts and her middle fingers tapping her elbows, informed me wordlessly that I was stupid. Maybe I was, and I stood to contradict everything that she was saying or implying. When she asked me in a business-like tone to sit because I was "acting like a child," I exploded. I shouted at her to shut up. I shouldn't have, I know, but the insanity had gone too far, and I wanted her to understand that the old man was lying to her and everyone else and that he was manipulating everyone to destroy me. Yes, me, for I was now convinced beyond a shadow of doubt that the old man was doing whatever he could to take away from me everything I loved, everything that made my life worth living.

"How dare you talk to me like…," she started to say but immediately fell silent when I insisted with even more vehemence for her to shut up.

"Don't you understand what's happening?" I insisted. Despite my best efforts to appear in control, I could feel my body shaking and my hands were involuntarily tightening and contracting. "Can't you see what that the kindly old man is doing and doing to us? We never argued before, and…"

"He's not doing anything to…"

"Listen to me. Listen to me for a change. Do you have any idea of what's going on at my workplace? Do you?"

She was silent for a moment and looked at me as though my questions insulted her intelligence.

"He's firing everyone and blaming me," I continued. "He told the entire staff that he was our father and that he's terminating everyone I didn't like. Don't you get it? One of the employees he fired threatened me with a box.

Another one scratched the word 'pig' on my door. One employee, a person I've known for quite some time, challenged me to fight him in the parking lot. It's only a matter of time before someone finds out where we live."

Tara took a deep, condescending breath and calmly re-crossed her slim legs. "Tell me, were you there when he said this? No? Jeff is your only source?"

"No, there were others. Practically the entire staff was there and heard him. Don't belittle Jeff."

"I'm not. I must say, though, there's often concern and anxiety over change, and these emotions will frequently color our perceptions and understanding of things. I wonder if it's possible that some of the people, perhaps those that weren't there, misunderstood your father's intentions with respect to the firm and the way forward that I'm sure he outlined. Their misperceptions, if held vehemently, could easily influence the thoughts of others, even those who were there. But regardless of how the situation appears to you, you must be able to see that his intentions were good."

"What do you mean 'good'? There's nothing good about the old man's intentions. Do you understand what's he's doing to me? Is that good? Is that okay with you? And he's going to do the same thing to you and everyone else unless I stop him."

Tara was cool and collected. She was back in her element. In her mind, she was trying to control one of her unruly patients, and so there was nothing that I could say now that would register on her face much less get a rise out of her. "How do you propose to stop him, assuming it's necessary to stop him?"

"I don't know. But if someone doesn't stop him, our lives and the lives of others will be destroyed."

There was a slight chuckle and an almost imperceptible smile on the right corner of her lips. "Don't you think you're being a little histrionic? Nobody is going to be destroyed. Your father is not a monster, and he doesn't need to be stopped, as you say. Have you tried to see his side of things?"

"More so than you. I can see how much he hates me. I'm his competitor, and he's doing what he can to eliminate me."

She shook her head. "He doesn't hate you. Quite the opposite. You're his son, and he's only working through…"

"For once in your life, cut the cheap psycho-bullshit."

Tara a closed her eyes and took a deep breath. When she opened them, I was once more the patient who refused to understand what had already been explained, more than once. "All right. As I said, your father had purchased the company for all the right reasons. He may have made a mistake or two in the execution, which I doubt, but I can assure you that it wasn't intentional. I can also assure you that his goal is to do everything he can to help and support you. He told me that nothing can make up for the past, but now that he's able to help he'd like to do whatever he can to show his love. Yes, his love."

I didn't quite know how to respond to this rubbish. I suppose that if we had been at the kitchen table dispassionately discussing the news, I might have come up with something more considered, compelling. But regardless of how it came out, I was only trying to help Tara understand that we were dealing with a stranger who was a pathological liar and quite possibly a homicidal maniac…or at least had violent tendencies, judging by how he threatened me when he was in my office. You can understand my point of view, right?

"Are you out of your bloody mind?" I screamed. I leaned forward and was practically off the couch. "Do you dish out this kind of mindless shit to your fucking, looney patients? God, if you do, I feel sorry for those fools."

The consummate professional finally showed a crack in her otherwise icy demeanor. Tara jerked up and glowered at me as though I had thrown a glass of water into her face. An instant later, her face darkened and I thought that she might actually lunge at me.

"I'm sorry," I grumbled. Despite her obstinate refusal to see the truth, I controlled myself and spoke in her kind of measured, calm voice to defuse the situation. "I didn't mean to speak that way. I was only trying to say…I mean, what I was trying to say is that I don't know what you see in that piece of garbage. You can't trust him, and, you're not going to want to hear this, when he's done with me, he'll come after you and Tom."

Tara appeared to take my apology as a sign that the tables were turning in her favor. "Please sit back. I deal with people who have problems. Part of my job is to understand these people and to get to the bottom of their motivations. I believe I have a little more insight into these matters than you do, and so when I tell you that your father…"

I gritted my teeth to keep from going off the deep end. "Stop calling him our father. If you had only a fraction of the insight you claim, you would have seen through the old man the first time you saw him. Jesus Christ, you're as delusional as your pathetic patients."

That was the last straw, for both of us. Tara came at me and furiously slapped me in the face and on the head, shoulders, chest, and everywhere else she could that might cause injury. Her aberrant behavior at that moment, along with the fact that she was continually taking the old man's side against me, nearly pushed me over the edge, too. Look, you have to understand, the unexpected appearance of the old man in our lives was driving me out of my mind. Father or not, his presence and spurious claims pulled me back into a time that for decades I worked to forget. It is hard to explain all the emotional turmoil I faced then and now because of our father. I was being torn apart by the things that the old man was doing in our father's name, doing to drive a wedge between Tom and me into which he was skillfully inserting himself. Do I need to highlight the wedge that he had already inserted between Tara and me? Well, I didn't touch her. At that instant I might have hated her, but I didn't lay a finger on her. I put my hands and arms in front of my face and crouched over to avoid the worst of her blows. It was only a temporary solution, because when she saw that she wasn't hurting me, she began pounding my back and then kicking me in the shins. Tara stopped swinging when she began to tire, and for a couple of moments I stared up at her as she stared down at me, both of us waiting for the next thing to happen. I remained sitting but slowly straightened up and tried to calm her. I smiled and uttered a number of soft inanities such as "it's okay, it's okay." Nothing worked. She shook her head (I thought she might even spit at me), and sat back down in her chair. I wanted to placate her, but as I inched toward her, she put her hand and arm out like a football player and growled at me to go away if I knew what was good for me.

"Tara, please…"

"Go," she hissed like an ocean wave coming ashore. "Just go. I don't want to see you ever…"

That was enough for me. I don't know if it was the last straw, but I do know that I had never been as angry with Tara as I was at that moment. There certainly had been times when I was irritated with her, when I was put off by her various attitudes, but never really angry, never anything close to the hatred that was now igniting my present emotions. But the hatred I felt wasn't just for my wife. It was also for the old man, who was systematically destroying our lives, and to a slightly lesser degree for Tom, Belinda, and everyone else who was happily, blindly enabling his actions. Since I was no longer confident that I could continue to control myself if Tara went on with her mindless, ignorant blather, I got up and briefly raised my hands as if I had been arrested. It was a stupid gesture. It was merely a way of saying that I was done with her and all the rest of insanity.

"I will. I'll go right now," I said loudly, unable to leave without the last word. Like a child, I stomped to the front door, and hesitated. I half expected Tara to call me back so that we could discuss things more calmly (isn't that what psychologists do?), but after waiting for what seemed an interminable amount of time for a response that wasn't going to come, I told myself that this was the end and yanked open the door. I reiterated what I had said as I stepped outside, but as I was closing the door behind me, my heel got caught between the door and the frame and my shoe came off. Once I retrieved it and put it back on, I slammed the door and, to avenge my shoe, I kicked the door twice with my heel and stormed away from the house.

I didn't know where I was going until I pulled away from the curb with a loud tire screech. I rounded the first corner, merged onto a larger street, and headed directly for Tom's house. I didn't call, I didn't want to give him a chance to hang up, I wanted to confront him personally so that I could help him understand what was happening behind his back.

It seemed as if it had taken me only seconds to get there. Once in his driveway, I charged across the pavement to his front door and rang the bell furiously several times. Belinda answered. She didn't expect to see me (I could see it in her face) and didn't have enough sense to say more than "living room" when I demanded to know what Tom was. I pushed past her and charged right into the living room where Tom and four gruff-looking individuals in pretentious business suits were sitting and pretending to discuss something of great importance. There was one other individual in the room. He was dressed like the other four except that he was wearing sunglasses. It was the old man, and like the others he was smoking a cigar. They all stopped whatever they were doing and stared at me.

I lost control when I saw the old man. He didn't move or flinch or even pretend that my unexpected presence there meant something. Blowing a ring of smoke in my direction, he smirked as if to let me know that he had won, that I had lost, and that this is what happens when someone like me butts head with someone like him. That did it. With everything else on my mind, that was all it took. I screamed at him, "You stinking son of a bitch," and charged toward him. It was a stupid thing to do, but I wanted to take that cigar from him and wipe that smirk off his smarmy face. I wanted to show him what it's really like being slapped around, I wanted to make him understand what happens when you destroy the kinds of relationships I enjoyed with Tom and Tara, and I wanted him to feel the pain that he had caused me and everyone else with his vile, criminal actions. I wanted to kill him, and I wanted to kill him in front of everybody, so that they could see the kind of louse they were dealing with. In my blind fury, however, I had failed to take careful consideration of my surroundings, and before I could get within an arm's reach of the old man, I was grabbed from behind in a chokehold and dragged out of the house. As I was being pulled from the room, I noticed the passive, unconcerned expressions on the faces of all the men, including the old man's. It was obvious that they didn't share my concerns and that to them I was little more than a bug being pulled into a spider's lair. The only face I didn't see was Tom's.

The grip was impossibly tight around my neck and I couldn't breathe. I couldn't stand or resist, either. With my heels dragging across the floor and my hands holding onto the arm around my neck, I felt as though the only thing I could do to protect myself was to hold on and keep the noose from tightening and strangling me. An instant later, I was yanked outside and slammed against the outside brick wall. But even then, the strangulation didn't cease. Instead, I was held against the wall with the same arm under my chin. As my eyes began to focus, I saw my brother, Tom. He was the one who had removed me from the house, and he was now the one who was now choking me against the wall.

It's hard to express how I felt when I finally understood what was happening. This wasn't simply another example of my brother taking the old man's side against me. Tom was manhandling me the way he used to manhandle me when we were children. It was his way of belittling me, of drawing my attention to something, or, and this is perhaps a more accurate way of putting it, of controlling me and taking away my resistance so that I was powerless to do anything except what he wanted me to do. Then as now, he was much bigger and stronger than me, and I have often thought that he revelled in his power as a puppet master. He enjoyed it like a bully enjoys the power he has over people. It's impossible to forget how he used to grab me when we were kids, grabbing me just like he was doing now, to show his friends and others that he could break me and force me to do whatever he wanted. Sometimes, it was only to show his friends that he could make me eat dirt. Other times, it was to get me to do something far worse. We were immature then, and now he was doing something that I thought that he had outgrown decades ago.

"What the fuck are you doing?"

His grip was so tight that I couldn't do anything but gag and gasp. "Can't...," I managed to say before again struggling to breathe.

He loosened his grip just enough for me to gasp out a response but not enough for me to free myself.

"I'll ask you one more time. What do you want?"

"I want...I want to tell you what was happening to me, what the old man was doing to me."

"Yeah?"

"My firm is falling apart. My marriage is in shambles. And the old man..."

He acted as if he was tossing something around in his mind. Shaking his head, he said, "You're responsible for your own life. Do you know what you just did?" Tom briefly pressed his arm tighter against my neck. "Dad and I are on the verge of making a major business deal, and you may have destroyed it. Do you have any idea what your antics could cost me?"

"I didn't mean…"

"I don't care what you meant. I care about this deal and what it will do for Dad and me. Can you get that through your thick skull?"

I don't think he had any idea of the pressure that he was putting against my neck. I was afraid that any second my vocal cords would be crushed and, if I were lucky, I would only pass out. What was worse was that my beloved brother, my best friend and guide throughout my life, the one individual I needed more than anyone else in my life, my brother, my dearest brother, was now making it clear that he had weighed me and the old man in the balance and that he had chosen the old man. As a result, I was therefore being banned from his life. Tom may not have said as much, but I felt it in his tone of voice and in the violence he was using against me–violence which began in front of the old man. In front of the old man, of all people. My knees were beginning to buckle, and I dropped my hands.

"Stand up, goddamn you. You've been continually badgering my father, you slapped him around, and now you're sticking your nose into my business. I thought you knew better. I thought you'd be more grateful for all the things I've given you. I gave you your wife, and now you're telling me you fucked up your marriage." He briefly gritted his teeth as he glanced to the ground. "She promised to control you. She promised…but she's as worthless as you. Okay, listen to me. This is it. I'm not going to tell you again–stay away, and leave my father alone. The next time…"

I didn't respond. I don't think that I could have responded even if he released me and flashed one of his large, brotherly smiles.

He was about to say something else but stopped and glowered at me. An instant later, there was an eruption on the left side of my head, and I collapsed onto something hard and unforgiving. My ears were ringing as I got onto my hands and knees, and I felt a searing, hot flame rush through my body before it centered on my head and neck. When my eyes were almost clear, I glanced to one side and saw Tom's pants' legs as he hovered next to me. I thought for a moment that he was going to kick me, but he must have changed his mind, for he grabbed me by the back of my shirt collar and held me partly up so that he could look down into my face.

"No more excuses," he whispered in my ear. "This was the last time. Do you understand? Now, get the hell out of here." He shoved me to the pavement and stepped back.

I struggled to my feet and staggered to my car. Tom didn't move as I made a U-turn in his driveway around him and left his property.

22

I didn't go home. I couldn't go home. Apart from the old man, Tara was the last person in the world that I wanted to face, and she probably already knew what had happened and, for all I knew, was packing her bags and waiting for Tom to give her to someone else. Maybe the old man. Wouldn't that have been fitting? I drove around for an hour or so and then pulled into a hotel on the outskirts of town. I checked in and immediately went to my dimly-lit room, where I plopped onto the bed and slept for the rest of the day. When I woke up, my throat was sore, my ear was swollen, and I had scrapes and bruises on my face and knuckles from the impact with the rough pavement. My back was also painful, though I couldn't tell if it was from the incident or something else. I didn't go back to work. I didn't call in, either. What was the point? I either had a job or most likely I didn't. Even if the old man allowed me to keep my job, I couldn't go back and work under his thumb. I couldn't go anywhere he was at even if I hadn't had the altercation in Tom's house. But having made this simple decision, I didn't know what to do next and I quickly fell asleep again and didn't wake up until hours later.

I eventually eased myself out of bed and went into the bathroom to wash. Under the bright, sterile bathroom lights, I admired all my bruises and touched several of them to test the limits of my tolerance for pain. When I was done and dressed, I lowered myself into in an oversized chair next to the only window in the room. The room was pleasantly dark, and I didn't attempt to open the heavy curtains and let in the day's bright light. I had seen enough light in the bathroom, and I wasn't in the mood for any more, especially because my head and side were throbbing and making practically every movement stiff and painful. I stayed in the chair for most of the day (I even told the housekeeper, when she softly knocked on my door, to come back later in the week), reflecting on what had happened and wondering what the old man was going to do next. He had to be plotting something, if for no other reason that he hadn't yet finished me off. In the early evening, as the sun started to descend behind the hotel, I struggled painfully out of the chair and made my way to the hotel restaurant. As soon as I had finished the tasteless, overcooked meal, I went back to my room and slept the night. The following day, I was up early and ready for some fresh air and for a distraction to clear my mind of everything that had recently happened. I was still sore and bruised and definitely not ready for an extensive outing, and so I confined my excursion to the hotel grounds, where I did my best to admire the red and blue flowers and the short, green bushes in front of the building. In the open area behind the hotel, I relaxed under a gray sky on one of the long, wooden benches and watched the elevated section of the highway where the cars and trucks were pointlessly racing from one place to another. Later in the afternoon, I spent some time admiring the empty swimming pool and then went through the reception area to check out the equally deserted exercise room and, afterwards, to inspect the locked doors of the convention hall. I ate dinner at the restaurant, and even struck up a pleasant conversation with the waitress and, later, with one of the cleaning crew who was pushing a large crate of linen down the hallway near my room.

These insignificant interactions along with the passage of the day tempered my anger a little. I still couldn't forgive my wife or set aside the fact that she had some sort of secret connection with the old man. I didn't think she had a sexual thing for pestilent old men, but I did wonder if she was connected to one of his schemes or simply working with him in some capacity that Tom had dictated. It didn't matter either way, because any inclination for the old man was a betrayal of me, and Tara made it abundantly clear whom she preferred. With Tom, it was different. I was still mad at him, I was humiliated over what had happened at his house (and, yes, as I'd like to emphasize, in front of the old man), and yet I couldn't turn my back on him as easily as I could my wife. He was still my brother, and I owed him my gratitude and loyalty for the many years that we had been together. In other words, I still loved Tom and I was willing to do anything I could to protect him and remain close to him, and I was fearful that whatever he and the old man were cooking up, nothing good would come of it. And I knew without the least doubt that if the old man was involved in something, that something had to be nefarious and illegal. But, as I said numerous times, I loved my brother, and I was going to stick with him through thick and thin, and I was determined to do whatever it took to prevent him from following the old man off the irremediable deep end.

Unfortunately, I didn't know exactly what I could do that wouldn't blow up in my face. I couldn't call him and try to explain things. Even if he did pick up and, for some odd reason, refrained from informing me that I was a dead man, I didn't know what I could tell him that would convince him that he was making the biggest mistake of his life–the biggest mistake of all of our lives. The only other option was the police. If anyone or anything could remove Tom's blinders when it came to the old man, the police could. They could provide objective, scientific facts–facts that could withstand Tom's desires and suppositions–regarding the old man's crimes and incorrigibility, and they were in the best position to convince my brother that he needed to dump the old man before it was too late. What made me reluctant to take this first, necessary step was the possibility that Tom was now so deeply involved in the old man's schemes that he would go down with the old man. This would not only defeat my intention, but it would also destroy whatever remnants of a relationship that I still had with my brother. Since I saw no other options of immediately changing things, I was going to reach out to Jeff to see if there was anything happening at the office that might give me another avenue through which to approach my brother.

When I dialed his line, there was a message which stated that his phone had been disconnected. It was strange, and so I redialed it to make sure that I was calling the right number. The same message came up. It was troubling to think that Jeff of all people was gone, and so I called the firm's main number to see if I could reach him that way. I didn't have any better luck–either the phone had been disconnected or it was out of order. With nothing else to do, I drove to the office to see if there were any visible changes to the building (possibly the phone numbers had been changed to save costs). I had no intention of going inside–I didn't have a job while the old man was in charge–and so I drove to a place where I could observe the main doors for people coming out that I knew and, if I happened to speak to any of them, I might be able to get the skinny on what was going on inside. But an anxious sensation came over me when I drove inside the parking lot and parked near the front door. The parking lot was empty, and the building seemed almost dark and deserted. Since it wasn't a holiday, I went inside the lobby, rode the rickety elevator to the third floor, and stepped out in front of the main glass doors of the firm. There was no light emanating from the offices, there were no employees scurrying in and out of the door, and there was no one in sight either in the offices or on the floor. The doors were locked, and there was a sign just above eye level which stated that the offices were available for lease. Cupping my hands on either side of my eyes, I pressed the sides of my hands to the glass door and looked inside. The place was dead. I returned to my car and when I was back at the hotel, I used one of the hotel's computers to check the firm's website to see if there was anything to explain what had happened. The website confirmed my worst fears–it wasn't online.

Enough was finally enough. Even if Tom didn't want to hear from me, he needed to understand what was going on behind his back, and he needed to know that the old man wasn't going to stop until he got what he came for and that I and everyone else in our family was destroyed. Back at the hotel and in the chair by the window, I took a deep breath, dialed his work number and immediately hung up. I initially thought it best to reach him at his office, but then had second thoughts about interrupting his business, especially after he got so mad about interrupting it at his home. That was stupid, I told myself. There was no place where I could call him without interrupting something, and this time the issue was important enough for him to stop whatever he was doing if only for a few minutes. Taking another deep breath, I dialed the number again and a secretary answered. She informed me that Tom was unavailable and that she could take a message. I hung up. I wasn't going to leave a message for something like this, and so I called his home phone. While the phone was ringing, I was beginning to hope that he wouldn't pick up, because I didn't want him to get mad at me again. To my surprise, Belinda picked up the line.

"You have your nerve," she said vehemently after I identified myself and explained that I wanted to speak to Tom on an urgent matter.

"What? Tom's not still mad at me because I interrupted his business deal, is he? It was a mistake. I didn't know...Belinda, what's the matter?"

Her voice was thick, and she seemed to have difficulty controlling it. "You...you know what's the matter. I thought...I thought you loved Tom, and now I see that you're no better than the garbage that walks the alleys at night."

"Good God, what are you talking about? I'm not like that. I'm the same person you've always known."

"I don't want to speak to you ever again. Goodbye..."

"Please, please, don't hang up. What's going on? Please, tell me."

There was a prolonged pause, and I was beginning to think that the connection was dead. Before I could ask Belinda if she was still on the line, she came back and this time spoke to me in a distant, emotionless tone. It sounded as though she standing a mile away from her phone. "You sure did a job on Tommy. He's in the hospital. I came home for...but you had already taken care of things. You bludgeoned him up for kicking you out of our house, and now he's in a coma and nobody can tell me if he'll make it. You're despicable."

"What happened? My God, no. Belinda, you have to believe me, I didn't touch him. I wouldn't lay a glove on him. I don't know how you could think such a thing. When did this happen? Where? Is he at Saint Mercy's?"

"You stay away from him."

"Belinda, I'm telling you the truth. I had nothing to do with this. Why are you accusing me? Did you speak to Tom after..." I had trouble finishing. I couldn't believe that he was in a coma. And I couldn't believe that anyone could have taken on someone as big and athletic as my brother. "Please, Belinda, you have to believe me."

"I don't."

"Who accused me of this? The old man? Don't you know by now, he's a liar?"

She hung up without answering, and she didn't pick up the next three times I called. Since I was over an hour from Saint Mercy's, I called the hospital to get an update on Tom's condition. The hospital didn't have any patient with my brother's name, and there was no way for the hospital to locate him at another facility. When the call was over, I felt that I had no choice but to call the police. As I dialed the number, I made a short, silent prayer that Tom was okay or at least that he would recover, and then that he wasn't involved in anything illegal. I also asked the same higher power to force the courts to let him off for testifying against the old man, who was doubtless the real culprit. The call turned out to be as unexpected as everything else. After I gave my name to the desk officer and informed him that I wanted to report a crime and a criminal, I was put on hold for a few minutes until a man came on the line and identified himself as a detective. He asked for my name and address and handful of other, related questions. All this seemed reasonable enough, but what he said next didn't.

"We've been having trouble finding you. Where have you been?"

"You've been looking for me? Why? Do you already know about my brother?"

"Your brother? No. We only want to hear your side of the story. You can tell us all about your brother later on, if you wish. By the way, where are you now?"

I told him the hotel and my room number. Seconds later, I began to have doubts about the advisability of providing such information at a time when the detective seemed more interested in answers to his questions than in what I had to impart. My doubts grew when he asked me to come to the station to make a formal statement. He wanted me to make a formal statement? To what purpose? Since my only other experience with the police happened when I was a child, I couldn't fathom why a trip was necessary. I could easily impart everything I knew over the phone.

"Am I in any trouble?" I was by this time focused on the police than I was on my brother's health. There were, after all, people looking after him.

"Why would you ask that?" he replied pleasantly, as if he were dealing with a child.

"I called to report a crime. I don't understand why you're asking me these irrelevant questions when you could be listening to my story and asking me questions about it. It's the old man. He's responsible for all of it. Look him up in your databases. I'll bet he has a criminal record as long as a baseball field."

"Interesting choice of words."

"What is?"

"Your reference to baseball. Do you like baseball?"

"Yeah, sure, but what does that have to do with anything? Do you understand what I'm saying? I want to report a crime, that's all."

"Yes, I understand. But, if you don't mind, let me ask you one more question."

"Okay, one more."

"Do you own a baseball bat?"

It was one irrelevant question too many. I hung up. The detective and, by extension, the police weren't interested in anything I had to say. It was at that moment that I also understood why the police never located my father–they get bogged down by irrelevant details while they're out chasing the next shiny object. Well, I wasn't going to waste my time conversing with the police, and I also wasn't going to wait until the old man located me and did to me what he had done to my brother, and so I picked up my few things and got ready to leave the hotel. My first stop was going to be Saint Mercy's to see if Tom might be there. Maybe they changed his name to protect him. I placed my hand on the door handle but didn't immediate open it. It was disturbing to think that my brother would ever need protecting. He had always been so strong and confident and, throughout our lives together, he was the one who protected me. I couldn't conceive of how my life might have been had I not enjoyed his protection, and his love. Apart from everything, his love, which protected me against the world. I turned the door handle and stepped into the hallway. Before I could determine the direction of the exit, I was surrounded by several police officers who handcuffed me and hustled me out of the building and into a waiting police car in front of the hotel. It was my first arrest.

23

I was booked on some vague charge and placed in a holding cell for a couple of hours before being moved to a small room in another part of the building. The walls, floor, and ceiling of the room were covered with a non-descript gray. In the center, there was an equally nondescript table with a nondescript chair on either side and a large, nondescript mirror on one of the side walls. With my handcuffs and shackles still on, I was eased into one of the nondescript chairs (the two officers who had escorted me to this room made sure that I was seated to their complete satisfaction) and told to wait for the detective. The two officers who had escorted me to the room and ensured my comfort silently backed away and stationed themselves behind me out of sight. Shortly after this, a man in a gray suit came in and sat down at the table across from me. He was average in height and slightly stocky, and he sported a full head of closely-cropped gray hair. Judging by the lines of experience radiating out from the corners of his eyes, he was probably in his mid-fifties.

"You've been comfortable, yes?" he asked after introducing himself as the detective in charge of the case and noting that I already been introduced to the two officers behind me.

"No, I've been in a jail cell. Would you find that comfortable?"

"I meant in here. I'm sorry for being late. I was held up by a little man who had something very important to tell me. Sometimes you just can't help yourself. I'm sure you understand."

"I don't. Were you the detective I spoke to on the phone?"

"Yes," he replied and smiled gently. It turned out that he often smiled as he spoke. "We had a lovely conversation, don't you think? You mentioned something about a baseball bat, as I recall."

"You brought it up, and the conversation wasn't very nice. You didn't have to arrest me. All I wanted to do was to report a crime. The old man attacked my brother."

"I'm sorry to hear that. We'll get to that later if we have time. Right now…but let me point out that you hung up on me. That wasn't very polite on your part, and so you'll have to forgive me for assuming that the only way for us to have a serious conversation was to meet here, where we could sit across from each other and hash out the problems."

"Fine. We're here now, sitting across from each other. Why am I still handcuffed? Why was I handcuffed in the first place?"

"To answer both of your questions–it's a requirement. Think of it as a precaution."

"A precaution for what?"

"You know, people get upset. I don't want my officers getting hurt. I'm sure you understand."

"Are you serious? They're bigger than me, and they've got guns."

"Still, things do happen."

"Fine, fine. I don't understand why I'm here. I just wanted to report a crime. What do you want to talk about?"

"Didn't you listen to the officers when they arrested you?"

"I sure did. They told me to turn around and put my forehead against the wall and my hands behind my head."

"Excuse me?"

"They weren't very kind about it, either. They pushed my head against the wall while they were handcuffing me. My head still hurts."

His smile momentarily faded as he glanced at the two officers behind me. "I apologize for that. I'm sure it wasn't intentional. But you know how it is in the heat of the moment. Now, tell me," he began as he turned back to me, "Do you remember our phone conversation?"

I wanted to look back at the officers to see if there was something I was missing, but the chains prevented me from turning completely around. "I remember part of the conversation. But you were asking so many irrelevant questions I couldn't stand it anymore."

"I'll try to do better. I can assure you, however, that none of my questions were irrelevant. Now, before we begin, you were read your rights, were you not?"

"I suppose so."

"You don't mind speaking to me for a little while?"

"Sure, if it gets me out of here. I don't know why I'm here."

"It will certainly help and, if you bear with me, we'll get to why you're here in just a moment." He cleared his throat. "Okay? Good. Now, where were we? Ah, yes, I believe you mentioned something about a baseball bat. You told me you liked baseball, right?"

"I guess I like baseball, but you brought it up, along with all the nonsense about a bat. Is it a crime these days to appreciate baseball?"

"Certainly not. I love the game, too. Tell me, do you own a baseball bat?"

"No. Well, yeah, I guess so. It's my brother's Little League bat. I haven't touched it in years, though. I'm not even sure where it's at."

"Are you positive?"

"Positive? I don't know where it's at, and I haven't touched it since I was a child."

"We'll come back to all that. Can you tell me about your wife?"

"Tara?"

"Yes. Do you have another one?"

"That's a stupid question."

"I guess it is. But you'd be surprised by the kinds of valuable information I get from my stupid questions."

"Fine. What about my wife?"

"Did you have a fight with her on the day of..." He glanced upward as though the date might be hovering in the air behind me. One of the officers out of sight caught it and gave him the information. It was the date that Tara and I had our last disagreement.

"Yes...no. It wasn't an actual fight. It was a disagreement."

"I see. So, tell me what the disagreement was about."

"Why are you asking me that? It's none of your business."

"Ordinarily, I would agree with you, but everything is my business when you're staying with us. If you'd humor me, I'm sure we could get to the heart of the matter fairly quickly. Does that work for you?"

I felt a moment of deep sadness. I missed Tara, or at least I missed the person she was during the first years of our marriage. The sadness, my sense of loss, immediately dissipated when I recalled the old man and remembered Tara's unrelenting support for him. Did she know what he did to Tom? "We disagreed about the old man. She refused to accept what was he was doing to me and the people I work with. Given everything else, she should have been concerned for me and everyone else. she should have been frightened over what he could do to her. She should have been...but she wasn't. Tara wasn't in the least bit troubled by these events or anything else regarding the old man. In her lovely eyes, the old man was simply bringing goodness into the world. He was making my life better. He couldn't do anything wrong. The son of a bitch could have stabbed me to death in front of her, and she'd put a positive spin on it. I'll bet Tom thinks differently about him now."

"I see. Your fight...excuse me, your disagreement, it got rather heated, didn't it?"

"I don't know. Maybe. I suppose it ruined our marriage."

"Really? Tell me about it."

"Isn't it obvious? She turned against me. She took the old man's side against me. She was always taking the old man's side. I'll bet you didn't know Tom paid her to be my wife."

"No, I didn't..."

"Yes, but the joke was on her."

"The joke? What joke?"

"Don't you get it? Tom wasn't happy with her, because he wasn't happy with me. She was supposed to keep me under control, and he was mad at her because she couldn't. As if I needed to be kept under control. Did he think I was some kind of loose cannon?"

"And this...exacerbated your anger?"

"I'm not a loose cannon, and I resent the idea that someone needs to keep me under control. But I could have lived with this. I might even have been willing to take Tara back, assuming things were different and I wasn't just another...I don't know. You know what troubled me? You know what I couldn't accept? It was Tara's unwavering devotion to the old man. I could have lived with anything but that. Not that. And so, I ended things. Do you understand?"

The detective sat back and eyed me as though the impasse in our conversation had finally been broken. There was a nearly imperceptible smile on his lips, and I felt that he was beginning to understand what had been happening to me.

"So, you ended things."

"Would you have done anything different?"

"I'm afraid I'm not in your shoes..."

"What does that have to do with it? Can't you see what's happening and how it's affecting my life? Isn't that enough? Do you have to be in anybody's shoes to understand the obvious?"

"I agree, it was an extreme situation. I've seen strong people break for a lot less."

"We disagreed...okay, we argued, and it came to a head and I went to a hotel. What else is there to say?"

"I just want to be clear. You had a fight–a disagreement, as you say–and things got out of hand."

I heard one of the officers whisper to the other and both slightly chuckled.

"Things didn't get out of hand. It was an untenable situation, and I first went to the guest room. I didn't feel comfortable being there while she was…well, I had to leave. What do people do when their lives are crumbling around them?"

He nodded. He smiled, too, though it didn't appear to be a sincere smile. There was something on his mind. "That's a good question," he said, rubbing his square chin as though he didn't believe it. "So, tell me about the baseball bat."

"What bat?"

"The baseball bat you used to…you know."

"Bat? Are you accusing me of stealing it? My brother gave it to me years ago when we were kids."

He gently shook his head like a benign old uncle. "Okay, let's see if we can approach things from a different angle. Don't you think your fight…I'm sorry, your disagreement. Don't you think your disagreement got a little out of control? I mean, is it possible you overreacted. Maybe a little? And I'm not talking about sleeping in the spare room."

"You're not making sense. I told you what happened. Don't you see that I'm the victim here? The old man is responsible for everything. Look, if he hadn't conned Tara into believing everything he said, things would have been fine with us. We wouldn't have had a disagreement. Tom wouldn't have suggested she was a prostitute, and she and I would still be happily married. Do you understand now? Do you see that it was the old man's fault? He ruined my relationship with my brother, he ruined my relationship with my wife, and he ruined my relationship with my employer. Why don't you harass him?"

"I get it. But don't you think some of the responsibility is yours? Tara, for example…"

"Tara? I'm the one that got hurt. I'm the one who was brutalized. I thought she was smart enough to know that bad things would happen because of her relationship with the old man. She thinks she's a psychologist, and yet she didn't have a clue what happens when you play with fire."

The detective placed his elbows on the desk and leaned forward. "So, you are admitting to what you did?"

"How many times do I have to say it? The old man was destroying my life. He was destroying everyone's life. I'll admit that he brought me to the breaking point. I wrote two texts. I think my response was mild compared to what others might have done in similar circumstances."

"I'd rather save our discussion of the old man for later. Now, you admit you reached your breaking point."

"Sure."

"You broke, and you attacked her. Your response in not uncommon in situations like these."

"Situations like what? I didn't attack anybody."

"You were enraged. I'm sure you didn't think about how things would turn out, especially when she fought back. The marks of your struggle are still on your face and neck. Things escalated, and…"

"Wait a minute. I don't know what you're implying, but it didn't happen that way. The marks on my neck have nothing to do with what happened between us. She hit me, several times, in fact. I protected myself, that's all."

"You protected yourself with your baseball bat."

"Stop calling it a baseball bat. It's just a bat. And, no, I didn't need it to protect myself. I crouched down and let her hit me until she was tired and stopped. After that, I left. End of story."

"Did you suffer any bruises or scratches from where she hit you?"

"I don't think so. Nothing hurt. She's not that strong."

"Okay, so tell me about the marks on your face and neck. You just indicated that they didn't come from her. Where did they come from? How did you get the bruises on your knuckles?"

I looked at the detective and for a few seconds couldn't say anything. I didn't know how to explain them, and I didn't want to implicate my brother. He was still my brother, after all, and he was probably suffering more than me for the way he pushed me around. "They're irrelevant. They had nothing to do with Tara."

"I think it's best that I determine the relevancy of your information. Please, tell me how you got them? It must have been an unpleasant experience."

"I'm telling you the truth. The marks had nothing to do with Tara. Listen, I'm madder than hell at Tara, but I didn't touch her. I'm not sure that I could even look at her if she came into this room, but I would never hurt her. I wouldn't hurt anybody. Did she tell you that I hit her? I can't believe she'd say such a thing."

"It's interesting that you should say that about yourself. Did you know that Tara called us shortly after your disagreement? She said that you were having trouble controlling yourself and that, sooner or later, you were going to attack her or someone else."

"She's nuts. I've never attacked anybody in my life. Wait a minute. Did you say Tara called the police? I don't believe it." I couldn't recall if he had mentioned it earlier, but the idea of Tara calling the police suddenly struck me as odd, out of character. She, Belinda, Tom, and me were all one big happy family, with Tom as its de facto head, and if she had a problem with me, she would have gone directly to Tom to handle it, not the police. She was his employee, for God's sake. Besides, it didn't make sense that Tom would have approved calling in the authorities. He had always had a mild aversion to the police ever since the day our father had gone missing. An instant later, the old man came to mind. Since Tom was in the hospital, it could only have been the old man who convinced Tara to call in the police. A shiver ran down my back as I sensed the fat fingers of the old man manipulating everyone around me, maybe even the police.

"Yes, she reached out to us," he continued. She was desperate. Now, I'd like to believe you're innocent, but the evidence seems to suggest otherwise."

"Innocent? What evidence? What are you talking about? I can't believe Tara would call the police and say something like that. Are you sure it was her and not the old man? Have you talked to him? I can tell you that he's a lying swine, and you can't trust a single thing he says. Do you know what he did at my brother's house? Do you know what he said to me in my office? Do you know what he's doing to my workplace? I'll bet you didn't know he exaggerated the number of threatening texts he got on his cell phone. If you don't know any of this, I don't see how you can begin to understand what happened to Tara and me."

"It was Tara. We confirmed it. She asked us for protection."

"From the old man?"

"No," he replied in a low voice to make sure I understood the gravity of his words, "from you."

"You got it all wrong. Where is she? I'd like to talk to her. I think we could straighten this whole thing out pretty quickly."

The detective leaned back and crossed his arms. He squinted and for a moment there was a peculiar, accusatory expression on his lined face. Leaning forward and placing his elbows on the table, he stared at me and practically challenged me to confirm what he thought he knew. "Do you know what we found when we went to your house to get her statement? No? Are you sure?"

"Why isn't Tara here to confront me? Why isn't she here to tell me to my face all the things that you claim she said? If she made those accusations, they're false. You should be holding her instead of me. You should be holding the old man. I don't know why you're holding me."

"Do you know why she's not here?"

"How should I know?"

"Do you know what we found at your house?"

"Evidently not the old man."

The detective was again silent as he examined my face for clues to something. When I glanced downward toward the table (I don't like people staring at me), I began to feel increasingly nervous. Prior to this moment, I was merely angry that I had been arrested for some unfathomable reason. But looking at the tired, gray-haired detective and then hearing the momentary shuffle of one or both of the officers behind me, I couldn't help thinking that there was something more to my arrest than I knew, that there was something that the detective was trying to elicit from me that he was reluctant to ask outright. Was he asking me to confess to something?

"Say what you're trying to say, and then let me out of here," I demanded. I was tired of the nonsense, and my wrists were beginning to hurt from the cuffs.

The detective sighed quietly and shook his head. "All right, let's have it your way. The police came to your door to follow up in your wife's call. There was no answer, and when they started to leave they noticed signs of a violent struggle on your door. Would you care to explain this?"

I became nervous. I would have shrugged this off as being of little consequence, but I quickly realized how it could be misinterpreted to my detriment. "There was no struggle," I replied and tried to laugh off the suggestion that the damage was anything other than it was. "Not at all. The damage happened after our disagreement. I was leaving and, out of frustration, I kicked the door. I may have kicked it twice. It was no big deal, and there was nothing sinister about it. If you want, I'll pay to have my own door repaired. That should make Tara happy."

"Do you know what we found when we went inside?"

Did I know what they found when they went inside? I was about to respond to the detective when it occurred to me that the house might be a mess. Tara and I had a disagreement, an argument, a fight–who cares?–and things occasionally get messy when you're arguing. It was becoming clear to me that his misperceptions were fueling his concerns.

"No," I said. "I don't have a clue."

"You don't? We found your baseball bat."

"Good. I've been looking for it for years."

"I suspect it hasn't been missing that long," the detective replied and sighed as if he were dealing with a recalcitrant child. "But you know the one I'm talking about, the one you bludgeoned your wife with. There are blood stains on it, and..."

I felt a nauseating sensation welling up in my stomach, and I struggled to understand what the detective was saying. "What…what are you talking about? I didn't bludgeon anyone with anything. What happened to Tara? Where is she? Are you joking?"

"If only I were. You took your brother's Little League bat–the very bat that you wanted to use to emulate your brother's heroics–and, graduating to the big leagues, you hit Tara over and over with it until she was…over. Mr. Reid, you might as well tell us where you dumped the body. We're going to find it sooner or later, and I promise you things will go much better for you if you cooperate with us."

I stared at the detective for a minute or so, waiting for him to inform me with his best smile that he was kidding, that the whole thing–the arrest, the interrogation, the accusation–the whole thing was a joke. Tara, I wanted him to say with a grin, was doing well and had set up this fake arrest to bring me back to her so that she could apologize for everything and assure me that she had finally discarded the old man. But as I waited for him to explain that Tara had made the "biggest mistake of her life" in siding with the old man, I noticed that the expression on his face didn't change. It was impassive, and nothing about it suggested that he was going to signal for Tara to come into the room and help me out of my chains. It was an expression that was telling me something I didn't want to hear.

Unable to respond, I leaned forward to the degree possible and looked down at the table. The thought of Tara being dead was too shocking, too unbelievable, and I had trouble accepting it. I couldn't accept it, not right then. And it wasn't because I had once loved her. It was simply that I had never thought of her as either dying or being dead. Sure, we had married with the idea of "'till death do us part," but like everyone else who has ever uttered that line, we didn't really believe it; we didn't take it seriously, because we didn't think the time would come, at least not this early in our lives. And especially not now, despite the fact that death is never convenient when we are talking about loved ones or the ones we used to love. I just…I just couldn't accept it. He had to be wrong, and he had to be crazy to think that I would ever do anything to harm Tara, even though I hated her for blithe acceptance of the old man and her equally blithe rejection of me.

"Are you sure?" I gasped without looking up.

"Am I sure she's dead, or am I sure you killed her?"

I couldn't answer the question. I don't think that I could have cogently answered any question at that moment. As I recall, he answered it for me, though I don't remember exactly what he said. I tried to focus on the notion that Tara was no longer here, that she was no longer in a form to hate, but I couldn't even do that. It was too disorienting. I don't recall how long I was sitting there with my head down struggling to come to grips with the world surrounding and suffocating me, but it must have been too long for the detective's patience. He loudly cleared his throat and, when I slowly raised my head to look at him, he smiled in a friendly way and informed me that "we" could end most of "this unpleasantness" if I signed a confession. He raised his right hand and briskly, loudly filliped his thumb and middle finger twice to one of the officers who immediately handed him paper and a ballpoint pen.

"This is a mere formality," he said in a pleasant, reassuring tone. "We have all the details, but a signed confession will make you feel better and help you through this whole, arduous process. I'm sure you want to get things over as quickly as I do." He slid the paper and the pen toward me. "If you please…"

I remember being horrified by the blank sheet of paper in front of me. Its featureless, neutral tonality almost beckoned me to pick up the pen and confess to something I didn't do and wouldn't have done no matter how angry I was with her. 'Come, sign,' it sung like a Siren, 'Sign, and things will be better for you and Tara. You will be out of the old man's reach, and Tara will sleep better in eternity knowing the violence surrounding her is gone.' An instant later, I recoiled from the dirty sheet of paper and the detective's repulsive request. I couldn't demean Tara's memory by confessing to something that was both untrue and disgraceful. And, apart from her association with the old man, I couldn't think of anything that would tarnish her memory more than being brutalized by her husband. Kill her? Was he joking? I would have killed myself first. But while these thoughts were fleeting through my head, something unrelated came to mind. It was the stupidity of the detective's request. My hands and arms were shackled painfully behind me. I was practically immobile. What did he expect me to do? Pick up the pen with my teeth and sign it that way? Maybe there was something else going on in my mind, I don't know, but I couldn't help chuckling to myself over this wrinkled piece of paper and the detective's ridiculous request, and shortly after this I started laughing, louder and louder and more and more uncontrollably, until my whole body was convulsing. When at last the detective thought he understood the conundrum, he went around the desk and unshackled one of my arms. It was then that I started to scream, and the two officers behind piled onto me and, with some difficulty, re-shackled my arm. They hauled me out of the room and threw me onto a bed in a different cell than the one I had initially inhabited. When the cell door slammed shut, I rolled onto my stomach and tried to suffocate myself in the pillow.

I woke up when I felt the heavy cell door rumble open. Shortly after this, I heard what resembled the dull thud of a flat, metal object hitting the floor. A scraping noise followed, which sounded like someone was pushing the object aside with the edge of his heavy boot. Before I could twist around to see what was happening, two or more guards came in through the open cell door. One of them grabbed me by my hair and shoulders and forced my head into the pillow while another sat on my legs and unlocked the chains holding my left arm. When I was about to pass out from asphyxiation, they got up and left, and I slowly, painfully raised myself and turned around. The metal object was a tray that contained my food (breakfast, lunch, or dinner, I didn't know), and, judging by the mess inside and surrounding it, I could tell that somebody had stepped into it on his way out of the cell. I wasn't hungry, anyway.

Sometime later, probably the following morning, two guards entered my cell. I couldn't tell if they were the same individuals who had entered earlier. One carried a shotgun, which he aimed at my face. The other, apparently unarmed, held me down while he unlocked the chains and cuffs on my right arm. Once he was off me, the other silently motioned with the barrel of the gun to indicate that I was to get up and go about my morning routine. When I was done, the unarmed guarded informed me that my cell stank "like shit" and added, with a sideways motion of his head toward the floor to his left, that he was disappointed I hadn't eaten my dinner. "I guess our fine cuisine ain't good enough for the likes of you, is it, shithead?" he practically shouted, while the shotgun held by the other guard was now only inches from my eyes. When I didn't respond, the unarmed guard swooped behind me, and, grabbing one of my arms and the collar of my shirt, slammed me face first against the bars and again secured me. Yanking me back around so that the bars were at my back and the shotgun leveled at my eyes, he informed me with a snarl that I had a visitor. With the unarmed guard at my side and the other behind me, they escorted me through several long, noisy, cell-lined hallways and then shoved me into a large, bright, nearly empty room with blank, white walls. Before I could say anything, the unarmed guard grabbed my arm and forced me into a hard chair in front of an empty, rectangular, cafeteria-style table in the middle of the room. Having accomplished this repugnant task, both guards retreated from the room as a large, slightly overweight guard that I had never seen before appeared and stationed himself in the back corner where I could see him over my shoulder.

Since no one gave me the name of my soon-to-arrive visitor, I thought that it might be Tom, who was coming to rescue me from this abyss. Like most siblings, we'd had our differences, especially of late, but in our heart of hearts we were brothers to the end and loyal to one another, just as we had been throughout our lives. An instant later, I realized that Tom wasn't likely to visit me any time soon, at least not until he was out of the hospital. It was a puzzling situation, because I couldn't think of anyone who might want to see me apart from the detective (who was probably still interested in the bat and the signed confession) and possibly Jeff, but only if he had some good gossip to share. Before I could come up with another name, I noticed the sound of a heavy, metal door opening behind me, some muffled talk between two or more persons, and then a sucking thump as, I presumed, the door closed. An instant later, a grayish, middle-aged woman dressed in a gray business suit appeared in front of me and sat down on the other side of the table. Apart from the faint hum of the heating system, the room was deadly still as she placed a notebook and mechanical pencil on the table and then adjusted herself in the chair.

24

"Mr. Reid," the woman said as she carefully flipped through the pages in her notebook. "Mr. Reid, I'm Counsellor Rondell. The court appointed me to be your attorney." When she found the right page, she scribbled something on it and underlined whatever it was with a bold flourish. "Mr. Reid," she reiterated, this time looking directly at me. She had a rough almost masculine voice that didn't match the softness of her sagging skin. "Unless you instruct otherwise, I'm here to help you."

"Yes, thank you," I replied, genuinely happy that someone was going to help me. "You're going to get me out of here, right? I didn't do anything. I didn't touch my wife."

She stared at me, and at once I could feel her observing my injuries as if they were telltale signs of the crime of which I stood accused. "Mr. Reid," she continued, her voice flat and unemotional, "I am not here to judge you. In the eyes of the court, you are innocent until proved guilty." The manner in which she articulated the sentence made me think that there was nothing I could say to convince her that I was innocent.

"I get it. But I think it would help if you understood my side of things."

"As I said, Mr. Reid, I am here to help you through the system, and I will do that to the best of my ability. But you also have to understand that you are not my only client. I have other people depending on me and, in order to provide the help they need, I can't spend all day with you. I am not making a judgment, you understand. This is merely a practical consideration."

"My innocence or guilt is therefore immaterial?"

"Correct, Mr. Reid, as it is with all my clients."

"Can you at least hear my side of the story if I promise to keep it really short."

The woman's aged face didn't change as she reluctantly nodded.

I told her everything from the moment that the old man slithered into our lives to the second that I had been shackled into the chair I was sitting in. I kept it short, but laid everything out so that she could judge for herself. The only thing I initially omitted was what Tom did to me. When I was finished, I could tell from the look on her worn face that nothing I said accounted for the marks on my face and neck.

"One question, Mr. Reid," she began. "If you didn't touch your wife, how do you explain those injuries?" She used the eraser end of the pencil to point to the marks on my neck and face and hands.

"I'm sorry, but I can't...," I began, seeking to change the direction of the conversation. She didn't give me an inch.

"You need to understand two things. One, as I suggested up front, I'm going to defend you to the best of my ability regardless of whether you're guilty or innocent. Two, as it is equally imperative for you to understand, everything you tell me is bound by attorney/client privilege. Our conversations are not admissible in a court of law. You can tell me that you killed your wife, but that statement will not see the light of day and will not affect my efforts to defend you. Is that clear? Now, how did you get those marks? What you say may help me deflect the DA's interest in them—and the DA will be interested. You won't be able to hide what's on the police photographs or in the police reports."

I looked at her and, for a few seconds, wondered if the criminal cases she had handled had psychologically incised the lines and furrows across her forehead and under her eyes. When she started to stir, I gave in. I guess I had reached a point in which I simply couldn't hold back, especially if it helped me to get out of this obscene place. I noted that I probably looked much worse in the police photographs, and I described with great reluctance the origin of the marks and what had happened at Tom's house. I emphasized that Tom wasn't a "bad guy" and that I may have called down some of the violence on myself. Nevertheless, I wasn't willing to expose Tom's actions in any forum in which he could be hurt as a result. "However this shakes out," I insisted, "He's still my brother and I love him more than life itself. He's all I got left."

"Understood," she replied and slipped the notebook back into her briefcase, which was at her side on the floor. I thought that she was packing up to leave—after all, she claimed to have had limited time to engage with me—instead, she pulled out a yellow legal pad and made notes on it while asking me questions about my arrest, what the police said to me, and what they did to me while in custody. When it appeared that we were finally coming to an end, she offered what she called some strong advice. "I don't want you to say anything to anyone about our conversation or about what had happened to you. As a general rule, you don't have to tell the police anything that might incriminate you. When you continued talking after they read you your rights, you were putting everything you said into the record and building a case for them. Do you understand?"

"I guess."

She dropped her legal pad into her briefcase. But instead of getting up and leaving, she paused and, after a few seconds of silent meditation, asked me where the police had found the body.

"Pardon?"

"The body of your wife. Did they tell you that they found it?"

"They didn't tell me. The detective accused me of dumping her body somewhere, and he wanted me to tell him and the others where it is. There were two other policemen in the room. I couldn't tell him, because I didn't do it. You have to believe me. In the heat of things, I might have been happy to see her dead, but I didn't touch her. I told you, I'm not that kind of person."

"Are you sure they asked you that?"

"Absolutely. They said they could prove everything with my bat, though I'm not sure they've finished analyzing it for blood stains. They would have told me, right? But I don't know how blood could have gotten on it. Resin, yes. It has kind of a reddish stain. But blood? I haven't played with it in years, not since I was a child. My brother gave it to me as a souvenir. I told the police I didn't know where it was."

"Are you sure about what they said?"

"One hundred percent."

"Where'd they get the bat? You didn't give it to them, did you?"

"No. They said they found it inside my house. I don't know where they found it. Like I said, I haven't seen it in years."

"Did you confirm the bat was yours?"

"No, they didn't show it to me."

She pulled out her yellow pad again and scribbled something into it. "I don't understand," she said with a bewildered look on her tired face. "They don't have a body, and so how did the issue of the bat come up? Did you tell them about the bat?"

"No. They asked me about the bat, but I couldn't tell them anything about it."

She eyed me critically, her mouth hanging on one side and her penciled-in eyebrows raised. "Let's be clear about this. They said they found it in your house. Did you give them permission to search your house?"

"They didn't ask. I didn't know they had been there until they told me. The detective brought up the subject of the bat, not me."

"Are you sure about this? Are you sure you've told me everything?"

"Yes, absolutely. Did I make a mistake?"

She shook her head, wrote something else on her yellow pad and then dropped it and her mechanical pencil back into her briefcase. "No, not at all. But from now on, don't say anything else to them. You do not have to speak to them without your counsel, me, at your side. Do you understand? Did you say anything about this to anyone else?"

"I didn't think about it until just now."

She reached for the handle of her briefcase, and then set it back down. Sitting upright with her arms across her sunken chest, she asked me to repeat what I had already told her. "This time, think back about your interactions with the police. Don't look at the guard. He can't say anything. Tell me again what they actually said. Tell me what the detective said before he started asking you questions. Don't worry, I've got time for this."

Shortly after I began, she retrieved her yellow pad and mechanical pencil. We spoke for maybe two or three hours more. During this time, she peppered me with question after question and, when we were done, she told me to sit tight (presumably in my cell) and that my case could be resolved sooner than expected. When she left, two different guards led me back to my cell, where a new tray of food awaited me on the floor. This time the food looked untouched.

The following afternoon, Counsellor Rondell and a rather heavyset guard that I hadn't seen before came into my cell. The guard silently and gently removed my shackles, and he and my attorney escorted me down a long hallway lined with cells occupied by jeering, sometimes spitting inmates and led me into a lobby-like area where I was "processed," given back the things that had been taken from me when I was brought to this place, and finally allowed to walk out of the heavy, metal front door on my own. Once outside, my attorney smiled and shook my hand.

"It's over. There's currently no evidence against you. There's no evidence that your wife was killed, and, regardless of what's on your bat, the police seized it illegally. There's nothing on which to hold you. Consider yourself very lucky. It could have gone the other way. My recommendation is that you go home and keep a low profile."

An unusual feeling engulfed me. For what seemed to be the first time in my life, I felt free, truly free. All the problems that had been darkening my life–from Tara's absence to the old man's presence–were finally behind me, locked away in the cell that I had fortunately vacated. Tara was probably alive somewhere, and while I knew that the old man would be up to no good as long as he was living, I sensed that with my incarceration, I was no longer the object of his attention. My imprisonment had been his way of destroying me and, having accomplished this, he had moved onto other execrable things. Breathing the fresh and unencumbered air, I was ready to go out and enjoy what other free people enjoyed–exotic food, engaging company, exciting entertainment, and all the rest. Turning to my attorney, who now seemed smaller than she did before (probably because we spent most of our time together at eye level), I thanked her profusely for what she did for me and then watched her step off the sidewalk and hail a cab. When the cab was out of sight, I started to walk away from the building (I was going to take a short walk to find a good place to eat) when two uniformed police officers and a suit-wearing detective approached me.

"Mr. James Reid?" the detective asked. When I nodded affirmatively, he said, "Mr. Reid, you are under arrest for the murder of Thomas Reid."

25

Since my original attorney wasn't available (or hadn't heard of my second arrest), I was assigned representation from a different firm. He was a pleasant, idealistic young man who, if I remember correctly, had just passed his bar exam. I don't recall a lot about him, though. I think he spent most of his time unsuccessfully fighting the court's ruling on bail (it was astronomically high). One of the few vivid memories of him that I still have is watching him on the other side of the table scribbling into his yellow pad the details of my arrest. But he seemed far less concerned about the true reasons behind my incarceration. He wasn't interested in what the old man was doing to me, for example, and he dismissed with a quick shake of his small head the evidence I proffered to prove that the old man was the only one with the motive, the opportunity, and the whatever to have killed Tom. Had he only stopped scribbling for a few minutes and actually listened to me, I am convinced that he could have crafted a defense that would liberated me from my hellhole and defined his fledgling career. Admittedly, I contributed to his failure, for I was pretty much useless during most of the hours we spent together. When I wasn't in a deep funk over Tom's death, I was raging over the kind of justice system that could be manipulated into incarcerating an innocent man while letting a murderer go free to prey on other innocent people. I guess he didn't understand that what I needed more than his legal services was someone to help me cope with the loss of my beloved brother, and the only thing that the prison could do was offer a different cell or the services of an idiotic priest who insisted that my suffering could be alleviated by converting to his ignorant fantasies. I chose the former. If there was a positive side to my situation, I suppose it was this: My shackles were removed, and I was allowed to move around in my cell just like any other prisoner.

Sometime later–three days, three months, three years, I couldn't say–the young man was removed from the case and replaced with a much older, more seasoned attorney by the name of Ted Baker, or Baker, as he liked to be called. Baker, a large, heavyset fellow who breathed noisily and sweated profusely, had been in the "business" for over forty years and, as he frequently said in his bass voice, had seen it all, "twice over." He didn't smile, or at least I never saw anything like a smile on his sagging face, but he was a genuinely pleasant man and had a way of engaging and probing me with his big, basset-hound eyes that encouraged me even in the darkest times to talk. At his pleasant, almost monotonous insistence, I gave him everything–everything that I knew about my family, my brother, and especially the old man. Baker understood–he'd seen it all, after all, and "twice over"–and with his gracious help (and I should underline that he was as concerned about me and how I was holding up behind bars as he was about my case and ensuring that justice was done), I pulled myself together and came to grips with Tom's untimely demise. This is not to say that I accepted it. I couldn't do that, but at least I became rational enough to know that my shouting and moaning wouldn't do anything to bring him back to me, and I knew that if I wanted justice–if I wanted to make sure that his death wasn't just another meaningless statistic–then I had to work with Baker to the fullest of my ability. During the first of our many productive sessions, I felt comfortable enough with Baker to tell him about the suffering I had endured throughout the years without a father and about the pain I was experiencing because the old man was pretending to be our father.

"It's clear," Baker huffed sometime later in the conversation, "The old man is the key to our defense." I was pleased with his statement. He was the first person to understand my situation, and I was satisfied with his characterization of my defense as "our defense," for it helped me that I wasn't alone like I had been during Tom's last days and that my case, my situation, was as important to somebody else as it was to me. One time, during one of our more recent sessions, I asked him what he was going to do once our case was over. I wanted to know more about the man who was the key to my longevity. He rose clumsily and, shakily grasping the top of his chair to keep from collapsing, assured me that he was going to see our case to the end and, after that, consider retirement. "I've been in this business far too long. I'd like to spend some time in Reno and really enjoy gambling for a change."

Despite his preposterous, rumpled appearance, Baker's legal mind was as sharp as a tack. He saw through what the police had either missed or misrepresented. For example, contrary to police assertions, there were some serious questions about what I think was termed due process (it may have been something else, for I couldn't keep up with Baker's blather of legal terms and precedents). Had I been arrested because I was the only credible suspect of a crime or because the police were eager pin something on me after failing to get me on Tara's murder? While the court was deliberating on this, my attorney had brought up another set of serious questions that forced some additional deliberations. Had the police considered all the possibilities why blood might be on the pavement next to Tom's house? My explanation was the only reasonable one. Tests proved that it was my blood on the outside pavement, not

Tom's. The blood he shed from the brutal assault was inside the house, not outside. Then there was the old man himself. He was missing. Why hadn't the police looked for him? He was, after all, the core of my defense. And why hadn't the police looked into my allegation that the old man had waged a systematic effort to upend my entire world, beginning with his behavior at the hospital (why hadn't they checked the hospital records for his stay?) and continuing with his efforts to turn Tom against me, his destructive acquisition of my firm, and his success in ripping apart my marriage? Did the police really think this was all irrelevant? If this weren't enough, where was the evidence concerning Tara's death that had been taken from my home? A different case, of course, but the two cases were related, and any evidence which suggested that the old man had killed her might have weighed in my favor with the current case. But while the police and the DA's office were reeling and rationalizing the gaps, Baker obtained evidence that virtually eliminated my bouts of melancholy and psychosis–he got copies of the hospital records of the man who purported to be William "Bill" Reid. This was enough proof, contrary to what the police had been asserting, that such a man actually existed. Naturally, the proof didn't demonstrate that the identity was either true or false (my attorney was working to show that the man had stolen Reid's identity) or that William "Bill" Reid had anything to do with me or Tom's murder. It was only a first step, but it was a first step that the police and the DA's office, in their misjudgment, had difficulty accepting.

Shortly after this, there was another major break in the case.

26

According to one of Baker's sources, Belinda Reid admitted during another police interview that a William "Bill" Reid had been living at her house for quite some time before leaving for reasons and places unknown. She claimed not to know of his whereabouts at the current time, and she also stressed that they had not been in communication for several weeks, or, as I mentally calculated, from the time that Tom was beaten. While she spoke highly of the old man as a houseguest and as the father of Tom and me, she admitted that she didn't know much about him. She didn't even know what he did for a living or who his friends, if any, were. Belinda also confessed that he and Tom may have been involved in a business deal or two, but she stressed, implausibly, that she couldn't provide details because she wasn't privy to her husband's professional affairs. With a weak backhanded motion, the DA dismissed this evidence as irrelevant, and he suggested that my attorney was merely using the old fraud to deflect culpability from where it should properly belong–that is, me. Baker, breathing heavily and using a linen handkerchief to wipe the sweat from his forehead, insisted that this wasn't the last word, and he said that he had engaged the services of a consultant (the private detective that his firm had on retainer) to locate and identify the old man and to expose the "business activities" that he was allegedly engaged in. Baker felt certain that if the old man were found and brought in for questioning, then the truth would be revealed–and, I had to believe, my release would be imminent. In my excitement over these modest successes, I failed to consider the possibility that with each step forward in my case, there might be two steps back that could either delay progress or derail it altogether.

"Now that the DA's office believes the old man, or at least someone calling himself Bill Reid, actually exists," Baker said to me one uncomfortably warm afternoon (the air conditioning system in the interview room must have been turned off), "They're using Belinda to prove he's harmless and irrelevant." His chair groaned pathetically as he adjusted his huge body. "She insists that there was nothing but a warm, loving relationship between Tom and the man he called his father, and therefore it doesn't make sense that he would do something so senseless to your brother."

"It makes more sense that I would kill my own brother?"

"In a manner of speaking," he replied while taking a deep breath and again mopping the sweat from his thick brow. "Fathers do kill their sons at times, but they're far more like to torture them and then abandon them. You know what I'm talking about. Vicious fights between close relatives, siblings killing siblings, brothers at each other's throats...I have to tell you, it's far more common than you think. In murder cases, secondary relatives are often the prime suspects."

"Incredible."

"We'll try to wean everyone from this unfortunate assumption."

There was a momentary pause while we both sought something less painful to discuss. "If Tara is dead," I offered, emphasizing the verb, "I'll bet dollars to donuts the old man killed her, too."

"Why?" The inside corners of his eyebrows rose, and a strange, perplexed look came across his puffy face.

"He's a violent man, that's why. Remember, he threatened me on more than one occasion. But Tom didn't believe it. Neither did Tara. Belinda...she's so besotted by him that she entrusted her daughter to him. Insane, isn't it? I tried to tell them, many times, and they always refused to listen. They always had excuses for his reprehensible behavior. But who had the motive and the opportunity to go after Tom and Tara if it wasn't him? Sure, Tom had enemies, and Tara was surrounded by crazies. That's the price of success. I can tell you, though, neither of them had the kind of enemies that would do something like..." I stopped. Tears filled my eyes and I briefly turned away. "If it wasn't the old man," I continued when I was under control, "then you tell me who it was."

"I don't know. But alive or dead, I'm almost positive the DA's going to use her against us. He dropped the ball the first time, and he's too smart to make the same mistakes he made then. You should know there could be additional charges."

"All right, but we've got to show the DA and everyone else that the old man is a murderous phony and scoundrel."

"We'll try. It's not going to be easy, not with all the support he got from your family."

Baker paused, and his normally placid features seemed strained, as if something terrible had unexpectedly come to mind. "Jim, I got to level with you," he wheezed. "Even though we're making positive progress, everything could end up hinging on the old man. Unless we can uncover his true identity and his motivations, we could be up the proverbial creek without a paddle."

I respected Baker's openness. When he spoke, I knew without a doubt that nothing was hidden and that things were exactly as he described. But this wasn't the moment that I wanted brutal honesty. Given everything that was happening to me, I would have preferred words that were a little less direct and a little more upbeat.

"All right," I began with a great deal of reluctance. "How about…how about digging deeper into Tom's finances." I wasn't comfortable suggesting this. I felt as if I were betraying my brother. But after Baker's words, I started to become a little desperate, and I told myself that it was impossible to betray a dead man.

Baker stopped writing and looked at me. "Are you sure?"

"Now I am."

"I mean about your brother. We could find something unpleasant."

"It's critical to the defense, right?"

"It certainly looks like it. Before we get too optimistic, I have to tell you that it's going to be a little tricky. His business interests could be intertwined with Belinda's, and she hasn't been charged with anything. I know, she claims to be ignorant of her husband's business, but we're going to have to do some digging to determine how uninvolved she actually is."

"How about the private detective? Has he come up with anything about the old man?"

"One thing at a time. He came up with everything we know so far. I haven't spoken to him in a couple days, so I'm not quite sure what else he has. Don't worry, he's good, and when he's ready, he'll give us the scoop."

"Aren't the hospital records enough? There's got to be a lot there we can use. Blood type, DNA, and I don't know what else. Skin samples, maybe. Do you think they took dental records?"

Baker cleared a deep obstruction in his throat. "The morgue takes dental records, and as far as anyone knows, he's still alive. All we were able to glean from the hospital was essentially a name and the time of stay. It's valuable information, it confirms that someone calling himself Bill Reid was there, but it's not enough to make a connection between this Bill Reid and the old man, and it's not enough to connect the old man with anyone if we can't get his real name. Right now, we need more information, but you can rest assured we're working on it."

I had a feeling, judging by the harried look under his overhanging brows, that my situation might even be worse that he had earlier led me to believe. "Use your detective to find my father," I pleaded. "If he's dead, then we can at least show the old man's a fraud. Wasn't there a social security number in the hospital records? I don't know what our father's social was, but surely that would tell us quite a bit. What is your detective doing if he can't find that?"

"The social wasn't available. I should tell you," he said, using the handkerchief to wipe the sweat from his forehead, "I should tell you that he's overworked, and we don't have unlimited funds to pay him. But, yes, I'll keep pushing him to see what else he can come up with."

"How about crowdsourcing? I mean, to get him the money he needs to do his job right."

Groaning, Baker slowly pushed his large bulk up and out of the chair. Before he took two thunderous steps, he turned and silently looked at me. I thought for a moment that he was simply catching his breath. "How are you holding up?" he asked. "It's been pretty stressful, hasn't it?"

I was touched by the sincerity of his inquiry. "Some nights are bad. But I can deal with anything as long as you get the old man–and get him before he gets me."

He nodded, and there was something on his face that suggested that he would have reached over and patted me fraternally on the shoulder had he been allowed to do so. I didn't hear from him for several days after that.

27

I tried to remain calm during Baker's absence and ignore everything around me, including the jail's foul smell and the unnerving, nighttime shrieks of one of my neighbors. I told myself that everything was going well and that it was only a matter of time before the nightmare finally ended. And yet I couldn't help wondering if something had gone wrong or, worse, if the old man had run a charm offensive on him and he was no longer my advocate. When I finally saw Baker lumbering into our meeting room and slowly approaching the table, however, I was relieved. I almost cried. I could see, or I thought I could see, proof that he was still in my corner and that if he had encountered the old man, the old man hadn't been victorious. How could I see such a subtle thing in Baker without a single word being exchanged? Simple. There was nothing in Baker's sagging face or in his slow, ponderous mannerisms to suggest that something had significantly changed. He was the same person that he had always been.

"I've got interesting news," he gasped as he slowly eased his massive bulk into the squawking chair on the other side of the table. It was clearly important news, because it wouldn't wait until he was finally settled in. "I've got interesting news," he repeated once he was ready and had a legal pad and a ballpoint pen on the table in front of him. "Well, I suppose whether it's good or not depends on how you look at it."

"I was worried." I promised myself that I would remain as calm and professional as he was, but an instant later I couldn't help blubbering, "I...I wasn't sure you were coming back. You don't know how it is here, alone and...anyway, I know the case is a bad one. I'm innocent, though. I swear on my brother's life. I didn't hurt anybody. Baker, you've got to understand. You're all I got." I glanced at the pimple-faced guard, who was fiddling at something on the front of his shirt.

"Let's not panic before we need to. I'm ready to pursue the case to at least its initial conclusion."

"Okay." I nodded hesitantly, not wanting to hear what he meant by the 'initial conclusion.' "Okay, okay, so what's the news? Don't tell me if it's really bad news. No, I guess bad news is better than no news, right? I mean, even if it's bad news, we can work with it, can't we? What do you do with no news? No news is nothing. You can't deal with nothing. Nothing is..."

Baker took several deep breaths before beginning. "I should have reached out sooner, but we were running down some possible leads. More importantly,

I was at the DA's office today, and I caught wind of something very interesting. I don't quite know what to make of it." He pulled out a large handkerchief and wiped the moisture from his face. "While we were there…" He paused again, this time to clear his throat and rub his heavy chin with his thick fingers.

"What is it?" I urged him on. "I can take bad news."

"Your bail…"

"I know, it's a lot of money. It's more money than I make in a year."

"Yes, it sure is. The interesting thing is that someone's putting up the cash. You could be out in two or three days."

I leaned back and stared hard at his pliable facial features. I couldn't tell if he was joking or telling the truth. When he nodded to confirm what he had just told me, I felt like jumping up and screaming at the walls and bars, and at the other inmates in their cells, that I was leaving and that the prison facility and the prison authorities could all go fuck themselves. I didn't, of course. The guard would have been on me in seconds.

"God, are you sure? Of course, you are. I can't believe it. I don't know why it took this long, but who cares? Why the long face? This is wonderful."

Baker was silent, and for a few seconds I thought that he might actually smile and congratulate me on my good fortune. He didn't do either.

"It's wonderful," I repeated. "It's wonderful. No, it's more than wonderful. I don't have a word for it. So, who's bailing me out? Your firm?"

"Like you said, it's a hell of a lot of money," Baker replied and shook his head slowly. "We don't have the cash."

I leaned as far back in my chair as I could and stretched out my legs. It's hard to describe my feelings at that moment. I was finally going to be set free. I had endured incarceration, the guards and the other prisoners, and all the other indignities of prison life for what felt like years, and I was now going to be leaving all of it. I was going to be getting my life back. I was so excited that I failed to consider the possibility that my freedom might be temporary. I didn't consider much of anything, except getting out of my fetid-smelling cell and enjoying the streets and the people and the food. It occurred to me that there was a breakfast place not far from the jail that advertised real buttermilk pancakes. I had to go there. I had to have something other than the slop they fed us on the good days, and I was practically salivating over a large plate of pancakes, scrambled eggs, and hash browns when I glanced at Baker and noticed that his eyebrows and lips were drooping more than usual.

"What's the matter?" I asked, slowly coming back to the real world. "This is great news. I'm going to be free. We're coming to the end of this madness."

"No," he breathed heavily. "The madness isn't over. The bail only means you'll have temporary freedom with a lot of restrictions. It has nothing to do with dropping the charges or winning the case. I know it seems like I've been working the case for quite some time, but…" He took a big gulp of air. "But we still have a long way to go."

"Okay, but even if my release is temporary, it's still a good thing, isn't it? How can it not be? And if you fix everything while I'm out, it would mean that I didn't have to go back, right? What's bad about that?"

"Nothing, I suppose."

"I don't understand. What's the problem?"

Baker was silent for a few moments and stared at me as if he wasn't sure about something. "The problem is with the money. We don't know who's putting it up."

"Really? Does it matter? A good Samaritan is putting it up."

"Perhaps," Baker ponderously agreed.

"What is it? Am I missing something?"

"Well, there's more. We have some new information that might be important." Baker seemed even less enthused about this information than he was about the bail money.

"Did you find the old man? It was only a matter of time. This will change everything."

Baker adjusted his bulk as if it might take a long time to lay out the details. "Not exactly. My detective ran a few preliminary background searches on your brother, and there wasn't a lot there. No recent arrests, warrants, or convictions. Tom had a speeding ticket a few years ago as well as a smattering of parking tickets, but that was about it. Nothing serious in this fluff. It's rather commonplace given the kinds of resources we have to work with. Something else came up, though, that's a little more disconcerting."

"It can't be anything bad. Tom liked to talk tough about his competitors, other businesses, and I don't know what else. It was all boardroom posturing. The kind of stuff that businessmen use when they're trying make people believe they're tough and masculine. You can't take it seriously. Despite our scuffle, Tom wasn't a mean person. He was strong and confident, but he wasn't a criminal. There can't be anything bad about him."

Baker nodded contemplatively. For a moment, I couldn't tell if he actually believed me or was merely humoring me. He sighed and adjusted his round shoulders as if they were sore. "These searches, as I said, were fluff, in other words, merely preliminary. I have another source in the DA's office who told me about an investigation into several individuals associated with organized crime. What's disconcerting is that over the past year or so, your brother's name came up in connection with a number of these individuals. According to my source, Tom appeared to have been serving as a front for some of their illicit activities, though the extent of his participation is unknown at this point."

"Are you sure it's Tom? It's probably the old man. He appropriated our father's name. He could have appropriated Tom's."

"It was your brother."

"And they're still investigating him? I mean, why would they continue to investigate him now?"

"I don't know. It's true the DA can't do anything to Tom, but he might be interested in these other individuals, and Tom's relationship with them could help make connections that he wouldn't have otherwise been able to make."

"Fine, I'm not sure I believe it. But why does that matter in terms of the case?"

"It might not. But a jury might be persuaded that if your brother is involved in this kind of business, it only stands to reason that you are, too."

"Wait a minute. The people the DA's investigating, is one of them the old man?"

The thick furrows overhanging his eyes momentarily levitated. "It's possible. It appears that one of the individuals is a character called Bill Reid. Now, before you jump to conclusions, I have to tell you that we got this verbally from our contact. We haven't been able to confirm the spelling of the person's last name or even if we got the name right. We're working on it–this is one of the reasons that I've been away– but we're still a long way from confirming the name and making the connection to the old man." He inhaled deeply and a long, leisurely exhale.

"It's got to be the old man," I insisted. "Who else could it be? He's using the name, and I saw him with those people. Did you check criminal records?"

"It's not quite that simple. We need to verify his name and identify first. We've done some Internet searches for a Bill Reid. Do you have any idea how many people in this world are named Bill Reid or some variation of the name?"

"Are there pictures? I can identify him through a picture."

"We're working on it."

I stared at Baker for a moment without really seeing him. "You know, when Tom and I supposedly met the old man for the first time at the hospital, there was something peculiar about that meeting. I had the feeling that Tom and the old man were practically friends and that the meeting was staged for my benefit.

Maybe Tom was introducing me to the old man so that he could be more open about his dealings with him. Maybe he wanted me to get involved, too. He kept telling me what a great guy the old man was and that I'd love him, too, once I got to know him. How about Tom's friends? What have you been able to find out about them?"

"Slow down. First things first. We need to identify the old man in order to connect him to Tom and the possible criminal elements at your brother's house." He shakily wiped his mouth with his handkerchief he coaxed out from the inside of his jacket. "Once we make this connection, we'll hopefully be in a position to show that the old man was the kind of person who could commit a terrible crime and that he was well-positioned to kill your brother. Belinda, of course, will state that a Bill Reid was living at her house, but this might not be enough to link her Bill Reid to your old man, much less demonstrate the old man's criminal tendencies. We've got to be careful here, otherwise we'll end up making the case for the prosecution. Tell me again: How long had he been staying at the house before Tom was killed?"

"Too long."

"Did your brother feel threatened? His wife and child were in the same house at the same time. If they weren't prisoners, then their statements about the old man will be the only ones sticking with the jury. Do you see what I'm getting at?"

"I suppose. But I'd bet my life that he's a criminal, and I have no doubt that he was one of the criminal types that were at Tom's house."

"Unfortunately, you are."

"I'm what?"

"You're betting your life."

A shiver ran down my spine, and I told myself that I shouldn't have gone with Tom to see the old man at the hospital. I should have stayed home, and…and…but it wouldn't have changed anything. I would have been pulled into this morass regardless. "If you can get the information you need, I'm positive everything will fall into place. It'll be as simple as one plus one."

"I hope so." Baker half-coughed, half-cleared his throat, the sound resembling a rumbling coming from a deep tunnel. "I'm afraid we've exhausted most of our resources. If we could get him in a lineup, possibly. But I don't know who could identify him."

"What do you mean? I could identify him anywhere."

"Your identification won't mean much under these circumstances. You're accusing him of a crime of which you have no first-, second-, or even third-hand knowledge. A single witness, even a bad witness, is worth more than that. It's got to be someone who had actually seen what had happened. Do you see what I'm getting at?"

"Sure," I said with hesitation.

"You have to know," Baker added after inhaling deeply, "Belinda will also testify that you and your brother were constantly arguing and that when things got out of control, you took it out on your brother. I don't know what Tara's going to say when she comes ashore."

"Do you think she's still alive?" There was a moment of hope followed by the thought that I didn't care.

"I don't have the slightest idea. But if she's anything like the person you described, I hope she doesn't return until our case is over. Right now, though, we're also trying to understand more about your brother's connections with criminals. If we can't implicate the old man, we may be able to premise your brother's death on a deal gone south or something like that."

I agreed with a slow nod of my head. I reminded myself that I wasn't betraying my brother and that if he had been connected with criminals, then it was his own fault if his posthumous reputation got sullied.

Baker, sensing my internal conflicts, explained. "It'll work like this. Your brother had fallen in with some questionable business associates. He may have been ignorant about who these people really were. Business, after all, is business, right? He was accustomed to questioning businesses, but not business people. It's standard practice among business people. Do you investigate your neighbors, your children's teachers, the people who mow your lawn? Do you see where I'm going? Anyway, you, Jim, went into your brother's house like you always did and found yourself in the midst of a strange meeting. Your brother was upset by your unexpected presence. From his perspective, you were inadvertently interrupting what could have been a once-in-a-lifetime business agreement. It was a sensitive deal, touch and go at times, and maybe he didn't recognize anything underhanded about the venture. It was too big to examine head on. One of the participants at the meeting, a career criminal if there ever was one, was afraid that Tom couldn't control the people around him—you or others like you could expose the undertaking for what it was—and decided on the spot that Tom himself couldn't be trusted and, as often happens in these kinds of illegal deals, took it out on your brother. He bludgeoned Tom to death. It doesn't make sense but, like I said, it's not uncommon in these sorts of rarefied circles. Don't worry, if we can connect the old man to any of this, we certainly will. So, what do you think? About our defense, I mean."

I closed my eyes for a few seconds to calm my nerves. "Every time someone gets close to catching the old man," I replied, looking into Baker's eyes, "He manages to slither away untouched. Look, Tom did whatever Tom did, but I hope we can at least hold the old man accountable for what he did, and I'm almost positive that whatever Tom was involved in had to be at the instigation of the old man. You see that, don't you?"

"We might get more information that will solve our problem. But until that happens, we don't have a lot of viable options."

"I sat up. "For God's sake," I practically hollered, "Why isn't your detective working harder to find something on the old man? Why do I always have to prove my innocence?"

The guard grumbled and took a few steps toward me before Baker waved him off with a slow, paddle-like motion of his right arm and hand. "It's all right," he said to the guard. "He has a right to be upset."

The guard said something that I didn't catch.

"But what I believe doesn't matter. Look, contrary to what you've been taught in school, our justice system isn't about uncovering the truth. It's not about establishing guilt or, as people wrongly assume, innocence. Our justice system is nothing more than a debate club, one with the same kinds of rules as every other debate club, and the goal of this and all the other debate clubs is simply to win the debate. Truth is irrelevant, especially if it's unfavorable. You need to understand that to win this debate against the DA, we need to be prepared to do it with or without the old man. If we prevail without implicating the old man, you'll have the opportunity to seek justice through some other means."

I looked down and shook my head. While Baker was breathing heavily and wiping the sweat from his face, something else came to me. I again leaned forward and this time asked him, "Are you sure about Tara. Are you sure she hasn't been picked up? She could corroborate everything I said, if she isn't trying to protect the old man. If she's found, there's got to be serums or punishments that will force the truth from her."

"Not in this country. Once again, we don't know if she's alive or dead. I asked my source at the DA, but he didn't have anything on her." Baker adjusted his feet and dabbed the corners of his mouth with his handkerchief. "I suppose you know that Tara was employed by your brother or your brother's company."

"She was employed there when I met her, but not after that. She was a trained psychologist…"

"We couldn't confirm it. All we could confirm was she studied accounting in school, and until her disappearance she apparently worked on the financial side of your brother's business."

"He said he gave…" I couldn't finish.

"What are you talking about?"

I shrugged my shoulders noncommittally. "Are you investigating her, too?"

"Not really, at least not right now. We came across the information while following a line on your brother. We're not giving up on the old man, but we also have to keep our facts straight. My bet is that the DA knows everything we know about Tara."

That was it. I was mentally and emotionally exhausted. I had nothing else to contribute.

Baker understood this, I think, and he struggled up onto his feet. "Well, that's about all for now," he said, breathing deeply. "We'll talk more later. I'll see you tomorrow or whenever your bail is posted."

28

I was up early the following morning and allowed to dress in the clothes that I had been arrested in. I was then instructed to wait in my cell until someone came to escort me to the courthouse. Late in the afternoon, I was awoken from a nap and taken to the courthouse where I was placed next to Baker at the defendant's table. The legal proceedings were a blur, and after we left the courtroom, Baker tossed a heavy coat over my head as a "precaution" and, breathing laboriously, walked me to an awaiting car. Baker's detective, as I learned later, was behind the wheel, and in no time we pulled up in front of a tall, shimmering apartment building and rode the glass-enclosed elevator to the tenth floor, where Baker lived in a large and luxurious apartment. Baker informed me that he wasn't married (though he did have a grown son, who practiced law in another city) and that his significant other lived out of state. He gave me the temporary use of a large bedroom, one wall of which was a bank of windows that looked out onto a noted park.

After placing my small bag of possessions on the floor near the foot of the bed, I washed my hands and face and then met Baker and his detective at a long, ornate wooden table in the dining room. My first interaction with Phil was, as I noted, in the car. At that time, I could only see the back of his head. He could have been anybody then, but as I looked closer at him in Baker's apartment, I could see that he was probably in his mid-forties, had pronounced lines skidding across his forehead and radiating outward from the edges of his narrow eyes, and was very thin and very tall, much thinner and taller than me. Phil's black, featureless clothing seemed to match the dourness of his facial expression and his overall lack of physical movement. At times, he seemed to move about as much as an old tree.

I started to thank Baker again for all his efforts on my behalf, but he waved me off and insisted that we had more pressing things to attend to.

"Things are moving in directions that I cannot fully understand or control," he began, looking down at his lap while Phil eyed me. "The bail situation is troublesome. Who the hell put up the money? Why did he or she do it? We had started to think that we might be on the verge of something in terms of identifying the old man, but we ran into a complete roadblock. We can't find him or verify his existence. And let's not even talk about Tara. That's a potential headache in itself. Phil, do you have anything to add?"

Phil shook his head silently and unsmilingly.

"I don't understand," I replied, glancing at Phil and then looking directly at Baker. "I agree, the money is strange, but I don't know any more about it than you do. I don't know why it matters. Money is money. I also don't understand why you haven't been able to place the old man among the crooks at Tom's house. I don't know why there's any doubt that the old man duped Tom into meeting those people. Haven't I given you enough about Tom and the old man to make your case? Christ, if it hadn't for the old man, none of this would have happened, and Tom would still be alive." Something dark and vague tugged at the back of my mind. "I don't want to talk about Tara anymore."

"Is there something you're not telling me?" he asked, narrowing his eyes at me.

"No, of course not. Do you think I'm lying to you?"

Baker took a deep breath of air, which seemed to calm him. "I'm just annoyed, that's all. Our case is frustrating, though I suppose most cases are frustrating at some point. We haven't lost yet."

"How frustrating are you talking about?"

"I wish I could have given you a better sense of things while you were incarcerated."

"What? I don't understand."

"I didn't feel comfortable talking in front of the guard."

"I thought…"

"I didn't want to worry you. I didn't trust him."

"What?"

"You never know these days. Look, besides the murder of your brother, the DA and his minions are working overtime…"

"Minions?"

"The police. They don't want another embarrassment on their hands, and so they're out to get you one way or another. My source says they're trying to connect you to the criminals your brother was working with. Except at the very end, you were close to your brother, and in their eyes it doesn't make sense that you could be shoulder-to-shoulder with Tom and not be involved in his business activities. Tara's still one of the cards in their hands. Just because the charges were dropped doesn't mean that you can't be tried for her murder if new evidence unexpectedly crops up. We're facing a Greek phalanx with the DA's office, and so we have to find a way to counter their resources and put them on the defensive. I guess I'm rambling. I'm frustrated that we can't even find out who posted your bail. The bail could have a significant bearing on this case. Are you sure you don't know anyone who might have posted it?"

"No, only my brother, and he…"

"Belinda?"

"In a pig's eye. She still believes I attacked him. I wouldn't be surprised if she's using her money to dig up dirt on me."

"Is she going to find any?"

"No, absolutely not. But that doesn't mean that she can't spend a million to find or invent something."

"Yeah, I suppose. You can't give me anything more on Tara, can you?"

"Nothing that you don't already know. Besides, she wouldn't have any more money than I do."

Baker nodded and silently gazed at something on the floor. "Fine," he said as much to himself as to me. "Fine," he added, this time looking directly at me. "We'll figure it all out sooner or later. In the meantime, Phil and I need to get back to work."

"Wait. What do I do now? Now that I'm free, I can help. Can I go with you to meet your sources?"

"No way. If you want to help, stay inside here and relax. The outside world's not a safe place for you at the moment, and I don't want you taking one step out of this place until we know what we're dealing with. Clear?"

Baker slowly looked at Phil, and the latter pulled a cell phone out of the inner pocket of his suit coat and handed it to him. Taking a deep breath, Baker handed it to me. "I know you're going to be safe here, but I want you to keep this by your side. This phone will only be used by you and me–and only by you and me. No calls to anyone else. Turn off your phone, if you have one, and don't use the phones in the apartment. You know what I'm saying?"

"I guess."

Baker nodded to Phil. Phil, who reminded me of a coatrack covered by a detective's trench coat, silently got up and left.

"He's off to do his work," Baker said when he noticed me looking at Phil. "He'll be back a little later today to give us an update. While he's doing what he's doing, I have to make some phone calls and then do a little research of my own. We can talk later."

"In the meantime, I'm supposed to relax."

"Correct. You know where the bedroom is, and you can stretch out and watch TV in the living room. Remember, don't leave this place. Any problems whatsoever, use the cell phone I just gave you. Questions?"

I shook my head. Despite what he had just told me, I wanted to ask him how much longer it might be before there was some resolution in my case. I wanted to know how long I would have to stay at his apartment and when I could go back to my own home. I wanted to know when I could resume a normal life, one with friends, a job, and all the rest. I wanted to know when I could have a dog, because at that moment a dog seemed like the greatest thing in the world to have. I wanted more, including an assurance that I would never again have to sit behind bars, that I would never again be chained like an animal, and that I would never again experience the stench of the cells and the vileness of the both the prisoners and the guards. But I didn't ask these questions. I didn't ask anything at all. It was obvious that he was too busy to sit down and discuss the issues that were percolating in my consciousness; to be honest, I wasn't sure that I wanted answers to my questions if there was even the slightest chance that his answers would be unfavorable. I had more than my share of bad news lately, and I wasn't eager for any more. Baker's apartment at least gave me the sense that he believed me, and believed in me (and why host me if there was slightest chance that I deserved to be behind bars?), and at this moment I was willing to take this as a temporary answer to these pressing questions.

I watched Baker as he stuffed some papers into his old, beaten-up briefcase and, after again reminding me to stay put, he headed for the door.

"Wait a minute. I thought you were going to make some calls," I said, worried that I was losing my lifeline before I had a chance to become comfortable in his apartment.

"I am," he replied with a deep, labored breath and left. Seconds later, the door opened and he poked his elephantine head in. "Stay away from the windows," he added and closed the door, locking it from the outside.

The snap of the lock didn't trouble me. It was a familiar sound, and it was comforting to know that I was just as safe from the dangers lurking outside the apartment as I had been safe from the dangers lurking outside my cell. But as the minutes and seconds ticked off, I began to feel anxious and every now and then my hands and shoulders shook. I wasn't thinking about the possibility of facing significant jail time or reflecting on the destruction of my life. I was troubled by the silence in Baker's apartment. Unlike jail, there wasn't a sound anywhere–not the groaning of the foundation, not the hum of an electric appliance, not even the muffled voices of my neighbors–nothing to suggest that there was life outside of myself and my little space. I knew I wasn't alone. I knew there was a lively, vibrant city just outside Baker's windows, and yet it troubled me I couldn't hear a thing inside this beautiful palace–not the cars, not the people, and not the millions of other things that should permeate the walls and jolt the senses–and I wanted to hear these particular sounds. I wanted to see and hear the city in all its liveliness and feel what its bustling, decent people felt. Because I now had at least a modicum of freedom, I wanted to go out and shake an honest stranger's hand and ask him how his day was going. I wanted to be part of normal life again. I wanted to forget the stench of incarceration. I wanted to forget the groans of the prisoners and the shouts and howls that reverberated throughout the prison walls. I wanted to forget the tapping of the guard's shoes as they approached my cell and the coarse barks of the guards as they told me to do this and that or insisted that I "shut the fuck up" whenever I asked a simple question. I wanted my life back.

As I got up and went back into the bedroom to shower (the bathroom had an enormous marble-covered shower where one could sit down and experience the prickling of water from every direction except up), I noticed on the stand near the bed a stack of new clothes (slacks, shirt, socks, and underwear) that Baker had thoughtfully acquired and set out for me. Once I was clean and in new clothes (they all fit), I went into the kitchen and made myself a fine meal (lunch or dinner, I don't remember, but the refrigerator and cupboards were full), and stretched out on the couch watched TV as though I hadn't seen it in ages–as though it was something that only free men could enjoy. I don't know how long I had been alternately watching the mindless shows and dozing off when I noticed that it was getting dark inside the apartment. The outside windows were black, and the entire apartment was engulfed in a dusk that was alleviated only by the garish light emanating from the TV and the dull, overhead lights near the door. I got up and went around the apartment turning on all the lights that I could find, and then went back to the TV and did my best to relax

Since I didn't have a real sense of how long Baker had been gone (I hadn't checked the time when he left), I was beginning to feel a little uneasy that however long he had been gone, it was probably too long. I wasn't going off the deep end like I did in jail when I hadn't heard from Baker for several days, but because he had pumped me full of concerns before he left about my safety, I couldn't help being concerned about his own safety as he worked on my behalf. 'The old man,' I told myself, 'was willing to destroy Tom, Tara, and everyone at my office to get at me, and so it's not a stretch to believe that he might do the same to Baker if it served his purposes.' I angled my shoulders to remove the stiffness in them. 'But this is absurd,' I countered to the demon resting on my shoulder. 'If the old man didn't pay off the prison guards to reach me, then he's certainly not going to attempt anything against someone as visible as a court official.' To get all the suffocating, counterproductive thoughts out of my mind, I started flipping through the channels to find something distracting. After settling on a silly sitcom, I stretched out on the couch and promptly fell asleep.

I was still in grade school that day when Tom walked me home from school. Normally, he wouldn't have bothered, but he had heard from someone that two boys about his own age were going to accost me along the way and rough me up because I was a fatherless child. As planned, Tom hid behind some large bushes seconds before the boys appeared and started calling me names and telling me that our father wasn't coming back.

"Tommy says your old man ran away because he hated your guts," one of the two said as Tom quietly approached the boys from behind.

The taller of the two pushed me to the ground just as Tom snuck up behind him and grabbed him around the neck. He forced the boy to his knees and then face down in the dirt. Tom rubbed dirt violently into the boy's face and wouldn't let him up until he started to scream. Even then he would let the boy go, and he pulled him up by his shirt collar and held him while he kneed him several times in the back. I thought the boy might collapse, but Tom wouldn't let him fall and kept kneeing him until he agreed to stay on his feet. Once Tom accomplished what he wanted to accomplish and allowed the boy to hobble away holding his back, he turned to the other boy, who had been too shocked to move, and grabbed him by the hair. When the boy started to protest, Tom pulled him closer and whispered in his ear to be quiet, and that stopped him. Holding onto the hair of the now-trembling boy, he told him that if he ever saw him again, he would be sorry he ever opened his mouth. He asked the boy if he understood and, when he nodded that he did, Tom pulled out a handful of his hair and set him free. Tom gave me the hair, but refused to say a word to me on the way home. Later that evening at my instigation, he told me that he was ashamed because I wasn't standing up for myself. "Are you going to spend the rest of your life letting jerks like that push you around?" he said and walked away. Just then, I heard a noise and woke up. There was a movie on TV during which two cowboys were fighting. One landed on his back and the other hovered over him, angling his gun at the prone cowboy's face. "I'm tired of seeing your face around here," the cowboy with the gun snarled, while the other pleaded for mercy. "Only God is merciful," the cowboy insisted as he slowly pulled the trigger, relishing the other's futile efforts to protect his face and gain a reprieve from judgment.

Just as the hammer snapped forward, Baker came into the room and dropped his heavy briefcase onto a coffee table. The resulting bang of the briefcase resembled the peal of a gunshot, and I jumped up. When I came to my senses and realized that Baker was back, I ran to meet him and hear the good news.

29

Baker shut off the TV and motioned for me to sit back down. After positioning himself somewhat unsteadily in front of me, his wide shoes and short legs straining to hold up his massive torso and broad head, he angled his hang-dog eyes down at me. There was a slight tremble in his jaw as he apparently waited for me to respond to a question that he seemed to think was unnecessary to articulate.

"What did you find?" I asked. I was beginning to feel uncomfortable before his sad, penetrating eyes.

"Have you told me everything, Jim?"

"Yes, I think so. What else do you want to know?"

"I want to know if there's anything that might have slipped your memory?"

"Slipped my memory? No, I told you everything. What did you find? Is it about Tara?"

Baker plodded slowly into the kitchen, poured himself a drink, and came back and sat down in a nearby chair. He held his glass briefly to the overhead light and then took deep drink. "Nothing about Tara. Does she matter to you?"

"I guess not," I practically whispered.

"I didn't think so. So, tell me about this old man. Is he your father?"

I was taken aback by his question. "No. What are you talking about? I told you all this before. There's no relationship unless you're referring to his attempts to kill me."

"Okay, let's walk this back a bit. What makes you think he's trying to kill you? What makes you think he's trying to kill anyone?"

"I don't understand what you want me to say? Don't you believe me?"

He took another long drink from the glass. "It's never been a question about what I believe. So, let's do this. Let's start by helping me understand things a little better."

"What?"

"Humor me. Let's begin by assuming that everything you told me is completely accurate. An old man shows up one day claiming to be your father. Tom buys into it, you don't. Over a very short period of time, this old man and your brother become very close. You object, of course—vociferously, in fact— that he isn't. 'He's a complete stranger,' you say, but Tom doesn't care. He believes that the old man is his father, and nothing you say makes a difference to him. All right, but now things start changing. It's not simply that Tom believes the old man is his father. He's obsessed with the possibility, and he's doing everything he can to turn that possibility into reality. We shouldn't forget the old man was destitute when he showed up at the hospital, and Tom, wanting to help his long-lost father, was going to do everything he could to get the old man back onto his tired, old feet. Right so far?"

"I think so."

"Now, over a short period of time, your brother and the old man become very close. They develop what can only be called a father and son relationship– hear me out–a relationship supported by both Belinda and Tara. Not by you, of course. You think the old man's a fraud–a valid assumption given his unexpected and peculiar arrival at Mercy–and you do everything you can expose him in front of your brother. The problem is that neither he nor anyone else believes you. Even after you tell them that the old man barged into your office and demanded that you stop coming between him and your brother, they take the old man's side and write off this incident to your imagination, jealousy, or whatever. But the old man is as smart as a fox, and he uses this turmoil to turn the family against you. He wants you gone, for while you're there, you're the only one with enough intelligence and foresight to see through the old man's intrigues, which peak when he buys your firm, fires everyone, and shuts the firm's doors."

"That's right, and I and everyone else suffers as a result."

"And then he kills your brother. It's not clear why…"

"Who knows? He was probably planning it all along."

"To get something from Tom that he couldn't get while your brother was alive?"

"Yes, exactly."

"Okay," Baker mumbled and slowly shook his heavy head. He inhaled deeply and took another drink. "There may be something there, but let's consider things from another angle. The DA certainly will. Let's say you're having money problems. You don't make much as a graphics artist, you're living beyond your means (how much did your car cost you?), and your job is in jeopardy. Remember, you told me once that you were underemployed and that you weren't doing anything an intern couldn't do. Jobs are tight in your market and, while Tara has a dependable income, this isn't enough money for the two of you to live on if something catastrophic happens. Because of your situation, because of your fear of financial humiliation, you start hectoring your brother for help. You've done it before. It isn't the first time you've been in such straights. But this time he keeps putting you off. He doesn't want to give you any more money. He's tired of handing out money to you only to watch you fritter it away and end up in the same situation. How much did you say that car cost you? Never mind. Anyway, he's got other ideas for his money. It's about this time that the old man is factoring large in his life. It doesn't matter whether he's your father or not. Tom thought he was, and that's all that mattered. Tom wants to help his old daddy out, and he has some big plans with the old man that call for big bucks. And these plans might not come to fruition if he has to bail you out again. It was at this point that the problems escalated."

"None of that's true."

"It's not really clear if you care one way or another about the old man's story. Father or not, you don't give a damn either way. But what you do care about is Tom's money. You're afraid that as the old man works his way into Tom's life, your lifeline is going to be cut off. It's this, this fear, that drives you over the edge, and you do everything you can to get the old man out of Tom's life, and yours."

"No, he came into my office..."

"Of course, he did. You claim that he threatened you, and I'm sure that he'll say that he came there with an overture of peace."

"Peace, like hell."

"Your brother, probably at the instigation of the old man, is reluctantly willing to give you one last opportunity to make good. But how to do it? How to set you up in a way that will keep you from becoming besotted with the money and, like you always do, frittering it away. It's the old man who has an idea. Since he and Tom are on the prowl for investments, it occurs to the old man that your firm might be useful in many ways. It's got investment potential–it's a small company on the verge of bankruptcy in a fairly decent market–and there's a good chance that he can make some pennies off it while ensuring you respectable, steady employment. In other words, instead of buying the firm and scrapping it for parts, as Tom usually does with the tiny companies he acquires, he and the old man are going to use it to make some easy money and keep you under control. Belinda will almost likely testify to this and everything else."

"I thought she didn't know anything about his business."

"Not the inner workings, certainly, but this might be something he told her over the dinner table, or maybe she heard it at a party as he was pontificating about his business prowess. I would also expect that if Tara turns up, she would confirm what Belinda says. She's a close friend, and everything she did in life seems to have revolved around Tom. But let's get back to your firm for a second. Tom's not going to run it himself–that's not what he does–and so he needs someone he can trust to keep the firm going and an eye on you. Who does he get? Who else? It's the man with the idea. It's an old man going by the name of Bill Reid."

"You should see what's happening there. Or–should I say?–what happened."

"It doesn't end there, does it?"

"I don't know what you mean."

"Sure, you do. Just when everything's in place and working the way it was designed, something happens, something doesn't go your way, and you leave the firm. You don't even have the guts to quit. You just walk out. You've done this kind of thing before."

"No, no, it didn't happen that way. The old man's not our father, and he was firing everyone at the firm. He was telling people that I made him do it. I had nothing to do with any of it, and I left because there was no point is staying if he was going to fire me, too. Don't you get it?"

"Oh, I get it, but what we have to worry about is how the DA is going to get it. Stay with me on this, though. You're the only one who gets upset over the old man and his relationship with your brother. You're the only one who finds him objectionable and wants him out of Tom's life. Remember, we're talking about Tom's life, not yours. The old man–and let's just call him Bill Reid–Bill Reid didn't want anything from you unless it was for you to stop hectoring your brother. I'm not sure there's anyone who will say Reid criticized you."

"I wasn't hectoring anyone. I was trying to make them all understand what was going on. Of course, he wasn't going to criticize me. He wanted everyone to feel sorry for him. That was his game. You can call him whatever you want, but that's not his name. He's not related to me."

"It's funny, no one else is troubled by Bill Reid's presence, not even Chelsea. You're the only one who's upset and you're the only one who takes it out on the man. It started with arguments and then moved onto threats. Remember those e-mails you sent him? You can't claim to be an innocent party if you sent those."

"They were phone texts, and I explained that. It was an aberration. I wasn't thinking right. I just wanted him to stop and go away. I'll bet you'd do the same thing…"

"You slapped him around, more than once. He's an old man, and you took it out on his friend, too, another old man. Do you like to beat up old men, or do simply lack the guts to take your frustrations out on men your own age and size?"

"That's a lie. They're all lies. Lies." I momentarily placed my hands over my ears as though this would keep all the lies from penetrating my consciousness.

"So, it all comes to this. You get wind of something going down in your brother's house. It's a business deal, and you're furious that Tom, your beloved brother, is going to enrich himself and leave you hanging. Remember, you're desperate for cash. Your car isn't paid off, is it? So, you barge in there with the intention of demanding a cut, and you see Bill Reid there, the old man, and you go apoplectic."

"What?"

"You get excited. It's obvious that the old man has succeeded in severing you from your brother and his money, and you lash out."

"No, that's not what happened."

"Tom, not unreasonably, is beside himself. You're interfering in his business and you're wrecking an important deal. You're also demonstrating to him and whoever else was there that Tom cannot control his unruly, younger brother. You've always had control problems, haven't you? You were the wild one, you were the one who couldn't adjust to absence of your father, and you're the one who couldn't handle the everyday problems of living."

"If you say so."

"It's not what I say that matters. Anyway, you rush into the meeting, break everything apart, and Tom, your beloved brother, finally snaps. Your behavior is problematical at any time, but this time it goes beyond the pale, and Tom does what he should have done years ago. He throws you out. He might even have put a chokehold on you to get you under control. You know how you can get. The following day, Tom is beaten senseless with some kind of solid object."

"You're out of your mind. Why are you saying these things? I told you how everything happened."

"I'm afraid it doesn't stop here. Belinda notified the police when it was clear that Tom wasn't going to revive, and when the police went through the crime scene, they found a bloodied bat. This is where it gets interesting. The police took the bat and subjected it to a detailed analysis. They matched the blood on the bat to your brother and, when they compared the bat to the photographs of a bat possibly used in another one of your family squabbles, they determined without a doubt that this particular bat was the same bat that they had once seized from your house."

"It was Tom's bat."

"It doesn't matter. It used to be in your possession. There's no denying it. In fact, you're on record having claimed that Tom had given you the bat."

"Is Belinda going to testify to that? Did she actually say that I was carrying a bat when I went to see Tom?"

"I don't know what she's going to say about this. It's easy to conceal a bat. Who knows? Maybe Tom had taken it back earlier. However, there will be fingerprints on it, and they will be identified..."

"Sure, I used the bat, a long time ago, and I guarantee you the fingerprints will have resin on them, not blood."

"I hope that can be established. The bat's being examined it as we speak."

"Wait a minute. They can't use it. Remember, it had been obtained illegally. The police thought I had used it against Tara. They came into my house without asking."

"That was a different case, and this is a different ballgame. The bat was obtained legally this time. Let's hope for your sake that Tara's blood isn't found on the bat."

"Fine, but you're twisting everything around. None of it happened the way you said. I told you what happened and how it happened. You have to believe me, the old man is at the heart of everything. If his fingerprints aren't on the bat, then maybe he was wearing gloves. He's a career criminal. Don't look at me like that. I'm telling you the truth. But it doesn't matter whether I'm telling you the truth or not, does it? You said your job is only to defend me to the best of your ability. For God's sake, you don't have to believe me. Just take my side and help me."

Baker inhaled deeply, meaningfully, and coughed as through he had been smoking. "I am defending you," he sputtered, "for now. I have to tell you, though, I'm discomfited by the slipperiness of this case. I have to be able to control the debate, and I can't do that if there's an equally viable alternate explanation for everything. You need to understand that for me to defend you, I need to have the whole truth and nothing but the truth. Without this information and your complete honesty, you and I are both losers."

"What are you saying? I've always been honest with you. What do you want to know? I'll tell you the truth, and what I say will be consistent with everything else I said. Come on, ask me something. Ask me anything."

"All right, explain how the bat went from your place to Tom's. Remember, Belinda's going to have a story, too."

I felt as though I was being backed into a corner with my own words. "I can't."

"It's your bat, right?"

"I don't know. I haven't seen the one the police have. Maybe it's mine, maybe it isn't."

"You have a bat, right? A Little League bat that is or isn't your brother's. Did he give it to you?"

I stared at him for a few seconds, hoping that we could change the subject.

"Did he give it to you? Yes or no."

"No."

"But you had it. How did you get it?"

"Please, please, I don't know why any of this matters. I didn't touch Tom. I didn't use a bat or anything else against him or anyone else. Can't you see what's going on here? Who cares about the bat? You should be concentrating on the old man. His true name isn't Bill Reid, and he's setting me up. He conned Tom and my wife, and he's conning you, too, if I have to tell you a hundred times what I've already told you. Don't you see how he's sowing doubt between us? If he succeeds, I lose. Listen to me. Listen to me. I don't know why my father didn't like me, I don't know why he preferred Tom over me, and I don't know why all of this is happening to me now."

Baker was momentarily as motionless as a giant Buddha on a pedestal. "It still doesn't help with the bat," he finally said in an old, tired voice. After slowly placing his empty glass on the table next to him, he folded his gigantic arms over his voluminous chest. "All right, you know what else doesn't help? It's all this stuff you told me about your firm. Do you remember? You said everyone was being terminated and the company shut its doors–and all because the old man wanted to punish you."

"Tara refused to believe it. She said it was all in my mind. I told her the old man came into my office. I told her he came into the building while I was out. He came in and announced to everyone that he and I had acquired the company and that I was firing everyone. She refused to accept it. It went against her idea of who and what the old man was. She wouldn't accept the facts."

"You were upset."

"Goddamn right I was upset."

"You see, this is another instance in which your story is problematical. The DA will rightly point out that the firm is still in business. Nobody shut it down.

It was indeed sold, and immediately after the deal it moved to a new location. There may have been some downtime because of the logistics, but it's in a bigger building now, and, as far as I can tell, most of the people previously with the firm are still there, at the new location. A few people were let go or refused to move to the new location, but that's common in these situations. If your brother were here, I'm sure he'd say the same thing."

"That doesn't make sense. I don't believe it."

"You can check it for yourself. Do you know something else that's interesting about your firm?"

"The old man was doing that just to mess with me. If it's there as you say, do you know what will happen to me if I come inside? Do you?"

Baker hesitated while keeping his eyes locked on mine. "Are you sure you don't know about the move?"

"No. Absolutely not. This was the first I've heard about it. I knew about the old man's acquisition of the firm, though."

"That's not going to help. Let me approach it from another angle. Do you know who the firm's vice president is?"

I gave him the name and told him that I was fairly certain the individual had been terminated.

"Wrong on both counts. I take that back. The person you named is gone, but he retired just before the move."

"I guess I heard something about his retirement. I wasn't invited to the party."

"That's strange. You should have been. Do you know the name of the person who took his place?"

It was my turn to hesitate. I was almost positive that the old man had installed himself as president, which meant that he had brought in one of his criminal cronies to fill the position. "No."

"Sure?"

"Stop playing games. Who's the new vice president of the company?"

"You're right. Let's stop playing games. Your office is right next door to president's office. Phil verified it."

"What? No, he made a mistake. He was in the wrong hallway. I'm just an artist, and my office is little more than a broom closet. Ask Jeff, if he's still there. Did Phil call him? Jeff knows everything, and he'll vouch for me."

"You're probably confusing the old building with the new building. But, yes, Phil contacted him, and he confirmed your new position and title with the firm. Jeff, by the way, is doing quite well these days."

"Did you speak to the corporate secretary? He gets all his information from her."

"This is not the time to go through the employee list. I have one last question before we move on." Baker paused to take a deep breath of air and run his stubby fingers through his thick, gray hair. "How come you didn't tell me that Bill Reid made your bail?"

30

I didn't tell Baker, because I didn't know who had made my bail until Baker told me. And I was as surprised as he was by the situation, maybe more so, though in hindsight bailing me out made a kind of perverse sense. I was more vulnerable on the outside than I was on the inside. Yes, most of the people in the jail, including a number of the guards, were bad people, and there more than a handful who would slit my throat for a pack of cigarettes. But I was lucky enough not to have been placed in the general population, and so only a few people had access to me (my attorney and the guards with whom I interacted on a daily basis), and overhead cameras monitored my every movement every second of the day and night. Still, if someone were determined, I have little doubt that they could find a way of getting me while I was inside. For the right price, one can buy prisoners as well as guards. It would be much easier, though, and the risk much lower, to attack me on the outside, where there were no bars and guards to protect me or cameras to record the act.

The bail also benefitted the old man in another way that I hadn't anticipated–it soured my relationship with my attorney. Baker was already upset with me over what he perceived was my lack of candor, and the bail was in his eyes one more thing that I had been hiding from him. More than once, Baker told me that he couldn't mount an adequate defense if I wasn't entirely open with him or if I lied to him. The last thing in this world that he wanted was to be hung out to dry at trial because a client had deceived him. And yet, despite his evolving assumptions about my honesty, I had told him everything, I had been consistent in what I had said, and I had never once tried to deceive him. No, and what was becoming patently obvious was that, consciously or not, he was taking the old man's side as the latter began subtly manipulating events, information, and perceptions. Baker certainly had a right to be upset with the way things were going (his legal swan song was beginning to look like a hog call), but I'm convinced that had he given more credence to the things that I said–had he seen the old man for what he was–everything would have gone more smoothly for both of us.

"Fine," I retorted when Baker told me that he was having second thoughts about pursuing my case. It was no longer our case. He added that he could have been making more money and feeling less stress with any number of other clients that he could have taken on instead of me.

"Don't defend me then," I countered heatedly. "I don't need an attorney who won't believe me." I jumped up from the couch and glanced at the bedroom. "It was the same with Tara. Whatever the old man said was gospel to her, and whatever I said was a lie or a distortion or a misunderstanding, even when the facts were on my side. It's happening here, too. The old man is manipulating things and, because you're blind to what he's doing, you're taking his side over mine. I don't need this anymore. I don't need to prove my honesty and integrity. If you're not willing to accept what I say, then don't."

Phil, who seemed to have appeared out of nowhere, stood next to the seated Baker like some dark, minatory statue, and together they stared at me as I charged into the bedroom, picked up my bag, and threw it over my shoulder. I stopped at the front door on my way out. Both men were wide-eyed and quiet as I thanked Baker for the work he had done and promised to pay him back for the clothes I was wearing.

"Wait," Baker commanded from his chair. It was clear that my departure wasn't cause enough for him to haul his massive bulk up onto his beleaguered feet. "If you leave, you could end up violating the terms of your bail."

"Everyone knows how to find me," I replied and pointed to my ankle.

I should have given Baker a chance to reply. If I had been a little more cognizant of my predicament, I'm sure that I could have worked with him to come to an understanding that didn't jeopardize the best opportunity I had of making my legal problems go away. But I couldn't speak to him or anyone else at that moment. I'd had my fill of people who doubted my word and who assumed, without proof, that there was an alternate explanation for everything I said. In other words, I was being the Goofball that Tom often accused me of being. Instead of waiting for Baker or even Phil to stop me verbally, I shut the door (I didn't slam it) and hurried to the elevator. Even then, I might have taken my time and let Baker or Phil come after me to coax me back into the apartment, but, as I said, I was being the Goofball. I allowed my anger to control my intellect. I didn't want to be sensible and work through their issues. I just wanted to be done with them like I was done with everyone else. Actually, I was a little afraid of Phil following me. Baker wasn't a threat. He was too heavy, too slow, too weak, and I wouldn't have had any trouble pushing him off despite his enormous bulk. Phil, though, was different. He was trim and probably physically fit, and I was positive that he could reach me as quickly as an Olympic athlete. I was afraid that he would try to hold me back physically, and I didn't want to tangle with someone so tall and menacing, someone who reminded me of one of the machines in our father's factory.

Once I was safely out of the building, the cool, night air embraced me and tried to lick a thin layer of skin off every exposed part of my body (I didn't have a coat). As I quickly looked around to get my bearings, I was inexplicably enraged over the temperature and the weak, pallid glow of the street and store lights, which in my estimation should have illuminated everything with a sun-like brilliance. Luckily, I found a cab right in front of the building, and as I closed the door I saw Phil exiting the building and heading directly toward me. His gate was stiff, and I noticed for the first time that he moved with a slight limp. 'Had he been injured in some desperate, wartime battle?' I asked myself. I realized then that I didn't know anything about him, which made his looming presence and his imperfect gate all the more formidable and disturbing. I shouted several times for the driver to move. As it turned out, though, there was no need to rush, at least not from Phil. He stumbled over something on the sidewalk and, in an effort to retain his balance, he crumbled pathetically backwards onto the seat of his pants. Turning back to the driver, who was now vociferously demanding directions, I gave him the address and described how to get there. Like an angry child finally getting a treat, this seemed to mollify him and we took off without incident. I must say that I felt bad for not helping Phil off the pavement. He had worked hard on my case, and I suspect that both his professional pride and his slender body had been injured with the fall. I also felt slightly uncomfortable for refusing to engage with the driver, who did exactly as I instructed and who now seemed to be as pleasant as his youthful, unmarked face. It was a long, lonely night for him, and I'm sure that even a few appreciative grunts from me might have made his time pass more agreeably. It couldn't be helped, none of it, and, like a criminal fleeing the scene of the crime, I sank low in my seat to keep Phil, if he got up in time, from seeing and following me, and to prevent the old man, the very last person in the world I wanted to encounter, from trailing me as the driver and I passed through a number of familiar streets in the city.

Once outside the commercial district, we angled onto the highway and continued for another forty minutes or so. I was thankful that the highway lights were brighter than the city lights, because they enabled me to see all the cars around us, and there were several times when a passing car was so close that I could see the driver's face and outlines of the passengers, if any. In the end, I decided that I had nothing to fear from Phil. He was a decent man, and I suspect that his pratfall quelled any desire on his part of following me and preventing me from violating the terms of my bail. It was the old man that I had reason to be worried about. Out of jail and fleeing my benefactors, I knew that he would see this as his golden opportunity to catch me and finish me off. He was desperate to find me, and if he noticed me leaving the city, I was positive that he would be hot on my tail, quite possibly in one of the cars behind us, just out of sight. But after a half hour of pointlessly twisting and turning so that I could see every car around us, I began to think that he hadn't seen me, after all, and so I tried to relax a little before we arrived. My relaxation was short lived, however. It occurred to me that I didn't have a single penny in my pockets and, though I had a wallet full of credit cards, I wasn't sure if any were still valid. It had been quite some time since I had paid any bill. When we exited the highway a few minutes later and stopped at a familiar corner, I put aside my concerns and instructed the driver to turn left and continue straight for another couple of miles while we passed through several pleasant, middleclass neighborhoods to our destination. I gave the driver an extra tip for pleasantly processing my card (he had to go through three before finding one that still worked), and stepped onto the curb. As the cab pulled away, I stood on the sidewalk and scanned the quiet neighborhood for signs that the old man had followed me or that he was skulking around somewhere waiting for me. When I felt at least momentarily safe, I strode onto the walkway that led to the front door of my house.

The house and most of the front yard were faintly illuminated by a nearby streetlight. As I walked across the same pavers that I had traversed countless times over the years, I was surprised by the desolation of the front yard, which I had seen even more times than I had touched the pavers. Instead of a lush lawn and a neat row of evergreen bushes in front of the house, there was a mass of dark, uncontrolled weeds, and if the evergreens were still there, they had long ago been subsumed by the same weeds that seemed to cover everything else. The house was even more disappointing. The place somehow looked different, smaller, than I recalled. Instead of the large, expansive home where Tara and I stretched out on the front porch to enjoy the warm weather, there was a small box of a place with a single-door entrance in the center and a modest-sized window on either side of the porch. One of the windows opened into the living room and the other into the bedroom, and neither seemed large enough to illuminate adequately the happy life inside that we had once enjoyed. There was also a loose gutter above the bedroom window, and it was obvious even in the dim light that water had been leaking under the gutter and rotting sections of the siding. (I remembered repairing the gutter a couple summers ago, or maybe I had only planned to repair it.) I hesitated after I stepped onto the narrow stoop and faced the front door. It was still damaged, only now it was also covered with dirt and dust and, in the upper, righthand corner, a spider had crafted a well-used, happy home. I remember thinking that Tara would have been appalled. She had always taken such care to make our place look "inviting," as she used to say, and it now looked anything but that. Taking a deep breath, I fished the keys out of my front pocket and was just about to insert the key into the deadbolt when my hand shook and I had to step back to calm my emotions. Once I was sufficiently ready, I inserted the key and opened the door, which after a slight resistance backed inside with a faint, protesting squeak.

Instead of good friends and holiday cheer, I was greeted with a stale smell that vaguely reminded me of a moldy cardboard box. The place needed airing out, and it was probably the case that the faulty gutter was allowing outside water to seep inside. I didn't investigate, though. I wasn't ready to make home repairs, especially in the absence of light (how long had it been since the utility payments were up to date?). Fortunately, there was enough light from the outside streetlamp streaming in through the parted curtains to bathe the living room and parts of the kitchen in a cool, dusk-like silver. But as the door closed behind me and I stood on the threshold observing the room that had once held so much happiness for me, I started to wonder what I expected to find here. Why did I come back? Did I feel that I was safer in my own home than in Baker's apartment? Did I think that I could come back and pick up where I left off as though the old man had never come into my life? Did I think that Tara would come out of the unlit bedroom and welcome me back into her arms? Or did I want to see what the police had done to my place in their quest to find something incriminating? I didn't know why, and I didn't know what I expected. I'm not sure I thought about it one way or another. But as I looked around the room and noticed that everything was as it should have been, a sense of loss welled up inside of me; I felt as if I were looking at a museum exhibit of another time and era in which the people living here led happy, productive lives–lives that would one day be destroyed by a Pompeiian volcano in the guise of a duplicitous old man. The furniture was situated where I remembered, the knickknacks were where they were supposed to be, and the pictures on the walls looked exactly like they did when I, the former tenant, occupied the place. Had the police actually been here?

I picked up the silver-framed photograph of Tara and me from the table next to the couch. It had been taken early in our marriage when we were on a trip to the Rocky Mountains. We were standing together on a large boulder near the summit of a mountain. Tara in front of me, my arms around her waist and my chin perched on her shoulder, we are smiling, we are in love, and we are on top of the world. We are also blessedly ignorant of the chasm that would one day open in front of us. I wanted to recall more about that day, that time, but I couldn't. I could only see what was in the picture. It was hard to fathom how that part of my life had simply ceased to exist. I was here, and yet a part of me, most of what I thought was me, was dead and couldn't be resurrected no matter how badly I needed it or how long I lived. Years ago, I would have gone to Tom for advice or thought about what he or John, our mother's cousin, might have said, but they were gone now and, like people from ancient city, part of a past that seemed remote and unconnected with me. Placing the picture back down, I felt the table wobble slightly. Should I have slipped something under one of the legs to stabilize it? I looked over my shoulder and the stale smell of the place came back, more intensely than before, and I wondered if that was a sign for me to leave.

But for some reason I couldn't leave. My legs began to tremble, and I sat down on the couch to rest for a few moments. Leaning my head back, I closed my eyes, though I wasn't sleepy. I didn't want to see the room anymore. I didn't want to see anything else in the house, either, because it would bring back memories of a life that had once been worth living and remind me of everything that the old man had taken from me. Somewhat irrationally, I was also afraid that if I looked around more carefully, I might discover the old man crouching in some dark corner like a bug, waiting to spring up and call me a loser because I wasn't like my brother. After inhaling deeply several times to control my anxiety, I opened my eyes and stood up but immediately plopped back down. I reached under the couch for Tara's journal–the book in which she recorded her professional thoughts about me and, I presume, everyone else, maybe even including the old man. I don't know why I thought that it might be under the couch when every other time that I checked for it, it was missing. But I suppose I thought that this moment was unique, because Tara wasn't around to keep it from me. To my surprise, it was there, and I took it over to the window where the light was the brightest.

The book, as expected, was black, carefully bound (there was white stitching around the edges of the covers), and secured by a stretchy cord. I yanked the cord off and opened the notebook to the first page. Actually, in my haste to see what Tara had written about me and the old man (and I have to admit that I was also a little curious about what she had written about her patients), I managed to rip the cord from the book. I didn't care anymore. The only thing I cared about was her words, and, since I didn't know where to start in order to find what she had written about me, I began with the first page. I was practically giddy with excitement when I saw Tara's cramped script. My hands shook slightly as I recalled Tara diligently bending over the book and inscribing what I had always thought were extraordinarily profound observations on life, even if these observations might not have been entirely flattering to me. As I immediately discovered, her handwriting was hard to read (it appeared to be the kind of scrawl typical of a seasoned healthcare professional) and I was forced to angle the book more toward the light so that I could decipher her words and sentences and, once again, hear the sound of her soft voice. The script was small, and so I practically pressed my nose to the page to read what she had written.

Despite my excitement, I was fully prepared to read something glowing about the old man and, conversely, something critical about me, Tara's wayward, temperamental husband. That was Tara's style. She was a psychologist first–though maybe only a pretend psychologist–and so in her best pseudo-professional opinion I could expect to find something about the husband who failed to appreciate the guidance and love of his long-suffering wife, the husband who ignored the love and endless support his brother provided, the husband whose response to intimacy was deception and denial and violence, the husband who ignored his father (the old man) and refused to accept his freely-given love and support, and of course the husband who couldn't hold down a decent job because of some silly, irrational childhood trauma. Sure, I could expect some harsh comments, but this was part and parcel of who Tara was, and to anticipate less would be tantamount to demanding a different person. But what I saw took me completely aback. On every line and on the first and every other page were nothing more than meaningless swirls, lines, and dots. Tara hadn't written a single word much less a single phrase or clause throughout the entire book. I couldn't believe it, and I ran through every page several times to make sure that the light and my eyes weren't deceiving me. They weren't. I leaned against the wall. Had Tara actually been analyzing me all these times she pulled out this damned little notebook, or had she been pretending to study me while daydreaming of something else? Was she trying to control me with her book, or was it insanity on her part, the kind of insanity that would melt when that grotesque old man opened his flabby maw? Only a crazy person would have gone to this much effort to doodle page after page within the lines–no, not doodle, for doodling requires an image or design of some kind, something at least vaguely recognizable, and there was nothing of that in this insane little notebook. I was about to toss the book across the room when something slipped out from between the last page and the cover. I didn't know how I could have missed it. It was a sealed envelope, slightly smaller than a business envelope and intensely red in color. My name was on the outside, and inside was a letter from Tara to me. She apparently knew that I would seek out her damned notebook when she was gone, and so she probably reasoned that there was no better way of sending me a message that I would actually read and possibly take to heart. Why not? It worked.

The letter had been printed on two plain sheets of paper and folded in half to fit the envelop. I remember being surprised that the paper was so thin. It was as if she had purchased the cheapest paper available to explain to me that everything was over. Surely, a letter like that deserved something better, elegant borders or perhaps heavier stock. What was even more surprising was that there was no salutation. There was no "Dear Jim" or "Dear Jimmy," or anything to indicate that this was not a letter to just anyone but to someone who had agreeably shared her life for quite a few years. We had been husband and wife, we had lived as one, and yet there was nothing to suggest that any of this meant anything. To be fair, Tara had never written me more than a few lines on birthday, anniversary, and Christmas cards, and so maybe this was her style. And her style? It was cold and clinical. She was laying out her assumptions– the old man was our father, he loved Tommy and me, and I was the cause of everyone's problems–while getting in a few pointless jabs. That was Tara, all right. When she wanted to convey something, she was the cool, distant, unimpeachable expert, even when she knew nothing at all about the subject (especially when she was pontificating about our father and the old man). But, I suppose, there was an upside to the letter. It wasn't just a couple of stale lines. She had something to say, and to me. More importantly, it was proof that she was still alive. She wouldn't have known some of the things that she mentioned in her letter if she hadn't been alive to know them–if she had been dead at the time I had been arrested for her death. Still, there was nothing in the letter that would have made a difference to me, to my life, such as it was. I would never see her again, I would never see my brother again, and I would never get rid of the old man, unless he did everyone a favor by ceasing to exist. Pointless, right?

31

"Things did not work out so well did they," the letter began and continued in the same sardonic tone to the end.

"All you had to do was accept Bill as your father. Things would have been fine then. We would not have quarreled and Tommy would be having us for weekend dinners. Why for Gods sake did you have to make things worse by barging into Tommys house and breaking up the meeting? You destroyed a business deal. You ruined Tommys relationship with these men. These are not the kinds of people you want to mess with.

"Your father was not responsible for any of this. He was always trying to protect you. He tried to keep you away from Tommys kind of business. At the risk of his own safety he even interceded in this fiasco to assure them you were not a threat to their business and this deal. It was not enough. Its true Tommy should have stayed away from them in the first place. I don't know why he thought he could do business with them unscathed. I guess the money was too good to turn down. Perhaps it was the excitement. Perhaps it was something else. He had a chance until you wrecked everything. Can I tell you something ironic? The day before this went down I gave your bat to Tommy for protection. He laughed. He said the bat looked exactly like the one he had as a kid. He also said he didn't need a bat because he has plenty of knives and guns at his disposal. I said it would give him the upper hand if he needed it. Who would think twice if he pulled it out from all the other sports equipment around the house? I guess somebody did.

, "Now that Tommys gone you are probably more obsessed than ever with your father. I know you think he is fooling everyone but I am more convinced than ever he is your father. He said so himself and he told me a lot of funny stories about you when you were a kid. God you were as hardheaded back then as you are now. By the way you did see me downtown those times you asked about. Bill is leasing an office not too far from your building and Tommy and I frequently visited him while he was working there. This is where I heard the best stories about you. Before you start carping about Bills veracity you should know he showed me his drivers license and a picture of him holding you when you were two years old. You sure looked different then. You had an ugly grimace on your face which almost seems to predict the future. Perhaps it does. But I did not need any of this to convince me Bill was your father. Neither did your brother.

"I guess by now you know the meeting at the hospital was not the first time your father and your brother had spoken since your father left home. Bill had been in touch with Tommy over the years and it was only when he fell ill and was hospitalized that he came into the open. He once had business problems too. When you and Tommy were children. He was convinced the only safe thing to do was to leave home and wait it out until his business acquaintances either forgot him or died. Remember your mothers cousin John? Bill told me he was a real problem because he was one of the men who was after him. John had somehow managed to get close to your mother and stayed at your house while he waited for your father to return. One day years later when everything seemed safe and John and your mother were long gone Bill surfaced and reached out to your brother. He and Tommy did some minor deals together before Bill became seriously ill and went into the hospital. Do you know why your father did not immediately reach out to you like he did your brother? Do you know why they pretended this was the first time they had seen each other since your fathers disappearance? Bill had been watching out for you at a distance and he knew the dangers of Tommys business and wanted you to stay away. He wanted you to be the one in the family who was clean. But when he got sick and thought he was dying he wanted to see you and Tommy one last time. He wanted to apologize for leaving and he wanted to spend his last days with his boys if possible. It was not.

"Let me tell you something else. You sure are sensitive about your silly car. Bill likes to make jokes and he did not know you well enough to see you did not have a sense of humor. I explained things to Bill and tried to help but he did not want me to say anything. He thought you would come around on your own and be nice. After he and Tommy bought your company it became obvious you would never change. The acquisition was not a joke. It was done for you. I told your father about your employment issues and he wanted to do something to help you remain honestly employed at a job you liked. I suppose mistakes were made but they were not intentional or mean spirited. Bill did his best to fix them. By that time it was too late. By that time you were spitting fire and brimstone and would not listen to anyone except yourself. You were ungrateful and violent. And stupid. Anyone else would have dealt with the issues and come through the process better if not unscathed. But not you. Not James Reid. Not Goofball.

"So why am I telling you all this? Who cares since none of it matters anymore? I am just trying to help you understand what happened so you can begin to deal with your problems on your own. I cannot help you now. I cannot support you any longer. Ive been with Tommy long enough to know when men get mad in this business like they did at Tommys house they tend to spread the blame. I do not think you are safe and I am not going to stick around and end up like your brother. You will never hear from me again and it is okay because we were having too many problems. I have to tell you the truth. I was not looking forward to spending my golden years with you. Things might have been different if Tommy was still with us. Hes not and I am not going to risk my life for you or anyone else.

"Of course this is all bullshit isn't it. You never take anyones word for anything. Your word is the only thing which matters. Fine by me. Remember my warning about these men."

There was something else after this. There were some hard, circular scratches on the page which suggested that she had something else to add—a conclusion that at least acknowledged our past relationship?—but her pen had run out of ink before she could finish. It was disappointing that she couldn't have found another way of offering me those words, and to this day I wonder what she might have wanted to convey at the end of the letter and everything else.

32

With respect to what she did write, it was indeed all bullshit. Well, most of it, anyway. You know, when I started reading this letter, I felt a little wistful as I thought about my still-living wife. It was a mean letter, certainly, and yet I couldn't simply forget all the great times we had together or pretend that all our future planning was done as a kind of joke (and, in this sense, I don't have a sense of humor). But when she started spouting off about what really happened and what I presumably would have trouble accepting, whatever feelings I had once had for her began to evaporate. Her claims about my relationship to our father had no validity. Who is she? She wasn't there at the time. Who cares if the old man had a picture of some squirming kid in his lap? Can you really look at an old picture of a grimacing baby and match that image with a mature adult? And the driver's license? I never saw it, and, as I'm sure Baker would attest, there are millions of Bill Reids in this world, and the odds of coming across one or two old ones in our metropolitan area are pretty good. I'd say that it would be peculiar if there weren't dozens all within spitting distance of my house.

Believe me, Tara was the old man's tool from the beginning to the end. He liked her because she lapped up without question every stupid, ridiculous thing he spewed, and because she was more than willing to gloss over all his lies, gaffs, and inconsistencies. But you know this, right? Is it a surprise? Okay, I admit that I sometimes sound paranoid and looney, but the facts are the facts regardless of who says them, and all I ask is for you to listen to the facts and not accept or reject them on the basis of how you perceive me. Do I have to say it again that Tara had no way of determining the old man's veracity, she had no special psychological insights into the old man or any man, and she didn't grow up in my household? She wasn't there when our father deserted us, she didn't hear our mother's pathetic cries, and she didn't witness the relationship between my mother and John. I grant it's possible that she could have gleaned some insights from Tom, but she didn't mention those in her letter (she relied exclusively on what she wanted to see in the old man and what the old man had told her) and, even if she had, his insights (note that I say insights and not facts) were no better than mine despite our age differences. They were worse, judging from the insights and facts that I have. So, yes, I had a moment of wistfulness when I began this letter (and this despite the absence of both a salutation and conclusion), but I was disgusted by the time I finished it. I remembered that ours had been a sham marriage, and she was now leaving not to protect me or our relationship, but to protect her own precious, silky skin. If there were any regrets on her part, it was clear from the letter that they revolved around Tom and whatever relationship she had with him. Good luck to her.

But as I leaned against the windowsill, I kept thinking about Tara's cold words and her specious assumption that because she is leaving my life, I should now give her thoughts credence. It was ridiculous, and it bothered me that I couldn't explain to her that her words were beliefs, not facts. I should have let it go–it didn't matter anymore what she said–and yet I couldn't help thinking that she was smiling at what the old man, through her, was pulling over me. "Does she think she's actually deceiving me?" I asked myself out loud, and, with my irritation rising at the thought of her playing the old man's game, I tore the red envelop into little pieces and dropped them onto the floor. Temporarily satisfied with that puerile action, I turned and noticed the letter, both pages of which were still in my right hand. 'Tara could think whatever she wanted to,' I told myself, 'I'm not going to live a life of fantasy.' I was ready to ball these up and heave them across the room when I had second thoughts about leaving them behind for someone to smooth out and absorb Tara's delusions. Hesitating, not knowing whether to take the papers with me or to toss them some place outside of the house, I impulsively ripped them apart just as I had done with the envelop and tossed the pieces to the floor. Seconds later, after the thrill of destroying both the letter and, metaphorically, her in one fell swoop began to wear off, I regretted my actions. I wasn't concerned so much that someone would find the pieces and put the letter back together as I was about the possibility that I might again be charged with her death, and the letter, though it wasn't signed or dated, might somehow help me prove my innocence (there might be something in the words that, when combined with other evidence, would show that she was alive and well and living somewhere else at the time I was supposed to have murdered her). Dropping to my hands and knees in the dark room, I hastily picked up every little scrap of letter I could find and stuffed them into my jacket pocket. When I was finally back on my feet, I told myself that I was finished with Tara and, as I was savoring the idea that she might be running for quite some time to get away from the men she was so afraid of, I started to wonder if she was still in contact with the old man. If she was as scared of the men as her letter implied, it didn't make sense that she would dump relationships with the very people who might be in a position to help her. After all, the kindly old man was trying to help everyone, wasn't he? "Would she actually keep in touch with him to protect herself?" I asked myself.

I continued standing there, not sure what I wanted to do next, until I began to feel uneasy. It was a vague feeling, though Tara did suggest that I needed to be wary of the businessmen at Tom's house, the old man's good old buddies. I tried to laugh it off. She was only being stupid (she wasn't smart enough to see through the old man, right?), and I was in my house–my own house, even if the lights were out, and nobody knew I was there. Yes, I was in my own house, and yet for some unaccountable reason I had a nagging sensation that I shouldn't be there. It was a feeling that had nothing to do with the police or the DA or the men who had frightened Tara. I had no fear of these people. I guess the best way of describing this is to say that I didn't feel as though I belonged there. I felt like an intruder in the very house that Tara and I had worked so hard to acquire. Others now possessed it, and they were sleeping contentedly in the very room where Tara and I once slept in each other's arms. This unaccountable, groundless feeling was intensified by the surrounding darkness and stillness, which amplified every creak and groan that would have gone unnoticed in better times. It was a ridiculous feeling–I still owned the house, and I knew that I only had to go into the bedroom to prove that my imagination was getting the best of me–and yet I couldn't quite reject it. The contradiction was like a living, breathing organism that kept coming back to me and, no matter how effectively I beat it off with the facts, it wouldn't leave me alone. "You don't belong here," it said, taunting me and challenging me to prove it wrong by looking into the bedroom or turning on the lights. Seconds later, unable to stand the absurd challenge to which I had no effective answer, I walked quickly toward the door and, without a single backward glance, left the place, forever.

33

Just as I turned after having locked the front door, I spotted my cherry-red kid's car in the driveway. I didn't know how I could have missed it as I approached the house or even how it got there. Maybe my first attorney arranged to have it returned to my home or maybe… It didn't matter. The only thing that truly mattered was having it once again in my possession. And it was beautiful, as beautiful as it had been the first time I saw it in the car lot, wedged in between two lovely cars that looked pedestrian by comparison. The overhead streetlight illuminated its gracious lines and its sleek, sexy shape, and the twinkling stars in the dark, night sky made nearly every square inch sparkle, filling my mouth and mind with the most delectable fruit in the world.

I walked across what used to be a lawn and placed my right palm on top of the hood. It was cold and dusty, and yet I could sense the vibration of the engine inside of me. I unlocked the door and looked inside. It had none of the mementos that filled the house, none of the detritus that can make an otherwise immaculate home look shabby and in disrepair. I slipped inside and gently pulled the door closed after me. The seat was soft and perfectly adjusted, all the controls were exactly as I had left them, and the upholstery…well, the upholstery smelled like genuine leather though it was a combination of velour and Naugahyde. I turned on the engine and, after a couple stuttering sputters, it caught and emitted a deep, lusty roar that reminded me, as it always had, of a wild beast demanding to be free. The car was the only thing I had left in life that hadn't been fouled by the old man, although after a minute or so I began to question its exquisite purity. The upholstery was abraded in places, the paint looked dull in spots, and I noticed several tiny dents and scratches on the hood. If these things weren't enough, it was beginning to smell unpleasantly. The smell wasn't overwhelming, but it was strong enough to help me locate the source, which was the passenger's seat. It was the stink of the old man, who had come into our lives with death and destruction in his wake. Since I was hopeful that the odor would grow fainter over time and eventually disappear, I rolled down the windows, backed out of the driveway and, after blipping the engine a couple times to keep it from stalling, took off.

I drove around the neighborhood streets for a while. After stopping to roll up the windows because of the cool outside air, I continued, passing a small, green park where Tara and I liked to walk in warmer weather and then the strip mall with the lovely little shops that we visited but rarely spent money in.

Around the corner, there was an independent jeweler who had sold me Tara's wedding rings. Tom referred me to the place, and, on my brother's recommendation, the clerk, a roguish-looking, middle-aged man with dense, green tattoos covering both exposed forearms, went into the back of his shop and found a ring set that he hadn't yet displayed. "Practically new," he said in his harsh, gravelly voice, and I immediately bought it and presented it to Tara a week later. I stopped at the light and, instead of turning right to see other parts of the area that I once loved, I turned left and then another left, after which I angled right and, twenty minutes later, ended up across the street from Tom's house.

The monolith was dark. The lights inside were off, and the little beams at the base of the structure were black. I was a little surprised, because Belinda and Chelsea were now living there alone and would have appreciated the lights at night. 'Maybe they're gone for the evening,' I thought, and then it occurred to me that they would have wanted the lights on when they returned, for security purposes. I turned off the engine, which rumbled a few times afterwards as if it wasn't ready to stop, and rolled down the window to have a better look at the place. I stopped thinking about the lights and started ruminating on the property surrounding the place. There was a pagoda in back under which we had dinner when the weather was right, and there was a wide area on the lawn in front just out of sight where we would relax in lawn chairs and watch Chelsea gambol in the grass. Tom was at his best and most loving during those times. On the driveway across from the garage, I was certain that there were still vestiges of the oil that my car dripped every time I visited my brother. Turning around in my seat, I recalled all the other places that were connected to Tom's house though not part of the property. There was a gym, stores, and of course that blasted hospital, where I drove Tom to and from on more times than I could remember. But the second I recalled that, I also recalled the old man, who tainted the hospital, the house, and everything else in my life. I might have driven to one of the cheap joints that Tom and I used to visit for a pizza or a sub sandwich, but the old man kept coming back to mind, and I became concerned that my presence at any of these places would be another violation of my bail (it wouldn't have surprised me if, in laying out the terms and conditions of posting my bail, the old man had singled out these and other businesses as places that I should under no circumstance visit). It was when I recalled the money that I vaguely toyed for a few seconds with the idea of killing myself to fix the old man for fixing me. I knew that he'd weep over the loss of his money, or Tom's money, or the money of the person from whom he stole it.

I turned the key, and my wonderful car sprang back to life, gasping and then throbbing with a determination to scream onto the highway. I pulled slowly away from the curb, I was a little reluctant to leave a place I knew so well, and then stopped. As I was taking one last look at Tom's house, probably the last I would see for quite some time, I noticed near the entrance to the driveway a 'For Sale' sign. I backed up and angled my car over for a closer look. The sign said that the house was for sale, all right, but on the top of the sign was another sign that said with bold letters "SOLD." If that weren't enough, next to the 'For Sale' sign was another sign that said "NEW HOME" and provided an image of what the new home would look like. Tom's family was not only out of the house, but the new buyer was going to raze the edifice that Tom had taken so much pride in and put something entirely new in the same spot. I was stunned. I had always thought that if anything could have stood the test of time, tainted or not by the old man, it was this house, and yet the new owner was going to wipe this place from the map and erect something new and unrelated in its stead. He was going to remove Tom's last vestiges from the face of the earth. Once this was complete, it wouldn't take long before my memories became unanchored and I wouldn't be able to distinguish myth from reality. I shuddered. I thought that I was now approaching my own end and that it was only a matter of time, days maybe, before the only thing I had left for the old man to take was my very existence.

I sat still for several minutes listening mindlessly to the choking rumbling of the engine's cylinders and feeling the heavy vibration in the seat and on the steering wheel as the car waited for me to give the order to charge. Finally, taking a deep breath as though I was going to dive into a bottomless pool of black water, I tapped the throttle a couple of times and was just about ready to go seek my fate when I felt another vibration, this time in my shirt pocket. It was a text message on Baker's phone. I had not forgotten his phone. I had intended to send it back to him once I landed someplace where I felt in control of my own destiny. I didn't know where that place was or when I would finally arrive, but since I didn't have anything particular to do at the moment, I pulled out the phone and read his message. I wasn't, however, interested in anything he had to say if it was premised by my return to this apartment. Baker was a good guy, and there had never been a question in my mind about how much he had helped me, but at the same time I wasn't ready to throw myself at the feet of the justice system while it piled charges on me and let the real malefactor go free.

"Jim," the message read, "Don't do anything stupid. Stay in the area. We'll talk tomorrow."

Don't do anything stupid? After all the stupid things that had swirled around me, he told me not to do anything stupid? What exactly was stupid in his tired eyes? I dropped the phone back into my pocket. I wasn't going to contact him again this night or any other night, for that matter. I'd had enough of everything–the case (my case), the old man, Tara, my brother, his wife, Phil, and, yes, Baker. I was grateful for his efforts, but I had reached my limit with him and his distrust of me. Don't do anything stupid, huh? Well, I'd had my fill of him and everything else, and I needed to find someplace where I could relax and clear my thoughts. Maybe after that I could come back and…I don't know, take care of things with or without Baker.

Tapping the throttle to hear the rumble of the engine and to make sure that it would continue running once I started moving, I again pulled away from the house and this time I headed directly to the highway. No, I didn't know where I was going, and I wasn't thinking of relaxing or clearing my head. After taking the first entrance onto the highway, I carefully maneuvered into the center lane and kept at a steady, legal speed. I was careful not to exceed the speed limit or weave from one lane to another. I didn't want my freedom to be circumscribed prematurely. With nearly a full tank of gas, I followed the highway for what seemed like hours if not days. I drove through the city, past the entrance where I fled from Phil, past the outskirts, past the suburbs, past all the ramshackle buildings with their garish lights, past everything that had bound me to a place I had once called home.

34

I didn't know how long I had been driving or how far (I hadn't once checked the odometer), but after a while I began to tire and I could sense the car leaving the lane every now and then. I was still engulfed in a deep darkness that was alleviated now and then by the yellowish headlights of an oncoming car and the occasional road sign, which reflected my car's lights. There was still no evidence that the sun was hovering beneath the horizon, and as far as I could tell I was either driving through a rural area or in a less densely populated space that was still asleep. I felt a rumble and a loud, whining noise, and I pulled back onto the road. I was wide awake. I was certain for a few moments that I'd had all the sleep I needed and that I could continue driving for another few hours, or until the sun rose. As I traveled, I tried to listen to the humming of the engine while watching the edge of the road, which was now down to one lane in either direction. I wasn't worried about going off the edge and driving into a field (as far as I could tell, there were wide fields on either side of the road punctuated now and then by the faint lights of a building or the glaring lights of a gas station); I was concerned with monsters running onto the road and forcing me off the pavement to avoid their grasp. What kinds of monsters were these that were running free in the night? I didn't know, but from time to time I spotted shadows on the side of the road that looked like old men running beside me. I thought that I had been doing pretty well, driving past one black field after another, when my eyes opened in response to another rumble and whine. This time I was almost entirely off the road. I slowed for a moment to calm my nerves and then continued as though I was in the proper shape to drive. But I was anything but in the proper shape, and I struggled to keep my eyes open and the car squarely on the road. A short, indeterminate time later, I spotted a sign for an upcoming rest stop. When I finally approached the turnoff, it was all I could do to keep my eyes open while I maneuvered through the entrance ramp and into one of the parking lanes. There was a darkened building maybe a hundred feet in front of me and farther down, near the entrance to the highway, there were some large trucks and trailers. The rest of the place appeared deserted. Tilting my seat backwards, I told myself that I would close my eyes for a half-hour or so and then get back onto the highway. I still didn't know where I was going, but I felt certain that I had to be going somewhere, and quickly. I hadn't given a second thought to Tara's warning.

Practically the instant that I had closed my eyes, a bright light bathed my face and seared portions of my flesh. I opened my eyes and immediately covered them with my right forearm. Turning my head to one side, I slowly opened my eyes again and looked out the window at the rest stop. I was in the center of a large, bright parking lot that was no longer deserted. There were other cars, many of them, parked throughout the lot, and people–young, old, children with their parents–were coming and going into the sprawling building, which was now clearly open and alive with the sounds of footsteps and chatter. I didn't know what time it was–I didn't have a watch, and my car's clock hadn't worked as long as I had the car–but it was surely midday, given the number of people I saw and the traffic on the highway, which I could see between two large trucks. I sat up, forced my seat into position, and then felt a sharp pain in my stomach. I didn't know when I had eaten last. It was also at that moment that felt something struggling to get out of my front shirt pocket. I jumped and retrieved the phone.

It was Baker with another important message. "Jim, I need to speak to you. We may have something. Call me."

I suppose because of the old man's inexplicable but pervasive influence, I couldn't help wondering if the call was a ruse. Was he setting me up to deliver me to the police or, worse, to the old man? I would never have expected something like that from Baker, but when the old man was involved, even the most stalwart people bowed to his will. No, I told myself, Baker wasn't like that. If there was one person in this world whom I could trust, it was Baker. I dialed his number, and he immediately picked up.

"This better not be a setup," I said before he could explain why he was calling.

"A setup? No, absolutely not."

"So, what's going on? Don't give me any warnings about where I should and shouldn't be."

"I got a call this morning."

"Wonderful."

"It was from a Chelsea Reid. She knows about your case and my relationship to you. She found my number and called to say that her grandfather, Bill Reid, had passed away the day before. Apparently, he died of heart disease."

I was silent. I didn't know what to say. If this wasn't a setup (and could Tom's daughter be trusted?), then it was practically the best news that I had heard in my entire life. Unfortunately, it didn't change much of anything. Tom was still dead, Tara was still gone, and, I had to believe, the goons after Tara were still probably after me. But, if it was true, it was good news, and seconds later it lifted a heavy weight that had been forcing my head to the pavement.

"Are you sure?" I asked, afraid that he would retract his statement and inform me that the old man knew exactly where I was and where I was heading.

"Phil just confirmed it at the coroner's office. This was the old man we've been looking for, right? Of course, it's right. There isn't another one, I hope."

"No, that's the one. God, I can't believe it. I can't believe it's finally over."

Baker cleared his deep throat. "It's not over yet."

"What do you mean? He's dead, right? He's no longer coming after me. What else is there?"

"There's the matter of your brother's death."

"Does everyone still think I killed him? The old man's dead. What's the deal?"

"His death doesn't exonerate you. But it could give us an opportunity to find out the true identity of the man. If he wasn't who he claimed to be, then it's a whole new ballgame in terms of demonstrating motive, means, and all the rest. Do you see what I'm getting at?"

"I suppose."

I jumped when something hit the side of my car. It was a child's bright red ball, and the girl's mother rushed over and apologized. With annoyance, I waved her off.

"Don't get depressed. From a case-management perspective, this is potentially some of best news we've had for quite some time."

"I'm happy he's dead," I replied, "but I don't see how this is going to help us identify him and prove that he was a fraud and that I'm innocent. Tom's family is convinced that he was the real McCoy and, if Tara turns up, she'll say the same thing. I'm positive about Tara." Tara's letter came to mind though I didn't mention it to Baker. I didn't think that it was germane to my case, and I also feared that if it was introduced at trial, it might become one more proof that the old man was whom he claimed to be and that I therefore was the only plausible suspect in Tom's death.

I could hear Baker breathing heavily before he replied. "It's not going to matter if we can prove scientifically that he wasn't your father. Phil has a contact in the coroner's office, and he's working with him as we speak to retrieve fingerprints, DNA, and any documentation they have that will help us establish his identity. Like I said, if this old man isn't Bill Reid, then the DA's going to have a job keeping the case from falling apart like a deck of cards."

"What if Phil can't establish his identity?"

"Don't worry about Phil. He'll come through."

"What if he can't? What if the source doesn't come through? What if there're no records on the old bum? Where does that leave me? Everyone's going to believe Belinda and the rest."

"Let's not worry unnecessarily. I think we're in a good position. But if we can't identify him, we're still in a better position than we were before, because he won't be around to testify against us. Here's…hold on. I'll call you back in a few minutes."

It was getting hot in the car, but instead of rolling down a window, I got out to cool down and stretch my legs. I may not have been as excited about my legal status as Baker seemed to be, but I was still elated that the old piece of garbage was gone. He was finally out of our lives, and there wasn't anything more that he could do directly to me. I wouldn't say that I had ever been afraid of him, not physically, but I felt calmer, unconcerned that he might pop out from behind a corner to ruin the rest of my life. Even Tara's goons seemed a lot smaller, less threatening than before. Since Baker seemed to be taking a lot of time, I walked to the building to see if I could find some food. I was hungry, and I didn't care what kind of food the rest center served.

It was my lucky day. My credit card still worked, and I ordered a large hamburger meal that I brought outside to my car. Instead of sitting inside, I sat on the hood and relaxed against the windshield to eat and soak in the sun (I still didn't know the time). When I was done, I slipped off the hood, walked to a trashcan to deposit my trash, and walked back to the car. Baker still hadn't called.

Since I still didn't want to get back inside the car–I wasn't ready to go anywhere–I leaned against the door and watched the people coming and going and milling about the parking lot. I noticed, for the first time, a small playground next to the building. There were several children there playing on the slides and swings. One was a little boy with what appeared to be his father. The boy was balanced somewhat unsteadily in one of the swings, while his father was carefully pushing and pulling him. The boy, who was maybe three years old, was nervously smiling, and the father, a youngish man in jeans, was clearly enjoying this time with his son. Neither the son nor the father looked like people I knew, and yet I felt an inner warmth watching them enjoying their time together, and for perhaps the first time in my adult life, I regretted not having had a child to whom I could provide the love and joy that I lacked as a child. I wanted to walk over and praise the man for loving his son, but my phone again came to life. It was Baker, of course.

"Sorry it took so long," he said breathlessly, "But there was a lot of information to go through. Phil got the coroner's results and..."

I strained to hear everything Baker said, every word, every inflection, and every nuance. After a short break during which he hoarsely caught his breath, he detailed the work that both he and Phil would now do for our case. When he was done–"for now," he said in a cheerful tone that I don't think I had ever heard from him before–he advised me to come back ("before the sun goes down") so that "together" we could begin forcing the DA to retreat. I hung up, pocketed the phone, and looked out at the distant highway, which was still packed with cars and big trucks. Nothing had changed. People were as oblivious to my existence as I had been, until that moment, of theirs. When my hands stopped shaking, I reached into my coat pocket to retrieve my keys. Instead of keys, I found a mass of paper shreds. I pulled them out and held them in my open palm so that I could see them in the bright sunlight. They were the remnants of Tara's dark letter. It was surprising that these dull pieces of paper, which were covered with even duller scribbles, could have had such an emotional effect on me. It was surprising that they could have had an effect on anyone. As I stared at them, though, I wondered vaguely how Tara was making out. Where was she going? Did she find another protector? Did she know about the old man's death? Of course, she did. Belinda had to have told her, and I wondered about the kinds of clandestine communication they had to keep Tara safe and probably Belinda, too. As I was musing over the ways that Tara and Belinda were communicating to avoid the attention of the kinds of people you don't mess with, something else came to mind, which I rolled it over and over until it was finally crystal clear. Seconds later, I tossed the shards into the warm, clear air and watched them tumble through the warm air and then drift onto the pavement, where they danced across the parking lot.

35

I remember walking into my parents' bedroom one afternoon a few days after my father and I visited the factory. My father wasn't home at the time, and my mother wasn't in sight, and, when I happened upon the partially open door, the temptation to violate the inner sanctum was overwhelming and I slipped inside. As soon as I was in the room and protected by the door, I stuck my head outside and looked up and down the hallway for signs of someone approaching. When it was clear that I was momentarily safe, I closed the door and tapped the doorknob thinking that this was enough to lock it. The room was dark and filled with even darker shadows though there was a slow, pale light filtering in through the curtains. I should have flipped on the overhead light, but I was afraid of advertising my presence to either my mother or my brother, who would use the occasion to inform my mother of one more crime that I had committed.

For the first few minutes, I leisurely strolled around the room, looking at this and that as though I were slowly making my way through a farmer's market. I studied my parents' bed, gently caressing the heavy, patchwork comforter, and patting firmly one of the oversized pillows against the headboard. I wasn't exactly sure whose side was whose (I assumed that my mother and father each had their own side), but after studying the pillow, sniffing it for the sweet smells that characterized my mother, I came to the conclusion that it was my father's. I raised my eyebrows and nodded my head in affirmation of my clever discovery, and then moved on, the eagle-eyed explorer looking for a new discovery, a new adventure.

I was on the other side of the bed when my foot touched something soft, and I stumbled backwards and nearly fell to the floor. Stepping cautiously to one side, I turned my head toward the disturbing and unexpected apparition. It was big, as big as a wild animal, and dark, as dark as a black panther, and from the manner in which it crouched and stealthily observed my movements, I was certain that any false movement could spur an attack. As I slowly started backing toward the door (I wasn't going to spend another second in that room), a slender ray of light poked out from a gap between the curtains and, streaking across the floor, illuminated a section of the beast that I fervently wanted to avoid. I froze, and I stared for what later seemed an inordinate period of time at the fiend as it defiantly returned my motionless stare. I practically strained my entire body to determine what exactly was lying halfway in and halfway out of the light, and, when it didn't move or respond to my presence, I stomped on the floor to get a reaction out of it. It was uncharacteristic of me to do something so bold and rash, especially since I half expected it to charge at any moment, but I was confident that if the worst should happen, I had enough time to leap onto the bed to elude the thing's grasp. It didn't move, not even to shrug its shoulders or lick its lips. Feeling braver now and sensing that I might have the upper hand, I slowly approached, one hand on the bed to fuel my courage. Barely inches from it, I was almost certain that I could see its wide-open maw and its straining, sweaty sides, and at that moment I couldn't tell if it was going to lunge or slither under the bed because of some grievous injury. But it didn't move. It became as still as an object in a photograph.

As I was weighing moving an inch closer to it, I spotted out of the corner of my eye a similar animal gnawing at the outside edge of my left shoe. I pushed it violently away with my shoe, and when it rolled over and played dead, I saw that it was nothing more threatening than a lifeless sock, one that was nearly as big as me. I picked it up. It was my father's sock, and its wonderfully masculine heft brought back memories of the towering giant who gently led me by the hand through the maze of darkened machinery and soot-covered men. After considering what my father would do in similar circumstances, I picked up the sock and hurled it at the mysterious animal, hoping that this would be enough to scare it away. It still didn't move. I took a deep breath like my father would have done and slowly squatted down to have a better look at the thing. It was then, as I reached out and patted what I thought was the top of its head, it was then that I recognized the animal–it was one of my father's slippers. Its mate was cowering under the bed.

Without taking off my own shoes, I slipped my feet into the slippers and tried to imagine what it was like to be my father as I tromped around the room. "Tommy," I whispered, "Go to your room. Jimmy, son, help your mother in the kitchen." As I moved to one side of the room, I came up to a chair and noticed a newspaper on it. It was my father's, of course (in our house, he was the only one who read the paper), and I picked it up and looked at it. It didn't mean anything to me, I wasn't even interested in the pictures, and yet I pulled myself up onto the chair and, paper in hand, pretended that I was my father at our evening dinner. "Mother," I said in my best fatherly voice, "This is an interesting story. Martians have landed, and they're going to break into the grocery store to steal the chocolate ice cream. Well, I have to go to work now. Don't expect me for dinner, because I'm going to stop this folderol on my way home before it gets out of hand." "Folderol" was a word my father liked to use.

Where most fathers used foul language, my father used "folderol" and sometimes "rot." I don't think I ever heard him use what my mother termed "bad words."

There was a noise in the other room, and I jumped down and stepped out of the slippers. I ran to the door and placed my ear against it to see if anyone was coming. When the noise didn't repeat itself, I spun around and noticed my father's desk. It was a massive, dominating structure that was full of drawers with strange golden handles across their faces. Even from my angle, I could see papers stacked up across the top, and there was a dish that was precariously poised half on, half off the desk. As I reached for it (I was going to take it into the kitchen), I noticed on the walls above his desk several frameless drawings, children's drawings. There was a mountain scene with pointed peaks and fluffy white clouds floating over them. There was a picture of a bird, the animal that used to sing outside our window (Tom and I shared a room). And there was a picture of what looked like our father's factory. I couldn't tell for certain, the picture was out of reach and partly hidden by a deep shadow that leached down from the ceiling, but I was positive that it was the one that I had drawn while sitting at our father's desk as he operated the adding machine and filled in his ledger books. I could almost see the gigantic, screaming monster machines that were demanding to be fed. In the center near the right, now covered with a shadow, should have been the smiling man who said something that appeared to have annoyed my father. The man couldn't have been that ominous, I reminded myself, and I guessed that the interaction between them had to have been more cordial, an off-color joke from employee to employer. But as I stood there trying to see the picture, I felt the need to look at it close up if only to understand why my father had chosen this particular drawing to grace the wall above his imposing desk.

I stretched upward with my right hand and arm fully extended to retrieve it, but no luck. The picture was hung at a height that suited my father, not someone as small as me, even if I were on my tippy toes. I wasn't going to give up, however. I wanted to see that picture in its entirety. I wanted to retrieve the memories of the event that seemed in some unconscious way to have a direct bearing on my young life, and to accomplish this, I needed to hold it in my hands. I glanced around the room for a solution, and then I weighed the possibility of climbing up onto the desktop as a possible way of reaching it. It was a sound idea, but there was no immediately observable way of achieving it. The desk was too smooth to offer a satisfactory foothold, and when I tried to pull out one of the drawers to use that as a ladder, the drawer wouldn't budge.

It appeared to be locked, like all the other drawers. Just as I was beginning to despair that I would never find a way to raise myself to the level of the picture, a picture whose significance seemed to grow in proportion to my inability to reach it, I became cognizant of the wooden office chair resting on the other side of the desk. I was surprised that I hadn't noticed earlier. Using both hands, I pulled the extraordinary heavy chair over the thick carpet and positioned it almost directly under the picture and then carefully pulled myself onto the hard seat. The chair was shaky–once or twice as I balanced myself I thought it was going to collapse under me–but I somehow managed to balance myself on my knees and, gripping the back of my chair as though my life depended on it, I slowly and unsteadily raised myself upright, albeit facing the wrong direction. I cautiously turned around, trying to keep my feet steady and still, and there it was, just a little over my head, though still mostly covered with a dark shadow.

Keeping my feet and body as still as possible, one hand tightly gripping the of the chair, I reached up as far as I could and managed to touch the bottom of the picture. It was a strain, and I was afraid that at any moment I would topple over before achieving my goal, and just as victory seemed at hand, an invisible yet powerful force propelled me back from the picture and caused me to tumble out of the chair onto the floor. I wasn't hurt, or at least the shock of the event made me numb to the sensation of physical pain. And so I got up on my knees, and, as I looked blindly around, I noticed that the bedroom door was open, letting in a brilliant rush of light. I turned to the picture and standing in the light with the picture in his hand was Tom. Without moving his tall, angular body, he held the picture high over my head, waving it back and forth as if was now permanently his. Perhaps it was, for a second later he flashed a wicked smile and then shoved it into his mouth, chewed it up, and then hurled the soggy mess across the room where it stuck on the wall. I might have lunged at him, but I was so surprised and frightened by his unexpected appearance–hadn't I locked the door?–that I couldn't immediately move, especially seconds later when he called out in a voice that sounded genuinely offended, "Dad, Jimmy's in your stuff again, and he destroyed one of your pictures." I could only surmise that our father had returned home earlier than expected.

I don't recall much after this. I can't even remember if my father was actually at home. Once, during one of the numerous heated arguments that we had over the years, I reminded my brother of this incident to prove to him that I, too, had memories of our father. Tom informed me, in his characteristic way, that I was "full of shit" and that the only drawings our father kept were those that he, Tom, had drawn. Our father, according to my beloved brother, thought that my drawings weren't worth keeping because they were shit, and the only reason they were shit was because I was shit. When we were young, Tom often told me that our father ran away because I was shit. Later, as an adult, he denied saying that. He accused me of making up things to supplant the gaps in my memory, and he told me, as though I needed to hear it again, that I was "full of shit." I guess I was full of shit. I am full of shit.

Now, I think I've managed to insert a bit of humor in this otherwise bleak tale. Tom's tautological utterances of "Goofball," for instance, are very funny, as is my incoherent, atavistic howling over my brother's death. On the other hand, the fact that I omitted a passage from Tara's letter in which she asked me if I had gone after my brother and then concludes that I probably didn't have the "guts' to do something so insane is itself amusing in a slightly different way. Yes, it was all quite funny, and so I think it's only appropriate for me to add one last joke before the curtains come down and everything goes dark. It goes something like this. Over the years, I managed to convince myself that I didn't care whether our father was dead or alive, and I was positive that I had got over the opprobrium of being called a bastard. When the old man arose from the dung heap, I was convinced that I was as indifferent to him as I was to any stranger living on the other side of the world and that my central concern, my only concern, was what he was planning to do once Tom's back was turned. Contrary to what Baker alluded to, my reaction had nothing to do with Tom's money or with the remote possibility that he would usurp Tom's position as the putative head of our family. Sure, I had monetary problems over the years (artists like me don't make a lot of money), and I often, perhaps too often, looked to my brother to make the decisions that I had trouble making. Do you want to know what was more important to me than any of this? Do you want to know why I couldn't tolerate the old man and refused to accept his assertions of paternity? It was because–and here's the punchline–it was because his unexpected presence in the flesh resurrected the mental and physical anguish that I had endured over the years, rendering it impossible for me to tolerate him even under the best of circumstances. As I noted earlier, Tom had always been in some pathetic way the father or father figure that I desperately needed, and so over the years I did everything I could to keep my feelings toward him untainted by his cruelty to me both as a child and as an adult. But the old man's presence upended all that, and at the end I was forced to accept the fact that he had never been interested in playing such a role in my life. (Despite my appreciation of John, it was the old man and what he conveyed to Tara that destroyed the few, precious illusions that I had about him.)

Punchline? Maybe that's not the real punchline. Maybe the real punchline goes something like this. It didn't matter to me whether the old man was our father or not. I was doubtful, certainly, since he was so unlike the father residing in my imagination, and I didn't care if Tom wanted to worship at the altar (did he?). It was Tom's business, not mine, if he wanted to give all his money to the old man. What bothered me, and what made me react to all the things that under normal circumstances I wouldn't have reacted to, was not the old man's presence or what he said and did. It was the fact that he cozied up to Tom and not me. He chose Tom to father, not me, and this brought back my childhood memories in which Tom was the favored son. I was the bedraggled kid who bothered everyone and seemed to lack the ability to behave appropriately. I was the little shit that neither our father nor anyone else could stand. No one ever seemed to understand that I needed at least an outward demonstration of our father's love and that I needed something more than punishment or indifference. When the old man arose seeming from the dead and offered himself as the father, his loving behavior toward Tom and his unconcealed disdain for me brought back all the unpleasantness, all the suffering, that I had endured over the years, and it made it easy, perhaps natural, for me to hate him and resent the relationship that he was developing with Tom. I felt as if I were reliving everything that I had tried so hard to dismiss and forget. I have asked myself many times if things would have been different–Tom still alive, Tara and I still happily married, and I still had my goddamn kid's car, which I sold to meet expenses–if I, not my brother, had been the favored son. Would I have been as willing as Tom to open my arms to the old man even if I suspected that he was a fraud and a scoundrel? Would it have made a difference if the old man had looked upon me as he appeared to look upon Tom? Would I have gone back after Tom with a fireplace poker because of what he did to me in front of the old man? I don't know, but it's pretty funny, isn't it?

Acknowledgments:

I offer my sincere thanks to my good friend, NK. Without his invaluable advice and suggestions, this book would have been in a pretty shoddy shape and would have befuddled even the most determined reader. In fact, without NK's efforts, this book may not have been completed.